IMMORTAL ALLIANCE

Book 1 of 4

Immortal Alliance Series

First published in the United States of America in August 2021 by Kindle Direct Publishing (eBook kindle edition) & Ingram Spark (paperback)

Cover Design: Aubrey Blair

Print ISBN 978-1-7374401-0-9
E-Book ISBN 978-1-7374401-1-6

Author's Note

The religious depictions and discussions in *The Immortal Alliance Series* are inspired by religions and cultures from various parts of the world. None are intended to be a faithful representation of any one culture or religion at any point in history.

To *Ian*,
for all the long hours of brainstorming and refining that made this story what it is. You're the gravity that holds me to the earth.

PART ONE
CRISIS & PARLEY

ONE
Heather

I LIKE LEARNING ABOUT old and dead things.

At least, that's the short explanation as to why I study Anthropology and Religion. Something about the history of religious mythology and symbology really resonates with me, even in early childhood. So it was only natural to pursue a career in the subject I felt such a connection with.

"*Heather*." I whipped my head up, but not one face was turned towards me. My imagination, it's nothing.

I remember when I first took the Intro to Anthro course during undergrad how interesting it all seemed. I meticulously took down notes and spent my weekends reading further ahead in the textbook. A dedicated student, gearing up for a long scholastic journey.

It took me five and a half years to complete my undergrad, and now I was finally in my third and final year of grad school.

"*I know you can hear me*." That voice again. This time I looked around, even behind me. My dreams have been coming with me into the waking world.

God, I'm so sleep deprived.

Just grade these papers, get through this class, and then a nap. I took another long gulp of coffee from my thermos and then went back to scratching red ink across the paper. The professors voice background noise.

Before taking courses on symbology, I dreamt of symbols, markings, and sigils. I still have the journals I used to enter them into. Some symbols I found in my studies, but occasionally some weren't anywhere to be found.

I can't count how many libraries I've been to, how many long nights spent on the world wide web searching for the mysterious symbols in my dreams. I had an amazing opportunity to spend a year abroad in Peru, studying ancient Mayan culture. But alas, some of my searching proved a fruitless endeavor.

I still record symbols from my dreams, hoping to one day find their source, and learn more about them. However, over time I began to just accept them as my imaginative mind creating its own unique language.

I wish that getting my master's degree didn't involve assisting in undergraduate courses. I've taken Intro to Anthropology upwards of four times since deciding on this field of study, and by now, grading papers of students who are only taking the course to fulfill a Gen Ed requirement is a real downer.

"*I don't have much time, I need you to listen.*" Shut up. Shut up. More coffee, need more coffee.

Today was the last day this class would meet before finals. Most of it was spent reviewing previous sections for students who needed a refresher, or really for those who didn't pay enough attention and would likely fail the final exam.

My presence wasn't too important, aside from answering a question here and there, I mostly sat in the back, grading the last of this week's essays.

But my focus was always getting off track. My tired mind resurrecting last night's dream. I still hear it, the strange yet familiar voice echoing in my skull like it was right next to me.

"*Please*." I jolted in my seat when a dark hand gripped my shoulder. But when I turned in my seat it was gone, and only a wall stood behind me.

"You alright, Heather?" Professor Chacon asked from the front of the room.

I brushed off my pounding heart with a breathy chuckle, "I'm fine, ha. Perhaps too much espresso this morning."

Students responded with small huffs and snickers. "Or not enough," one muttered, followed by more laughs.

"Alright, alright, we still have fifteen minutes, what else do we need a review on? Christy?" The professor continued.

With a steadying sigh, I turned my pen back to the stack of papers on my desk. My hand was shaking. I gasped when a sharp pain hit in my belly. A cramp?

"*Help me.*" It was almost inaudible. I whipped my head around to see who it was—but still, there was no one.

Again, I heard it, distant—yet right next to me. Chills crept down my body like tiny spiders. The hair on my arms rose. My legs felt wobbly, and the muscles in my body tensed, suddenly feeling fatigued.

Then everything began to slow.

The sound of the professor's voice lightened and muffled, as if cotton filled my ears. I looked to the front of the classroom where Mr. Chacon stood, his lips were moving, but they were moving much slower, more so in slow motion.

The fatigued feeling increased and it felt surreal. It wasn't my weakness that I was feeling. Like a heavy fog moving over me, it choked my air supply, making my vision clouded.

All the sensations in my body changed, replaced with terror. My eyes filled with tears, the fear threatening to rip apart my insides.

But as quickly as the feeling came, it was gone. An unbearable scream that wasn't my own resonated through my skull. There was pain biting down on my head like teeth. I held my hands over my ears trying to shut it out. I felt a warm, sticky substance trickle from them.

When I tried to stand, my legs buckled beneath me—slamming my knees hard into the floor. I saw blurry figures moving towards me, but I couldn't hear what they were saying past the screaming.

My vision blurred further until everything became white. I was no longer in the classroom, instead I was in an all-white space, no sense of up and down, no doors or windows.

Where am I? Am I dead? Did I pass out?

A slight movement made me turn towards it—a curled-up figure lying on the floor weeping. I managed enough strength to crawl towards it.

As I reached his crumpled body, without so much as a hesitant thought, I placed a hand on his shoulder. A sense of familiarity swayed in me—and in that feeling his name appeared in my mind.

"Mason."

He continued to weep, whatever pain he was feeling was so intense that his tears were coming out red, spilling down his cheeks without end. There was a wound in his abdomen. A deep one. Blood percolated from it.

It looked like he had been stabbed. Blood loss with this kind of laceration could kill him.

The back of my mind remembered the basics of first aid, moving me to press my hands against the wound to stem the bleeding. Apply pressure, that's the most vital thing you could do with a stab wound, *right?*

I felt like I was experiencing his pain, feeling the anguish that consumed him.

He was afraid to die.

Wet streaks slipped down my cheeks as I watched him stifle his own tears. His dark skin chalked from blood loss, and already I could feel the heat leaving his body.

I tried to breathe, even as I felt his life begin to dwindle away with each exhale.

"Please, what can I do? Let me help you," I begged.

He choked on a sob, blood spurting from his mouth and dripping down his nose. I pressed harder, but the thick liquid continued to pool around my fingers.

“I don't have anything; we have to stop the bleeding,” I muttered.

Breathe. We both needed to breathe.

“You have to stay awake.”

Panic and dread were threatening to puncture what little resolve I had. I'd never been in this situation before.

What if this stranger died right here in my arms? Maybe I should've studied medicine instead, then maybe I could actually do something.

He tried to take a breath, but it turned to a wet cough as blood filled his lungs. Some of it splattered onto my face, but I didn't care. I looked around the white expanse, looking for anyone who could help.

But there was no one.

"Help! Someone please help! Call 911, please!"

He rested one of his hands on top of mine. The flow of blood slowing, but not from the pressure.

No…his blood was running low, too slow to spill anymore.

My eyes were blurry from my infernal tears as they locked with his.

"Heather," he said. Even while dying, his voice offered a bit of warmth and comfort.

I continued to apply pressure as hard as I could, barely feeling my numb fingers at this point.

"You're going to be okay, you just have to keep breathing. Just a little while longer." My voice cracked, knowing that it was all a lie. A merciful, horrid lie.

His head shook. "There's nothing—" he winced. "—that can be done. Heather, listen to me. You have to find Malachi, don't trust—" He was cut off by a pained cough.

The bleeding from his wound stopped entirely, and his skin grew unnervingly cold. I cradled his head with one of my hands.

I didn't know this man. And yet, I felt like I was dying alongside him. He looked like he wanted to say something else but couldn't. One last teardrop fell from the corner of his eye, and his mouth formed words, void of sound. *I'm sorry.*

A final shuddering breath escaped from his lips, and then the light left his eyes completely—his body going limp.

My chest shook with a broken sob. "No, no, no. Oh god, no, come back." My words barely a whisper, but broken all the same.

For a moment, all was quiet and still, leaving me alone leaning over his cold, lifeless body.

Suddenly light began to break from his eyes and mouth.

I yelped and ducked out of the way as the light shot out of his body upwards, pouring out of him in a rush.

The air whipped around us like a hurricane, whipping my hair all over. I crouched low to shield myself from the bracing wind. The light filled the room. So blinding, I had to close my eyes.

Then a string inside of me tied to every muscle, bone, and nerve pulled and stretched until it was ripped out of my body, shredding as it exited. I screamed at the pain, but as quickly as it came, it vanished. The last thing I remember was collapsing into darkness, with the echo of my scream fading into it...

TWO

IT WAS A SHRILL ALERT THAT rippled through the realms.

Piercing every immortal soul right down to the very core of who we are. It was heard across the entire supernatural web, silent only to mortals. Pure and evil spirits alike succumbed to the sound of this deafening scream.

A catalyst.

Unexpected and foreign. It was as if the universe had fractured open, and no one had any idea what caused it.

But the Balance had been tipped in its wake.

It lasted only a moment, and once it ceased the preservers of the Balance abandoned their posts. Angels and demons alike fled to their bases of operation, all who were able took flight, others winnowed, and those who could not waited and listened for answers their leaders could provide.

Heaven, a sanctuary and beacon of hope, was quickly overwhelmed with angels from all divisions; Guardians, Scribes, Reapers, Watchers, all desperate for answers.

But the almighty did not greet them.

Instead, he summoned his archangels to a closed meeting. They gathered in the grand courtyard, separate from the Empyrean Manor. Pillars lined and walled off the inner garden. Marble stonework intricately designed into archways, benches, and fountains. Private, but open for immediate flight if needed.

The archangels Michael, Gabriel, and Raphael were the first to appear. The enforcers of heaven and earth. Flying in from overhead with wings, Michael's of gold, Gabriel's white with an aura of gold, and Raphael's white with flakes of dusty indigo. The three of them magnificent symbols of righteousness.

Azrael and Uriel chose to winnow directly inside. Rarely did Azrael show her wings, but she had them all the same and unlike the others, hers were as black as a moonless night.

Uriel's wings, like the remainder of their siblings, were smaller, resembling something closer to the wings of an owl. They were brown in color with spots and streaks of white and black. Jophiel was Uriel's twin and had similar wings, but their similarities stopped there.

Zadkiel, Jophiel, and Chamuel had winnowed outside of the compound and simply walked into the courtyard.

Zadkiel's wings were unique in that they were more red and orange than brown. Chamuel's wings usually took a more exotic look, varying in vibrant blues and greens.

It had been an age since all of the almighty's children were in one place. Even longer since he'd seen their wings in all their glory.

Lucifer would not be at this meeting. He remained restricted from entering the Heavenly realm, but his opinion would still be heard and weighed later—just not here.

And as much as God wanted to relish this special reunion, the event that brought them together still echoed through the universe.

The almighty was a simple being. After being in existence for so long, he'd lost any need for extravagance. For a time, it was up to him and his companion to hold the fabric of this universe together, to keep the Balance intact.

When the archangels were born, he was able to delegate and lessen the responsibilities on himself. And over these billions of years, the growing population of angels and the skills they brought with them had allowed him to serve more as a figurehead.

His archangels ran the system like a well-oiled machine. For the billions of years they've held the reigns, the Balance has more or less remained even. His creations thriving in the mortal realm.

They all stood in the courtyard, trained commanders of a glorious kingdom, patiently waiting until their father, the creator—the almighty spoke.

"Thank you all for coming so quickly," God started with, receiving curt nods in response.

The three that had arrived first retreated their wings, concealing them with their power. God turned towards Gabriel, his youngest, and already one of his most powerful and loyal archangels.

"What we all felt…it was a Guardian—murdered."

"How?" Raphael asked even before Gabriel could.

Gabriel's division directly trained and oversaw the Guardian angels.

God answered Raphael and all of the questioning eyes around him.

"I don't know. A unique weapon of great power perhaps, or a creature of great power. Whatever it was, I couldn't see it."

"Something powerful enough to kill an angel? That isn't a very long list. *We* make up most of the things that would fit that description," Azrael stated. Some of them darting their eyes at one another.

Michael folded his arms across his chest. A warrior ready to spring at any moment. "Could Lucifer be sparking another uprising?" he challenged.

"Or his Heir?" Uriel added with a venomous tone.

Jophiel asked, "He hasn't utilized his son in the three-thousand-years he's been alive, why would Lucifer unleash him now? And only to kill a Guardian?"

"Perhaps he's been waiting until he was at his strongest? Training him and preparing him so when the time was right he would have control over a powerful weapon," Zadkiel theorized.

Azrael shook her head. "As much as Lucifer might think he has control over that boy, he doesn't. Besides, if he were going to weaponize the Heir, it wouldn't be done this way. Lucifer only takes calculated chances, this kind of erratic, messy disturbance would be foolish and lead us right to him."

"Lucifer plots and schemes, he could very well just be trying to jostle things enough to expose a weakness in us," Michael pointed out. He locked eyes with his father. "It may be wise to disperse the growing crowd of angels in heaven back to their positions. With all of them rushing here, the mortal realm is vulnerable and open for his hellborn to move in on the unattended souls."

"Lucifer's not an idiot. He may be cunning, but you really think he'd be so irresponsible as to do something that would immediately put suspicion on him?" Azrael argued.

Michael only met her gaze, leveling it with conviction. "I wouldn't put anything past him at this point. We'd be fools to immediately acquit him for being the obvious suspect."

Azrael snorted, dull amusement written on her face. "Already itching for another duel with him, brother?"

Michael arched an eyebrow. "Aren't you?"

"I'm afraid the desideratum for violence wasn't inherited by all of us," she joked.

Though Michael maintained his calm, a slight pulse of frustration flickered in his eyes—echoed by the tension in his shoulders.

"Why don't we just talk to him?" Chamuel added, his first contribution to the conversation.

He had since sat on a bench on the side. The most docile of the archangels, peaceful and compassionate.

Chamuel clarified, "Father could summon him, include him in our discussion."

"I intend to meet with him individually following this meeting. He hasn't atoned enough to be allowed back in this realm just yet," the almighty confirmed. "Be that as it may, I don't believe this is his doing, nor his Heir's."

"Would you like me to join you when you meet with him?" Michael offered.

A knowing smile ghosted onto the almighty's lips. "I don't need protection, and he cannot manipulate me. But I appreciate your offer, Michael."

God took a moment to look at all his children. The most powerful beings aside from himself that still remained in this universe.

"Back to the matter at hand. All we know is that a Guardian is dead. We need to find out how, who killed him and whatever else is needed to correct the Balance. Most of you have realms to watch over, inform your angels to keep an eye out for anything strange. But we must continue on as normal." He made eye contact with Gabriel. "Would you go find out who the Guardian is for me? We'll wait here until you return," he instructed.

Gabriel nodded, extending his wings and without another pause took to the skies.

"If it was a Guardian, that leaves their humans unguarded. Does the Guardian Master have a contingency plan to fill that missing hole? I know Guardians are stretched thin as it is," Raphael asked.

He was the most intelligent of the archangels. Always thinking five steps ahead, preparing for any setbacks or alternative measures.

"All the angels are stretched thin," Chamuel argued quietly.

Indeed. With the mortal population increasing at an alarming rate, the angelic forces were taking on more than they could bear. Guardians and Reapers made up the majority of the divisions, but even so they took on more than one mortal at a time.

New angels came in slowly, and required training before entering the workforce. There were thinned areas in every division as they sought to catch up.

When the almighty created this incarnation of humans, he gave them the ability to procreate easily, and their lifespans were meant to balance the populations out.

But with modern technology and better health practices, as well as a disregard for resource management, they'd grown beyond capacity.

"If they need additional forces, I can spare a few Cherubims," Chamuel offered.

He was always the most willing to help, even if losing a few of his own angels would greatly hinder his own division. He wouldn't voice those hindrances, instead he would actively work in the field alongside his angels.

Every division was struggling to keep up with the mortals—and with the growing demonic presence on earth.

God shook his head. "No. I think they'll manage, though when it comes to the humans left unguarded, we don't know the exact nature of what killed their Guardian. We may need one of you to guard them until it's sorted out."

He was doubtful that it had anything to do with the humans themselves, but better to be on the safe side.

Michael immediately took a step forward. "I can do it."

"Your willingness is admirable, Michael. But maybe it'd be best if Gabriel takes this one," Azrael replied.

Uriel narrowed her eyes. "This is a big deal, maybe Michael is the best choice. He is the strongest among us."

"Second strongest," Azrael muttered.

"Second to Lucifer," Uriel countered, her voice edging on a snarl. "—and if he is at fault, it would only be fitting for Michael to be the defense, given their history."

"Guardian angels are Gabriel's division. Besides, Gabriel has exceeded all expectations of his abilities," Jophiel defended.

Gabriel was the youngest, and therefore should've had the least amount of power. But he trained hard, and his power grew enough to match Raphael on the power scale.

"Guardians may be his charge, but maintaining the Balance across all the worlds is mine. I could handle this—" Michael said.

"All of us have that charge, Michael. Yours only specifies to go beyond this planet." Raphael cut him off. "I agree with Azrael. Gabriel should serve as the mortals' temporary Guardian and look into this. And if it gets to be too big for him to handle, then you may be prompted to step in."

Michael conceded to listen to Raphael. Azrael and Raphael weren't very different, both logical and calculating. But Michael notoriously listened to Raphael's opinion more willingly than his other sisters.

Perhaps it had to do with Azrael's own unique position and power. Or perhaps it was simply a closer sibling rivalry. Either way, Azrael never let it bother her.

Within moments, Gabriel's winged form lowered back into the courtyard. Once his feet touched down, he receded his wings.

"The Guardian's name was Mason. He was young, had only been a Guardian for just over two hundred years," he explained. He looked around to his siblings. "What did I miss?" he asked.

God moved towards Azrael, who now leaned against an archway. "Would you go check the Gates and see if his soul makes its way there?" he asked.

She blinked in surprise. "Would it? He was immortal—if anything his soul should've returned to you."

"I haven't felt anything yet, but it can't hurt to check," God said. "I'll come visit after I meet with Lucifer."

Azrael nodded, and then she began walking out. "I'll disperse the crowd on my way out." she shot a pointed glance at Michael, to recognize his earlier suggestion. And then she was gone.

Chamuel stood from his bench. "Back to work then, I suppose. Lots to do. It was good to see you all." This time Chamuel chose to winnow rather than walk out. A shimmering cocoon of vibrant amaranth light followed in his wake.

God nodded to the others. "Report back with anything out of the ordinary."

That was all the dismissal they needed. Zadkiel, Jophiel and Uriel disappeared in their own signature columns of light. Raphael and Michael remained.

"What would you like my Scribes to write on this event?" Raphael asked God.

"Only what we currently know, I suppose. I will try to relay any vital information I receive as it comes to me," the almighty replied.

Raphael nodded, extended his wings, and took to the sky without another word.

Drawing the almighty's attention, Michael said, "I suppose I'll just go check on the other worlds?"

Michael held his expression to be stoic and indifferent, but God could see the frustration underneath.

More, he wanted to do more.

God nodded. "I'll call when I have need of you."

Michael's wings beat only once, and he shot into the air like a missile. Gabriel watched him go, waiting for his instructions. All of the archangels, save for Lucifer, were fiercely loyal and reliable, but were sometimes...more like *often,* competitive.

Gabriel was young and had missed a lot of the most influential parts of their immortal history, but he had earned his place amongst them.

The almighty at last turned towards Gabriel, who remained collected, despite his worries having lost one of his angels so suddenly.

"Gabriel, I need you to be the humans' Guardian for a little while. Check on them. See if anything is amiss," the almighty instructed.

Gabriel knew a little about Mason's charge, most of the Guardian's human assignments were already venturing out of Mason's assigned stage of life, so they might be better off receiving their new Guardians immediately.

But there was one human who wasn't yet ready for that transition.

Gabriel nodded. "Alright."

"I'll speak with Lucifer and figure out where to go from there. But this is your assignment, find out what you can, and I'll see about giving you help."

"What should I be looking for?" he asked as the almighty began to turn away.

"Anything, everything. Start with the mortal's subconsciousness, I assume you've been practicing your dream-walking?"

Gabriel nodded. "I'll take care of it." he looked back to the now empty skies where Michael ascended. "Would I be right in guessing that the reason Michael left in a huff was because *he* wanted the honor of this task?" he asked.

The almighty grinned. "Your older brother tends to forget that he isn't the only champion of heaven."

"I'm grateful you're giving me the opportunity."

"Some of your siblings, Azrael, Raphael and Jophiel vouched for you, it's them you should offer your gratitude. You have yet to experience the chaos and challenges that this world can spur, my son. Having lived through so much peace, this might be your chance to gain some respect from Michael and the others."

God clamped a strong hand on his shoulder.

“Safe flying.”

God didn’t wait for a response before he left the courtyard, returning to the manor beyond.

As for Gabriel, he chose to walk out through the other exit. Some of the gathered angels remained but in smaller quantities, most of them had dispersed back to their divisions. Gabriel greeted a few on his way out to the edge of heaven, the drop off point into the mortal realm.

Gabriel took one deep breath and then let his body free fall towards the Earth below. Wind whistling past his ears, his wings out but tucked in tight to achieve maximum speed.

He felt the veil between realms push against him, felt the hidden wards built more to keep unwanted beings out of the Heavenly realm than in. Leaving was much easier.

An orb of golden light wrapped around him for only a moment, the power slicing through the veil into the next realm, leaving behind the soft warmth that never ended in heaven. He was falling through the icy thin air of the atmosphere.

Below him, surface grew closer and closer, the cities, plant life and ground, growing more detailed.

Before impact, Gabriel extended his wings, and just an inch from the ground he came to a stop.

He was hovering above a desert. He shifted into the Ethereal realm, a direct parallel veil from the mortal realm to conceal his presence from any mortals. It was in this realm that if he wanted to move from one place to another faster than he could fly, he could winnow.

But he didn't want to winnow now. No, now he wanted to fly, still faster than most modes of travel, but slow enough to give him a view. So, with a twist of his feathers, his vector changed from vertical to horizontal, moving like a bullet toward a town still asleep as the first rays of dawn began to break over the eastern horizon.

THREE
Lucifer

LUCIFER WAS WAITING on top of the Golden Gate bridge for the almighty to arrive.

Since he was not allowed in Heaven, and God wasn't a welcome visitor in Hell, they would meet on Earth.

Lucifer was sporting his signature dark suit. It was rare of him to visit earth these days. Hell tended to be a chaotic place and required a considerable amount of his time and attention. Keeping all the hellborn in check was a full-time job. His most trusted first-and-second generation demons handled the soul-snatching on the surface.

A lot had changed since his uprising. Long before that he had been the almighty's right-hand when keeping the Balance and righting the wrongs of previous creations. But Lucifer had always been free spirited.

Rebellious in nature, he always longed for more agency, for his own domain.

He had a proclivity for cruelty and the immoral. Taking more after his mother than his father, he supposed.

His fall may have been brought about as a result of his selfish intentions, but not one part of him regretted it.

Even as he continued to cooperate with heaven, his realm of sin and fire served as the counterbalance to the righteousness of heaven, and therefore he remained a working participant in the engine of the universe.

The most powerful archangel turned devil. A welcome title for the king of the underworld.

As Lucifer sneered down at the mortals buzzing through their mundane day-to-day lives below, he felt the familiar aura unique only to the almighty himself arrive behind him.

"Let me guess, my dear brother Michael has placed me firmly at the top of his suspect list?" Lucifer stated.

He glanced over his shoulder, God had dressed in a tan trench coat, a navy suit visible underneath.

The almighty placed his hands in his pockets, peering down at the mortal world as well.

“Can you blame him? You were always at each other’s throats, even before The Fall. He is arguably, your archnemesis, yes?” he quipped.

“He should find other hobbies.” Lucifer turned fully to his father. “I know I certainly have found more meaningful distractions from our endless quarrelling.”

A long history between them, but Lucifer could no longer find a scrap of devotion left inside himself. Satan had long abandoned emotions such as admiration and reverence, only callousness and rancor remained.

God leveled an equally assessing gaze upon his eldest. “You’ll be pleased to hear that most of us consider this act to be beneath you.”

Lucifer smirked at that. “It was a bit too obvious for my tastes.”

“And none of your rogues…?” God asked. Lucifer chuckled.

“No. They’re cowards, not nearly capable enough for this. What of your gilded workforce?”

God adjusted his cuffs. "I'm afraid they are just as much in the dark as the rest of us," God responded.

Lucifer’s smugness grew. "Not quite as much, my friend," he teased.

God viewed the lights below, letting out a sigh. “Then we have a real mystery on our hands. And something out there is tipping the Balance, it must be restored.”

“If you ask me, I think it’s a nice change of pace.”

The almighty frowned. “This isn’t some minor human dispute. An *immortal* was murdered. The effect it had on the Balance was exponentially larger than anything the humans could do. And even that pales in comparison to the threat of what could still happen. Something out there was able to pull this off—without our knowledge. No immortal, angelic or demonic is safe. So I condemn your humor in this situation.”

Lucifer scoffed, “Still sounds amusing to me, but thank you for reminding me how boring heaven is, nothing but the status quo. I’m missing my Inferno already. So, what do you want to do about this, oh almighty one?” he mocked.

God threw a wary, accusatory glance his way. "Are you behind this, Lucifer?"

Lucifer placed a hand over his heart dramatically. “Oh daddy-dearest, you have no faith in me.”

“Not too long ago you used the kernel of the cosmos you inherited to bring your Heir into being. His talents are considerably intense. Convince me that you haven’t unleashed him upon our universe.” his voice was firm.

Lucifer fought the urge to sneer at him, instead he enacted his serpentine arrogant smile.

“Believe me, if I had unleashed Kaleus on this universe, it wouldn’t result in a singular immortal death. It would be *nuclear*,” Lucifer emphasized.

Keeping his straight face, he continued, "No matter how much I’d enjoy wiping out your precious garrison of angels, like you—I have a higher obligation to keep the Balance. I've spent a great deal of time building my realm into my pride and joy, getting it organized. I would not jeopardize that for one stupid Guardian angel," he explained.

The almighty stopped short. “I never said it was a Guardian…”

Lucifer didn’t fluster from the accusation, instead he crossed his arms and smiled confidently.

“The Opsalis filled in the blanks.”

The almighty knew that Lucifer had stolen away multiple valuable objects from heaven’s vaults during the Fall. The Opsalis being a direct link into the supernatural web without a personal connection. Among the treasures of the Eternals, it wasn’t badly missed.

God sighed, holding Lucifer’s gaze, looking for any signs of deceit within him.

When he was satisfied that there was none he said, "Very well. So if it wasn't you and it wasn't me, any idea what might have caused this? The fallen Guardian—his soul hasn't returned to heaven, as it should have following his death."

"Are you considering the humans he was guarding in your search? If they might be related?" Lucifer inquired.

"Do you have a theory?"

"This Guardian, I assume they weren't innately important, just another cog in your machine?" Lucifer asked.

"I consider all of my angels important," God countered.

With a roll of his eyes, Lucifer continued, "What I mean is, if there was no logical reason why anyone would kill the Guardian themselves, then perhaps this has something to do with his assignments," he explained.

God pondered this for a moment. "I'll have Gabriel look further into it. He's been assigned to the mortals still without a Guardian."

"Gabriel? You think that golden-boy can handle it?" Lucifer chuckled.

The almighty shook his head with disapproval. "He'll do fine. Guardian angels fall under his division, and it's time he be given a more challenging assignment anyhow."

"Let's just hope the youthful brute doesn't find himself too attached to the mortal. Those Guardian bonds can be intense if I recall," Lucifer stated.

Lucifer would know. During the new mortal creation after The Tear, he himself served as the Guardian over the first mortal woman, Lillith. That ended well…

A knowing glance from God sent a spark of fury through his cold blood.

“Gabriel was born without your astounding need for lust and violence,” the almighty stated.

Lucifer snorted. “From what I hear, he can be a little reactive, like Michael. So I wouldn’t be so sure about the latter. We’ll see how he fairs against such a unique bond.”

Lucifer thought back to their current predicament. The main question to ask was, *why*?

Why would someone or something kill a Guardian? They have a simple job that doesn't interfere with others, they simply guide a human through their stages of life. They keep humans from their death before their specific time. They guide them towards paradise, though they aren't allowed to interfere if their humans go astray, their Guardian presence is watchful and sheltering.

What would a Guardian be sheltering someone from that could kill them to get to the mortal they’re protecting?

Of all the immortal creatures that roamed the realm, Guardians were some of the least worrisome and remain relatively neutral. Not even demons waste their time with them. So why a Guardian?

"What are you thinking?" God broke him out of his thoughts.

Lucifer kept his eyes on the world. "It's strange that a Guardian would be killed. Do we know how he was killed yet?"

"Not yet. I’m hoping Gabriel may be able to figure that out."

Lucifer nodded. "It's so unusual, and the impact it made was massive, everyone on the web heard it. One would only make such a show if they meant to send a message. That or they themselves didn't realize they were capable of such a feat."

"You think it might have been intentionally done to tip the Balance?" God asked.

He shrugged. "Perhaps. Or maybe it wasn't intentional, maybe whoever or whatever caused it hadn't intended it to be so public."

God theorized, "They had to know that something that large might draw attention. If it were unintentional, they might be long-gone by now."

They both observed the earth below them. The mortals went about their lives completely heedless to the event that had occurred. Their lives were brief and insignificant in the grand design.

Yet, the almighty put them on a pedestal. He controlled an entire universe, entire worlds. His archangels were the only true offspring he had, but angels and humans were his *creations*.

For the humans he would do anything. The archangels pretended it didn't bother them, but Lucifer hadn't been so willing to be set aside.

"Finding out who and why should be our priority," God said.

This mystery was an exhilarating change in routine for Lucifer. Intriguing enough that he felt tempted to invest his own time into it. But then again, his hands were full down in the pit.

Lucifer had his demons, creations of his own blood. Along with the angels that sided with him and inevitably plummeted with him during the Fall.

He had an entire arsenal at his feet. The legions served more specific purposes and also allowed more freedom than the Fallen. Those strong enough to make it through to the mortal realm had a pension for causing havoc every once in a while, keeping those angel patrols good and busy. On occasion giving the enforcers like Gabriel a chance to stretch their wings a bit.

The angels of heaven and the hellborn didn't get along one bit.

There was a natural and delicious rivalry between them. Demons weren't as immortal as angels, though to kill one an archangel would need to smite them. Otherwise, angels could only banish them from the mortal realm using runes and spells when need be.

Angels were a lot harder to kill, in-fact the only things capable of killing them aside from a being as powerful as an archangel themselves would be…

It was then that an idea glimmered in Lucifer's mind.

A fortuity that could drive towards a promising destination.

"What are they trying to tell us? That we can be killed, that immortals are no more immune to death than humans?" God asked.

Lucifer hadn't been paying attention to him, key elements of a plan were coming together in his mind.

“Shall I propose an idea?” Lucifer inquired. God lifted an eyebrow, his sudden change in demeanor made him skeptical. Lucifer cocked his head to the side, a cunning mind ready to work.

“I always was the best with ideas.”

“Raphael would beg to differ,” God added.

A shrug. “There is a difference between precocity and just being crafty.”

“I don’t know if I like where this is headed.”

Lucifer waved his hand in the air.

“Humor me. What if, now think about it before you say no, what if we brought our foot soldiers together on this? Say, I send some of my greatest and most reliable demons, and you send your angels, and they work as a sort of team to overturn every possible stone, and find the answers to this new riddle, so to speak.”

The almighty chuckled. “A team? Of angels and demons?” his laughter grew. “That sounds more problematic than helpful.”

“An alliance then, a temporary parley.”

God knew better than to trust Lucifer right away, especially when he appeared to be overly cooperative.

"Demons and angels quarrel like cats and dogs, you believe they could manage to collaborate without any major altercations?"

Lucifer smirked. “Oh there will be clashing, but I think they can manage, especially while under orders. Or are your angels not as obedient as they appear?”

He crossed his arms across his chest, looking Lucifer up and down. “You’re up to something with this…”

“You’ll just have to play along if you want to find out.” His grin was wide and cunning.

"If I agree to this, there will be rules in place.” God pointed.

“I’d be amazed if there weren’t.” Was Lucifer’s only response.

He sighed audibly, “I mean it. We may each employ someone to hold charge, an *equal* and professional group. Don’t send someone who will only cause trouble.”

Lucifer pouted. “Aw, but that takes all the fun out of it.”

“This isn’t about fun. If this is really going to happen, you need to take it seriously,” the almighty snapped.

“Fine. Fine.”

Another deep sigh. God paused to reconsider, thinking about all the possible ramifications of this agreement. Lucifer plastered his cool, calm look, hiding the grinning wildcat underneath.

God conceded, “Alright. A temporary alliance, only until this is rectified."

"Of course." Lucifer bowed mockingly to his father. "Now, if you'll excuse me, I must be off to brief and prepare my chosen damned. I’ll have my messenger notify yours of the time and place to meet.”

“You already have some in mind?” he asked.

Lucifer stepped up onto the brim of the tower platform, his feet balancing him from a sheer drop.

“Haven’t you?” His hand lifted to give him a final salute. “Always a pleasure working with you. I look forward to more of it."

With that he simply leaned his body and fell headfirst off the bridge. His hands and legs tucked in tight, gravity bringing him down quickly. But not one hair or piece of his clothing moved in the wind.

Just before his body would slam into the gray water below a plume of smoke and lightning appeared, opening into a pitch-black rift. Without breaking his speed Lucifer plunged into the fissure between the realms. It closed behind him, the smoke dissipating into the air and mist.

The almighty once again looked down at the mortal realm below him, shaking his head.

"He always did have a penchant for the theatrics.”

God’s next destination was to visit Azrael at the Gates of Judgement. Afterwards he would return to heaven. There he would try to curb the panic growing among the angels, but also to call his own chosen company of angels for this joint venture.

FOUR
Gabriel

THE MORTAL WAS SLEEPING.

Being only two in the morning, it was only natural she would be asleep. Her home was a small one-bedroom apartment, on the third floor of a tall building complex. From the look of it, she had chosen the place for its price, rather than its luxury. No doubt she was on a student's budget. Making barely enough income from assistant teaching to make rent and pay for basic groceries.

I had been with her for a few hours, during which I had learned some things about her. Where she was going to school, how long she'd lived in Phoenix, and so on. Having just started, the Guardian bond hadn't yet clicked into place. But I'd wait as long as needed, the bond was a necessary mechanism of defense to help Guardians protect their assignments.

Heather Coleman. A twenty-six-year-old graduate student at Arizona State University.

From the outside, she appeared an average young woman. An ordinary human with an ordinary life. Olive skin, shoulder-length dark brown hair, with light honey-colored ends that matched her eye color.

From a surface point of view, there wasn't anything special about Heather or her situation.

In the mortal realm, an archangel needed to suppress their grace. However, the occasional creak of the walls inside the small apartment spoke to how much my power still strained against the tight space. It was manageable, but tended to cause strain on my emotions as well. Making them more intense, eager to burst.

So I busied myself, picking a book off of her shelf and reading the pages while she slept. Staving off the building storm within me.

Heather began to stir, her heart picking up its pace. A vivid dream, or a nightmare.

I couldn't enter her conscious mind, my mental abilities like most angels were limited to the subconscious. Some could break through the protections the almighty's bit of soul offered the mortals. I was not one of those born with the gift, however.

But dream-walking was something most angels could do. Guardians would use it sometimes to soothe their mortals during times of extreme distress or trauma.

I knelt softly next to her bedside, her features were twisted, entangled in a nightmare.

I lifted my hand to her temple, having to cross enough into the mortal realm to make physical contact, and focused my mind on her subconscious barrier. My touch soft enough that our skin barely made contact.

Mortal minds were already fragile and unguarded, but more so while in REM sleep, which is why dream walking was easy for gifted immortals.

I could see the walls that guarded her mind, low while she slept. With only a focused thought I was gliding inside past the barriers.

All at once I was there with her. We were inside a dark cave, the walls looked to be made out of volcanic rock. The large cave had a vague dome shape, and in the center there was a dark pool. The only sources of light were low-burning streaks of embers along the walls and floor.

Heather was first just staring into the dark pool, her eyes almost blank, as though the black pool of water had drowned her soul in its depths.

Then she turned to face one of the far walls. The embers burned brighter as she approached, revealing various symbols, runes, and other markings. Some looked like Egyptian hieroglyphics, others like Mayan texts. But there were runes too, from ancient languages long forgotten.

She lifted her hand to the wall and began to trace circles and lines, the symbols glowed and pulsed on the walls with her fingers. She drew Enochian symbols and Zibu sigils—languages of angels.

“Darkness dwells where one can’t see…" Heather recited a short passage. Translating it as if by memory.

"Strange," I spoke.

She jumped and whipped toward me, shocked that she wasn't alone.

"Who are you?"

I ignored her and approached the wall. Tracing the Enochian symbols.

"Loose this bond of endless light…?"

"You can read it too?" Heather asked. My eyes remained on the wall, the passages weren't familiar to me. As if they were written elsewhere, not meant for angels.

"...escape, bend the whole…open mind…Hmm. This doesn't make a lot of sense."

"Please, I don't understand. Who are you?" Heather begged. Her voice edging with desperation.

Finally dropping my eyes to hers I asked, "Do you often see these markings in your dreams?"

Her eyes a swirling storm of gold and deep brown, staring at me as she had never seen anything like me before. Even in here, my power was dampened, but maybe she could see some of it.

I waited for her answer, but it never came. She was motionless, my presence overwhelming her senses. I faced her more fully.

"Heather."

I heard her heart skip a beat when I spoke her name. Her heart beating faster now, my gaze deepened.

I tried again, with more command. "I need you to focus, Heather. Have you seen these in your dreams before?" Her eyelids blinked. Once. Twice. She broke contact to peer at the markings on the wall, scanning up and down before returning to me.

"Yes. I've seen them before."

"Has anyone else been in here with you? Have you seen anyone else in here? Anyone you may not have recognized?" I asked. Perhaps her Guardian, or someone else…maybe his murderer. A fool's prayer, but a chance, nonetheless.

Her only response was a short shake of her head.

“What about while you're awake? Anyone or anything stand out to you? An unexplained event or behavior?” I prodded.

It was unlikely that she would have experienced anything out of the ordinary.

But then her eyes sparked with shocked recognition. "Mason," she whispered.

I stiffened. “What about Mason?” She had seen him—her Guardian. But how?

She looked away distantly, as if seeing that far away memory and its every detail.

“I was in class. And then I wasn't. He was…dying.” Her voice broke off at the end.

My chest tightened, watching her Guardian die must have been truly difficult to witness. I wouldn't wish that pain, that accompanies such a bond, on anyone. Although, it did peg the question of why only Heather felt it…

I took another step towards her. She froze—unsure if she should move or stay.

"I need to see your memories, Heather. Will you allow me further in?"

I slowly raised my hand to her face, touching a finger to her temple. This was a more complicated technique, one that I wasn't well-versed in. It would take a lot of concentration to not leave any damage.

She remained frozen, waiting in what I could only think was reluctant fear.

Only while in her subconscious would I be able to view her conscious memories, while her mental blocks were already down. But it would put a lot of strain on my own abilities. If she were conscious, I would need to find someone more adept in mental exploration.

She stared at me, a tiny flicker of fear and confusion crossed her expression, but then she nodded.

I closed my eyes and gently dug deeper into her subconscious, past the dreams and into the shadowed area of her memory palace.

I searched for Mason, any sign of him, using what she had already said about the memory to try to locate it. But like the almighty experienced, even from here, I found no sign of him.

Even if she hadn't remembered him, there should have been a beacon of light inside her where the bond would have been. But there were only shadows and darkness. As if when he died, every trace of his soul was wiped out.

The information only added to my long list of questions. How was she able to remember it when speaking with me, but it was nowhere to be found when I looked for it?

I gently began withdrawing from her memory palace, sliding back through the dreams of her subconscious, and exited fully into the dream we both stood in.

I opened my eyes and watched her face. "I don't understand," I muttered.

The ground rumbled, the very walls of the dome shook. Heather and I both crouched a bit to steady ourselves. Bits of rock tumbled off the walls as the quaking grew stronger. Then it stilled for a moment.

Heather's eyes were wide. "What was that?" she asked, barely above a whisper.

Then all at once the scenery changed. The dome stretched and pulled as if being ripped away. Light flooded in, grass reached up and met our feet. Heather's body was pulled away from me by an unseen force.

I tried to grab her but missed.

Within seconds we weren't in the cave anymore, now we were on the edge of a cliff. Below the cliff, there was only darkness where I would imagine a sea to be.

Quickly after surveying our new location I turned back to make towards Heather—only to see she was no longer alone.

Behind her stood a hooded figure, its tattered cloak flowing outward like smoke and liquid. I couldn't see its face, but its hands curved to sharp talons. Those talons were wrapped around her neck, holding her hostage. She stood there, still, and seemingly unaware of the figure behind her. Enchanted in a way to remain calm.

A nightmare, this was a nightmare.

It leaned in close, whispering in her ear, and when it finished her vacant eyes locked on me. The golden/brown color of her irises shifted, consumed by a liquid onyx, completely overcoming the whites of her eyes, leaving them void of light.

"What are you?" I asked the figure.

Its free claws clicked together; its figure still hidden behind Heather.

“Good to see you Gabriel,” it said.

The voice was wet and raked, inhuman. Chills ran down my spine, but I kept it straight. Ready to surge my power at it if I needed to.

“Do we know each other?”

A sloppy, raspy chuckle. “You shouldn’t go poking into things that aren’t your business, archangel.” It traced one of its sharpened talons down Heather’s hair.

She remained still, unflinching.

“It became my business when you killed Mason.”

“It must be frustrating, a being of endless light to be in the dark. Still young and ambitious, still naïve,” it rambled.

I rallied some of my power, feeling its cleansing burn just underneath my skin. This wasn’t just a nightmare, and it couldn’t be allowed to stay here inside of her.

“Why don’t you enlighten me?”

From what it was implying, perhaps it wasn’t Mason’s murderer, but an accomplice.

"You are strong Gabriel, but impulsive. Even now, you're preparing your mighty power to strike me down. But you are powerless here." The words of this creature came from Heather's mouth.

It had her under its control and if I attempted to strike it, it would result in striking her.

A show of force then. I unfurled my wings and let the light of my power bring more light into the space. A shadow remained surrounding Heather and the creature, my light couldn't penetrate it, the creature answered my display of power only with an amused hiss.

"I won't ask again, tell me what you are and why you're here." I let my glow pulse to emphasize my words.

The last thing I wanted was to hurt the mortal, but if I had to in order to banish this thing, I would have no other choice. In the end, what was one mortal life to stopping a potentially cosmic threat?

When it didn't answer me, I continued, "Are there more of you?"

The more I looked at it, the more familiar it seemed. An ancient creature that shouldn't be in this realm, one that had been locked away long ago.

It only let out a hissing chuckle, tightening its grip on Heather.

My jaw tightened. "Release her immediately." My voice was strong and vibrated the walls of the dream world. The walls of her subconscious rippled like fabric.

"You have no power over me, archangel. It's been a pleasure."

With a sickening hiss the figure pierced Heather's neck with its talons and she lurched forward. The blood that seeped from her wound was black, and it poured out like a river breaking from a dam.

When I went to lunge for her the blackened, oily blood flooded the earth and rushed towards me in a wave. I braced myself, curving my power into a protective shield in front of me.

When the force of the wave hit, I could feel myself being pushed back. I had to expand my shield until it became a bubble surrounding me to keep the liquid at bay. Still, it carried me back as if I were caught in a current of the ocean.

When it receded, I was no longer in her mind. And my energy was low.

Gasping, I looked around, I was back in her room.

"What in heaven—"

Heather remained asleep, her eyes fluttering as if the nightmare carried on for her. Her body twitched and shuttered, but she was alive despite what those talons did to her inside. I hadn't realized that my wings had come out during that ordeal. They consumed most of the room, luckily the room hadn't collapsed, only a few things had been knocked aside, things easily restored to their original place.

"Gabriel."

I shot hot light toward the sound, the beam enveloping the room in golden light. Ready to defend against anything that came near the human and me.

"Gabriel! It's just me!" The angel Duma blocked the light with all his might. He wasn't an archangel but could shield against a smiteful blow well enough. At least one that was weakened.

I breathed, easing the light. "Duma. I'm sorry, I acted on impulse."

"Why so defensive all of a sudden?"

I relaxed, retreating my wings back into myself. Bringing my power back down to a more manageable level. A few cracks in the walls, however, needed repairing before she awoke.

"I think I just encountered a wraith inside the human's subconscious."

"A wraith? Are you sure?" He was right to be doubtful.

"No, I'm not. It looked like a wraith but was immune to me. Maybe it was simply posing as a wraith to hide its true form." I began mending the broken pieces of the apartment. "What news from heaven?"

"The almighty and Lucifer came to an agreement; they're assembling their best to work together as a team. They meet in two days in a secure location in the desert not far from here. He sent me to notify you," Duma explained.

"They're assembling…? He expects us to work with the hellborn on this?" I asked.

Duma shrugged. "The almighty works in mysterious ways."

I couldn't help but smile. "Indeed. Was it his idea or Lucifer's?" I already knew the answer. Duma only gave a shrug. "That's not leery at all."

Duma leaned against the doorway, observing the sleeping human. Both of us hidden in the Ethereal realm now.

“Jade’s upset,” he muttered, his eyes scanning Heather, but distant, “Mason was a friend of hers. You and I trained him way back when, you remember?” he asked.

I nodded. “He was a good one.”

Biting his lip, he said, “I can’t think of anyone who would’ve wanted to hurt him.”

I peered at Heather’s sleeping body, the sight of that wraith still fresh in my mind.

“I don’t think this is as simple as just someone with a grudge. It’s something bigger, darker.”

Duma dipped his chin in understanding, his eyes filled with grief.

This was new territory for us. Angels lived long enough lives that their natural decline towards death wasn’t abhorrent. But this, it was an open, gushing wound of mourning that we immortals weren’t accustomed to experiencing.

“Do you know who the almighty is calling for our end of this…assembly?" Wanting to distract Duma.

It appeared to work; the warrior calm returned to his eyes. He straightened.

"You’re to be in-charge, obviously. He’s asked me to join, as well as Iaoel, Jophiel and Jade." Those were strong angels. Some of the best in their fields in heaven, but a strange combination.

Duma seemed to read my thoughts. "I think he believes that a variety of abilities will have a better chance of finding and eliminating whatever the threat is. It doesn't hurt that we all know one another and have worked together before, less chances of internal disputes."

As if we would be the ones worrying about that.

"Plus," he added, "I think he is hesitant to trust Lucifer and his hellborn, he wants a strong yet adaptable team to offer a unified front."

I laughed lightly. "I would hardly consider Jophiel adaptable." My sister had a temper, and overall was very intolerant of demons.

Duma smiled with amusement as he shook his head. "I think she's more for brute strength than anything."

"Jophiel and I are the only archangels on that list, perhaps Raphael or Michael would be better choices."

Michael was as strong as they get, and Raphael was a planner, he made calculated decisions that would benefit an alliance such as this.

Even if Mason fell under my jurisdiction, it doesn't necessarily mean that I was the best choice. As much as I wanted to prove myself to be.

"Michael is probably the worst choice to make for this. Working with Lucifer and his cronies…it'd be anything but productive." Duma chuckled at the idea.

It was true. Michael and Lucifer each considered the other their nemesis, and likely would forever.

“Besides, I assume they’re both the cavalry waiting in the wings, they’ll be used if stronger fighters are needed. No offense, of course.”

I nodded in understanding.

Duma and I were partners in my division. He knew my strengths and my weaknesses. And though I matched Raphael in raw power, I was nowhere near equal to his mind.

“He’s being strategic holding them back. Here’s to hoping they won't be needed," I added.

I fought against the twist of jealousy in my gut. My brothers have been around a lot longer than me, they’ve been tried in battle and in the development of this universe.

I would get my chance too, and perhaps this was it.

Sibling rivalry was natural in our family. Michael was a symbol of power, he made us all feel small in a way. Being the second oldest, his inherited power was more potent. The only ones of us who seemed to pay no mind to the power structure were Azrael and Chamuel. Their gifts made them neutral, indifferent.

A blessing, I suppose, to be so specifically gifted that you never have to fight for your place on the pyramid.

"Do we have someone assigned to guard the human while we meet?" I asked.

Her dreams concern me, all human life is something to be cherished, but my instincts told me something was different about Heather.

Duma studied my eyes carefully but answered my question without hesitation, "Jade intends to assign her second and third to watch over her. Since Guardians can be killed, more than one watching over her may be better."

I nodded in agreement.

Two Guardians weren't nearly as strong as an archangel, but they should be able to protect her and each other for a few hours.

Pairing up two Guardians would stretch our resources. All of our angels would be working double time for a while, and that may render them more susceptible to attack.

"I have to go, many angels are requesting additional combat training in hopes to better prepare for threats, so I've got a lot of work to do. But I will see you in a couple of days." Duma grasped my forearm with his hand.

"See you then, brother."

Light flashed in his wake as he disappeared. I turned back to Heather, who was still stirring in her nightmare.

I sighed and knelt beside her bed again. I lightly touched her head, smoothing her hair down.

"*Rauha sinun unelma.*" *Peaceful be thy slumber.*

I recited a simple yet effective spell and used a little of my powers to further soothe her dreams. It would wipe away lingering pain and fear.

Her face calmed, and she drifted into a soft slumber.

"*Mitä sinä enkeleillä ja demonilla olet*, Heather?"

What are you to angels and demons, Heather?

FIVE
Azrael

THE ANGEL OF DEATH, Azrael, wasn't like the other archangels.

Her duties dealt with souls more than all the others. She was in charge of all the Reapers and Thrones that roamed the earth, messengers and guides of death.

Azrael was organized by trade, with an ever-growing number of souls reaching their end each day as the global population continues to grow, without organization souls could slip through the cracks instead of finding peace.

Azrael's job was pretty simple in the broad scope of things, she hasn't had to interfere with living souls since the time of Exodus. However, the Balance was a large factor in her everyday existence.

She determined who belonged in the Elysian estates of heaven; who deserved peace and who was beyond the grasp of heavenly redemption.

Her Reapers were like worker bees, always working and adjusting where needed. Azrael has a spiritual connection with each and every worker, sending signals to point them in the direction they need to go.

Reapers don't just hang about waiting for a human to pass away, they are specifically assigned to deaths, they're only purpose is to grab hold of a soul once it has left the body and guide it to the Gates for judgement. Thrones are a lesser form of Reaper, lending assistance during mass deaths when necessary. But their main job is to guide those souls who will become angels upon passing, mostly young children who are still blessed with the innocence of youth.

The Gates of Judgement were sort of like a waiting room in an office. Souls would come in and wait to be called. Azrael was progressive in that way. Back during the height of the Egyptian empire, Azrael was referred to as Anubis, and the Gates involved balancing their good deeds against a feather.

Now, it's like a doctor's office, every soul has a chart categorizing their good deeds, sins, and overall influence on the lives they touched. Every human is given a chance to defend themselves or have a loved one vouch for their redemption.

Azrael, with the use of her Book of Order, would see the soul exactly as it was and it aided in the final judgement.

The death of a Guardian was unheard of, and when it happened Azrael heard it louder than most.

A soul not meant for judgement had broken the system.

When an angel's long lifespan reached its end, the soul would simply pass right back to the almighty to be redistributed. No pain, no grief, just a part of the cycle.

But when the Guardian, Mason, passed unnaturally, it was cause for concern.

When his soul didn't return to heaven, Azrael waited for Mason's soul to find its way to her gate, hoping for an explanation. But it never came.

Azrael actively sent her Reapers to look for any signs of his soul heading for hell, but they found no evidence of it. She knew God would be visiting her for answers, and she would have to disappoint him.

Azrael flipped through her book, finding no answers to their endless list of questions. She looked at her tablet, scanning through the ever updating list of incoming souls, but didn't find the one she looked for. She slammed her fist against her desk. She felt restless and began pacing her office.

"Damn it." She peered through the glass walls of her office down into the large room where souls came in and out.

She tapped her chin, tugging on a few threads in her mind linking to her head Reapers. "Anything?" she asked out loud, the message going down to each of them.

They buzzed back similar-to-identical responses.

Nothing. We're still looking.

Her assistant waited just inside the door, patiently quiet during her frustration.

She turned to him, "Nile, go see about the other souls downstairs. Report back if anything requires my personal attention." He nodded and left the room without a word. The door shut with a quiet click.

Azrael gazed at her book again, grateful for its resolving influence. Even the moderate nature of hers could sometimes feel overwhelming anger, but an outburst from her would be deplorable beyond reason.

She had to remain calm during this endeavor.

“Azrael.” The almighty’s warm familiar voice filled the room, his presence brightening the monochrome office.

“I don’t have news for you,” Azrael explained without turning to face him.

“I feared as much.” God was always a patient leader, but his concern influenced the atmosphere. “Lucifer knows nothing as well.”

“I’m not all that surprised,” She stated. Her eyes remained on the souls below.

“You seem to be the only one willing to believe him.”

She turned to him slowly then. “I know him better than most. We do work in tandem quite a bit.”

Azrael and Lucifer both handled the aftermath of death, their relationship was always respectful. And even though she didn’t agree with his uprising, she understood it. The Fall was more disappointing for her than it was for her siblings.

God sighed, not looking at anything in particular. “It would be nice to work with him without having to keep one eye open for deception.”

She nodded. “It’d also be nice if Michael weren’t always itching for a fight.”

God gave her a knowing smile. “You all have your key traits. Lucifer the cunning, Michael the mighty—"

“Azrael the just,” she finished for him.

Her thoughts drifted to the first millennia of their existence. So much about their world was fresh, ripe for corruption. When it was just the three of them, things were simpler. Power pulsed beneath their feet as the fabric of this universe still settled and built into life.

Even as more of her siblings came into existence, the realms trembled as they were stitched together. It wasn't until the dust settled when their rivalry really began roaring. Powerful beings having to share space, share duties.

They needed purpose, needed regular tasks to distract them from competing against one another. For most of them, that need to ascend eventually dulled and settled along with the universe. For others, it only festered into something unending.

Azrael sat at her desk, her fingers scanned mindlessly through her book. Mortal souls seemed so minuscule compared to the issue at hand.

"Gabriel coming into his new assignment alright?" Azrael asked.

"He's being professional about it." Azrael shot him a perceptive glance. The almighty clarified, "I have no doubt that he'll rise to the occasion."

Azrael nodded in agreement.

God asked, "Where could a Guardian's soul go if it didn't return to me or here for judgement?"

Azrael hadn't ran into a problem like this in all the many years she'd been in charge of soul retrieval.

"There are still forces in this universe that are beyond our knowledge. I wouldn't be shocked if something eluded me, but you're the almighty, one of the Eternals. If anyone knew of something that powerful, it would be you. Perhaps you've forgotten something?" she asked.

God could think of others powerful enough, but the possibility of that was unfeasible now. Long departed from this universe. It had to be something else.

Azrael's assistant came running in. "Azrael, your presence is needed." He looked to the almighty, embarrassment and shame replaced his worried expression. "Oh, I'm sorry for intruding" He bowed before turning back to Azrael.

"What is it Nile?"

"Some of the Reapers, ma'am, they haven't been reporting back. And human soul arrivals have slowed, our data indicates that deaths are increasing but the souls aren't reaching us."

Azrael's eyes widened. She looked to her father. "You're sure none of Lucifer's demons aren't involved?"

"He gave me his word," God responded.

"How many Reapers are missing?" she turned back to Nile.

"Five are not answering so far, but were losing more, some of the others are going to their last locations."

Azrael tapped her book, seeking its stable equilibrium. It answered back, soothing away the most frayed pieces of her sanity.

She looked back up to Nile's waiting face. "We're pulling them back. Reapers and Thrones must return to the gates immediately. Tell them to not linger around their assignments, only grab and go. If souls refuse to come, leave them to Purgatory."

God's head snapped towards hers, she met his wary gaze.

"We'll go back for them when we can. When they get back here we'll begin pairing them off, no one goes out alone." She nodded towards Nile to carry out the order, he dipped his chin and exited.

"A Guardian dies and now Reapers and mortals are vanishing out of sight? I don't like the direction this is going." Azrael conveyed her dismay to her father with her eyes. "I'll have to notify Uriel that her realm is going to have increased occupation—temporarily."

God agreed. "When this is resolved, we can readjust as needed. If the disappearances continue, I recommend ceasing your Reapers completely," he said.

A thought crossed Azrael's mind. "This feels an awful lot like the beginnings of a war. You think there is a chance of combat?" she asked.

God met her gaze, nothing but calm seriousness in his eyes. "It wouldn't hurt to prepare for it. Some of the other divisions are already refreshing their combat training. Maybe your Reapers and Thrones should do the same."

Azrael began shaking her head. "I don't think the Spectrals would be able to accommodate for all of us, not all at once."

Spectrals, the trainers of angels. Gabriel's division already overwhelmed as it is, a large influx of returning angels looking for additional training would cripple them.

"Perhaps it would be best if they came to you instead. I'll send a message to them, see if they can send trainers to the divisions. Reduce the bottleneck," the almighty reasoned.

Azrael sighed, worry weighing heavily on her shoulders. She didn't usually let it affect her, but even this she couldn't hide from her father.

"I was really hoping we were done with fighting after The Fall."

"This is eternity, Azrael. Peace is only a portion of it. But let's hope it doesn't get to that point." Azrael and God stared at one another.

"Hope for the best, prepare for the worst," she recited. He smiled at her.

He waved his hand in the air. "I always thought our next conflict was going to be caused by Lucifer's Heir," he mused.

Azrael snorted. "Lucifer's losing his grip on that boy's leash. I don't see him doing Lucifer's dirty work for much longer."

"I assume he's going to be the one leading Lucifer's caravan." God shared with her.

"Oh, Gabriel is going to *love* that," she chuckled.

God chuckled with her. "I don't know. I think it'll be good for him, for both of them."

"If you say so." She shrugged.

Her eyes scanned the edges of her book again. Thinking about her Reapers, about the angels that were now at risk. For the first time in a long time, Azrael felt the cold, dry feeling of dread.

“We may need your help as we move forward,” the almighty amended.

The angel of death was a powerful being, and she may offer unrivaled assistance in certain circumstances.

She dipped her chin in response. “I’ll be there when I’m needed. Just tell Gabriel to call me. But I have faith in him. He’s smart and dependable. If anyone can see this through, it’s him.”

“I’m sure he would be grateful for your immoveable confidence in him.”

“If only some of that confidence would transfer to him.”

The almighty smiled to himself, “All of my archangels have exceeded any expectations I had for them, especially Gabriel.”

“Even Chamuel and Lucifer?” she teased.

Chamuel was a romantic naturally, a bit eccentric, but most importantly docile in comparison to the other archangels.

“Tell me someone else who could’ve done Chamuel’s job better? Lucifer, like all of you, has his part to play in keeping the Balance. The Fall a necessary evil in the path towards change,” the almighty explained.

Lucifer was always the epitome of free will and rebellion, it wasn’t all that surprising when he started the Uprising.

Though Azrael would love to continue this invigorating conversation, her Reapers were going missing, and that was pressing on her mind.

However, Azrael wanted to end their interaction on a relatively positive note.

“It’s good to see you, I wish it was in better circumstances, but I’ve missed home anyhow.”

The almighty embraced his third oldest, kissing her cheek.

“Heaven misses you as well. You know you are always welcome to visit? You don’t need the excuse of a supernatural crisis.”

Azrael chuckled, “Yes, because I have time for those *lively* family reunions.”

“I will reach back if I find answers,” he said.

She nodded, as if to say that she’d do the same.

The almighty vanished. The light of his presence faded and the shadows that crowned the room returned. Leaving Azrael alone to fret and ponder what tasks lay ahead.

SIX

THE SUPERNATURAL WEB was a universal communication tool that angels and demons used to speak to each other. In the web, when an immortal chooses to open their mind to another then they may communicate that way. Though rarely do demons and angels open that line of connection with one another.

This particular situation was one of those rarities. Duma had served as the main messenger of the angel cohort, so it was he that coordinated the meeting with Lucifer's chosen group.

It was a Thursday evening; dusk was setting on the horizon. A small, abandoned cabin in an old, barren town was their rendezvous. After the initial meet-and-greet, they would establish a better headquarters.

Gabriel was the first to arrive because of his close proximity. At least here he was able to release some of his power without fear of breaking the buildings.

The old cabin wasn't large, but it lacked a lot of furniture. A rotting table sat against the far west wall underneath the window. A rocking chair and a deteriorating coat rack sat on the south wall.

Duma and Iaoel appeared in the doorway together, having winnowed into the town.

Iaoel was an Angel of Sight, seers of the fates of mortals and resources for Reapers and Cherubim's. The information they gained with their ability were an essential piece that made up the chain of destiny.

Angels of Sight were gifted with premonitions, and Iaoel was one of the highest ranked angels in the division. A good choice for this mission, an angel with Sight might give them an advantage against their adversary.

"Gabriel, long time no see." Iaoel shook hands with him.

"Indeed," Gabriel responded. "You've changed since we last spoke, Iaoel. I like the haircut."

Iaoel self-consciously brushed the short fuzz with their fingers.

They exchanged smiles that didn't quite reach to their eyes. Iaoel wore a button up top, bowtie and suspenders connected to black capris. Their hair a chestnut brown, cleanly combed back.

"It's been a while since I've been in this realm, I didn't want to be too far behind the fashion," Iaoel said.

Duma, dressed in a simple blue t-shirt and worn jeans, having only seen Gabriel a couple days prior, felt no need for an introduction.

"Do we know which demons Lucifer sent?" Gabriel asked, the question mostly pointed towards Duma, but there was reason that Iaoel might know, with their abilities.

Iaoel smirked. "Of course we know, but that would ruin the surprise," they teased.

Gabriel chuckled.

“I don’t even get a hint?”

“Mmm, I think I’d rather see your reaction.” Iaoel was used to having their abilities spoil every inch of surprise, sometimes it was refreshing to leave things to the unknown.

“You’ll just have to be patient,” Duma recanted.

“Gabriel may be patient, but I’m not.” Jophiel’s voice alerted her presence, she was standing by the back door, a distasteful frown painting her archangel grace with gloom.

“Jophiel,” Gabriel greeted with a nod.

She wasn’t an affectionate or cheerful type. So he wouldn’t deign to behave as such with his older sister.

“Gabriel.” She nodded back. Jophiel jerked her chin towards the outside of the cabin. “Jade should be here soon.” Jophiel picked a piece of loose dust that had floated onto her Prussian pantsuit.

“We haven’t all worked together for some time,” Iaoel stated.

Duma chuckled, “Some of us work together quite frequently, Iaoel.”

Gabriel ignored him and grinned at Iaoel. “You are always welcome to come back to training. A refresher course couldn’t hurt you.”

Iaoel waved their hand idly in the air. “As much as I’d love to stretch my legs in the ring. I have other things I have to do in my leisure.”

Jophiel grumbled, “Like socialize with demons.”

Iaoel didn't face Jophiel fully, only shooting her a sidelong glance. "They're interesting creatures, I find them incredibly intriguing. You'll forgive me if I choose to be open-minded towards our fellow keepers of the Balance."

"You'll forgive *me* if I don't share the sentiment." Jophiel picked at the chipping door frame, not looking at anyone.

Her resentment of the demons ran deep, and her chilled temperament was always such a joy to have around.

None of them gave a response—not seeking to rouse her fury any further. Iaoel, however, rolled her eyes at Gabriel, forcing him to bite his lip to keep from chuckling out loud.

"This place is so dry," Jade said as she appeared next to Jophiel.

She slipped past her in one smooth motion and walked towards the others further in the cabin. Worry was shrouded over her hazel eyes, but Jade tried to hide it with her positive attitude.

"I'm not late, am I?"

Gabriel shook his head. "You've never been late a day in your life."

She grinned wider, shrugging. "Punctuality is a virtue."

"Well, I wish the demons felt the same way. Leave it to the hellborn to be consistently tardy," Duma teased.

Perfection was a well-known expectation of angels, often without a lot of room for individuality, some room, but not much. They were soldiers, a part of one synchronized machine. Even something as silly as tardiness made the hellborn stand out.

The sound of revving motorcycle engines stirred the silence of the decaying town, drawing the attention of the gathered angels. Their roar grew louder and louder until they were right outside of the cabin. Though the cycles had stopped, the riders revved them again for good measure. Sending a loud, obnoxious noise around the cabin before they cut the engines.

There was one specific individual who liked to ride motorcycles as a mode of transportation. The realization hit Gabriel along with a coiling of an old grudge in his gut.

Though he shouldn't be surprised that Lucifer chose him for this group, it didn't make Gabriel any happier about it. The archangel locked his gaze on Iaoel.

"Not him?"

Iaoel only grinned with amusement, mouthing an apologetic *Sorry*.

The front door of the cabin opened by a phantom wind and in walked two figures. The first was dressed in a worn t-shirt, leather jacket and ripped jeans, though he sauntered in wearing his signature smirk, the temperature rose from his presence.

Accompanying him was a short female, her dark skin tattooed immensely, contrasting starkly against her almost white coiled braids. She wore skin-tight black pants and an oversized matching shirt that she had twisted and tucked tight to her body. Her specialized weapons barely glinting behind the various straps and flannel shirt tied around her hips.

"Smells like baptism in here, fuck, we must be in the right place," she chuckled.

Gabriel recognized them both from an older encounter. She was Seere, a lower-level demon with unparalleled weapon and combat skills, and right hand to one of Gabriel's least favorite beings in the universe. Kaleus.

"I feel like I'm about to be exorcised." They both laughed.

Gabriel flexed his fists at his sides to avoid glaring directly at the new additions to their party.

The demon, Seere, eyed Iaoel and moved towards them.

"I suppose hello is in order, especially for such an attractive specimen. I'm Seere, but I'm sure you knew that." Iaoel grinned, unafraid of her, and perhaps more intrigued than anything.

"Iaoel. Pleasure to make your acquaintance." They extended their hand, Seere took it and shook once, holding it for a moment longer than necessary.

"If this is your idea of pleasure, then I think a thorough education is in order." She winked. "Don't worry, I'm a great teacher."

Iaoel choked back the startled chuckle that threatened to escape their lips. Instead, just held Seere's suggestive gaze.

Gabriel cleared his throat. "You're late," he said to Kaleus.

"Well you know, traffic is a bitch." Kaleus took off his jacket and hung it on the old coat rack. "It's been a while, featherbrain, how's daddy?" he asked, popping down into the creaky rocking chair.

The air in the room went taut.

"Could ask you the same question," Gabriel retorted.

Kaleus gave him a crooked, knowing smile. Gabriel, with the angels still behind him, watched Seere walked over to Kaleus and stand just behind his shoulder.

Ever the obedient general. Kaleus cataloged it.

"I certainly missed *that* expression on your face, wonder-boy."

Before Gabriel could growl at him Duma asked, "Anyone else going to show?"

"Why? Feeling lonely?" A sultry female voice wrapped its silk elegance and arms around Duma's waist from behind.

Her hot, enchanting lips close to his ear. "I'd be more than happy to keep you company."

Duma stilled the second she touched him. The angel straightened his back to maintain his composure, even when the very feeling of her hot breath on his neck made his skin shiver.

Lillith, mother of demons, and the thing that motivated Lucifer to rebel against heaven. Her serpentine powers of temptation helped bring about the fall of humanity, and even angels struggled against her allure.

She leaned in closer to the nape of his neck. "What do you say we break down some of that purity?" Lillith's hand began to move down Duma's chest, towards the belt of his pants.

Brazen, that's what she was, and shamelessly in front of everyone.

Duma's hand caught hers and held it firmly against his belly to stop her downward motion.

"Go any further and you'll have to manage without your hand." His voice calm but firm.

She giggled under her breath.

"Who said I needed my hands? I prefer to use my mouth anyway." Lillith bit the lobe of his ear.

Duma's shoulder's stiffened further, but he couldn't stop his eyes from clenching closed. The others assumed his reaction to be of disgust, but Lillith knew better, his pulse had increased against the vein in his neck, and she could feel heat of his body shifting with the arousal.

"A little pain, a *lot* of pleasure, lover." She ran her tongue along his neck.

"Lillith," Kaleus commanded, his voice dropped low with authority.

She shot a sharp glare towards him but relented. Duma relaxed only a little when Lillith released her grip and moved past the group of very tense angels over to stand next to Kaleus and Seere.

"It's too bad, I almost had him." She smirked.

Duma lifted his chin, steadying himself both physically and mentally. "I was completely in control."

She delicately and sensually moved her hair to one side all while looking him up and down.

"Challenge accepted," she mumbled.

Duma hid his returning challenging smirk. He may not like the mother of demons, but if she wanted to challenge him, he wouldn't shy from the trial.

When he saw Gabriel's disapproving gaze, his cheeks burned a bit in shame, but he righted himself.

"Nothing like carnal temptation to start this little shindig," Kaleus cooed with a lazy sigh.

The final demon, Daevas, was the last to show. The ginger demon was quieter in his approach, having simply walked in the door and took his place behind Kaleus' other shoulder, his eyes monitoring the desert outside. His own weapons strapped to his back.

"We're all here now, featherbrain, can we get on with it?" Kaleus twirled a small karambit dagger in his hand, knowing full well there was a glare pointed in his direction from the archangel.

"I suppose the first thing to discuss is what you already know." Gabriel eyed the group, mostly towards the demons.

Seere spoke first, "We heard about the Guardian's death, and we've heard rumors here and there but nothing concrete."

"Lucifer said after he spoke with the big guy that no angels are to blame, and none of us obviously had any involvement," Lillith added.

"Obviously?" Jophiel snarled.

Lillith rolled her eyes and went on, "So as far as we've been told, we're all here to figure it out, be a rag tag team of angels and demons." The others nodded along, agreeing with her statements.

They all watched each other waiting for the other to make an unexpected move, conscious of every shift and look exchanged.

They were all highly trained and skilled in their fields. Lethal weapons to be used if necessary.

"I'm not so sure we should believe any of you, a demon seems like an *obvious* suspect to me. Wouldn't be surprised if it were the mother of demons herself," Jophiel muttered.

Lillith smirked and turned towards her. "Maybe it was me, you never know. All things considered, if I had a way of killing angels, I wouldn't start with a *Guardian*." Her disgusted emphasis on the word set Duma and Jade's teeth on edge.

"What's a mere foot soldier compared to the glory of slicing up a delectable specimen such as yourself?" Lillith continued, pointing to the archangels. Lillith's gaze shifted to Duma with a wink. "Not you, sweetie. I have other intentions for your deliciousness."

Jophiel couldn't contain her deep growl this time.

"When in doubt, be seductive. Honestly, Lillith, do you have any other qualities?" Jophiel gestured to Gabriel. "This is the best that hell could offer? A succubus, an angsty prince, and a couple of inbred demons? Really? Gabriel, you and I both could do the job better on our own."

The responses that concluded her statement came all at once.

"Hey, what about us?" Jade chimed.

"Well that was rude…" Seere said.

"Did she just call me an angsty prince?" Kaleus chuckled.

"Inbred?"

"Arrogant archangels..."

"Jophiel, you know this isn't my decision." Gabriel's voice rang over the others.

"We'd be happy to do our own investigation, featherbrain. There's really no need for your involvement anyway if you feel you're not up to the task," Kaleus retorted.

Gabriel sighed, a test of patience, that's what this was going to be.

"Look, we are all here because this isn't just about the death of an angel. If something out there can kill a Guardian, then they can easily kill demons too, and all immortal beings for that matter."

The collective silence was reluctant.

"We may not like each other, and this may be a disaster, but we are all obligated to keep the Balance. Whoever did this tipped it, and we're all at risk." Gabriel sighed. "We have a job. Let's get it done, and then we can go on hating each other for all of eternity."

"I think it could be fun," Jade chimed in.

Everyone turned at the sound of her cheerful and optimistic voice.

Voicing a particular elephant in the room. "Who are you again?" Lillith asked, clearly annoyed by the situation.

Jade stood up straighter, though it didn't help her height any.

"Jade. I'm the Guardian Master. I trained the Guardian that was killed and was a part of assigning his post. In the grand scheme of things, I was the last angel to see Mason alive, and was the closest to him among those of us here."

"So you can tell us a bit about him?" Duma asked.

She started to nod when Lillith yawned loudly. "Who cares about the stupid Guardian? His death was a message or a fluke, either way, who he was doesn't matter, who the killer is matters." She leaned against the window.

"For once, Lillith, just shut your fucking hole," Kaleus sternly warned. Gabriel noticed a difference in Kaleus when he addressed Lillith. He was cold, harsh. But with everyone else he was comical and relaxed.

She giggled. "Which one?"

Kaleus only lifted his hand signaling her to stop, she backed off in a huff. Everyone watching the encounter slowly turned back to Jade.

"Go on, Jade," Duma encouraged.

Jade moved more to the middle of the room, her size seeming so much smaller in comparison to the high-level beings surrounding her.

"Mason wasn't new, he was made a Guardian about two-hundred years ago. Before that he helped new angels-in-training, his guidance abilities led us to agree that he would make an appropriate Guardian."

"Who were the humans he was guarding when this happened?" Daevas asked, a trained warrior cataloging potential key information.

"He had a few, some of them were already transitioning to their new Guardians. The main one in question, the one that is of concern is named Heather Coleman. She's a graduate student at Arizona State University," Gabriel answered.

Jade nodded. "He's been her Guardian for about 8 years."

"Wait," Kale stopped her, "I thought Guardian angels are supposed to be for life. Why was he only guarding her for 8 years?"

"Not anymore, we've made some major changes in the recent millennia to our system to accommodate for the mortal's population growth. Every human goes through different stages of life, and therefore need a variety of guidance depending on their stage of life. Our Guardians are specialized for specific maturity groups, so as a human moves to a different stage of maturity, they are assigned a different Guardian angel. Mason took over when Heather was seventeen, as she began moving into young adulthood. We estimated that he would only stay with her until she was into her mid-thirties to early forties when she would move into the next stage of maturity," Jade explained.

"So any given human would go through like eight Guardians in their lifetime? That sounds like a lot," Seere chirped.

"No, if it were based on age that would be the case. But we base it off of maturity. Early childhood to adolescence, adolescence to early adulthood, full-adulthood and then after a human hits about seventy years old, they will live out the rest of their lives with one last Guardian. So really, most humans only have about five Guardians throughout their entire lives. We've only recently developed and integrated this method in the last millennium. Before that it was a Guardian for life, but as populations rose and the diversity our Guardians offered became more specific, it seemed the best idea to get the best out of our resources."

Gabriel was there when Jade presented this idea, its success was the deciding factor to anointing her Guardian Master.

"Okay, back to Mason. Had he given any indication that he might be in trouble?" Duma asked.

Jade shook her head.

"I met with him only two days prior to his death. He gave me a normal status report and seemed perfectly fine. It was routine, he even met up with a couple of his training companions. From my perspective, everything was as normal as it could be."

"And the human? What of her?" Kaleus asked.

"She seems normal; however, I did encounter something strange in her dreams," Gabriel answered.

Their eyes turned to him. He cleared his throat.

"I was instructed to take over as her Guardian for the time being. I went into her subconscious and there was a creature there, looked to be a wraith."

"A wraith? I haven't seen those since...are you sure?" Jophiel asked. Gabriel nodded.

"I thought you and the other arch-assholes locked them away for good?" Lillith asked.

"The wraiths were sealed up during *Kaṇṇīr*, The Tear," Gabriel clarified. "Michael, Lucifer and Raphael did most of the sealing, but my other siblings helped them. They were sealed in some of our realm prisons, like Tartarus, Nessus, Maladomini and such."

"Can wraiths even get inside a humans mind? I thought they were just soulless spirits created from misuse of dark magic?" Seere asked.

Clearly the demons had also been taught some of our histories, even though they didn't come into existence until after The Fall.

"Wraiths act like a parasitic entity, it's entirely possible for them to get inside an unguarded subconscious. I believe what I saw in Heather's dream was a wraith. However, what confused me about it was that it was able to resist—if not nullify my powers a bit. Wraiths don't possess that capability, especially against an archangel. Our particular strength is why we were the only ones able to entrap them back then."

Gabriel recalled the memory of the creature and its black talons slicing Heather's neck open.

"So, it wasn't a wraith, then. Just glamoured as one?" Daevas suggested.

Duma fidgeted with the dusty wooden beams that held the old structure up as he cataloged all this information and thought of explanations.

Jophiel broke through the contemplative silence. "Either way, it wouldn't hurt to look at the prisons to make sure they're still sealed shut. We could also check the different layers of hell—I know Lucifer holds a few well-enforced dungeons down there as well," Jophiel said, pointing her eyes at the others as if suggesting which ones should go where.

"I have something else," Gabriel stated.

"Well, don't spill it out all at once featherbrain." Kaleus joked.

Gabriel pointed a menacing finger at him, full of threat. "Push me, I beg you."

Kaleus threw his hands up in playful surrender, holding his signature smirk on his face and maintaining eye contact.

“Any time, any day. I like it when we play.” Kaleus replied *very* suggestively.

Gabriel sighed to regain his composure and returned his eyes to the others. “Heather, the mortal, knew who Mason was.”

“I’m sorry, what?” Lillith turned.

“How?” Jade gaped. Humans were never supposed to know the presence of their Guardians, especially not who they were by name.

“I don’t know to what extent, but it was clear that she had met him before, she knew his name and…she witnessed his final moments.”

Kaleus whistled. “Dang, that’s definitely a precursor to a psychotic break if I ever saw one.” He lifted his hand to Daevas, who nodded. Confirming that he’ll look into it in his own way.

“I’ll have to observe her more to see how much more she might know,” Gabriel finished.

But observation was a slow and often boring process, and patience wasn’t a trait the hellborn easily possessed.

“Why don’t you just ask her?” Kaleus suggested.

Gabriel’s head snapped in his direction. “Did you really just ask me that?”

“She’s a human. We can’t involve her in this.” Jade chimed in.

The Prince lifted his hands, shrugging. "I'm just saying, you think she knows who Mason was, maybe she knows more about our existence than we think. Maybe trying to skate around her trying to maintain her ignorance will just make things harder for everyone. Just cut out the middleman," he argued.

"She's *mortal*, the very fabric of her mind would break apart if she knew about all of this. A mortal mind can't fathom our existence. There's a reason the Principalities monitor and alter religious records to reveal no more than about a small percentage of the correct information. Anymore and the stability of human life would be disrupted," Duma explained point blank.

Kaleus let out a snort. "Is it really all doom and gloom with you guys? Seriously, you give humans so much, but heaven forbid they learn about the supernatural, pun entirely intended. Can't you just erase her memory after it's all solved? Your big bad almighty can do that, can't he?" he teased.

"Even if we did, it's against the rules to share that much with a mortal," Gabriel said.

He rolled his eyes. "You angels and your rules. So fucking frigid, no wonder y'all are stiff as boards. Whatever, it was just a suggestion." He gave up with a sigh.

The other demons chuckled under the breaths while Kaleus was talking, the angels were a little fazed, trying hard not to show it. They weren't accustomed to having their divisions and order questioned so brazenly.

Iaoel and Duma visibly adjusted their postures to look more relaxed. Lillith had made her way over to Duma, and when he adjusted, she couldn't help but whisper to him.

"Don't worry, baby. I like it when you're stiff." Duma didn't have his wits about him to stop from choking on his own breath in response, coughing hoarsely. Lillith giggled at the reaction she stirred.

Jophiel stepped towards her. "Get lost, filth."

Lillith scoffed but sauntered away.

"The almighty and Lucifer agreed that we are to work together," Gabriel stated.

"Unfortunately," muttered Jophiel, earning her a warning glance from Gabriel and a playful grin from the demons.

"None of us trust one another, but this isn't going to work unless we *all* try to cooperate." he looked at all of them one by one. "We'll travel in pairs, to hold each other accountable and ensure that we're on the same side," Gabriel suggested.

"Who made him boss?" Kaleus snorted. Gabriel glared at him. He shrugged. "Relax, pegasus, for once, I agree with you," he stated.

"Duma, you and Daevas should take a trip down to hell, Lucifer can help point you in the right direction," Gabriel instructed.

Lillith rushed over to Duma, clinging to his arm. "Let me go with them and there'll be no need for Lucifer. I know hell like I know my own—" she whispered the last word into Duma's ear, though it didn't take a brainiac to know what she implied.

Duma's raised eyebrows and pleading glance towards Gabriel said enough.

Weighing the pros and cons in his head, Gabriel conceded, sending Duma to hell with Lillith seemed better than having him interact with his older brother.

“Fine, Lillith, Daevas and Duma, go.” Gabriel waved off.

Lillith hummed and grabbed Duma’s chin and turned his face close to hers. “It’s you and me, sweet cheeks.” Duma suppressed a gulp.

Daevas gripped Lillith’s other hand like it could bite him at any moment, rubbing the back of his neck awkwardly. “Don’t mind me.”

The three having physical contact vanished together as one in a column of crimson smoke that looked more like liquid silk.

“Iaoel and Seere, you should go speak with other realms, starting with Purgatory, see if the Watchers have any relevant insight,” Gabriel ordered.

Iaoel nodded, agreeing with their leader. Seere looked to Kaleus, a silent conversation passed between them.

He nodded, “Keep in touch.” He smirked.

Seere smiled wickedly and held her hand out for Iaoel. “Purgatory, huh? Sounds like fun, how do we get there?” she asked.

Iaoel pressed their hand into Seere’s. “Reapers Creek, shall we?”

Seere wriggled her eyebrows with seductive delight.

“Lead the way, my enlightened friend.” With that they vanished in a pillar of light.

All that remained were Jophiel, Jade, Kaleus and Gabriel.

“What will you do?” Jophiel asked Gabriel.

“I should return to guard the human, keep watch. Though I think I might need to speak with a colleague of mine to see if they have any information.”

“I can take Guardian duty,” Kaleus offered.

Gabriel huffed, “Like I would leave you in charge of her.”

He grinned wickedly. “You sound awfully protective for someone who’s only been watching her for a few days. Guardian bond already beginning to chafe?” Kaleus teased.

Gabriel stepped towards him, tensing his muscles.

“It is a vital part of my mission to be her Guardian, I wouldn’t be a very good Guardian if I left her in the care of a hellborn, especially one such as yourself.”

“You said yourself we need to cooperate. That includes watching the human, yes? I promise I’ll only observe. And when you return, we can look deeper for clues. We are a team, are we not?” He raised an eyebrow to challenge him.

As much as he hated it, Gabriel couldn’t very well argue with him when it would go against everything he himself had said earlier. His disdain for Kaleus ran deep and working with him was the last thing he wanted, but since he had established himself as the leader of the demon hoard, it would make sense that they should pair up for their portion of the mission.

Gabriel sighed, releasing the tension in his shoulders.

“Fine. But I won’t be gone long. Keep your filthy hands to yourself. Only intercede if she is in danger, do you understand?”

"Whatever. Later, feathers."

Without saying goodbye to Jophiel and Jade, Gabriel too left the cabin, extending his golden-white wings and taking flight back up to heaven. A small amount of gold light lingering in his wake.

Jade walked out into the street and watched him leave, Jophiel leaned against the open doorway.

"Well that was pleasant," Jade remarked.

"Gabriel has a history with him. I don't see this going well." Jophiel shook her head, anticipating the brawls to come from this alliance.

"Let's go, I think we can start in Egypt, talk to some of the Scribes there, see if we find an origin to whatever it is Gabriel saw in that dream," Jade suggested.

Jophiel extended her owl-like wings, Jade followed suit. Like most of the lesser angels, she didn't have large wings like the archangels, instead they were smaller, cream-colored wings.

"Correct me if I'm wrong but isn't Kaleus…?" Jade began to ask but stopped when Jophiel nodded. "Hm. I expected him to be more…well, *more*," she chuckled.

Jophiel raised an eyebrow, her eyes looking out at the tracks left behind from his motorcycle. "You'll find that any son of Lucifer will have infinite ways of surprising you, especially when you least expect it."

With a mighty flap of their wings they took to the skies. Their flight stirring the dust and sand which surrounded the rotting cabin, some of the sand landed on the old wood of the cabin with a soft hiss, some of it disappeared into the dry air along with any evidence that anyone visited the old town to begin with.

All except Seere's abandoned motorcycle streaked with green and pink paint.

SEVEN
Kale

BORING DIDN'T EVEN BEGIN to describe what it was like watching a human go about their daily, normal routine.

For someone who only last week just had a major supernatural experience, to just continue on doing mundane mortal things was just insane. There's a reason demons only spend time with humans when they're engaging in more entertaining activities.

I had arrived to watch over the human, Heather Coleman, hours ago. And already, I was bored out of my mind.

She was pretty average compared to most humans her age—had a job, and apartment, scholastic responsibilities... When she wasn't pounding her fingers against the keys of her computer, she was tucked in a living room chair reading a book while sipping on cheap wine.

The moment that truly captured my attention was when she pulled a neon purple vibrator from her bedside table. As much as I would've loved to watch how she pleasured herself, it felt too creepy to do so without permission.

So, I left her to that sense of privacy, the same I granted whenever she showered or changed clothes.

While taking a break in the other room, I instinctively reached down the wide-open connection that became my tether to sanity.

Seere's comical quips keeping me distracted enough from the muffled buzzing noise behind the bedroom door.

Having fun I see. She teased.

Their bond so potent that she would feel his eyes roll back as though she had done it herself.

Oh yeah. It's Mardi gras over here.

I made myself comfortable on the couch, though observing meant staying out of sight, staying quietly in the Ethereal realm, I could be right in front of the mortal's face and she wouldn't see me.

Eventually she exited the bedroom, her cheeks having a fresh flush of color to them. From my spot, I watched as she ate stinky take-out food and streamed a few episodes of Law & Order on the television until well past ten o'clock, after which I followed her into the bedroom.

I fought the urge to release tendrils of my power to ease the building pressure underneath my skin. Perhaps volunteering for this particular chore wasn't a good idea.

Heather followed a bedtime routine as precise and practiced as a professional concert. Finally slugging herself under the thin covers to sleep.

When her breathing had become steady and long, I let a little heat release. Not enough to burn anything, but just enough to ease the growing headache against my temple.

Heather must have felt the heat subconsciously. She pushed back the blankets to free an entire leg to the open air. I opened her bedroom window to help vent the air a bit before I settled against the wall.

She was an attractive enough human. A mortal like her, a part of me wondered if she was single, and if so—why? But then again, I suppose her seemingly introverted lifestyle might've had something to do with it.

Featherbrain was right, from the outside she wasn't all that interesting—perfectly, painfully normal.

It was about three in the morning when I had just about died of boredom. I ventured out of the bedroom and towards the bookshelf against the living room wall and plucked up a book.

"America Pacifica, hm. Not a bad choice." I looked at the other options on the shelf: *Earth Abides, The Passage, A Clockwork Orange, Spoken Here, The Body Silent…* "Dystopian fiction and anthropological stories, surprise surprise."

With a shrug and a sigh, I took the book in my hand with me back into her bedroom where she slept. I sat down on the chair next to her desk, opened *America Pacifica,* and began to peruse its pages. I noticed a multitude of blue-colored post-its bookmarking specific pages. I opened to one of them to find she had highlighted a quote.

Maybe she had some sort of extraordinary quality, secret even to her. Maybe she did have the power to alter the things she'd always assumed she'd have to endure.

"Searching to find something in yourself mortal?" I asked out loud, knowing full-well she couldn't hear me, "Also, marking up your books, breaking the spine…" I clicked my tongue, peering at her sleeping form. "—what would the book community say."

I fingered through the pages blindly and left the room to pull another book from the shelf. Finding more blue tabs with quotes highlighted. Seems she had each of her tomes bookmarked that way. A bibliophile, at least she used to be. I carefully placed all the books back on the shelf in the order they were before. Though I doubted she'd notice the shift in dust.

Back in her bedroom, I looked out the window of her apartment into the city below. At this hour, the streets were relatively quiet and dull, only the soft orange glow of the streetlamps and the occasional gust of wind pushing desert weeds around the pavement.

For a moment, the quiet was peaceful.

Compared to the pits of the Inferno, this heat was paradise. The orange glow wasn't a sign of unending fire, but of a dry climate. No matter how boring this particular job was, at least it was away from everything else. And for a little while I could at least pretend.

A buzzing hum rang in the back of my mind, a signal that someone was reaching out telepathically with a message. This one had the familiar golden glow of my *favorite* archangel.

I loosened the shield in my mind, allowing in the message through to hear what Gabriel was sending me.

Haven't set her on fire yet, right?

I rolled my eyes. *There are other, more fun ways of keeping her warm.*

I could feel Gabriel's annoyance in his response, *I'm serious, you better have kept your hands to yourself.* Gabriel sneered.

Relax, featherbrain. I'm observing as promised. I see you're taking your time.

The almighty wants me to stay a bit longer. Angels are afraid and aren't cooperating when receiving new assignments because of it. I need to help alleviate some of the upset. Gabriel explained.

I chuckled. *All you buzzards are cogs in the large machine. So industrialist and boring. At least it's a good reminder of how much of a blessing our lives are, pun-intended.* I glanced back at Heather, still soundly asleep.

Her head was buried in a pillow and half of her body messily outside of the thin sheet. Her baggy t-shirt had ridden up revealing a large portion of her bareback.

Mm, charming.

Gabriel made a gruff noise in my head. *Need I remind you that I can read and see your thoughts while we're connected like this?*

A smirk formed on my lips; I couldn't very well miss the opportunity when it presented itself.

Connected? You make it sound like such an intimate affair, feathers. I mean, I'd totally be into it—if you know what I mean. But I didn't peg you for that type, though if you're truly curious, you know I'd be more than happy to peg y—

A feral rumble vibrated the inside of my skull, cutting me off.

I swear on all things heavenly I will rip you apart if you finish that sentence. Gabriel quickly shot down my suggestive commentary.

My sly grin widened. Another idea to mess with him popped into my head then...

Fine, I won't talk.

Using an extra amp of power I projected images from my mind to Gabriel's, only these were with Heather.

Images of me climbing into the bed with her, letting my calloused hands wander along her fragile, smooth skin. My mouth brushing slowly up her body. Heather moaning low as she lowered her hands to tangle in my hair, pulling me up further to the hot core between her legs…

I wonder if she's still wet from her earlier private session...

I winced as my images burned with a searing light and pain that spread across my entire head. I clutched my skull, gasping at the intensity.

Jesus fucking Christ, featherbrain.

Try that again, and I'll fry every neuron. The light subsided, and I could finally see again.

I took the chance to erect some additional mental blocks that I had originally left down to avoid it happening again.

I took a deep breath, regaining my composure. *So touchy, jeez. When was the last time you had your bill sucked?*

Ignoring my comment he said, *I should return sometime in the next couple of days, I'll keep you informed if anything changes.*

The arch-asshole dropped the connection without another word.

"Kay, bye," I scoffed aloud. "We need to give you dodo's lessons on phone call etiquette."

It was frustrating that Gabriel had the upper hand in that moment. I'll make sure it's the last.

Normally my mental abilities were almost unparalleled. It was among my large cache of powers that gave me an upper hand in hell and in all the realms. Not to mention I could hold my own in a hand-to-hand fight against an archangel if I needed to.

"Who's there?" Heather's voice filled the room.

I whipped towards her, shocked. Did she hear me?

I did a quick check, making sure I was still in the Ethereal veil.

Yup...I was.

Heather still laid there in her bed and, as I moved closer, I realized that she was sleep talking. Only dreaming.

Her eyelids twitched and the muscles in her arms tensed. She could be having another nightmare. Gabriel did mention that he saw a wraith in her dreams earlier. Perhaps she was seeing it again.

Maybe it's worth checking into.

I had promised I would only observe her until Gabriel returned. That should count towards her dreams, right? And if a parasitic wraith were actually in her mind, it would potentially harm her.

It was decided then, it was worth the risk. I sat cross-legged on the floor beside her bed and lightly touched her hand to establish a connection. Closing my eyes, I focused my mind on her, and within moments I was entering the gates of her mind, wide open and easy for picking.

And inside, a horror lurked.

EIGHT
Heather

"HELP ME!"

My eyes shot open, all around me was white. I had no sense of up and down. I'd been here before. The hairs on the back of my neck and arms rose. The air felt cold and wet, much like a foggy night.

I struggled to adjust to the disorienting white light but couldn't. My eyes searched for anything that could bring them focus, but there was nothing.

Even in all this nothingness, I felt I wasn't alone. I couldn't explain it, there was someone standing right in front of me, watching me, but I couldn't see them.

But I *felt* them.

"Who's there?" I whispered.

My voice echoed as though it hit a wall that didn't exist. I still sensed whatever was there with me, but they gave no indication of their presence.

It had to be another dream, but then again, the last time I was here I wasn't dreaming, and then someone was dying under my hands.

"Help!" I heard that familiar plea and whipped around, expecting to see his figure curled up on the floor as I had before, but there was nothing.

My heart searched for a name to the familiar voice. "Mason? Where are you?!" I yelled.

"I'm so sorry, Heather." Those words echoed at different levels, ping-ponging around like a spirit in the wind.

He was everywhere and nowhere. I continued to spin to try to find the source of his pleas.

There. A slight discoloration in the white drew my eye. It was subtle, like a shadow, only slightly darker than the bright white of the room. It hovered in the air in the shape of a person. Although I couldn't see its eyes, it was watching mine.

It wasn't Mason, it didn't feel like him.

"Is this real?" I asked tentatively. I sure hoped not.

The figure began to move into a circle, I turned with it, maintaining our distance—my instinct telling me not to lose sight of it. Its form began to darken, allowing me to see more of it. It floated and hovered like smoke—yet seemed almost like a liquid.

I felt something tickle my ankle, breaking my gaze I looked down to see dark smoky liquid swirling around. I gasped, it didn't hurt, in fact, it was in a way beautiful. The contact felt like a cold mist grazing my skin.

My heart jumped in my throat when I looked back up to see the creature much closer to me. The misty feeling it emanated touching my skin. It lifted what seemed like a hand and touched my face. I stood perfectly still, mesmerized by the thing that watched me like a predator watched its prey.

Was it a predator? *Was I its prey*? Why couldn't I move away from it?

This had to be a dream, things like this didn't happen in real life.

The creature moved its hand to my chest. Leeching fear crept into my body. What if it killed me right here? What if it had the power to stop my heart without breaking a sweat?

Staring at the creature, I almost felt its intentions, feeling the unspoken, stirring aggression that hadn't yet come from its essence. Was this it? Would this thing take me?

In a split second, the atmosphere changed, the whiteness around us began to blow away on a phantom breeze, replaced with a sky of deep red and black. It looked like the white was being torn away like fabric to reveal a darker, more sinister landscape.

The creature whipped its head around to look at a figure sitting on a black rock not twenty feet away from where we stood. The creature hissed and moved away from me, turning full-bodied towards the other figure.

The cold mist left my body and all my muscles felt heavy. I looked around me at the new place my subconscious created—the ground made up of black, sharp stone and glassy obsidian. The sky was red with black clouds and an eclipsed sun shown in the distance. The air no longer felt wet and cold, instead now dry and hot.

A sharp breeze blew coarse, black sand into my face. I shielded my eyes until the wind passed. When I returned my gaze back to the two figures, the distant one was still sitting, unmoved. The creature who had since been focused on me zeroed its attention entirely on the other figure. It looked angry, its liquid smoky skin looking jagged, less fluid than it was before.

The creature moved closer to the figure, who had its eyes closed and head bowed, as if in meditation. The creature hissed again and muttered something in a language I wasn't familiar with—the sound raspy. When the figure didn't so much as budge, the creature screeched and moved closer, only this time extending its shadow hands, shifting them into long talons to attack the figure.

The figure opened its eyes, which were a glowing orange and red, like churning molten lava. An aura of what looked like smoke and electric sparks shot out around the figure's body in short bursts. One of the sparks slammed into the creature, causing it to screech so loud my ears rang.

Another, stronger jolt hit the creature again, and this time the spot it hit disintegrated the smoky essence. Again, a jolt hit. Over and over, with each hit more and more of the creature broke apart. The figure didn't cease the jolts until the last of the creature had shattered and floated away into the wind like sand.

The fire and electricity retreated back into the body of the figure. Calming into darkness once more. The figure closed its eyes, hiding the molten glow they once had.

My breath was shallow, coming in short gasps. Who was that? How did they *do* that?

It was one *hell* of a weird dream.

The figure stood in one fluid motion and turned to walk away.

My feet acted on their own, following after it.

"Wait," my voice cracked. They didn't stop. I cleared my throat and spoke again more clearly, "Please! Can you tell me what that was?"

I was rushing to catch up with it when my foot caught on a sharp piece of rock and suddenly I was falling towards the shards of volcanic glass below. I braced my hands to catch my fall, and when I landed, they were cut. Stinging pain shot up my arms. My knees felt scraped up as well.

When I righted myself and looked up the figure was right above me. Did I really move that fast? Or did it come back to me?

It was looking down at me. I could see more details, though it was still shrouded by shadows. It appeared to be male, and its eyes weren't glowing red anymore, instead, they were just as dark as the rest of his body.

He just stood there, staring at me. I stumbled back to my feet, brushing off the dirt and sand on my pants. I winced, looking at my scraped-up hands.

Now that I was standing I could see that the figure was about a foot taller than me, his clothes were dark as well, he was shrouded in a cloak of shadow hiding his features. It made me wonder what he looked like outside those shadows.

"Care to share your name?" I asked.

He just watched me, no response. Even though his features were hidden by the shadow, I could still see a slight indication that he was confused. Maybe he didn't understand my language? But why wouldn't he? It was my dream after all.

"Okay, if you don't want to tell me that, could you tell me what that thing was?" I tried a different question. He still didn't answer.

"Really not a talker, are you? Okay, I'll start…I guess. My name is Heather."

"I know who you are," his reply was swift, blunt.

My eyes widened. "So you do speak." His baritone voice evoking electric shocks under my skin. "If you know who I am, then can't I know who you are?" I asked.

"No," he stated.

"Why not?" Instead of answering he turned to look next to him.

"I have to go," he said, turning to leave.

"Hey! Wait, you didn't answer my question." He turned back to me, and I swear a phantom smirk appeared on his mouth. He continued to walk away.

I huffed. "Where are you going?" He paused only for a moment to point at me.

"Time to wake up." Before I could understand what he meant I was jolted out of my slumber by the sound of my alarm beeping.

I looked around; I was back in my room.

I was always a vivid dreamer, but recently, it seemed my dreams were becoming even more active each night. I pulled out my journal sitting on my desk and started to jot down what I had seen. Every detail I could remember.

After finishing, I decided to look further back in the journal. I saw symbols, strange places, and horrible creatures in my dreams from about four months ago at the beginning of the year.

And then there was the entry from the previous week. When I had a nervous breakdown during class. I was checked by doctors and psychiatrists. One theory was that I may have been schizophrenic. After spending twenty-four hours sedated in the psych ward, they deemed it a stress-related breakdown and sent me home.

I stopped on a page in my journal, where three symbols were scribbled all over the page.

I traced the largest one on the page with my finger. Its swirls made it look graceful, but it had sharp points as if to add significance. For some reason, these symbols had appeared in almost all of my dreams, and I had no idea what they meant.

While tracing the symbol I felt a presence behind me, causing the hairs on the back of my neck to rise. I froze, feeling like it was hovering over me. I flipped around, but there was no one there. It was weird. I must've been going insane.

The image of the dark figure appeared again in my mind. He had refused to tell me who he was. The fire and electricity made him seem dangerous, but I wasn't afraid of him, apprehensive maybe.

But not afraid. Not the same way I was with the first creature. The first creature felt like it had been there for a while, almost like it was always there. The man was new, though I suppose my subconscious was simply fabricating images to deal with the stress of finals.

"I should give them names. Figure and creature are too similar, I'll get them mixed up," I said out loud as I jotted down the last of my dream in the journal.

I went to my closet to pick out an outfit for the day. I held up a navy-blue blouse on a hanger and looked in the mirror.

My mind didn't even focus on it. I mindlessly put it back and grabbed a white sleeveless blouse instead. I pulled on a pair of skinny jeans and tore off my pajama shirt to put on a bra.

For a moment I smelled cinnamon, I looked at my wax Scentsy against the wall. I was pretty sure I put lavender in there. I shrugged it off and put on the blouse.

As I went to work readying myself for the day in the bathroom, my mind kept flashing back to the dream, seeing those glass rocks, the eclipsed red sky…I brushed my hair, applied makeup, all the while letting my mind rake over every detail of it.

I need to get a life. I sighed to myself.

As I turned off the light to the bathroom I peered once more into the mirror. Just as the light went out, I saw a dark figure standing behind me. It looked eerily like the figure in my dream.

A squeak escaped me, my heart jumping into my throat. I whipped around, flicking on the light in one sweeping motion. No one.

What the…?

I turned back to the mirror, nothing.

I took a moment to catch my breath before turning the light off once more. This time there was no figure.

My mind must've been playing tricks on me, probably still affected by the nightmare.

"I need coffee," I voiced out loud, exiting my room. "Strong coffee."

What I needed was to get back to reality.

NINE
Heather

THAT DREAM MUST'VE REALLY RATTLED ME because I swear all day I had felt like I was being watched.

I'd never been a paranoid person, so why did I feel so uneasy? It made it difficult to focus on anything, I'd be grading papers and would constantly feel the need to scan the room as though someone were watching me. Even when I would speak with my professor, it felt as if I had a shadow constantly within a few feet of me.

It was normal as a woman to keep aware of my surroundings and automatically trust my gut when I felt followed. But this was different. It was…I don't even know what it is.

I was between classes with a big enough gap to take lunch. I went to the library and stopped at the little café just inside for a small mocha frap and a chicken wrap.

They had a small study area on the second floor, students called it the fishbowl because the entire floor had glass windows and you could easily watch people studying from the walkways outside.

I was sitting alone, munching on food while scribbling in my planner's past assignments and exams, trying not to let my mind wander into strange places.

I only had one more final before we'd be released for winter break. Three full weeks of relaxation. Though I should have spent those three weeks prepping for my summer trip abroad.

I had signed up to travel to Xian, China to see the Tomb of Qin Shi Huangdi and do some field experience in the other dig sites surrounding the area. It would be beneficial to get ahead of some of the research and readings required before the trip.

It would be my last trip before I completed my degree and it would play a huge role in the last sections of my thesis. I turned a few pages in my planner to the three-week break and wrote down which days I should spend doing those readings. I'd forget if I didn't write it down.

"Hey, Heather!" I was drawn from my planner to the familiar voice of an old classmate, Miles.

I looked up to see him sporting one of his typical plaid shirts and brown messenger bag.

"Hey Miles, how's it going?" I asked.

He gestured to his bag. "Just thought I'd get some studying in before my final at two. Mind if I sit with you?" he asked.

I shuffled some of my stuff that was crowding the tablespace. "Yeah, sure! Just let me get some of my crap out of the way. What final are you studying for?"

"African Studies with Dr. Arnold. It's one essay question with a two-hour gap to complete it. I hear it's brutal."

I winced.

"Ooh, yeah I took that class last year, and I can't give you any comfort. I hear she changes the essay question each term so that students can't work together on it. But on the bright side, you're that much closer to being done!" I tried to cheer him up.

"Yeah, one more semester and I can finish my MA and move on to get my Ph.D. What about you? Any more finals?" he asked.

"One more. Anthological Research, it's just a paper, not a test, thank god. But I haven't acquired enough sources for the theoretical portion. But hey, what's another four pages compared to the twelve I already wrote over the last week."

Miles chuckled. "I wish they told us how hard grad classes were gonna be, I might've reconsidered it."

"No, you wouldn't have."

"You're right. I wouldn't have, but I would have bought more wine." We both laughed.

I opened my laptop and logged on, he seemed to get the same idea and pulled his out as well. Opening my paper, I looked at my progress, one more discussion point to hash out over four pages before I could finally submit it tomorrow.

I sighed. "I'm going to find a book real quick for my paper, would you watch my stuff?" I asked, rising from my seat.

Miles snorted and waved me off. "I got you." I thanked him and left towards the stacks.

Luckily, the fishbowl wasn't far from the anthologies section of the library. Scanning the sections, I found a portion labeled for Native American symbology, which was the topic of my essay.

I picked up a couple of texts, looking at their basic information in the front to determine if they could be useful for my paper.

After stacking up about three books, I turned to leave the stacks.

"A little light reading?" a voice asked from behind me. I turned around, careful not to knock over the books in my hands. Each one over nine-hundred pages long.

I chuckled. "Anthologies always are," I joked.

The person who spoke stood about a foot taller than me and was wearing torn baggy jeans, a white shirt with a dark faded black leather jacket over it with a hood attached. In his ears were small, hooped earrings. His hair was brown, shaggy, and reaching just above his shoulders.

He had a black, thin beard line and mustache, his skin was light brown and even deeper rusty eyes. His look screamed rugged biker vibes. And though I've seen a lot of those types around this campus—as bikers in the desert are common, this guy was just…enchanting.

For a split second, my mind flashed back to my dream, and a sense of familiarity washed over me. I thought I saw an aura wrap around him that mimicked smoke and molten lava, but when I blinked it was gone.

I shook my head slightly to clear my head, I must've seen this guy before, and he somehow ended up in my subconscious somewhere. Although, if I ever saw this guy walking around campus, I'm sure I would've remembered it.

"Is it for a paper or something?" he asked, referring to my books.

His words brought me out of my curious thoughts that I found myself in while looking at him. He smiled, almost as if he knew.

I adjusted the heavy books in my hands, "Um, sort of, a portion of my paper I haven't yet finished. Are you um," I looked at the book in his hand trying to figure out what he was taking. "Are you taking a religious studies class or something?"

The book he held was titled *Christianity in East and Southeast Asia.*

He lifted it and laughed a little to himself. "Uh, yeah, you could say that."

I nodded, suddenly feeling a little awkward standing there with large heavy books talking to a stranger.

"Alrighty, then. Good luck with your finals!" I swiftly turned away and walked back to the table Miles was at.

He looked up from his laptop and noticed me rushing over awkwardly. "Did you get lost or something?" he teased.

I thought about the guy, and it evoked images of smoke, fire, and lightning. "Yeah, I guess you could say that." I put down the books and sat down, clicking my laptop back to life.

I glanced back to where I had just come from, to see that guy looking at his book with amusement before he lifted his head and caught my eye. He smirked and winked at me then walked behind the stacks, disappearing out of sight.

But I didn't know why there was something familiar about him. Again, my mind went back to the dream. His physique certainly matched that of the shadowy figure in it. But I swear I had never met him or even seen him before.

And his voice…that was familiar too.

It was forty-five minutes after Miles and I had started studying that he had to leave to go take his final. I had only been working on my paper for thirty of those minutes. Taking some time in the beginning to finish my lunch, needing the brain food.

Out of the three books I had chosen off the shelves, only two turned out to be decent sources for my paper. It would have to do for now. Writing an additional two and a half pages, I clicked save and took a long deep sigh.

My fingers and brain ached. Finals were always a tedious and stressful time of year. I missed the days when I could take a multiple-choice test, the higher the course numbers got the more and more finals were long essays requiring annotated bibliographies, footnotes, and case studies to back up theories you create on your own. It just made me dread having to write my final thesis.

Taking a break, I decided to browse the internet for a while. I scrolled through all the engagement, wedding, and baby announcements happening in the lives of my old friends.

Seeing all the feed filled with those sort of life updates, I couldn't help but feel behind somehow. Even though I made the decision during my early twenties that marriage wasn't a realistic goal for me.

Sure, if love found its way into my life I wouldn't turn it away. But I wasn't going to go looking for it.

I had all my research to factor in as well. In reality, the construct of marriage was built to suppress one of the parties involved, most notably women. Not to mention, my high expectations for people. I hated the masks people wore when dating, and how ugly their true selves turned out to be in the end.

I've dated before, but each time I let someone get remotely close enough to consider a lifetime commitment, they disappointed me. If only people were their truest selves from the get-go.

Honesty and transparency were rare finds these days. So while I scanned past Lyla Hill's pictures of her new engagement, the focus of the image set on the big rock on her finger and all the flashy things her fiancé did to make it memorable, I didn't feel resentment or jealousy. I felt pity.

"Mind if I sit with you?" A voice drew my attention away from my computer screen to the mesmerizing figure I had met earlier.

He was leaning slightly forward, holding the back of the chair across the table from me, waiting for a response. The grin on his face made something wiggle in my stomach.

I tried to answer, but my breath caught in my throat.

Crap, forgot to breathe.

I cleared my throat. “Um, yeah. Sure.”

I watched as he slid the chair out and slipped in it with ease. His eyes never breaking contact with mine. There was something challenging about his expression.

Was he waiting for me to say something else? Was he expecting a conversation icebreaker or something? I’d never been great at those.

As if sensing my struggle for conversation starters he asked, “How’s the paper going?” Motioning towards my stacks of books.

I flipped the open book closed. “Almost finished. I should be able to finish the rest before tomorrow. How’s your studying going?” I felt nervous, could it be the basic *stranger-danger* instinct that all women possess from birth when being alone with a guy?

No. It didn’t feel that way, I mean we were in a public library, almost every other table in the fishbowl was occupied by other students.

Additionally, he didn’t give me a dangerous vibe. At least not in the *I need to be careful* type of dangerous. Or at least not the *I need to be careful because I’m in danger* way, more like an *I need to be careful cause he’s kinda dreamy* sort of way.

And he was dangerous alright, dangerous in the *could show up in my sexual fantasies for eternity* kind of way, definitely.

Oh, god. Get it together, you blushing fool.

“I’m pretty confident I will pass,” he stated.

I scoffed. "Lucky you, if only everyone else felt that way." I stretched my hand across the table. "I'm Heather by the way." He stared at my hand for a second and a knowing smile came across his face.

A flashback, *I know who you are*. I nearly shuddered in my seat.

He held my hand and squeezed it. "Kale." When his hand released mine I felt like I had just touched hot coal, and the residual heat made it start to sweat.

I pressed my lips together and smiled meekly. Turning my attention back to my computer to avoid the awkwardness of my internal mess of reactions.

"Got any fun plans for the break?" I asked. I felt so stupid, small talk was painful to partake in.

He chuckled, the sensual sound of it drew my eyes back to his.

"Going hunting I guess." He chuckled some more as if it was a private joke. I decided to shrug it off and go with it.

"Gonna spend time with your family for the holidays?"

"My family doesn't celebrate the holidays. I see them all the time, so any time spent with them is always the same," he answered. "You going home for the holidays?" he asked.

I shrugged. "My parents live on the opposite side of the country and I don't like traveling that far in bad weather, so I'm just gonna stay here and work on research."

He laughed. "Isn't that time supposed to be spent taking a break from studies? Or are you just a highly devoted nerd?"

I rolled my eyes.

"I take 'nerd' as a compliment, thank you. I'm a grad student, we actually *enjoy* doing research. Anyway, I have a big study abroad trip coming up this summer that I need time to work on," I retorted.

"Where you going?"

"Xian, China. It's, uh, where the—"

"Tomb of Qin Shi Huangdi. I'm impressed," he finished.

I blinked once, twice.

"Um yeah. Wow, that's amazing. Most people don't ever know what that is unless they see a picture of it. Did you see it recently in a class?"

He shook his head.

"I've seen a lot of tombs in my line of work," he stated plainly.

My eyebrows raised. "What kind of line of work takes you to China? Better yet, to a lot of tombs? I mean, you're too young to be an anthropologist." Mirth edging in my voice.

He smirked and shot me a swoon-worthy wink that made my toes curl a bit.

"How old do you want me to be?"

Smooth…

I mean, I guess he had a point. I was assuming. But *he* was flirting. *Hard.*

But I didn't much like being played with by a complete stranger, who may or may not be bad news.

"Sorry, didn't mean to assume. You look like you're in your mid-twenties and the youngest anthropologists are typically in their late twenties to mid-thirties."

“And what if I said that I was over three thousand years old?” he asked.

Even though I knew he was joking, his delivery was so confident, it almost felt real. I laughed awkwardly, strange joke indeed.

“Pfft. Right, yeah, okay so you’re what? Immortal? Okay.”

I shook my head, chuckling. This guy was trying way too hard now to fulfill a fantasy that was meant for a much younger audience.

I returned my eyes to my laptop and opened up my email to scroll through my inbox. I could see in my peripheral vision that he was still watching me with amusement. I chose to ignore it and began replying to emails.

I snuck a glance back at him above my laptop. He was looking at the table, almost as if he were listening to something. *Doesn’t he have a phone or something to look at?*

Speaking of, I looked down at my phone to check the time. Two-thirty-three. Geez, I’d been here for longer than I had meant to be. I missed my last class.

I glanced back at the Kale guy. Who names their child after a leafy vegetable anyway?

With his biker gang vibe I would’ve pegged him for a Rufus or Mac. Even though my better mind told me that the ‘bad-boy’ energy he was emanating was overrated and juvenile, despite my inner teenager tickling with an attraction to it.

And I knew, somewhere deep down that I should take it seriously. My eyes scanned him while his eyes were elsewhere.

The immortal joke was amusing, in a flirtatiously cliché way. But there was something inhuman about him. I tried to imagine the silhouette of the figure and then imagined Kale with a shadow over him to compare.

Hm, sure they were similar, but was I just reading too much into it? I mean, why would someone I hadn't met before appearing in my dreams only to meet them in person the very next day?

That's impossible.

In all my thoughts I hadn't realized that his eyes had met mine once more, and we were just staring at each other. I cleared my throat and looked away quickly.

"Sorry, staring off into space," I mumbled.

He tilted his head to the side, almost like a predator sizing up its prey.

"See anything you like?" he asked.

I looked back at him to see another confident smile across his lips. He was daring, I'll give him that.

"Have we met before? I mean before today?" I asked suddenly.

For a moment, his eyes blinked quickly, surprised by question. Then they shifted to curious amusement.

"Where would we have met?" he asked playfully. Did he know something I didn't know? Or just more games?

"Well, I don't know. I'm probably just being paranoid. Finals' week has me having these weird dreams lately. And for some reason you resemble someone I saw in one, and the only explanation I can think of is that we've met before. Does that make sense? Or is that weird? I read in an article once that when you see someone you don't recognize in a dream, it usually means you've seen them in passing and your subconscious just holds onto it."

His expressions gave me mixed signals. They shifted from recognition to surprise, then from bright-wonder to excitement then finally to a playfulness demeanor. The quickness of every shift nearly made me dizzy, but I caught each one of them.

“Are you saying I’m the man of your dreams?” he teased.

Although his tone was that of flirtatiousness, his eyes betrayed him, telling me that he knew more than he was saying.

No longer in the mood to play along. I rolled my eyes and began collecting my things. “Never mind. It’s dumb. I should get home.”

He didn’t seem happy by that response.

“You’re leaving? We only just started talking.” He stood. I put my school bag over my shoulder.

I looked at him and sighed in defeat.

“Look, the whole flirting session was fun and all. But I’ve got a lot on my plate, and playing games only gets in the way of productivity. So, it was nice to meet you, Kale. Good luck with your finals and have a nice day.” With that, I left.

He didn’t appear to follow me, so I made the long trek across campus to where my car was parked in the school lot, keys between my fingers just in case. It was only when I was locked inside my car driving down university avenue when I felt some semblance of normal again.

TEN
Kale

PURE AMUSEMENT, that's what Heather's final words gave me.

She had spunk, a little plain otherwise, but at least she wasn't afraid to call out bullshit.

It was interesting that she recalled me in her dreams the night prior. Supernatural entities such as high-class demons and angels should be able to enter a human's subconscious mind and leave unnoticed.

I made sure to keep myself shrouded in shadow to be safe, since she had recollected the Guardian in her earlier experiences. She shouldn't have been able to connect my appearance in the dream to my physical form in the real world.

And yet…she did. That'll have to be something I mention to the others later.

While I was spending time with her in the library Seere relayed a message that she and Iaoel were headed to Reapers Creek to try to see what was happening in-between veils. I hadn't heard from anyone else, including Gabriel.

At least Seere was staying in touch as promised. Seere was my right hand, but more importantly she was my best friend. She understood me in ways no other could, Daevas came close, but not as close as her.

Seere shared my disdain towards my father and helped me vent all of my destructive emotions in more productive matters.

Rather than go on a cataclysmic rage like the last time, and the time before that.

While Heather may have walked away, I never truly left her presence. Easily shifting into the Ethereal veil to conceal my presence from her—I accompanied her in her car as she started for home.

The whole ride back she seemed lost in thought, occasionally grunting and scoffing as if she was reacting to her own inner monologue. I watched in amusement, knowing that it was likely me that was in her thoughts.

I never ceased to stir up humans and their fragile emotions.

"Three thousand years old, seriously? Does he think I'm some thirteen-year-old girl just waiting to be swept off her feet by a fictional book vampire who sparkles in the sunlight? Fucking joke," she said aloud.

I couldn't help but laugh, she wouldn't hear me while I was riding the border between the Ethereal realm and the mortal one.

"If anyone had a Twilight complex, it would be featherbrain," I joked.

She continued driving, completely oblivious to my presence.

Her nose scrunched up and she let out an aggravated sigh. "Ugh, why do I even care? He's not even my type, I don't know what's wrong with me. Just get over it Heather."

My smirk now permanently plastered on my face. "I have that effect on people."

The buzzing in the back of my head turned my attention elsewhere. Opening my mind to allow Gabriel to come in.

What's up, glitter-bomb? I asked.

How are things? Gabriel asked as a form of greeting.

Doing just fine down here. Human is safe and sound, living her boring life.

Good. I'm on my way back. Any news from the others?

Seere and Iaoel checked in, they're at Reapers Creek. But other than that, I haven't heard from anyone else. I answered.

Jade and Jophiel are leaving Egypt, bringing a few scrolls with them, I think they're going to stop in Siberia to speak to a couple of Scribes. Gabriel explained.

Naturally, they would report to him since they were both angels. I wondered what Daevas and the others were finding down below.

"What the hell is that?" Heather exclaimed. My eyes shot to the front windshield.

In the middle of the road, three hundred feet ahead, there was what looked like a human woman, but something was off. I looked closer to see the woman's eyes were slitted vertically and teeth were thin and sharp as needles.

Heather's car continued nearing it, getting closer by the second. It noticed her and the hair on its head began to shed off and its bones and joints bent in unnatural ways.

Whatever it was, it wasn't human.

In-fact, I vaguely recognized it from an old drawing in one of the realm histories I was forced to study when I was young. The slitted eyes and needle teeth gave it away.

A *vetala.*

I haven't seen one beyond historical texts in my lessons...because they were supposed to be locked up tight.

How was it here?

Heather was gawking at it, not fully knowing what she was looking at, and also not realizing that she was still driving towards it.

The vetala grinned an unnaturally wide smile as it eyed its oncoming prey.

“Shit,” I swore aloud.

What? What’s going on? I barely registered Gabriel’s distant response to the alarm simmering in my body.

I ignored him and broke past the film separating the Ethereal veil from the mortal veil. Heather screamed when I appeared out of nowhere in her car. I held out my hand and closed my fist, forcing the brakes to squeeze down the wheels, bringing the car to a hard stop, just a few feet away from the vetala.

Heather’s gasp was more like a choke, and then she was breathing in shallow heaps. The vetala snarled and jutted towards the car.

“Oh my god, what-what is that?!” she sputtered, clearly sinking into shock of what was happening right in front of her eyes.

The vetala gripped the hood of the car with its bony hands and ripped it clean off. Heather held her breath or forgot to breathe altogether—not fully registering that it was all indeed real. The vetala let out a nasty cry, eyeing at me with liquid menace.

I pressed my palms against the windshield and with a jerk of force it went flying towards the creature, sending it back until it slammed a good thirty feet away against the pavement, covered in the now shattered glass.

I climbed out through the open cavity of the windshield and stared back at the shell-shocked mortal still sitting in the driver’s seat.

“Stay here.” An order to be followed.

I jumped off the remains of the car and ran straight for the vetala, still trying to get up from the initial blow.

When it spotted me coming towards it, it moved—shielding as much as it could from the incoming blow. I hit the creature with my bare fist, it only grazed it and used it to help propel it over my body, landing behind my back.

Nimble little bastard.

What is happening? Gabriel forced hard enough to squeeze past my barriers.

I growled back at him. *Not now, featherbrain.*

Once it landed it instantly jogged back towards the car—towards Heather. Heather watched in horror as this deformed version of what she first thought was human woman was quickly closing in on her—ready to make a tasty meal out of her flesh.

She was frozen in her spot, unable to fully decide what she should do.

I grunted in frustration. I could use my powers to incinerate it immediately, but honestly, what I had in mind felt like more fun.

I was a skilled fighter, and these weren't difficult to kill if you knew where to aim. I whipped out one of my throwing karambit daggers from my jacket and with the flick of my wrist I sent it flying after the vetala.

Forged in the Hades' pit, its sharp blade made its mark faster than a bullet, piercing the vetala's back, stopping it in its tracks just a few feet from the vehicle.

The vetala cried out as the spelled dagger did its Infernal job and began to burn its skin. Welts and blisters formed and then were gone as its entire body erupted in a momentary flame before disappearing into a puff of ash.

Leaving only the dagger behind on the pavement, the sigils dimming from their use.

I had already been walking towards the creature while it burned. I bent down to pick up the dagger and wiped its blade against my pants to clean off any remaining residue before stowing it back in its hilt underneath my jacket.

I loosened a deep sigh, looking at the mortified young woman.

That was definitely more than she was supposed to witness. Feathers was gonna kill me.

However, vetala's out in the open were not a good sign, especially since they were supposed to be thoroughly imprisoned for all eternity.

Approaching the car, I opened the drivers' side door, reached in, and unclicked her seatbelt. She stared at me in horror and confusion but didn't resist. I grabbed her forearm to help pull her out of the car.

"Come on, we need to get you home." She stumbled out of the car and followed me. I held on to her arm to keep her steady.

"What-what just happened?" I ignored her and just kept leading her down the block until we reached her apartment complex.

Her questions, though stuttered and breathless, didn't yield as we worked our way up the apartment complex stairs.

"What was that thing? My car! My car is ruined, and just sitting in the street! I need to call the police! But—what would they say, they'd think I'm crazy!" Her breath coming in short burst of gasps, hardly taking in enough oxygen to speak.

If she kept this up, she'd soon faint.

I rolled my eyes and kept going. "Don't worry about your car, I slipped it between realms. No one will see it or mess with it."

Heather's voice got louder as we neared the third floor, echoing off the hallway walls.

“I’m sorry, *where*? How did you—you *killed* that thing?! You have to tell me what’s going on! What did I just witness?”

We reached her door and I, with only a sliver of power, willed the lock to flip and opened the door.

“Wait a minute, I locked that! What the hell! How do you even know where I live?!”

Did she ever shut up?

After getting her inside, I locked the door behind me. Then went to the windows and peered outside the curtains to check if anything else was near.

Heather began pinching herself, and pulling her hair, slapping her face to try to wake up.

“This is so insane! I must be dreaming. That’s it. This is just another horrible dream, I need to wake up! Oh, I’m going mad, I truly belong in a nuthouse now. Oh god, I’m gonna pass out.”

Once I knew the surrounding area was secure, I grabbed her hands, stopping her.

“No, unfortunately, this time you’re not dreaming, and you’re not insane.”

We both glanced at my hands holding hers, I released them in an instant as if I were shocked and put distance between us. I continued monitoring the apartment perimeter.

Heather must have noticed how easy it was for me to move around, as if I had been there before.

She and I locked eyes for a moment, and without thinking my gaze flicked to the bedroom door and then back to her. She saw the recognition in my face and then it spread across her face as well. Her cheeks turning a deep shade of pink.

"It was you! I knew it! I don't know how I knew that, but it was you—in my dream! It was real!" Panic started to set in. "But how is that possible?"

I threw up my hands and tried to calm her.

"Trust me, the answer to that question would take too long to explain. Plus it might fry your brain, so." I shrugged.

Her face pinched. "Fry my—"

Suddenly the whole room filled with a blinding light.

A strong arm held my throat, and a strong invisible force pinned my entire body back against the wall. Gabriel stood in front of me in all his glory, wings and all.

And he was furious. If it wasn't for the lethal glare he seared into my face, I might've been turned on.

"Are you out of your mind? You had one job. Observe and protect. I get here and you've revealed yourself and your powers to the mortal?! Do you realize how reckless this is! I could smite you right here, right now. Heaven would thank me for it." His voice echoed against the walls, amplified.

Clearly Gabriel hadn't realized that Heather could see him and all his glory.

Well, not ALL his glory. An amused demon's voice chuckled in the back of my head. Seere must've sensed the sudden distress and chaos and tuned in.

I could get out of this, easily. But the force of power…trying it might not end well for the mortal not far behind him, especially inside such a tight space.

So instead, I leveled an equally lethal glower at him, my smoke unfurling just enough to push his arm back so I could choke out.

"I'm reckless, huh? Turn around buzzard brain."

Gabriel's face that was filled with fury only a moment ago shifted. My comment registered, and he blinked with stunning cognizance.

He glanced over his shoulder to see Heather staring at us in what I could only discern as a mix of awe and horror, completely frozen in place.

Her skin was paler than death as she looked upon the archangel in her apartment. His wings completely engulfed the small room and his golden light of grace lit up the otherwise dark room like a hot summer day.

Gabriel instantly dropped his grip on me and turned his entire body around. Within a split second he retreated his wings back into himself and the light surrounding him dimmed to a more tolerant level.

I coughed. "Busted. Now who's the idiot," I muttered from behind him, sitting on the floor, exhausted.

Gabriel ignored me, instead slowing started to inch closer to Heather.

She stumbled backwards. "I, uh….um…you….him…..what….oh Jesus…" Heather stuttered.

I watched her skin pale and knew that she wasn't going to stay conscious for much longer.

Probably for the best. Seere giggled.

I shushed her internally. *Hush, beasty.*

"Heather, it's okay. Everything is fine, I can explain—"

But even as Gabriel was finishing his sentence Heather's eyelids dropped and her body collapsed.

Gabriel barely managed to catch her before she hit the floor. She was out. I'm honestly amazed she lasted as long as she did.

"Way to go, Lancelot," I grunted.

Gabriel glared at me but proceeded to carry Heather to her bedroom, gently lowering her unconscious body on top of the comforter, gently resting her head on the pillow.

He placed his palm on her forehead, a soft light appeared beneath his palm and seeped into her head.

A small spell most likely, to ward off nightmares.

Gabriel left the room, closing the door behind him and turning to me, his least favorite person in the universe.

"That should let her rest for a little while dreamlessly. Now, you have some explaining to do. Tell me what happened," Gabriel said.

I stood, shaking off the leftover bruising left behind by the brute, they would heal soon enough. I folded my arms across my chest and leaned against the wall.

"What? But all that foreplay got me in the mood." I pouted playfully.

I could see that he was trying not to lose control again. And it only made me want to push him farther towards that breaking point.

I'd certainly like to see that.

I smirked, *Such a bloodthirsty little demon.*

Her answering laugh faded into the vaults of my mind as I took a deep sigh and made myself comfortable on the couch before giving in to Gabriel's less-than-gracious patience.

I said, "The Nessus prison is open."

ELEVEN
Iaoel

THE MORTAL REALM CONTAINED multiple outposts and embassy-type locations specifically for supernatural use.

They eliminate the amount of traffic and travel between realms. Some of them are specific to divisions of heaven. In Siberia there is an outpost for scribes called Metalius. In a remote location, scribes can receive and transmit records of mortal and supernatural alike without being disturbed.

Reapers have an outpost in South America called Crepúsculo, but they nicknamed it Reapers Creek. A place for Reapers to take a break and meet with other Reapers outside of the headquarters at the Gates. It's also conveniently located near one of the biggest passageways into Purgatory.

Iaoel had only been there a few times during their early training years, but now as an Angel of Sight, they didn't find themselves crossing over into those areas often. Seere had never been there but had heard about it through the grape vine.

Hidden underneath the dense rainforests of Brazil, dark stones made up old, worn structures that looked like they housed a civilization thousands of years ago. But really, the civilization was only a front, covering the hub of supernatural travelers.

The churning ash of Seere's winnow signature circled them as they landed on the lower platform of the haunting ruins. The ash swirled upwards from the ground, revealing Seere and Iaoel back to their solid forms, in the mortal realm.

Seere was out of breath. Her powers, or lack thereof, left her winnow abilities scarce. Traveling such a distance took more time, and a lot of energy.

Seere looked around, seeing no Reapers. "Anybody home?" she asked.

Iaoel crouched down to the ground and pressed their palm to it.

"We have to be in the Ethereal realm to see them." Iaoel closed their eyes and focused on their ethereal soul, and when they opened their eyes the colors of the forest were heightened, slightly brighter, with more saturation. A sign that they were in the parallel Ethereal realm.

Every supernatural being had their own way of shifting from the mortal realm to the Ethereal and back. Most of the lower-class demons had to use their demon names to shift and remain stable, angels could shift much smoother and maintain stability with their angelic grace.

Seere had followed suit by tracing her demon name that was tattooed on her arm. When winnowing, she wouldn't need to do this to move from one place to another, but to be in the Ethereal realm stable she would need to anchor. Her demonic name was tattooed into her bones, serving as that anchor.

Stronger beings such as archangels and of course Kaleus could winnow without using as much focus or anchoring.

Now that they were in the Ethereal realm, they could see multiple angels, primarily Reapers conversing with one another along the pathways and steps leading up to the passageway. Beside the stone pathway, a small creek weaved through rocks and plant life, giving the place its nickname.

"I'm a little disappointed. I was expecting there to be massage circles, yoga sessions, and buffet-style feasts," Seere said while they walked further up the pathway, passing Reapers.

Some noticing the presence of a demon in their otherwise secluded location.

“Why were you expecting that?” Iaoel asked.

“Well, I mean, it’s like a getaway for Reapers right? That’s what I heard at least. I just assumed it was going to include some stress-relieving activities.” Seere winked at a pair of Reapers watching them closely, clearly not fond of her presence.

“So, this is supposed to be like a vacation retreat? Do we angels seem that stressed to you?” Iaoel chuckled, nodding towards any Reapers they noticed to reassure them that the demon’s presence wasn’t a threat.

“Yeah! You all look like you’re holding the world in your hands and don’t even get me started on the whole work-pyramid thing. I get that there has to be structure for things to run properly, but it’s so excessive, if anything it just sets itself up for failure.”

The two of them reached the staircase, leading up to the entrance of the passageway and began to climb.

“What are we doing here again?” Seere asked impatiently. Iaoel shook their head, ignoring her question.

Iaoel turned and looked back at the scattered Reapers.

“The crowd is a lot smaller than it usually is, Azrael must be keeping them busy,” they regarded, turning back to continue up the steps.

“You say that like you spend a lot of time here,” Seere responded.

Iaoel shrugged. “Not much anymore, but during my training years we’d come here to unwind after a difficult training examination. This may be named after Reapers, but the young trainees use it the most,” they explained.

Seere smiled, raising an eyebrow suggestively. "Oh, so really this place is where the angels party, let off steam," she said. "Maybe demons should join, we could liven up the place."

"I don't see why not. They're not banned from being here, but demons aren't the most welcome. Imagine the fights that might stir from angel and demon mingling. It would destroy a lot of this place's peace," Iaoel stated.

Seere scoffed, "Oh please, we're getting along aren't we? Maybe the problem is we don't spend a lot of time together in the first place. Demons and angels aren't that different from each other. You know, aside from you being created from dead babies and all, and we're actually born."

Iaoel chuckled. "'Dead babies'? I've never heard it put that way."

Seere shrugged her shoulders. "All I'm saying is, it could be fun."

"It could be. But not all angels are as open to the idea as I am. Take Gabriel and Kaleus for example. The two are a clashing force that can't be stopped. They hate each other. I'd be surprised if they aren't tearing each other to shreds as we speak. This place wouldn't be left standing if they were here."

Seere laughed at that.

"I don't know about that. I know Kale better than anybody, and I think he enjoys playing with Gabriel. Besides, I've never seen him hate anyone more than Lucifer, for obvious reasons…or Lillith—she gets under his skin like a damn leech." She sighed and put her hands on her hips. "Are you going to tell me why we're here? You didn't answer me before." Seere asked again.

They reached the top of the steps, looking straight ahead at the large stone archway into a dark entrance. A cold draft drifted from the darkness, smelling of moss and rotting wood.

"Gabriel tasked us with asking around. We will have an easier time speaking with Watchers and Caktis inside the realm they primarily operate in," Iaoel responded.

They moved closer towards the darkness.

“Right…and what realm is that again?” Seere asked, looking up at the large archway as they passed under it. Was the Ethereal realm not good enough?

“Purgatory,” Iaoel said bluntly like it was obvious.

Seere gaped. “Ghost land? What? Wait, am I even allowed in there? Demons who get stuck in there and never come out. If I go in there with you am I gonna get stuck?”

Seere gradually began to panic as they got further into darkness.

“What the fuck, Iaoel, are you trying to get rid of me?”

Eventually they could no longer see the light of the outside world, surrounded by darkness.

Iaoel grabbed Seere’s arm to stop her from walking further. Their skin prickled at the touch.

“Relax, Seere. I’ll make sure the Caktis let you out when we’ve finished our business inside.”

They stood in silence for a couple minutes. Listening to the subtle sound of wind coming from further in the darkness.

“What are we waiting for?” Seere whispered impatiently.

Iaoel sighed. “Purgatory isn’t like the Ethereal realm. We can’t just shift into it, not like the archangels, it’s more heavily warded because of all the wandering souls that reside inside. We have to wait until a Cakti comes to usher us in,” Iaoel explained.

Seere nodded.

“Ah, I see. Well can they hurry up? I’m bored.”

Not long after Seere spoke a soft flickering glow started to move closer to them, eventually revealing a pale bald figure wearing a brown dhonka and shemdap.

Their eyes were pale blue, the color leeched from them, adapting to the low light of their environment. The low-glow emitted from their outputted grace surrounding them acted as a torch, giving a small light to the otherwise pitch darkness.

“Iaoel, you wish to pass into Purgatory?” the Cakti spoke in a low whisper, almost as though it didn’t speak often and had lost its voice.

“I do, this demon is coming with me, we will both be returning together as well,” Iaoel explained.

Those ice-cold eyes landed on Seere. “Demon’s aren’t allowed to come into Purgatory or face entrapment,” it stated.

“I’d like to see you try and entrap me, pale-face,” Seere dared, her loud voice echoing in the darkness.

Iaoel shot Seere a warning glance to keep her from speaking further.

“I have permission from Gabriel, if you must check with him I’d understand,” Iaoel stated.

The Cakti nodded in response.

“I’ll trust your word, follow me.” It turned and began walking further into the darkness.

They were silent for a few moments, walking deeper towards a cold draft.

“So, how does this work exactly? Will there be a door? Or is it like a slide?” Seere joked, chuckling to herself.

The Cakti ignored her playful tone and simply answered the question.

"The passage isn't entirely hidden behind a door. As I'm sure you know it runs parallel with the mortal realm like the Ethereal realm does. This is why you feel the chilled air currents from Purgatory."

"Right, but that doesn't exactly answer my question, baldy."

The Cakti turned and gave Seere a sneer riddled with disgust then asked Iaoel, "How do you manage to travel with this filth, it never shuts its mouth."

Seere's answering glare was ignored by the Cakti.

Iaoel sighed, breaking the eerie silence they were filled in. "It isn't without difficulty, I assure you."

The Cakti continued forward. "To answer your rudely delivered question, demon, the passageway will feel a lot like passing through a bubble. You'll barely feel it, but once you're inside, the air will be colder and damp. You'll also be able to see, and travel to different parts of the world much faster and return to this passage with ease."

Caktis were the border angels of the realms. Those who watched and guided the Purgatory realm were the most strict, due to the high concentration of various souls going in and out. Demons had been known to use Purgatory to invade a poltergeist's soul, or if they were summoned in by a human opening a portal.

The mortals never knew that their childish games with unfiltered magic could open small portals into Purgatory.

Purgatory was where the lesser demons could cross into the mortal realm without excessive use of power. So, some warding and guarding was put in place to keep them trapped inside if they tried.

Most of the time when demons were given permissions to leave hell, they were restricted to using the Ethereal realm, and only those with more formidable abilities and strength could safely linger on the border between the Ethereal and the mortal realm and therefore interact and play with mortals.

Those with the capabilities of doing so were usually the Fallen and their earliest demon spawns, but as their generations lengthened, their power diluted.

Whenever demons were in Purgatory looking to gain easy and full access to the mortal realm, the Caktis were there to report their presence and occasionally cast them back to hell. If they were unable to stop them, their reports would reach the archangel Uriel, who would dispose of them properly in the mortal realm.

But even those angels under Uriel's division hesitated to call for her help.

Within a minute or so of the Cakti's explanation the air shifted, as if walking through a thin film into another climate. Coupled with the strong feeling of fog, the darkness began dissipating into a dim gray light.

The Cakti stopped just inside the realm, extended its hand out further into the fog.

"This is where I leave you. When you wish to return, simply summon one of us and we'll lead you out," it said.

Seere surveyed around, the complete darkness wasn't anywhere, as if it had never existed.

"Right, and how exactly do we summon you?" she asked.

The Cakti sneered slightly at her, then turned to Iaoel. "You may trust the hell spawn, but I won't exercise that same level of confidence. Iaoel, you know how to. I'll trust you to leave the demon here if it misbehaves." And with that the Cakti vanished.

Seere snorted, the sound slightly echoing in the mist. "So little faith for such a faithful group."

Iaoel ignored her and lifted their hand to the mist, looking deeper into it, but not really looking with her eyes.

“So, how are we supposed to know where to go, who to look for? If the entirety of Purgatory is like this, it must be impossible.” Seere walked a small circle around Iaoel, feeling the air on her fingers.

“To a demon, yes. There are very ancient and powerful wards in here that keep demons from navigating their way through, at least most of them. First-generation demons and the Fallen can navigate if they have the right gifts,” Iaoel responded, closing their eyes.

A shadow passed them, Seere reacted by withdrawing one of her blades. Ready to attack.

“Relax, it’s just a mortal soul wandering the mist. It hardly knows its own name let alone that you’re here.”

Seere sheathed her weapon.

“I don’t like it here,” Seere stated with a chill.

Iaoel’s eyebrows raised slightly. “I’d be surprised if you did.”

Seere snickered. “What are you doing anyway? Shouldn’t we be moving?”

“I’m locating Demetri. He’s a Watcher, a personal friend,” they replied simply.

“Locating? Are you like a GPS angel?” she asked.

Iaoel opened their eyes and had to turn a full one-eighty to meet Seere’s eyes. “I’m an Angel of Sight.”

Seere’s brows furrowed together slightly. “I thought those only saw the future?”

Iaoel shook their head.

“It’s more than that. And it takes a lot of concentration, and your endless chit-chat doesn’t help,” they stated pointedly.

Seere lifted her hands up. "Sorry."

Iaoel sighed, "It's fine, I found him already, only a few hundred miles from here."

Seere chuckled, shifting her boots. "Only a few, huh?"

"Don't worry, we can travel much faster than the souls can. We may not be able to hop, skip and jump like we can in the Ethereal realm. We'll just have to canter instead."

Seere looked around once more, still seeing only dense fog, and the occasional meandering shadow.

"Do you see this place the way I do?" she asked politely.

Iaoel gazed around as well. "Not likely. What do you see in here?" they asked.

Seere tapped the hilt of the blade sheathed to her hip. "Just fog, dense gray fog."

Iaoel dipped their chin in acknowledgement.

"There's fog, definitely, but it's mild, I see Earth, or a muted version of it. Living souls have an orb of color around them, those who are trapped here are void of color, dull and shadowed."

Seere looked around more, but any souls she saw were mere blurs of shadow.

Iaoel tilted their head. "It must be frustrating that you can't see all of it," they teased, earning a glare from Seere. "You must be much lower on the power scale in hell if you see so little."

Seere snapped, "I may be a low-class demon, but I'll have you know I can fight much better than most of the Fallen."

Iaoel didn't react to her snappy manner, only moving closer to her.

“Will you be able to canter then? I know a great deal of third-generation demons are unable, let alone a fifth or higher. Will I need to carry you?” they asked.

Seere started to object, but then looked down. Suddenly being aware that she didn’t in fact have the ability to canter.

When her and Kale needed to get somewhere quicker than a motorcycle they would winnow. Cantering was running, in a supernatural manner—faster than flying, but slower than winnowing, and an uncommon use of travel for anyone.

Iaoel was right, they hadn’t ever known a demon further down the scale than a third-generation to successfully canter.

Seere was lucky she could winnow, but even that required all of her focus, and if she had to carry another, it would often leave her winded and with a headache that lasted for days.

Seere shifted her boots in place, feeling inferior all over again.

“Is carrying necessary?” she asked.

Iaoel didn’t say anything, they only watched the wrath demon.

“I could…” she took a hesitant breath, “I could take your hand and hover maybe while you canter?”

Hovering? She was just making things up now.

It was already likely that Iaoel would need to winnow them back, Seere’s limited power was already waning from the initial trip here.

Iaoel narrowed their eyes, seeing a demon so insecure was so strange. They were always a picture of arrogance. Though they could suppose that the brutality of their training and upbringing forced them to use those attributes as shields.

Seere was a lower-class demon, serving as second to the son of Lucifer, she likely had to endure more than the average demon.

"I'm afraid you'll find hovering to be difficult in this realm."

They watched Seere fidget a bit, she looked around awkwardly. Iaoel too looked around, observing the mirror village just outside the foliage covering the ruins of Reaper's Creek.

A trapped soul lingered, watching a pregnant mortal with a purple aura carrying a basket of freshly harvested food into her small home.

The faded, trapped soul looked sad, feeling so close to his loved one yet so far away.

Purgatory was packed tight with saddened souls who chose not to go to the Gates. It was a sorrowful place. Watchers and Caktis had to have patient demeanors to spend all their time here.

Iaoel looked back at Seere, who was watching them closely, then looked in the direction of the souls, but saw nothing. Maybe she was hoping to see what they were seeing.

A vision sparked to life behind Iaoel's eyes, sending images into their head of the young wrath demon when she was a youngling in a fighting ring against a much older demon, blackened blood dripping down her nose over her bruised mouth and chin. She was on the ground, her clothes mere rags, and every inch of her visible skin was covered in bruises and cuts from multiple bouts of blows. The older and stronger demon standing on the other side of the ring was clean, aside from the bloodied fists, smiling at her like she was a piece of meat.

Seere peeled back her lips and snarled through her stained teeth and stood on shaking legs. She didn't hesitate to lunge for him.

That image blurred and shifted to another.

Of Seere gently tending to another young demon's wounds from a lashing. His back reduced to a slab of shredded meat. Smoke curled underneath his hands as he pressed them into the wall bracing the pain while she cleaned the cuts.

It was Kaleus, only just a boy, looking no older than sixteen. Seere was speaking to him, saying something to keep him distracted as she cleaned the wounds. But Iaoel couldn't make out the words.

Another flash and they were seeing her standing next to Kaleus, both looking not much younger than they were now. Kaleus wiping sweat from his forehead, smearing some of the ash on his hands in the process. He noticed and looked down, his expression turning from lethal chill to a mournful grief.

Seere reached for his hand, pulling his eyes to her. Seere sent him a sympathetic and understanding look. They both looked in front of them to a charred body.

The corpse's gut was burst open from the inside out, chunks of scorched organs spilled out but all other signs of flesh burned black to the bone.

And in the distant shadows an all-too-familiar figure stared down at them, his glowing crimson eyes and lips formed into a smirk of approval.

Iaoel blinked and all the images were gone, and they were once again in the foggy realm.

They hadn't realized that Seere was carefully watching them. There were a lot of stories in this demon that made them curious for more, so much more to her than what meets the eye.

Iaoel cleared their throat. "We should be going; I promise to be quick." Suggesting to Seere that carrying her was the only choice they had.

Seere looked regretful but nodded.

Iaoel was small, but Seere was slightly smaller. Iaoel reached down and scooped her up, one arm under her knees and the other around her waist. Seere couldn't help but cover her face with her hands out of shame.

“I swear, if you mention this to anyone I’ll fashion those all-seeing eyes of yours as keychains,” Seere mumbled.

Iaoel let out a small chuckle. “I’ll withhold this part of the journey in my reports.”

Iaoel lifted their feet, and then they were whooshing into the fog, the shadows and images a mere blur.

“You know, I actually find demons fascinating, you’re essential pieces of the Balance, as equally important to it as we are,” Iaoel muttered.

Seere kept her head low to avoid awkward eye contact.

“I don’t care what angels think of us,” she replied.

Iaoel shrugged. “Fair enough. What I mean is, I’ve spent a great deal of time with demons, and they never cease to amaze me. Very complex creatures, each one having their own cacophony of tales about battles, trials, conquests… If you wish to share any of yours while we’re traveling, to pass the time…it can stay between us,” they suggested, offering a safe space for confidence.

Seere rolled her eyes. “I know what you’re doing, and I’m not interested.”

“What am I doing?”

“You’re one of those vision angels, I figured it wouldn’t be long before you got a glimpse of something about me, and that distant look in your face a bit ago proved me right. I don’t know what you saw, and I don’t care. You’re cute, and I like to play, but I’m not about to share my deepest, darkest experiences with you. So, if you’re done with the ‘let’s get to know one another’ attempts, I’d rather ride out this embarrassing experience in silence,” Seere explained.

Iaoel for a moment was taken back by her candidness but spotted the small fidgeting movements she exhibited, like playing with one of her braids.

She was feeling vulnerable.

She was a demon, who had to fight tooth and nail to gain respect. Perhaps being in a position such as this was taking her back to some of the more vulnerable parts of her past in the pit.

Iaoel would make a point of getting to know Seere further, in time they could even be friends…maybe.

But for now, “Very well.”

The rest of their cantering was spent in silence. That is until Seere decided the silence was too awkward and started hitting on Iaoel with a newly energized fervor.

TWELVE
Heather

I COULD HEAR MUFFLED VOICES in the next room, sounded like they were arguing.

I wish they would be quiet so I could sleep.

Wait. I lived alone.

My eyes shot open as the memories flooded back. A woman in the street, who turned into something unreal. Kale, the flirty library jerk, suddenly appearing in the passenger seat of my car.

My car coming to a stop all on its own, Kale somehow pushing my windshield completely off and into the woman/monster in front of me. He *killed* it, or destroyed it, or whatever that fire and dust effect was.

It couldn't have been real, could it? If not, this is one *hell* of a dream I found my way in. One hell of a week, really.

I winced, my head throbbing. I sat up and realized I was in my bed, still dressed in that day's clothes. The light still coming in through shades of the window.

So I wasn't out for long. My attention went to the closed door, light flooded underneath it, and the voices behind it in the living room. Thank god for cheap, thin walls.

"Vetala's shouldn't be all the way out here, their place of origin was what is now Australia, which is why they were imprisoned in Nessus. One just showing up on the opposite side of the world doesn't make any sense," a harmonic voice muttered.

An image popped into my head, showing me the person behind the voice. Male, tall, dirty blonde hair cut short, and then there were the wings.

Wings. White. Feathers and all. Surrounded by an intense golden glow.

“We were lucky it was only a vetala, and only *one*. And yes, maybe I could’ve handled it better, but I was more focused on eliminating the threat quickly,” the other voice spoke.

Kale’s voice.

I took a deep breath. This couldn’t be happening. I lifted off the bed as slowly as I could to avoid making a sound. Holding still once I stood to make sure they didn’t hear.

When the next one spoke, I knew they hadn’t known I moved.

“Regardless, she’s seen too much.”

I managed to sneak over to my window, peering down. I didn’t have a fire escape, and the though the drop wouldn’t kill me, I’d break enough bones that I wouldn’t be able to run away.

“She’s seen more in her subconscious.” My eyes shot to the door.

My dreams…the shadow in my last dream, so closely resembled Kale, it had to be him. But how could it be possible? And how did they know about them?

Before I realized it, I was creeping towards the door. Slowly, not to make a sound.

“Dreams are one thing, but awake…” My fingers touched the doorknob.

I froze when a shadow passed the under the door.

Kale's voice much closer and clearer than it was before. "You're not in charge, you know? I get that you have your halo on pretty tight, but you're not the only one who gets to make the decisions here."

"As her standing Guardian, I make the final decision for her safety." The winged voice clipped.

I waited until the shadow moved further from the door before I slowly knelt, clutching the knob.

"You're really gonna pull rank? You're not the highest angel on the totem pole in this case, you wouldn't want me to bring my father into this, would you?"

A rumble sent vibrations through the apartment, making my stomach jolt.

A metallic ringing sounding a lot like a sword being unsheathed.

I pinched the doorknob to the right to begin opening it, one millimeter at a time.

"Or we could settle this right here, I've been itching to pluck a feather or two for a while. Of course, I *had* imagined it happening in a more naked scenario, but this will work just fine."

The knob clicked slightly, indicating it was open. But they hadn't noticed. I let the door ease open just a crack, just enough so I could peek with one eye.

No wings in sight, but the man stood by the kitchen table. He wore a simple, untucked, sky-blue button-down shirt and light denim jeans.

From the way he was standing I could see that he was fit, and compared to Kale, standing on the other side of the room by my tv, he was taller than him by almost half a foot.

The contrast between the two was staggering.

Kale had a dark and twisty vibe to him, shadowed. Versus the other who was almost aglow in light, and unnaturally still. Both of them attractive in ways beyond the human imagination, which only further made me think I may have just gone completely mad and or in a very vivid and long dream.

My mind had to be playing tricks on me because I swear he had wings the last time I saw him.

They hadn't spoken for a minute or two but had relaxed their tense positions. Kale twirling a small, curved dagger in his hand like the sharp weapon was as harmless as a fidget spinner.

They maintained eye contact however, almost like they were communicating silently. Kale's lips curved into a smirk, and the no-longer-winged one simply sneered.

"Maybe we should put it to a vote," Kale suggested.

The other scoffed in response.

"Well, if we want this stupid alliance to work, we're going to have to cooperate with each other. Acting like you're the boss of everything and everybody isn't going to start it out on the right foot."

A strange swirl of smoke and flickering embers filled a section of the room.

"I agree."

My eyes bulged out of their sockets when the smoke dissipated to nothing and in its place stood another person. Someone who was definitely not in the room a second ago.

The ginger-haired male who just appeared was wearing a large black and red oversized hoodie, gray sweatpants that gathered at the ankles, and converse shoes.

A large sword was strapped between his shoulder blades, slightly hidden beneath his hood.

Though most of his pale skin was covered by his clothes, I could see the edges of a tattoo peeking up onto his neck, looking almost like black tentacles or claws—I was too far away to know for sure.

His eyes were pale seafoam green, but they pulsed slightly when they briefly locked on mine, or maybe my eyes must have been tricking me.

He turned towards Kale, not acknowledging that he saw me and dipped his head slightly, bowing to him maybe?

“Where’s Lillith and Dumdum?” Kale asked.

“Duma,” the golden man corrected bitterly.

The new addition to my apartment shrugged, bored. “They’ll be along shortly,” he replied.

The golden man crossed his arms, a look of disapproval written on his face.

“You shouldn’t have just winnowed in here,” he stated. *Winnowed*?

Kale snorted. “You did the same thing just a while ago, and with more *pizazz* too.” He chuckled as he used jazz hands to emphasize his words.

“And she fainted as a result. All I’m saying is, she could’ve seen you and reacted badly.” Well golden man got that right.

Where on earth did he come from?

A shiver ran down my spine, and my skin felt like something was slivering along my arm. In the corner of my eye I spotted movement, snapping my head towards my bed my eyes landed on a female silhouette, her features shadowed, all except the crimson glow of her eyes on me. A barely audible gasp burst from my lips.

“You’re a nosy little mouse, huh?”

My heart jumped out of my chest and I let out a short scream, falling back against the door, causing it to loudly slam shut.

"Too late," Kale muttered with a chuckle.

The female let out a shrilling laugh at my reaction but was cut off when the winged-man appeared between us, light flooding the room. Her expression turning to a sultry grin.

I could see her features more clearly now in the light. Her hair was long and wavy, reaching her hips in a deep scarlet color. She had defined cheekbones and plump lips covered in a blood red lipstick. Her eyes in the light no longer glowing red, but black as night. Her skin was pale like the others, lacking any sense of imperfection.

She wore fishnet tights, knee-high suede heeled boots, high-waisted black shorts fraying at the edges and finally a strapless lace and boned deep-green corset, accentuating her defined collarbones and plump breasts.

She was the most beautiful woman I've ever seen— intoxicating and seductive.

She leveled her smile to me. "Sorry to scare you, little mouse, but your less-than-covert lurking and fear smelled absolutely delicious."

I couldn't look away, she was hypnotic. Her eyes twinkled with delight as I took her in.

"Mmm, I always love it when beautiful mortals undress me with their eyes. Do we need to send these brutes out for a little private time, sugar?" she asked.

I blinked, breaking from her trance. Having remembered that the winged-man was standing between us, and somehow the door had opened, and Kale was leaning against the door frame. I looked at him, his expression was bored if not annoyed.

"I nearly killed you, Lillith. I thought you were a threat," the winged-man stated with disgust.

Lillith?

She sighed, getting up from the bed to approach him.

"So quick to defend, the white knight angel. I was only having fun."

I'm sorry, did she say *angel*?

She trailed her finger along his shoulder and withdrew quickly after a searing sound resulted.

"Ooh, I live in hell, boy. I like a little burn." She continued past him, sending me another seductive smile before slipping into the living room.

She lives where? My thoughts were swimming from the small kernels of information that was being tossed around like they were nothing important.

The winged man leaned down towards me, still crouched on the floor. "Are you alright? There's nothing to be afraid of, she couldn't have hurt you even if she tried."

Up close I could see that his eyes were deep blue as the Pacific.

"Breathe," he said.

I did as he said, feeling less dizzy.

"Who are you people?" I asked, my voice raspy and broken. I swallowed, the whole action feeling unnatural.

He held out his hand, and against my natural instincts I took it. And when our hands met I felt a wave of warmth wash through me, calming the churning uneasiness of my stomach. The feeling was so familiar, and for a split second I thought of that man I dreamt of dying in my arms.

"That's a bit hard to explain, there's *a lot* to explain, and I'm not sure we should—"

“Cut the crap, Gabriel. Just tell her,” Kale snapped from the doorway.

Gabriel, that was his name.

“Her mind may not be capable.” An entirely new voice sounded from the living room.

How many people were in my fucking apartment?

Gabriel led us to the living room, Kale turning outwards to lean against the wall.

The new voice came from near the front door. He was about Kale’s height, same as the ginger-haired male. Only his hair was shoulder-length and dark brown. His skin was tan, and his features suggested Native American, his eyes a caramel brown color. He was wearing a simple black sweater and brown pants. A small scar curving above the curve of his left eyebrow.

This one must be Duma, assuming from their previous mention. He was standing with his arms folded, casual, but his stance was balanced, conveniently ready to move if necessary.

“So your vote is no,” Kale plainly put.

“We’re not putting it to a vote,” Gabriel snapped, releasing my hand but staying next to me, as if to prepare for another fainting episode.

I could see a difference in all of them, a similar contrast to Gabriel and Kale. Lillith and the ginger male felt shadowed and even had similar scents of chili pepper, cumin, and firewood.

Duma had an aura of light like Gabriel. Not only that, but even just looking at Gabriel and Duma I felt a sense of trust and warmth, whereas with Lillith and the others there was temptation and fear, like an adrenaline rush mixed with danger.

Though Kale felt…never mind.

"Why not? I'd like to have a say," Lillith purred, finding my couch to be a comfortable place to spread her body over. "Let's see how much her feeble mind can handle."

Gabriel tensed next to me. "Besides the fact that I'm in charge of her well-being, putting it to a vote would mean bringing everyone else here, and the apartment is already feeling crowded as it is." He turned to me apologetically. "No offense intended of course."

But I didn't care about that, what I cared about was that additional tidbit of information: there were more of them, whatever they were.

"If this is a dream, I'd really like to wake up," I rasped, my mouth feeling dry.

"I'd say that's another 'yes' vote," ginger chimed in.

Kale chuckled. "Indeed." He watched me with amused approval.

"Enough. All of you need to leave, we're overwhelming her." Gabriel's voice rumbled the apartment once again.

Lillith clicked her tongue. "Whatever, I don't want to sit here while you tell the story anyway, so boring." She motioned to Duma with her red manicured finger to 'come here'.

He nodded slightly and crossed the room, stopping short of Gabriel, placing a hand on his shoulder.

"We'll be at the warehouse, send us a shout if you need anything." Then he stood next to her, as she looped her arm through his, looking uncomfortable with the intimate touch.

The ginger male reaching to grab her other hand before they all disappeared together in a plume of smooth red fluid.

I gasped at their departure. My brain throbbed, not given enough time between surprises to prepare for the next.

"You should go too," Gabriel spoke to Kale, who still leaned against the far wall, unmoving, watching my every move.

A predator sizing up his prey, that's what it felt like.

He didn't bother to look towards Gabriel when he spoke, "I'm staying."

Gabriel shifted, tilting more towards Kale. "It may be easier if—"

Kale's eyes snapped to his at that. "I'm staying, featherbrain. Lest you tell a biased narrative. Or worse, choose to erase her memories while no one is here to stop you," Kale interrupted.

His eyes clicked back to mine, and my heart skipped a step. I couldn't tell whether I was grateful or disappointed that my memories of all this weren't going to disappear.

Gabriel grumbled, but didn't argue further, facing me.

"Where should I begin?" he sighed, though the question wasn't actually for me. But I knew where to begin.

"You had wings be-before," I stammered. I sighed to steady myself, "Let's start there."

THIRTEEN
Heather

IT WAS SURREAL WATCHING HIM pour me a glass of water.

Every movement was smooth, precise and, dare I say, perfect. I kept waiting for a sound, the simple clink of cups against each other in the cupboard, or the subtle squeak of the cabinet as it closed.

Or maybe even the familiar sloshing sound of the water pitcher as it was lifted from its regular place inside the fridge door. All human, normal noises that I once ignored, so mundane and natural, only now was I missing those sounds.

Not one of them captured my ears while Gabriel, *an angel*, moved in my kitchen.

Is that what it is to be human? Noisy, banal, clumsy?

Even as I watched him, I hardly believed what I was seeing was real. Even though his feathered wings no longer protruded from his shoulder blades, the ghost of them remained. And even though his faint golden glow had diminished, the essence lingered.

His very presence filled the room with warmth and gentleness. But it wasn't just gentleness, no, he seemed strong and purposeful. And yet, not one movement he made, no matter how solid, made a sound. Was that the major differences between humans and whatever they were…angels.

Surely, the energy he emitted was intended to be comforting, and in a way it was. But in another way it was fiercely intimidating.

I knew before they had told me anything, before most of them left, that my modest human life was about to be disrupted forever. And I already missed it.

I missed my ignorance.

Gabriel extended the glass towards me, I took it. Allowing the chilled condensation dripping down the outside of the glass to soothe my wracking nerves.

I was sitting cross-legged on my armchair. Kale lingered by the living room window, continuously peering into the street, watching for danger—or trying to make me feel less uncomfortable, I'll never know.

Gabriel chose to sit on the far end of the couch, keeping a safe distance from me. They both seemed to be trying to give me enough space to breathe, not wanting to push my nerves.

Gabriel's eyes remained on me until I at last took a sip from my glass. The cool water feeling foreign in my mouth. I forced myself to swallow and take a deep breath. Recounting what he had told me prior to getting me a drink.

"So…you're an angel. As in, halos, harps, white robes and of course wings?" I asked. My voice a little clearer thanks to the water.

His expression was nothing short of wary. He allowed the corner of his mouth to twitch upwards. A mask of calm, no doubt he was nervous as well, given how long it took him to tell me that little shred of information.

"That depiction of us is purely a subject of spiritual opinion. But in a sense, yes. You've studied many religions, correct?" he asked. I merely nodded.

"Then you're familiar with archangels." It wasn't a question. I thought back to basic Christian and Catholic religions, archangels being the top tiers of power next to God himself.

And one of those archangels, had been named Gabriel… My eyes widened, snapping me from my thoughts and back to his face.

"You're the archangel Gabriel?"

"I know, not as impressive in person, huh?" Kale joked.

Gabriel sent a glare in his direction. If I was in my right mind, I would've allowed that attempt at lightening the mood to make me smile, but laughter was far away from me at the moment.

"The other one…by the door, Duma? Is he an archangel too?" Gabriel looked back at me with surprise written on his face.

"No, he's a Spectral angel."

My brows narrowed in confusion. I've never heard of a *Spectral* before. Gabriel simply shook his head.

"We'll get into those details another time. But he is an angel."

I dared a glance at Kale, still gazing out the window. "The others aren't though, they're different."

"Demons," Gabriel stated.

Unnatural fear cramped my stomach. *Demons…*

"We don't bite, unless you're into it." Kale winked.

He was amused, but I stared at him and he met my stare fully.

He was a *demon*.

But that didn't feel right, not the way Lillith made me feel. With her and the other I could smell the brimstone and ash in their bones. Kale was something else…

"What are you?" I asked. His eyes darkened and he tilted his head, curiosity playing across his eyes, with a hint of bewilderment.

His response was swift and final, "He just told you."

My throat ached. I took another sip of my water, breaking eye contact. But I didn't miss them exchange side glances. An unspoken message conveyed between them.

"There are more of you?" I said.

Gabriel responded first, "Four others. Three other angels and an additional demon."

"I didn't know angels and demons spent time together."

Four demons and five angels made for a large group. And if my religious studies were correct, they weren't supposed to get along.

Kale replied, "They don't. Angels are boring, not great for enjoyable company."

A low growl-like noise came from deep in Gabriel's throat.

"Our dispositions aren't, shall we say, compatible." Kale snorted at that. Gabriel only went on, "This unique situation calls for an aberrant alliance."

I peered between them. "What situation?"

Gabriel sighed, rubbing a hand over his face. Hesitant to speak further. He looked towards Kale, who met his gaze.

"If we go much further and her mind breaks, I may not be able to repair it."

Kale didn't speak for a moment, only watching him closely. Moments passed, and eventually Gabriel sighed again, turning back towards me.

"You are going to learn a lot of things about the supernatural universe, things that no mortal is meant to know. We go to great lengths to make sure you never know. Mostly because mortals aren't able to tap into enough of their brain function to comprehend it. Humans have lost their minds, broken from the intensity of the information."

He paused, still considering if he should continue.

"You may be different, and I have reason to believe that you are. You may be able to withstand it. But as we tell you more, you need to let us know if you start to feel…odd. More than just nausea or nerves, but if your brain starts to *boil*, for lack of a better description. Do you understand?"

If the impact of those terrifying words didn't send my heart racing, his intense gaze certainly did the trick. Would my mind actually *boil*?

"I- what makes you think I could withstand it?"

"That will be explained, but for now I just need to know that you understand the risks," Gabriel reaffirmed.

Fear, insecurity, and foreboding clutched at my gut.

But beneath it, there was an eagerness, a thirst for knowledge. Deep in that part of me that drove my studies, that drove my answer from my already parched mouth.

"I... understand. Go ahead."

I took a bigger gulp of water, before setting down my glass on the coffee table. Gabriel still seemed wary, angling his head towards Kale, listening.

Kale, however, was looking at me from underneath his lashes. Approval and intrigue sparkled across his eyes.

Gabriel began, "Angels, among other supernatural beings, are considered immortal. Angels and humans alike are created from parts of God's soul, but in different quantities. This is why humans live short lives. Lower class angels can have lifespans ranging from a few thousand years to many Kiḷai."

"Kiḷai?" I asked.

"It's a unit of time, one Kiḷai is equivalent to about a million years."

Woah. Yeah, I can see where that might stump a few people, I don't even think I can do that kind of math.

"So, in comparison to a human life of one hundred years, angels are 'immortal'. And the higher the degree of angel, the greater amount of soul and the greater their life span. Demons are different. They live long lives, but aren't immortal, and can be killed."

"Though, we make it very hard to do so," Kale muttered.

Gabriel ignored him and went on, "The point is, it is near impossible to kill an angel. But recently…someone or something managed to do it." He stopped.

He watched me, waiting for something. I contemplated what he said. An image of blood, screaming, pain, and tears. A pure soul dying in my arms. His name emerging from an unknown place that I still didn't understand.

"Mason."

Kale's head snapped up, his attention wholly on my face.

"That was real?" I whispered.

Gabriel dipped his chin once. Mason's pain once again emerging, winding up my chest into a ball of rubber bands. I fought against it to focus back on Gabriel.

"He was your assigned Guardian angel. His death was sudden, and his scream was heard by all supernatural entities. His death was unnatural, and it shook the universe. He was nowhere near the end of his life cycle, and the cause of his death still remains unknown." Gabriel explained.

The sheer terror I felt during that experience inched back into my body.

"I saw him, felt him. I knew him, but afterwards I thought it was just a nightmare. But you're saying it really happened?" I murmured.

"We assumed it had nothing to do with you," Gabriel responded. "So I was sent to be your Guardian temporarily until we figure it out. God and Lucifer both have no idea how it happened. They summoned us all to work together and weed out the culprit. Angel killings aren't common, and their occurrences are taken very seriously. Something or someone having the ability to end the life of an angel poses a large threat to the Balance. Deeming it necessary for an abnormal and powerful coalition of two different realms."

Must be pretty serious then.

My stomach churned, bile daring to rise up my throat.

Kale jerked his chin at me. "Looking a little green there. You need a minute?" he asked.

I didn't find worth in acknowledging him, instead I cleared my throat to respond to Gabriel.

"What was that thing in the street? The thing *he* killed." Only nodding towards Kale.

Gabriel looked to Kale, waiting for him to answer.

"It was a vetala. An ancient primordial from the Ceyya period. It shouldn't have been anywhere near here, especially where you were. Its presence among others suggests that Mason's death was just the start, that maybe something bigger is happening. We aren't entirely sure yet," Kale explained.

He sounded like a leader, like Gabriel. And from what I witnessed earlier; he probably was in charge of the demon side of their affiliation. Maybe that's why he stayed, ensuring that Gabriel didn't take full charge of the situation.

They seemed to know each other well, a murky history perhaps.

"As a human, I was supposed to stay in the dark of all this?"

"Mortal's knowledge of the supernatural is purposefully limited. Our intention was to simply monitor you while we did our investigation, but the events today changed that," Gabriel answered.

Kale was again staring into the street. The sun was setting, a burnt orange sky dimming to a dark blue more and more every minute.

I thought of my dream, of the liquid mist that crept along my skin, paralyzing me. I thought of the shadow figure that sat on rough black stone. The red eyes, like molten ore coursing. The fire and sparks that struck down the smoky creature into nothing with one blow.

That figure was Kale, in a rawer form. His demon form, maybe. Dark, scorching, ignited in organic power.

The Kale standing in my living room was reserved, polished, refined. But like the golden glow itching to escape the barriers of Gabriel's skin, that smoldering power showed slightly. A curl of black smoke around his fingers, a flare of fire in his eyes.

A brief whiff of cinnamon and something sweet touched my senses, as if answering my thoughts.

He was there, inside my mind. He saved me from whatever lurked there. But he was *in my mind.*

He hadn't noticed me staring, but shifted slightly when I asked, "Was that creature in my dream real too? The one you *disintegrated*?"

"What dream?" Gabriel asked.

I clamped my lips tight. I guess he hadn't told him about that.

Kale ignored him, fiddling with the hilt of his dagger. "It was real. I merely banished it from your subconscious. You may see it again."

"You didn't want to mention this to me? When did this happen?" Gabriel demanded.

Kale rolled his eyes and looked back at the street. "I had it handled."

"Clearly you didn't. Because you neglected to erase the memory from her mind afterwards," Gabriel snapped.

Kale shot a cold sneer his way. "Memory wiping isn't my style, ass-feathers. She chocked it up to be a nightmare, there was no harm done. If it weren't for the vetala, she wouldn't have known."

"But…I did know. I asked you in the library if I had met you before. I recognized you."

Kale eyes filled with warning.

Gabriel folded his arms, his skin pulsing slightly. "The library?" His tone turbulent and accusatory.

Kale groaned, "Tattle-tale."

"I see the *observing* went all according to plan, then. You half-witted leech just couldn't resist, could you?" Gabriel pinched the bridge of his nose.

Kale smirked. “We invented temptation, pegasus, why should we resist it.”

They stayed quiet for a few minutes. Kale’s sly grin only grew larger, and shortly after Gabriel jumped to his feet and pointed a warning finger at him.

“Enough. This is not the time for your perverted imagery.”

My eyebrows shot up. What exactly just happened? As if hearing my thoughts Kale’s eyes flashed to me.

“Supernatural beings have a mental connection to one another. And they can choose to open their minds or keep them shut to messages going in and out. Demons and angels rarely converse telepathically, but our unfortunate alliance forces us to. And I personally love driving this high-and-mighty featherbrain nuts, so I sometimes send things that aren’t for the pure of heart,” he said with a wink.

“You mean you can read each other’s minds?” I asked.

“We can send messages, and if a connection is accepted, depending on the strength of it, then we can hear or see each other’s thoughts, yes. But just as easily we can sever the connection, or only allow in limited messages,” Gabriel answered.

Not lowering his glare from Kale’s amused figure.

“It’s like a thread, connecting us all that we can sometimes tug on or tap on.”

Kale leaned in towards me, as if to convey a secret.

“Imagine a spider web, and a simple tap sends vibrations to our minds. Buzzing in the back of our heads letting us know someone wishes to get in, their vibrations unique to each messenger, so we know who it is contacting us without opening our minds,” he clarified.

“Can you read my mind?” My face heated at the idea of either of them seeing any of my deepest darkest thoughts, let alone the dirtier ones…

Kale gave me a knowing smile; My worry must’ve been written all over my face.

“Not your conscious mind, your subconscious is more open and less guarded, and even then it takes great focus. Mortals have little power, and therefore little agency against a supernatural. For that reason, God added in certain…loopholes that keep mortals safe from our control. Blocks are set in place to protect the minds of humans. It would take a great deal of power, power only a few of us possess, to tug on and enter your conscious thread.”

I released a sigh of relief. Kale smirking in response.

They had already given me so much information, and yet I knew it wasn’t even close to the behemoth that awaited. But this small grain of rice worth of knowledge was making my stomach swirl, and my head feeling dizzy, but not boiling—thank god.

I could see why humans are kept in the dark. Our very existence would fall apart in panic if everyone knew these things. Religious beliefs really only scraped the surface, but perhaps that was intentional.

“I’m guessing I can’t just crawl into bed, wake up in the morning and all of this be nothing but a crazy dream?” I joked.

Gabriel’s eyes warmed, comforted that I could find some humor in all of this.

“I know it’s a lot, and there’s plenty more to come. But for now, I think we can stop. There’s time to learn more later on.”

His eyes drifted to Kale’s. Another silent conversation I couldn’t hear. Kale moved from the window, bracing his hands against the back of the couch.

"We should get going. You should take some time to pack a few things," Gabriel said to me.

I straightened. "I have to leave?" He nodded.

"The vetala knew where you were, which means your apartment may not be a safe location. Protecting you here, in the middle of the city would be more strenuous than if we moved you," Gabriel explained.

I looked at both of them. "But…I have finals, I can't just leave."

Well, one final, but still. I had responsibilities I couldn't just walk away from.

Gabriel stood, confident and poised.

"We'll take care of it. Hopefully, you won't be away for long."

Clearly I had no choice in the matter. What was the point in resisting? I mean, after all they were supernatural entities, and they were keeping me safe. Those thoughts didn't shake the anxiety churning in my gut.

I huffed, standing, my legs feeling wobbly.

"Where are we going? That warehouse mentioned earlier?" I asked.

Gabriel grinned. "Good memory. It's one of his safehouses. Big enough to accommodate all of us, and not crumble to the ground."

I gulped at that. *Crumble*? They were that powerful?

Kale once again answered my thoughts. "We're all among the best of our breeds. That much power doesn't bode well for small, fragile structures. But don't worry, we'll point that energy towards each other, not to you. Wouldn't want your small and fragile structure to break down, would we?"

He gave me his signature smirk, like in the library, it made my heart skip a step. I hadn't realized he had made his way so close to me.

Gabriel cleared his throat from a few feet away, breaking me from my trance. I stepped away from Kale and walked towards my bedroom.

The door was open, and I could see the outline of my bed. Little light now coming from the windows. I remembered seeing Lillith perched on it, her eyes glowing red, her sultry gaze paralyzing me in place.

I swallowed. "Are the others going to be there?" I asked carefully.

Gabriel exchanged a glance with Kale then nodded to me. "Jade is…preparing a dinner, to ease the tension," Kale snorted.

"Who's Jade?"

Gabriel offered me a sympathetic grin. "You'll see."

PART TWO
STEEL & CONCRETE

FOURTEEN
Heather

"WE'RE GOING TO WHAT?" I uttered.

Kale secured his dagger behind his back. Gabriel was facing me, with his arms slightly outstretched towards me. My left side heavier from the small gym bag I packed with a few days' worth of essentials, hopefully a few days would be enough.

"Winnow. It's what you saw the others do when they came in and out. It's the fastest way to where we're going," Gabriel clarified.

"And how does this work exactly?" I asked.

Gabriel stayed still, trying not to push me.

"We shift into the Ethereal realm, and from there we can go from one place in the mortal realm to the other in seconds. You'll have to hold onto me. The first time is usually pretty jarring. Once you're used to it, you will only need to have physical contact with one of us who can do it."

I peered at his open stance. Welcoming, warm, inviting. I glanced over at Kale who met my stare.

Kale shrugged. "If you'd prefer I take you, I'd be happy to sweep you off your feet." He winked.

I swallowed and returned my glance to Gabriel, carefully waiting for me.

"How far are we going?"

Much to my dismay, Gabriel shook his head. "Unfortunately, until we know your mind is secure, we can't tell you much about the location. It will only take a few seconds. You can even close your eyes if that will make it easier."

I nodded and moved closer to him. Suddenly unsure of the right way to *hold* onto him. I moved my arms and hands around awkwardly, trying to find the least uncomfortable position to take.

He must have sensed my discomfort, he took my hands and placed them on his chest. His hands then wrapped around my waist and he lifted me slightly until my feet rested on top of his. His arms finally wrapped all the way around waist, overlapping behind my back.

My face was beet-red being so close to him. The muscles underneath his shirt were firm and sculpted. His entire body warm.

He smelled faintly of sea salt, and roses.

My attention went to Kale when he clicked the light switch, turning out the last light in the living room and turning to us.

He smirked wickedly and stood next to us. "Heather and Feathers, sitting in a tree," he sang quietly.

Gabriel snapped his head towards him. "Grow up."

I merely hid my face, not wanting them to see my flushed cheeks.

Gabriel whispered closer to my ear, "We're going to go now. It'll feel strange, but don't let it scare you. We'll be there soon."

As if on cue, the ground beneath us disappeared, and the air around us was warped. A cocoon of gold and white light in thin vertical lines surrounded us. It felt like we were dropping, but my hair barely moved an inch. No, it was my heart, it felt like it was rising into my throat much like it did when on a tower drop ride at a theme park.

Before I had a chance to adjust to it, it was over. The ground met our feet softly, and the air around us stopped warping, the light falling away.

Now surrounded by concrete and steel pillars and arches.

I hadn't realized I was clinging closer to Gabriel until he cleared his throat, lowering his arms from around me.

I took a step back, planting my feet on the solid concrete floor. Looking around the warehouse I saw it was large and wide. The windows were spray painted with black and brown paint, artificial lights hung down from the ceiling of steel, giving the place a low warm light.

Further in there was a collection of workout equipment as well as a wall of various weaponry. And in the center, a better lit area, there was a square sparring space, outlined by the thin, muted blue mats on the floor.

Turning, I saw behind us was a large staircase leading from the warehouse floor up to an open archway, light leaking through from the space beyond it. A digital clock hung above it.

12:16 AM

When we left, it was just after nine. So we were in a different time zone, the other side of the country—if we were even in the same country.

A pillar of dark smoke with churning orange flame and lightning appeared for a moment a few feet from us, and then disappeared, leaving Kale standing there. His winnowing looked much different, not as bright as Gabriel's. He immediately began walking towards the staircase, paying us no further attention.

Gabriel gripped my elbow tenderly. "Are you hungry?" he asked.

A whiff of garlic and oregano hit my nose, making my stomach groan. Gabriel must have heard it because he grinned. He gestured to the stairs. Kale was already halfway up them when I gripped the handle to ascend.

"Your Guardian Master can actually cook right?" Kale asked, still not turning towards us.

Gabriel followed me up, keeping a couple feet away. "She's probably the only one who can out of all of us."

Kale snorted. "My father would have her beat, his culinary skills *almost* rival his affinity for cruelty," he mumbled.

As we got closer to the top of the stairs I could hear more voices, some familiar, some not. Kale disappeared through the doorway, his voice joining the others. Before my feet could reach the last step, I paused.

What am I doing here? This was all happening extremely fast, only a few hours ago I was simply planning for the end of the school year. Now, it all felt upside down.

"You alright?"

I forgot Gabriel was behind me. I angled towards him slightly. My facial expression must have given my thoughts away.

"I know this is a lot," he said, "but it's necessary to keep you safe. As soon as we figure it all out and fix it, I'll personally make sure you make it back to your normal life." I nodded.

The air in my lungs was heavy. Laughter sounded from the open archway, drawing my focus.

"This is overwhelming." Was all I could manage.

Gabriel raised a couple steps up to better face me. He didn't touch me this time, he only offered me comforting eye contact.

"At any point during this dinner, if you feel like you need to step out or take a break, no questions asked. Okay?"

I returned a smile and turned back to the archway, reaching the top of the stairs.

The large open room had an industrial kitchen against the back wall, and a large metal dining table to the far left of it, surrounded by different styles and colored chairs. In the other corner there was a dark blue sofa, a black futon, and a huge dark green beanbag chair, all surrounding a block of wood that served as a coffee table. Hanging on the wall was a large flat screen tv and two speakers suspended on either side of it. More of the hanging lights surrounded the space.

Hallways on both sides of the room leading to other locations. The walls were made of concrete and rusting steel beams. Some of the walls had faded graffiti written on them.

In the kitchen, behind the island counter, a small pale brunette had her back turned, stirring a pot heated on the stove. She wore a light-denim blouse and black leggings. Her hair was swept up in a messy bun, with strands falling out. She swayed when she stirred, humming slightly.

Another female sat on one of the island stools. She was really tall, had to be taller than Gabriel even. She wore a halter-top, sleeveless mustard pantsuit, finished off with peep-toe black heels. The yellow brought out her umber skin and jet-black hair that was swept all to one side.

Her eyes were big, dark as her hair, and she had a long clean nose with large lips. Her face was beautifully symmetrical, her arms sculpted and long like her legs and torso. Her expression broke through the beauty with disdain and contempt.

Duma, the angel I briefly encountered in my apartment was carefully setting the table for dinner. Kale had made his way over to the futon, sitting next to the ginger-haired demon who had a controller in his hand and was playing some kind of video game on the tv.

Lillith was nowhere to be seen.

Gabriel still hung back a foot or two behind me, as if he were waiting for me to decide if I wanted to leave.

The brunette cooking turned from the pot to pull out a couple bottles of wine from the fridge. Her skin was pale, but her face was covered in freckles, and she had bangs that reached below her eyebrows. Her eyes were light blue like her top, and she had a petite nose and lips. Her figure was also petite and almost prepubescent. But her square jaw and defined cheekbones were mature.

She went to open a bottle when she glanced upwards and caught sight of me. Her mouth instantly turned upwards into the most welcoming smile I'd ever seen.

"You're here! Come in!"

The other female on the stool looked towards me as well. Her eyes scanned me up and down, assessing. But the cook simply walked around the island and came straight up to be, holding out her hand.

"I'm Jade. I'm an angel, more specifically I'm the Guardian Master. Would you like something to drink?" she asked.

Her tone and demeanor were very maternal, I almost felt like I was meeting a friend's mom or something.

On instinct I took her hand and shook it.

"Heather. Nice to meet you. Um, sure, what do you have?" The words felt robotic, a human who had met loads of people and, as a result, introductions turned to muscle memory.

She held my hand tighter and brought her other hand to hold it too. The gesture was warm and familiar.

She used our hands to lead us over to the counter. “We have wine, chardonnay and even some merlot if you prefer. And of course, water, beer, even some apple juice I believe. It’s entirely up to you,” she explained.

She let go of my hands only to grab a wine glass from the cupboard.

I swallowed. “I’ll take some chardonnay, thank you.” She smiled, popping open one of the bottles on the counter.

I looked behind me, Gabriel had moved to the table to help Duma set the remaining tableware, keeping a side eye on me. The other female was only a couple stools away, and she was still watching me like a hawk.

“So, Heather, I’m sure you have loads of questions. But why don’t you tell me a little about yourself. You are going to school, right? What are you studying?” Jade conversed.

I got the feeling she might know all the answers already, but I appreciated the casualness she was trying to offer.

She placed the filled wine glass in front of me and went to open the other bottle. I tore my eyes from the other female to take a sip.

“Anthropology mostly, with a specialty in ancient religion and symbology,” I answered. Jade nodded.

“That’s really interesting, if not a bit ironic,” she mumbled the last part. She glanced over at the other female, who was still staring intently at me. “Jophiel, would you go fetch Iaoel and Lillith? Dinner is ready.”

The female, *Jophiel*, stood without a word and departed down the left side hallway. Jade waited until she was out of sight to speak again.

“That’s Jophiel, she’s Gabriel’s sister, another archangel.” My eyebrows raised at that.

I hadn't realized…her aura wasn't as strong as Gabriel's, I assumed she was a lesser-angel.

"We should probably go sit at the table now," she said. She turned to the boys at the tv. "Hey! Dinner time!" They rose from the futon in unison.

The table was large, it had four chairs on each side and one on each end. I walked towards the table, Gabriel had seated himself in the chair at the corner, so I followed suit and sat in the empty chair next to him, leaving two seats empty next to me.

Jade and Duma set the food down on the table. Kale sat in the head table spot, two chairs down from me, and the ginger sat on the other side of the table in the middle.

Jophiel re-entered the room, with two others in tow. She sat in the head chair opposing Kale, to the right of Gabriel. Lillith sauntered in, sitting next to the ginger male.

The other that came in with them looked female, she was half a foot shorter than me, her hair was pitch black and cut short, combed back. She looked Eastern, dark hair, dark eyes, and light skin. She wore black skinny jeans, a white button up dress shirt and a black blazer with the sleeves folded up her forearms. Her whole ensemble was very androgynous, making me question her gender a bit. She sat next to Jophiel and Lillith, across from Gabriel.

Jade put down the final dish and plopped down in the seat next to me, Duma sitting in the last seat on our side. Leaving one seat remaining between the ginger and Kale.

"Where's Seere?" the androgynous female asked. Kale smirked and simply pointed towards the right-side hallway.

On cue, an even smaller female walked in. The first thing I noticed was her platinum blonde braids, tightly woven and coiled, with the sides of her head buzzed. Her skin was a dark bisque tone, and her ears were pierced from the lobe all the way up the arch. She had a nose piercing as well.

She wore a black oversized t-shirt that was cut into a crop top, torn denim shorts with a flannel top tied around her hips and combat boots. Her arms, waist and legs had various tattoos covering the skin.

She was emanating major stoner-goth vibes that made me reminisce of high school.

She sat in the last remaining seat. Making direct eye contact with Kale. Kale nodded slightly as if they communicated mentally.

"Alright, we're all here! Dig in!" Jade said.

The demons didn't hesitate, but the angels restrained, watching them with various expressions of disgust, aversion, and hatred. Once the demons had their plates filled, then angels gracefully put various items on their plates.

The demons' plates were covered, versus the angels' were light and little in quantity. I watched in surprise as these ethereal beings dished and ate like they were humans at Thanksgiving. I hadn't realized they needed real food.

I hadn't moved and jolted when Jade nudged my arm with a plate of broccoli in her hand. I took it and put a couple of pieces on my plate. Taking the opportunity to put a couple other things on it as well.

A chicken breast, a scoop of pasta, a piece of bread. Even as I took a savory bite, I couldn't even taste it, my attention fixed on the people at the table, watching them, baffled at the casualty I saw.

The demons at least were casual, right at home. The angels were tense, like they were forced to eat dinner with their in-laws. They seemed to be trying to stay civil though, despite their combined powers and general dislike of one another causing a dry sauna heat to fill the room.

Or maybe it was just me who felt it.

Jophiel seemed to be the only one not trying to conceal her acrimony of the demons, eyeing them like they were vermin.

“How was Reaper’s Creek?” Kale asked the blonde next to him.

She tensed slightly and slipped a quick glance over to the androgynous one, then shrugged.

“It was fine. Not a lot of answers, mostly just more questions.”

The androgynous once spoke next, looking at Gabriel. “Demetri said that there are areas with tears between realms, small, barely cracks, but they tend to attract some of the souls near it. Sealing them is easy enough, but he doesn’t know why they’re happening,” she said.

Her eyes went from his to mine, noticing that I was watching. She cleared her throat.

“I’m Iaoel, by the way.”

“Iaoel is an Angel of Sight. They can see premonitions, futures, pasts, they tell us a lot about fate and help divisions like ours know where to go,” Gabriel clarified. *Oh, is that all?*

There was a lot to unpack there, that explanation only left me with more questions.

The blonde chimed in, “They tend to be very nosy.” Before anyone could retort Kale, gestured to her.

“This tardy spitfire is Seere, she’s my second, a demon—obviously.”

Seere waved mockingly at me.

I looked back at Iaoel, then between Jophiel and Gabriel.

“So…she’s an angel who can see things, and you’re both archangels?”

Iaoel cleared her throat. My eyes went back to her.

"Quick side note, assuming that you are progressive. I'm not a she, but they. The Angels of Sight have no gender."

"Oh. Right, sorry." *They* waved me off politely as if to say it was a common mistake.

Gabriel took a small sip of wine and then opened his position more to me. "I guess introductions are in order. Jophiel is my older sister, she charges over the creation division of heaven. Her and Uriel are twins."

Uriel, that was an archangel name I was familiar with from my studies.

Gabriel continued, "Jade is the Guardian Master; she essentially leads the Guardian angels. Duma, next to her, is a Spectral. They train new angels before they receive an assignment."

Gabriel looked at Kale, signaling him to introduce his own posse.

Kale finished the food he was chewing on and cleaned his mouth with a cloth before speaking.

"You met Lillith, mother of demons, Lucifer's first wife, blah blah blah."

"What a rousing introduction, thank you," Lillith scoffed.

Kale ignored her. "Seere is a fifth-generation demon, she and I trained together when we were young. And Daevas," pointing to the ginger demon, "is a first-generation demon, one of Lucifer and Lillith's first spawns. He's also my third."

I observed each of them, taking them in, saving Kale for last. He was relaxed, but still a little of that mysterious power leaked from him in sparks of electricity.

"You lead them?" I nodded. "So, what kind of demon does that make you?" I asked.

He raised one eyebrow and smiled wickedly. “The fun kind,” was his only reply. Again, he avoided the question. My head throbbed once more.

I took a deep breath. “You keep naming different types of angels and demons. How many are there?” I asked Gabriel.

Kale chuckled. “Too many.”

“There are nine archangels. You know the big ones: Lucifer, Michael, Raphael, but some of them have multiple names and have since been less included in historical records. Each of us oversees a division of heaven, these divisions establish and maintain what we call the cosmic Balance, keeps the realms intact, and protects the peace of mortal and immortal life alike. Going through the entire *paranormal pyramid* right now would take a long time and might be too much all at once for you right now,” Gabriel explained.

I looked over at Seere and Daevas. He was swirling the wine in his glass, not looking at anyone in particular. He was quiet, but it felt like he was perhaps aware of everything and everyone. A trained spy with keen listening skills.

Seere was nibbling on a piece of bread, her eyes remaining on Kale. His occasional sideways glance to her told me that they were in fact communicating, through that *web* they told me about.

Seere watched him with such intensity, like he was the thing that held her onto the earth. Kale had mentioned that she was his second, adding to the assumption that he was in charge of the demons that sat before me. Clearly the two of them had a history, history of *what*, I wasn’t sure.

I glanced back at Daevas, who now was watching me closely. His expression was emotionless, but his stare laid me bare. The tattoos that rose from beneath his shirt up his neck looked almost like they were moving, like a snake slithering. His green eyes pulsed like they did the first time I saw him in my apartment.

I focused on them, and the sound of forks on plates and voices faded to something else. I could hear my heartbeat, among the rushing sound of flowing water and wind. My peripheral vision turned black, and all I saw was the pair of green eyes that held me in place.

I felt cold, the anxiety and fear that had gripped me the whole time I was here dulled to nothing. Replaced with resounding numbness.

Those green eyes pulsed further, and I was no longer looking at them, but looking at a pair of golden-brown eyes, human eyes, *my eyes*. My olive skin was blanched, paralyzed. My hair's brown and blonde highlights were dull compared to the radiance of the ethereal creatures around me.

Whispers sounded around me, or *him*, Daevas, the eyes I was now looking through. Speaking different languages, mostly unfamiliar, but others weirdly familiar. And all eerie enough to raise the goosebumps on my arms.

All at once, it was gone, the water and wind ceased, and my vision returned to normal, no longer looking through those eyes, but through my own.

"Wraiths and vetala's aren't strong enough to cause rips between the realms," Jophiel said.

I missed the earlier parts of their new conversation. I blinked, letting in an unnatural breath to steady myself. Daevas no longer looked at me, but his mouth curved upward, knowing full well what he had just done. Whatever that was.

"That's why I think it has to be something else, disguising as a wraith to throw us off," Gabriel responded. "What did you find in hell?" he asked Lillith.

She rolled her eyes. “So bossy, you could say *please…*” she sighed when he simply waited. “The cells down there are still secure, so are the pits, no strange visitors or infiltrations so far. Good thing too, the hellborn aren’t the forgiving types. Even if something managed to get in, they wouldn’t get past the legions. Lucifer hasn’t sensed anything unwelcomed enter his realm, so from our side of things, nothing is out of the ordinary.”

“Legions?” I blurted out without thinking. They were talking about actual hell, Dante’s Inferno and all that, it was absolutely mind-boggling.

Enough of a distraction to take my attention away from Daevas and his whispers.

Kale nodded. “Demons aren’t as disorganized as you may think. Lucifer keeps a tight ship. Each legion is a generation, and they are trained in combat, magic, strategy. You could think of them as armies. They mostly consist of the lower-class demons who don’t have a lot of raw power.”

My eyes widened. “How many of you are there? Do you outnumber humans?”

Jade answered, “No, humans outnumber angels three to one. And there are even less demons. Maybe a few million. We aren’t created the same way as humans. And since we’re immortal, the need for more isn’t a priority.”

“Oh.” The questions in my mind were endless. “How are you created? Gabriel said something about being parts of God’s souls…”

Duma decided to answer, having not spoken since dinner started. “In a simple explanation, he takes pieces of his soul and uses it to create matter, to create us, the angels that is.”

"Demons are created the old-fashioned way. Offspring of other demons. But our abilities to procreate diminish the younger our generation is. Most fifth-generation demons and younger can't conceive. Angels can procreate if they bed humans, demons unfortunately can't. As much as we try," Seere explained.

She winked in response to my horrified expression. Demons sleeping with humans, *angels* sleeping with humans? My dinner was threatening to come back up.

Jophiel sneered, "Can we save the supernatural history lessons for another time and get back to why we're here?" Her voice full of irritation.

Gabriel put a reassuring hand on my lap. "We'll explain it further later."

The rest of the dinner was carried out with exchanges of information they acquired in their scattered scouting. Talking about places and people I had no knowledge of.

Eventually I stopped listening and resigned to simply taking in the full intensity of all of them together. I found myself watching Gabriel and Kale the most.

Eventually, I moved away from the table and helped Jade with the dishes to gain some sense of mortality back— finding comfort in the suds and flowing faucet. Lost in the process of washing and drying I hadn't realized that more than half the group had left the room.

Handing Jade the last plate to dry, Gabriel touched my shoulder, turning me around.

"Need some fresh air?" he asked.

Only Lillith remained in the room, flipping through channels on the tv. I faced Gabriel, who looked sympathetic and beautiful. I nodded.

He jerked his head for me to follow him. He led me down the left-side hall, passing a few adjacent halls and some doors before we reached the end, where a metal ladder led upwards to a ceiling door.

"It leads to the roof," he stated as he climbed up first, hauling open the door and we were greeted by a cool, crisp draft.

He peered down at me, and it was enough to get me to climb up the rebar ladder, my legs aching from a long day.

When I reached the top, he took my hand to help me step onto the roof. The sky was dark aside from a sea of stars. The city below was small, only a few lights to illuminate the quiet streets.

We must be much further north than Arizona, the air was extremely chilly, and the wind didn't help. Goosebumps raised on my arms, but I ignored it. The cold was refreshing compared to the heat I sat through during dinner and it helped calm my electrified nerves.

Gabriel walked to the edge of the building and looked out into the view. His mind elsewhere, distant.

"You did well in there. I'm sorry if it was too much, but we'll all have to get used to it for a while." His eyes never leaving the horizon. I neared the edge as well but kept a solid ten feet between us.

"What exactly am I to do here while you all carry out your…'mission'?" I asked delicately.

I didn't want to stew in this strange world, wondering if every day was to be my last.

He shrugged. “Whatever you like, as long as one of us is around to keep you safe, you’re free to do anything you wish. We’ll make sure some of your things are brought here, your computer, journals, a few books if you want. I want you to be comfortable.”

I snorted, “Comfortable. I just found out angels and demons exist. Been thrust into a reality of insanity, and now have to live in it. I won’t feel comfortable for a while.”

Gabriel chuckled. “Well, having a sense of humor about it is a good sign at least.”

I was to stay in this strange warehouse among five angels, two of which were *archangels*, and four demons. Beings that up until ten hours ago I didn’t even believe existed. This was going to bring on quite the existential crisis, that’s for sure .

My eyelids began to feel heavy, my mind fuzzy and exhausted. I took one last deep breath of cold air and let it out with a long sigh.

“I’m tired.”

Gabriel nodded, walking towards me.

“I’d be surprised if you weren’t. Let’s get you to sleep.”

FIFTEEN
Kale

AS SOON AS THE DOOR to my room was shut, I released the power I'd been pushing inside.

Fire and bolts of electricity streamed up the steel beams lining the walls. Crumbles of shredded concrete showering down in places where it was hit the strongest—swept away from the floor by the lingering shadows that followed.

The headache that formed under the pressure of concealing my abilities finally subsiding. I loosened a long sigh, my muscles releasing tension and my emotions dulling to something less lethal. The fire and electricity dissipated and fizzled out.

I cracked my neck and stretched my aching arms. I didn't usually have to keep my energy cooped up when it was just Daevas, Seere and I here. The place was large enough, and sturdy enough that I could continually drain the excess without harming others.

But it was way more crowded now.

The warehouse was my mortal getaway from hell and from my responsibilities. But its durability made it the ideal location for a large and powerful cohort to occupy without utter destruction.

Even then, I wouldn't have to shove my powers down as much if it weren't for the human being here. A small slip blasted in her direction could wither her to dust, so more restrictive measures were necessary. The only problem was, going too long under that amount of pressure usually led to unintentional violence and catastrophe.

A soft knock rapped against the door. I knew who it was.

"Come in."

Seere was inside a moment later, shutting the door behind her. Her eyes amused and curious.

"Well, that was fun. Think we scared her enough? I think we could've done better," she harped.

I chuckled. "There's always tomorrow."

I picked up a small finger knife and in one swift swing, sent it flying towards the wall. It jutted itself half an inch into the concrete.

Seere went to the wall and observed the knife, then turned to face me, pinning her head and back to the wall.

"You were uncharacteristically civil."

I groaned, slicing another knife towards the wall. It hit an inch next to her left ear. She didn't so much as flinch.

"I wish these feathered fairies would stop trying so hard to soften everything for her. It just wastes time." Another knife pierced the wall just above her right shoulder.

She smirked. "Says the person who suppressed their power to the point of bursting."

I sneered at her, "I think she should be involved, not dead, Seere. Though if Gabriel coddled her anymore, I might've burst." One lodged above her head.

She shrugged, her shoulder tapping the knife above it. "He's a softy. I thought Jophiel was going to rip Lillith to shreds when she kept sensually licking her fork at Duma." Seere giggled.

"I think we all would've enjoyed watching that." I smiled.

"The human would die of shock," she scoffed.

I walked towards her, stopping a few inches away and began pulling knives from the wall.

"She's smart, for a human."

"I suppose."

"She saw right through you—she knows you're something more than the rest of us. Don't know how, but she sees the difference. A lot like I did when we first met."

I turned my focus from the knives to Seere, staring up at me.

"Maybe I'm not doing a good enough job at keeping it all in," I stated.

Seere held my stare, her mouth turning upwards. "You like her. Admit it," she teased.

I rolled my eyes, pulling another knife from the wall.

"Sure, as much as anyone can like a helpless mortal. She's got kick, I'll admit. But she'll soon enough become a burden like all the rest."

"So leave Prince Charming to care for her."

I lifted my chin and let out a quick laugh.

"I can't let him have all the fun."

I plucked the last knife and walked away from Seere. She simply sank down to sit on the floor. Her fingers played with her braids.

A sigh broke from her lips. "There's so much vanilla in this place now, it's making me antsy." Referring to the angels that now occupied our home-away-from-home.

I nodded in agreement. Working with them was less than ideal. At least they had the decency to stay on a different side of the building, and they usually wouldn't all be here at the same time.

I laid down across my bed, twirling my dagger between my fingers, staring up at the ceiling. Tendrils of my powers streamed out into the halls and corridors of the warehouse.

The tendrils gave me a sense of the bodies within it. Lillith still lounged on the couch, now joined by Daevas who returned to his game. Jophiel and Duma had left, the Guardian master was in the training ring doing some reps. The power speared further, seeing Gabriel and Heather on the roof.

I sent my earlier *Heather and Feathers sitting in a tree* towards Gabriel's mind, but was only met with a solid crystal wall blocking me out.

Oh well. *I'll tease you later.*

Seere continued to play with her braids, fidgeting more like. I let the tendrils come back into the room, and instead focused them on creating a ring of smoke and fire, letting them float above my head.

The two forms swirling around each other like a tornado, perfectly in sync. Little activities like this helped keep my inner fire in check and manage the anger the roiled inside.

Seere's voice sounded in my head. *Any word from Lucifer?*

I sighed.

My mental blocks were always down for Seere. We grew up together, trained together. My best friend. I had no secrets from her, so our line of communication always remained open.

With Daevas, it wasn't open all the time. I trusted him, but he wasn't as dependent on our bond. I didn't mind his selectiveness. More likely than not, with his special abilities, he'd see the disasters in there and try to erase them and fill them with less terror.

A lot like what he did with Heather at the dinner. I don't think she fully realized what he was doing, but I saw it all.

Daevas was the Psychísąe. His unique abilities included being able to root out some of the deepest seeds of fear and anguish that grow within the mind.

He did such a thing in Heather, finding those in her from her most recent experiences with us. Only instead of amplifying or exploiting those seeds, as he was trained to do since the beginning of his existence, he tried to wash it away.

So Daevas tried to help Heather. Tried to flush away the fear. Not enough to make her forget—but enough to help her sleep better in this place.

I kept my eyes on the ring above my head when I answered Seere's question. *I've heard him nagging, but nothing actually helpful.*

I felt her shift, now laying on her belly on the floor with her feet perched up against the wall.

I'm not sure I believe everything Lillith was saying in there.

A little bit of my anger slipped then, causing the ring to jut out of alignment slightly.

She has her own agendas. Lucifer has the bitch on a tight leash. I'll likely need to speak to Daevas or Dumdum about hell later.

More of the ring lost control. I let it dissolve—no point in trying if I can't keep it in line.

I decided to change the subject. *You wanna talk about Reapers Creek? You seemed tense when I mentioned it earlier.*

Even from across the room I felt Seere's mood change. *It was nothing. An anticlimactic place, no naked Reapers getting massaged, it was disappointing really.*

Inappropriate humor was Seere's natural defense mechanism, a tell that she was experiencing feelings of discomfort. She knew as well as I that this was her way of avoiding what was really upsetting her.

But Seere never hid those parts of herself from me, I knew her insecurities and deepest shames.

She left her mind wide open for me. Not that she could keep me out if she tried, her mental shields are limited because of her lack of raw demonic power, but after a couple of decades working with her to build the little walls inside her mind, she was better protected.

I only stepped a fraction into her mind before I saw a glimpse of what had happened in Purgatory. And right away I could see one of her biggest insecurities poking at her insides.

I swallowed. *You're not weak...for needing Iaoel's help.*

She was the one to sigh this time.

I know. I mean, I really do know that it was stupid to feel that way. But I can't help feeling insignificant in all this. Compared to all these powerful beings, like, more than one fucking archangel is involved, it's not easy knowing that among all of us, I'm the least powerful. she admitted.

I sent a smirk her way. *Technically, the mortal is the least powerful.* I joked.

She giggled and plopped onto the bed next to me. Sitting with her legs crossed and jabbed me in the rib with her index finger.

"You know I wasn't counting her, smartass." We both chuckled together. Then it died, seriousness returning to her eyes. "I just don't need everyone here to think that I'm only a part of this alliance because I'm your loyal *puppy*."

Everyone in hell, especially Lucifer and Lillith called Seere that. Even after all the carnage she committed in the pits to prove her strength, they still saw her as a mindless grunt with a leash around her neck attached to my arm.

I raised up on my elbows, staring at her. "Did you already forget why I made you my second?" I asked.

She looked away shyly.

"Yes, we're friends, Seere. You were there for me when I needed someone. And if you weren't around, my dear ole' creator and the other hellborn grunts would have delighted in watching me engulf the world in flames. Hell, I probably would've liked it too."

When she didn't look me in the eye I gripped her chin and forced her to face me.

"But that's not the reason you're my second. You're the best combatant ever bred in hell. Even Daevas and Lillith can't hold you in a hand-to-hand fight. Yeah, sure, all of the rest of us have raw power on our side. In a fight, they will rely on their magic to do the fighting for them. But what happens if magic and power aren't options? If who or what we're fighting uses wards and runes that nullify it altogether? Then they're out of luck."

Seere nodded, some of the stuff I was saying sinking in.

I grabbed one of her braids and tugged.

Her head jerked, "Ow!" she squealed.

"You have just as much right to be here as anyone else. Own your strength, damn it! Don't let your demons eat you, kay?"

She rolled her eyes, and I tugged again on her braid.

When she yelled again, I demanded, "OKAY?"

"Okay! Jeez, do that again and I'll cut off your favorite part, and then you won't be able to seduce anymore archangels, you hot-headed-ass-wipe."

We laughed. Once our laughs died down, we both sensed Daevas and Lillith nearing the room. And at the moment they opened the door, our heads shot to it in unison.

Lillith entered first, unabashedly. Daevas slipping in and simply leaning against the wall right inside the door.

"I know you don't spend a lot of time in the mortal realm, Lillith. But knocking is considered a courtesy," I grumbled.

She smiled, her eyes playful and naughty. "Didn't realize we were interrupting such an intimate moment," she teased.

Seere and I only rolled our eyes—earning a glare from Lillith over the innate disinterest in her games.

"There's a report of a small wraith hoard terrorizing Cape Town. Figured you'd like to join us for a little anger management."

My inner fire burned at that. Lillith knew all too well that my powers needed siphoning, whereas hers did not.

And though I hated agreeing with her, some justified violence would do me some good.

I stood, grabbing a few extra daggers from my dresser. Or maybe, tonight I would fight the old-fashioned way. Seere and I followed Lillith and Daevas out of the room.

The warehouse was warded and covered in runes that prevented anyone from winnowing in or out except from/to the practice floor. Makes it a lot easier to isolate any unwelcome visitors.

Gabriel had since joined Jade in the sparring ring. Weaving and moving around each other gracefully. Mostly evading one another's blows rather than using brute force.

Such an angel thing to do. Avoiding conflict instead of facing it.

On the rare occasions they did manage to land a blow on the other, it wasn't hard. If Gabriel were to use his full energy, the Guardian master wouldn't stand a chance.

"What a lovely little dance. Should we install ballet bars into the walls and buy everyone tutu's?" I teased.

The others chuckled and snickered behind me as we walked down the steps.

Gabriel and Jade ceased their scrap. Jade simply shook her head and even showed signs of amusement. The archangel on the other hand, he held a stoic prick-like stance with his arms crossed over his chest. His regular casual business attire replaced with a pair of blue fitness shorts and a gray t-shirt.

"Where are you all off to?" he asked.

I winked. "Got an orgy appointment, can't be late."

Seere and Daevas coughed, covering their laughs. Gabriel obviously wasn't convinced—eyeing our weapons and fighting attire.

Rolling my eyes, "Wraith hoard, gonna go kill some. Don't wait up."

Gabriel straightened. "Do you need assistance?"

Almost in unison all four of us snorted. We gathered in the large pentacle in the far end of the space. Designated to be the area of egress for supernaturals.

"Just don't ruin anything while we're gone."

Seere and I linked hands, Daevas and Lillith did the same, Daevas placing his other hand on my shoulder. I speared my power to cross into the Ethereal realm, and then visualized our destination, using Daevas' mind to help narrow it down to where they received reports.

Smoke, fire and lightning—my winnow signature, wrapped around us as the air and space bent around us. Fifteen seconds, and then the space reshaped. I dropped us out of the Ethereal, letting my winnow signature float back to me. Daevas and Lillith broke physical contact, Seere lingering a moment longer to send me her signature 'good luck' squeeze then let go.

The reports were correct—ugly and bony hooded creatures screeched and wailed, shooting razor sharp claws outwards to scrape and lance the small gathering of angels and demons fighting them off.

The buildings were crumbling and broken. Glass windows shattered, roofs burning, and blood running down the gutters, splattered across the sidewalks and broken buildings.

No bodies in sight.

I forgot that part about wraiths—when they killed humans, they didn't leave much evidence behind. The angels that were present looked to be Guardians and Reapers, judging by their auras.

The two demons that were there were a part of the sixth-generation legion, utterly powerless aside from their combat training. When one of them noticed us he came running over to us. Blood was smeared across his forehead, and his sword was coated in a black tinted liquid.

He bowed to me when he reached us.

"They're nasty buggers. When we got here, the buzzards were already fighting them off. We managed to corner these five, but a couple scattered and got away. The rest of the town is secure, a few other patrols arrived and have been scouting to make sure of that."

I let my expression remain bored and didn't even bother to look him in the eye. Lillith was the one who stepped forward and met the eyes of the now gaping angels who held the wraiths in a tight corner.

"You golden geese can be on your way now."

One of the Reapers scoffed, his teeth baring. "Who are you to order us around? We're the ones who kept these things under control, *you* and your filth can leave."

A demon-hater. I muttered down the link between Daevas and Seere.

Typical. Daevas replied.

Boring. Seere added.

I glanced at Seere who had a knowing smile across her lips. Then I made full eye contact with the angel who spoke. "Go report to your keeper, we'll make sure they are punished accordingly."

He stared back at me, looking me up and down, recognition now crossing his eyes. He realized who I was. I grinned wickedly.

"I won't say it again."

His eyes widened. The other angels exchanged looks, then one by one they winnowed out, with the outspoken Reaper going last, pillars of light following in their wake.

Daevas, Lillith and Seere had positioned themselves around the cornered wraiths, the other two demons stepping back. They too, knew that these were our playthings now. I stepped up to the center position. The wraiths watching us, hissing, and clawing at the air, as if they stood any chance at surviving.

Seere and Daevas tilted their heads towards me, waiting for me to make the first move. I scratched my chin lazily, scanning the five remaining wraiths before us.

Until my eyes landed on the only one that didn't look away—the only one who held my penetrating stare. The only fear it displayed came when my signature smirk appeared.

I pointed at it. "This one lives."

The wraiths didn't even have time to scream before we attacked like wolves—gutting, slicing, tearing until the rest of them were mere ribbons of flesh.

SIXTEEN
Heather

THE PEACEFUL SLUMBER had allowed me to forget where I was, and what had happened the day before.

Even as I opened my eyes, my immediate thought was that it was all a dream. But when I saw the iron and steel framework on the ceiling of the room, and instead of smelling the comforting lavender of home I smelled metal and rain, I remembered where I was.

My chest tightened as I recalled everything. Yesterday was a long day, and the amount of information I was given in such a short amount of time was mind boggling.

The room I was given was no larger than my apartment bedroom. A twin-sized bed on a simple metal frame against the corner wall. The window was painted like the others, darkening any natural incoming light. A small dresser, a bedside table.

The space was simplistic, a guest room that had little purpose, probably put together last minute. I got the feeling this place didn't usually have visitors.

The floor was concrete, cold. I would guess that this entire warehouse might've been used to produce and ship products once upon a time. This room might've been an office.

My computer and a few notebooks lay on the dresser. Gabriel had them brought in late last night when I was settling in. I took some time alone to unpack the little personal belongings I brought with me.

I clicked my phone to see the time, *12:34 PM.* It was close to two in the morning when I had finally went to sleep last night. I guess I needed the rest.

I couldn't hear anything in the hall outside the metal sliding door. Nothing sound-related woke me. Maybe they were all gone.

I was half-tempted to stay in bed. Curl under the cotton blankets and forget the stark reality that awaited outside the concrete room.

But I was already feeling the grime and stress sweat that had accumulated from yesterday's ordeals. A shower was very much needed.

Gabriel had said the washroom was only a few doors down, by the end of the hall. With a heavy sigh, I lifted my wary body from the bed. I gathered a few of my toiletries and went to the door. The lock was a simple latch, I lifted it and it slid open with a metallic screech. The loud noise interrupted the silence that filled the entire hallway, making me cringe.

But there was no response. Nothing to suggest anyone was near. I paddled over to the door marked with a bathroom sign.

Inside there was a long counter with three sinks and a large mirror above it. The floor was covered in black and blue tile, differing from the concrete everywhere else. I walked further in, just past the sinks in the corner was a single shower stall with a blue curtain and a toilet stall on the other corner.

Why have three sinks and only one toilet? I shrugged.

A shelf was in between the two, and on it there were baskets of various soaps and fresh towels. Thank goodness, I didn't bring one along.

I turned the dial, and water flowed from the spigot. Feeling it with my hand until the water turned to a near-scalding hot.

Looking around, checking to see if anyone was coming in, I quickly stripped and hopped in.

The water felt *amazing*.

I went to work scrubbing and washing every inch of myself, and once that was done I allowed myself to just sit in the hot water for a little longer. The hot water relaxed my tense muscles and soothed my nerves.

It felt normal—and I needed normal right now.

Once I finished, I dried off, dressed, brushed my teeth, and combed my hair back to keep it out of my face. I packed pretty quickly before we came here, so my choice of clothing was limited to a pale-yellow t-shirt and overalls.

Almost immediately after returning to my room my stomach growled. I checked my phone once more before heading down the hall. I didn't entirely know where I was going, but I figured eventually I'd reach the main room.

It was so quiet, that when I entered the kitchen area I couldn't help but jump when I saw Gabriel standing by the kitchen island.

He turned at the sound of my arrival. "You're awake, would you like something to eat?" he asked.

I took a deep breath to calm my heartbeat and sat on one of the island stools. No one else was around.

"Where is everyone?" I asked.

He lifted the steaming kettle from the stove and poured its contents into a mug, then handed it to me. I took a sip, chai tea.

"They have things to take care of. This is what you would call an ongoing investigation. In addition to finding out as much as we can about what happened to Mason, they all still have to maintain their other duties as well," Gabriel explained.

He pulled out a container of eggs and a loaf of bread from the fridge. Cracking the eggs into a sizzling pan and plopping a couple slices of bread into the toaster.

“What about you? Don’t you have…duties as well?” I asked.

He nodded. Adding some spices and herbs to the eggs as they cooked.

“When Mason…passed. And we started this alliance, the position of your Guardian needed to be filled. Because we aren’t entirely sure what the threat is, it was decided that I would be your Guardian for the time being, to be safe. So, you’re my priority as of now. When I need to tend to my division elsewhere, one of the others will take over.” He flipped the omelet and took the toast from the toaster. “Butter? Jam?”

I cleared my throat. “Just butter is fine, thank you.” He scraped some on and then handed me the plate of toast and returned to the eggs.

“Are Guardian angels always with their humans?”

He nodded. “Nearly always, aside from the times when they need to report back to heaven in person.”

I gulped. “That’s just a tad creepy.”

He chuckled.

“I suppose it seems that way. But they’re merely there to protect you and guide you towards the next part of your life, then you are assigned a new Guardian. It’s like in school, when you finish elementary and move on to junior high with new teachers and new maturities, if that makes sense.”

“But I thought there were less angels than humans, how is it possible to cover every single one?”

Gabriel folded the eggs into an omelet. I finished the first slice of toast while he answered.

"There are a lot of things we can do that aren't comprehensible for mortals. Guardians in particular usually watch more than one human at a time, and they have *duality* abilities. They can shift parts of their soul from one place to the other without winnowing, and at much faster rates. They're so fast, that essentially they can be in two or more places at once."

The more I learned about the supernatural the more I thought that if all this was just a *sliver* of their world, it was no wonder they kept it to themselves.

"So…when an angel has these *duality* abilities, as you say, they are assigned to be Guardians?" I hope I got that right—they mentioned a *paranormal pyramid* yesterday.

It wouldn't be helpful to learn all these things and not remember them later. Not that I could, I spent a good part of the night and this morning going over every word, every look, memorizing the things I learned.

If I were going to be stuck here, I was going to learn all I could.

"Precisely. When we train angels, some of their natural gifts manifest, and those gifts tell us a lot about which division they would do best in."

While he was being so open, might as well dig a bit deeper, even though another headache was coming on.

"You said 'it was decided', did you mean that…God assigned you to me?" he only nodded.

I took the last bite of my second slice of toast.

"So he actually exists…" I mumbled through my chewing.

Gabriel paused, peering at me. "I'm guessing you weren't a religious person."

"No. I'm an atheist. *Was* an atheist, I guess. After studying so many religions, it becomes hard to believe in any one of them fully," I explained.

He gave me an understanding nod. "All religions only contain about three percent of the actual truth. We purposefully keep it that way to protect humanity."

"By keeping us ignorant?" The question slipped without warning.

Gabriel wasn't fazed. He scooped the eggs onto a plate and set it in front of me.

"You remember how intense yesterday was, how shocking the little bits of information we were giving you were? We haven't even scratched the surface, it'll take a long while to tell you everything, and even longer for it all to make sense," he stated.

"And you're a lucky one, your mind is open and educated, we can only assume that that is what's keeping the fragments of your mind from imploding. I've witnessed mortals shatter from just seeing an angel in all their grace, let alone knowing everything there is to know about them."

The memory of seeing Gabriel, wings unfurled and golden grace consuming my apartment came to mind.

"Mortals are built differently than the rest of us. Fragile. Imagine trying to explain the entire universe to a colony of ants." My nose crinkled at that. "*Not* that you are ants. It just means, that our reality wouldn't bode well for yours."

Though his explanation made sense, but it made me feel even more helpless.

I ate the remainder of the eggs in silence. Gabriel only waited patiently. But my eating brought up a question I had last night.

"You all ate last night. Do you actually *need* to eat?"

He shook his head, grinning at the more casual question.

"No, not really. We can eat, but it's not necessary for our survival. Demons indulge in mortal delectations such as eating more than angels do. But they have a different...*disposition*, as you might have noticed."

"So, the religious histories, like Lucifer and the Fall...they really happened?"

"Not exactly the way they were told no. Lucifer did revolt against heaven, but it was more of a strong disagreement and a negotiation. It lasted for a few thousand years. A lot of it had to do with Lucifer being restless with the structure of heaven. Some angels agreed with him that there needed to be some unrest in order for the Balance to truly be even.

This wasn't long into the period of peace and order following The Tear. So God made it happen, through Lucifer. Hell needed a full-time leader, and Lucifer served as the best option. Part of his compromise was the transformation of Lillith to a demon and the ability to procreate with her to build a species of their own. The Fallen were the sect of angels that chose to go with him."

"Wait, *The Tear*?"

Gabriel leaned his folded arms on the counter, the action was casual, human even.

"That creature, the vetala. That was just one of many ancient primordial creatures that once roamed the Earth alongside humans. They were made with darkness and were very corrupt. Think of them like the titans in Greek mythology."

"Okay."

"They were jealous of the mortals—who grew quickly and had a higher level of thinking, not to mention were favored by the almighty himself. So they reacted by going on a killing spree. We marked it as Paṭukolai, or *The Great Slaughter*. It was a blood bath, they wiped out the entire mortal population that existed back then."

Images of monsters from myths and histories of ancient civilizations flooded my head.

He continued on, "*The Tear* was when the almighty and the archangels rallied and imprisoned them in powerful prisons that they couldn't escape from. Places like Tartarus and Sheol. Once they were done away with, the almighty refined his design of mortals, created them again and without the primordials around they were able to live and evolve in peace."

I stared at my cup, baffled by what I was hearing, intrigued even.

"Sounds like what Zeus and the Olympians did against Kronos," I chimed.

He chuckled, sitting in the stool next to me.

"Our Scribes and Principalities were less restricted back then with how much they shared with humans. A lot of the ancient mythologies have a lot of truth in them, if you know where and how to decipher the truth out of the dramatics."

I fidgeted with the edge of the counter.

Awkward silence lingered between us. Even though I had many, many questions to ask. I think taking a short break from absorbing information would keep the headaches at bay.

Gabriel didn't seem to mind the silence. He didn't even stare, at least no more than a glance every now and then. Surely, he knew I was ruminating.

When he wasn't looking at me, I would look at him. Taking note of his clothing. He wore a blue/green plaid button-down shirt and dark jeans. Casual, yet professional. His hair was cleanly styled, neat and trimmed. He didn't wear any watches or rings. No tattoos, like the demons had.

Clean, simple, efficient.

Less of his light leaked today. Maybe he had let some it out to avoid it seeping through again. But even his eyes occasionally showed a glimmer of gold every now and then.

He was *beautiful*.

I suppose an archangel would be. His very essence made me comfortable, a soft melody meant to temper and soothe those around him. This close I could smell roses and brine. His scent—just as calming as his presence.

He glanced back at me and caught my eye—caught me staring. But he didn't mock me for it, didn't smirk like Kale would. He only stared back, completely calm and patient.

"Is there anyone who will worry about you if they don't hear from you regularly? Your parents, perhaps?" he asked quietly.

I sipped my tea, shaking my head.

"My parents live in North Dakota. We've never been close, they're intellectuals like me, focused on their work. We only talk on birthdays, and I only see them every other Christmas. It'll be a long while before they would even notice I was gone. But I guess, if you're all going to cover my tracks, then really I'm not missing at all." He dipped his chin in response.

"What do your parents do?" he asked.

I shrugged. "My dad is a mathematician—he freelances coding algorithms for apps. My mom is a botanist, she writes gardening books. Both of them are very invested in what they do."

"No siblings?"

"Ha! No, one kid was already too much work."

I tapped on the counter, now finding the crumbs on my plate entertaining.

Gabriel shifted in his seat. Was he even comfortable?

"Sounds like you get your intelligence and thirst for knowledge from your parents."

I grinned. "Along with an unrelenting drive and lack of social skills," I chuckled lightly.

His smile matched mine, along with some relief. Relief that I was not falling apart, perhaps…

My thoughts drifted from his beautiful face to Mason's. Even while he died, he was radiant. My chest tightened and throat bobbed recalling that painful memory.

Gabriel noticed the change and touched my hand, concern written over his face.

"Are you alright?"

My eyes brimmed with tears. "Why did I see him die? Is that normal?" My voice cracked.

His hand fully held mine now, his thumb gently stroking my palm.

"A Guardian has never died like that, so we're not sure if it is normal for humans to experience it with them. I have to assume it was probably because of the Guardian bond. It's a special connection that allows the Guardian to feel everything their human feels and sometimes communicate with them through."

I took a few deep breaths, regaining some of my lost composure, trying not to see the blood and feel his agony.

I looked down at our hands, his were so warm and soft. I raised my eyes to his, and though they were filled with concern and sympathy, I began to get lost in the deep blue colors, and the flecks of gold that flashed every once in a while.

He broke contact and turned towards the entry way. But his eyes were distant…that same expression he had when he and Kale would speak silently at the apartment.

"What is it?"

"Last night, Kale and his circle went and dealt with a hoard of wraiths. They left one alive, they're on their way back with it right now," he answered.

He stood and made for the archway, stopping just before it.

"It won't be pleasant to see. You may want to go elsewhere until we take care of it," he suggested.

Another monster, and they were bring it *here*.

"I'll just…stay in here, watch tv or something."

He nodded and walked out and down the stairway.

I had plopped on the futon when I heard a loud whooshing sound from the floor below.

A small, gurgled screech followed.

"Took you all night to bring that back? Did you go sight-seeing on the way?" Gabriel's voice asked.

A large thump, another sickening shriek.

"What, were you waiting for me tuck you in?" Kale's voice joked. "We took our time with the others, even cleaned up a little. But winnowing a primordial is like crawling through mud. And I was also carrying these three, so yeah, it took a while longer."

The sound of chains rattled against the floor, and then clinking accompanied by another blood curdling screech.

"What were you doing in Cape Town?" Gabriel asked.

A hiss answered. Footsteps reached the top of the stairs.

I whirled, Lillith and Daevas had come in, walking towards their hallway. Both of them were head-to-toe in dark, tight-fitting clothes, leather straps wrapped around their arms, legs, chests with various weapons.

The color of their clothing almost completely hid the liquid that was splattered on them, but it was noticeable on their weapons and on their exposed skin. Not blood, at least not a type of blood I've ever seen, it looked like used car oil.

Lillith waved flirtatiously at me as they passed me.

"You can go peek if you want, it's positively gnarly," she cooed.

Then they were both gone. My eyes drifted from the hallway they went into to the open archway, to the loud screech that sounded from past it.

"This will be a long and painful process, wraith. You might as well answer our questions," Kale said with an eerie calmness.

Another hiss.

Then a scratchy, inhuman voice said, "Chaos. We're causing chaos."

A chill ran down my spine from the sound of the wraith's voice. But I moved, touching the archway frame. I was half-tempted to just turn and run towards my room.

Taking a deep breath, I ignored that urge and walked into the large warehouse floor. The others hadn't noticed me, so I stayed low, going halfway down the steps before sitting and watching through the bars.

In the middle of the room, held down to the floor by bolted chains was a hooded creature. The hood was black and torn in places. Its arms were thin, skin and bones, no muscle. The skin was gray and had a glossy sheen coating it. Instead of fingers, it had long claws that stretched out, longer than my own forearms. Its head was low, the hood covering its face.

Seere was sitting cross-legged about ten feet or so from it, dragging the tip of her blade along the concrete floor lazily, wearing a similar attire that Lillith and Daevas wore.

Gabriel stood directly in front of it with his arms crossed, grounded and calm. Kale was also dressed for a fight, though he had retained his leather jacket and didn't have weapons surrounding every inch of his body.

Did he even need weapons?

Kale was crouched on the floor, his index finger tracing swirls, dots and jagged lines into the floor, and where he touched the lines would glow orange like burning embers.

"How did you escape from your prison?" Kale asked.

The wraith made a stuttered hissing sound, like it was chuckling. "Trick question."

Kale crossed another line in his current pattern and the wraith screeched again in pain. Whatever he was drawing was causing it pain.

"Fangelsi's doors were open," it gasped. It sighed when the pain stopped.

"How did you get out?" Gabriel asked.

"We were let out."

Kale prodded further, "By whom?" It hesitated, which was met with another shock of pain. "Answer the question."

It spat out some of that black, oily liquid. It's blood, then. "No," it sneered.

Kale grinned evilly. "That's not an answer we're willing to accept." It tried lunging for him, but it didn't get far because of the chains.

“You should be glad we’re here, Heir Inferno. Our return will clean the earth of those abominations, and this time the arrogant angels will go with them,” it said to Kale.

Gabriel turned his attention to Kale, who had stood and now squared the wraith straight on.

“So your plan is to what, slaughter humanity once more. How exactly do you expect to accomplish that, your wraith friends are specks of dust,” Kale stated. His voice still calm as death, bored even.

“There are things even your kind don’t know about the world, hellborn,” it hissed.

Gabriel spoke this time, grabbing its attention. “How did you kill a Guardian?”

Its mouth clicked. “That wasn’t us.”

“And Heather, the mortal, there was one of you inside her mind, how do you explain that?” Gabriel asked.

The wraith turned and caught sight of me. Its eyes were hollow and fluid at the same time. A bony face with slashes and uneven features that made it hard to look at without feeling my breakfast rising from my stomach. Its oily sharp teeth grinned at me. It looked like some of the things I’d seen in my nightmares. The chill ran down my spine again.

“*Darkness dwells where one can’t see*.” It screeched in pain as if struck.

But Kale wasn’t drawing on the floor anymore. Instead he was simply glaring at it. Did he even need those markings to torture it?

Kale tilted his head when the pain subsided. “I don’t see any further use for it. It’s not going to give us anything more, even its grotesque mind is blocked,” he said.

Gabriel nodded, sighing. “We should send it to the pits, or one of the still secured prisons for holding.”

“Like hell. Kill the damn thing,” Seere argued.

“You’ve done enough killing for one day. We may need it to answer more questions later. Besides, violence is corrupting, we don’t need any more of it here,” Gabriel countered.

Kale glared at the archangel. “Violence, as I’ll remind you, has settled more issues than any other factor, buzzard brain. You’re in my house, and therefore my rules.” His tone was predatorial and commanding.

Gabriel turned away, looking at me. Not entirely surprised I was there, more worried than anything.

“I don’t support this decision. But I’ll respect your authority as long as I’m a guest here. Do what you will.”

Kale grounded himself, and simply turned his hand in the air as though turning a dial. Then a jolt of fire and lightning speared towards the wraith, lighting it on fire. It screamed as the hood and its skin blistered and singed away.

The smell of cooked flesh and soot filled my nose, making me gag. Not long and the fire retreated back into Kale’s hand, and the only remnants of the wraith that remained was a pile of ash.

Even though the initial power that had struck out of Kale had since gone away, Kale’s power leaked more than it did before. Like a hot coal still smoldering. That amount of power was effortless, as simple as unlocking a door. What kind of power could he unleash if he were actually trying?

Kale turned and caught my stare. Fear must have been written on my face because he looked ashamed when our eyes met.

But he dropped the expression quickly and turned once more to go to Seere. She watched him, stepping into tow next to him as he passed.

Gabriel was waiting at the bottom of the stairs, observing my reactions.

“I did say it would be gruesome.”

I dragged my gaze away from the retreating demons, clearing my throat.

“Ugh, yeah. You weren’t kidding. It just makes me worry what the rest of these primordials are like.”

“Worse,” Gabriel muttered. “Much worse.”

SEVENTEEN
Heather

TO PASS TIME I DECIDED TO DO SOME RESEARCH. Looking back at some of my work during my undergrad and grad years on religion. All the more thankful that I had my laptop to do so.

Even looking for that drawing Kale used on the floor earlier. Maybe it was in one of the ancient texts I studied. I skimmed through some of the Greek myths, those were pretty easy to understand and could pull out some of what Gabriel was saying to me from them. I had a folder on my desktop for every religion/country.

I clicked on the Egyptian folder, a couple essays, a few articles and studies were inside. Some photos from various museums and archeologist reports. The deities they had were clear representations of the archangels.

Osiris, the God of the underworld, symbolizes death and resurrection. Lucifer perhaps? But then again, Christian religions depicted a completely different name as the Angel of Death. I clicked open my phone and made an electronic note to ask about that.

Isis, the wife of the God of the underworld, and depicted in Greek/Roman history as Aphrodite. But that didn't make sense, the wife of the God of the underworld in Greek was Persephone, Hade's wife. So maybe this was just a made-up tale rather than stemming from truth. Unless…it meant to depict Lillith?

I shivered—the idea of that temptress being depicted as Aphrodite or even Persephone for that matter just didn't sit well.

Horus—sky god, embodiment of divinity…Gabriel? Michael? I made a note of it.

Oh, but wait, Seth the god of chaos and violence, so *that* must be Lucifer, yes? Hmmm. Noted.

Funny enough the Egyptians were obsessed with gods of death, because even Anubis was in charge of caring for the dead. I took a break from Egypt and ventured into the Mayan culture.

Their creator' god was Itzamna. Ah Puch was their god of the dead. Chac was one of their oldest gods, associated with war and human sacrifice. Wow, it was amazing how much more all my studies meant now that I'd been thrust into the supernatural world.

While I was taking down a few more notes and questions to ask later, Jade and Jophiel entered from the main floor. I was using the dining table as a desk space to work on.

Jade came over to me right away, her smile warming some of my initial uneasiness. Jophiel, however, went to the counter and pulled out what looked like a few old scrolls from a bag I didn't realize she carried.

Jade peered over my shoulder. "What are you up to?" she asked sweetly.

I continued to glance over at Jophiel when I answered.

"Um, I'm just looking back at some of my religious studies."

Jade grinned and sat in the chair next to me, a knowing grin on her lips.

"Trying to find where we fit in?" She asked. I nodded. "Well, it's not awfully hard to find the obvious ones. God and Lucifer have *many* depictions. Even Azrael gets a lot of attention in nearly every religion."

I crinkled my nose. "Azrael…that's the—"

"Angel of Death," she said simply. My eyes widened.

"Oh! Well, that answers those questions. There were a few deities and gods that I wasn't sure were supposed to be Lucifer or…Azrael. Why aren't the rest mentioned?" I asked.

She looked back at my computer, seeing my Mayan section open.

"They are, you just have to know where to look. The Mayan god Chin, who was all about open sexuality, that is a rough depiction of Chamuel. He's the second to youngest archangel, he oversees the division of destiny. You could think of his angels, the Amors, as cupids and then there are the Cherubims." She winked.

"Chamuel? I don't remember learning about him." She shrugged.

"He's not a very…powerful archangel. And his personality is gentle. It's hard to be interpreted by mortals if you don't make a lot of noise, as the others tend to." She sent a smirk towards Jophiel.

Her eyes remained on the scroll she was reading, ignoring us completely. I don't think I'll ever get used to how magnificent all of them looked.

"Are all immortals so…polished?" I asked carefully.

Jade laughed.

"You mean, good looking? We have the advantages of not growing old, and I guess our angel grace does add some extra *sparkle* to our appearances. Don't feel intimidated by it, even the prettiest ones can have horrible tempers and even uglier dispositions."

Another jab at Jophiel, who didn't so much as blink.

I thought about Kale and Lillith, they too had unnatural good looks. Even Daevas and Seere were beautiful in their own way, but in a less divine manner.

"The demons…"

Jade smirked. "Their good looks are mostly hereditary. Lillith, was the first mortal woman created after The Tear, she was made to be as exquisite as she is. I mean, Lucifer was so infatuated with her that he paid a handsome price to have her."

An Aphrodite indeed.

"What price was that?" I asked.

This time Jophiel did look towards us, and I noted it—the careful wariness in her face.

"My eldest brother is arguably the most powerful archangel to exist. His perversions for that succubus cost him some of that power," Jophiel stated harshly.

Ah, so not only was there some *deep*-seeded hate for Lillith in there, but also an aversion to Lucifer—or of the decisions he made.

Jade didn't let any of her calm kindness waver, leaning her head in one of her palms.

"He was in love," she cooed, with a slight tone of taunting. A touchy subject?

Jophiel bared her teeth a little. "Lust and love are not the same thing, Jade. You know that. Besides, he eventually tired of her and demoted her—taking other wives even. So much for love."

Her reactions made me wonder if this was about her brother having to now rule over hell, or that his love connection didn't last. Not to mention, this must have happened millions of years ago, so why did she treat it like it was a fresh wound?

Or is it when you're immortal, disagreements and grudges tend to fester longer?

Jophiel met my gaze, and it was filled with distaste and resentment.

"I understand that you're new to all this, and you have a lot to learn. But we have more important things to do than sit around and explain all of our histories to you. Jade, we have work to do."

The bite in her tone eliminated any sense of safety and trust I might've felt towards her. I guess the angelic kindness doesn't extend to all of them, Jade did mention ugly dispositions.

Though I wouldn't say Jophiel's rudeness in any way dwindled her impeccable beauty.

Jade rolled her eyes, still calm. "Jophiel's a very straight-forward character, as you can tell." She patted the table with her hand twice. "Bring them here, Jo. I'm comfortable where I am."

Jophiel proceeded to dump a few dozen scrolls, various papers and even some books bound in a strange material onto the table.

Jade grabbed a small stack of papers and quickly rifled through them and then decided which ones she would read right now.

"You can carry on with your research. You won't be able to read the languages these are written in," Jade said, gesturing to the pile.

"What are they?"

"Records. Scribes are a division of angels that record everything that happens in time. Both immortal and mortal. We went to a few of the Scribe outposts to gather anything on immortal deaths. Some of this goes back to before more than half the archangels existed. And the languages are *old*, which means we'll be working pretty hard to translate what we can," Jade explained.

Jophiel said, not looking up from her current reading. "Yes, and less talking would speed things up."

Jade rolled her eyes and mouthed *rawr* while clawing the open air. I giggled a little but silenced when Jophiel glanced up through her lashes. I bit my lip and went back to my laptop.

I liked Jade. She was a lot more human than the others. If we had met in my…regular life, I think we would've been quick friends. I'll have to ask her more about her position and her life. I just know that talking to her, even if her stories were about immortals, she would make it feel normal and human.

Though I was trying to focus on my own work, curiosity got the best of me. I'd peek at the papers laid out on the table. Both angels fully engrossed in whatever pieces they were reading. Jade was right, a lot of it was in languages I didn't understand.

I did recognize a couple, a French document here, a Greek scroll there.

But my eyes locked onto one paper in particular; the dark-brown, faded paper had singed edges, and there were only six lines on them, and whatever the symbols that were written, they must have formed words or a text of some kind.

They reminded me of hieroglyphs or Norse runes. But these, something about them was familiar. One I recognized from a dream I had a few days ago, I would need to look further back in my journal to find where it was noted.

"I'll be back," I said quietly to Jade. She nodded and went back to reading.

I ran down the hall to my room, snagging the fabric coated journal on the bedside table and walked briskly back. All while flipping through the pages until I came upon that symbol again. I flipped again, and on the next page I had noted other symbols that looked like the ones on that paper.

I walked back into the dining room, and stood in front of my laptop, peering down to compare the images. They were the same.

I read some of the notes and the dream I had written in those particular entries. In my dream I knew what those symbols meant, and I wrote it down. I looked back at the paper and spoke out loud.

"What does a *transition* have to do with a dead angel?"

Jade and Jophiel's heads snapped up, noticing that I was looking between my journal and a paper on the table.

"What?" Jade asked.

I picked up the paper. Pointing at it. "This symbol, it means *transition* doesn't it? And this one here means *will*, and this one *awakening*. Or roughly means it at least."

Jophiel stood from her chair and snatched the paper out of my hand, her brows furrowed together.

"You can read this?" she asked. She showed it to Jade, who looked at me shocked.

I eyed them warily. "Um, sort of. I dreamt of them and wrote about them in my dream journal. Why?"

Jophiel glanced back at the paper. "This is Zibµ, it's an angelic language. An old one. There's no possibility that you should be able to read it."

"Incredible. Gabriel had said you were having strange occurrences in your dreams. But seeing Zibµ, *I'm* not even fluent in the older ethereal languages. What else did you see?" Jade asked.

I shrugged. "I—I don't know what they are. But you're welcome to look in my journal."

She slipped it out of my arm before I could finish the sentence. She began flipping through the pages, her eyes bulging as she spotted something else.

"Enochian?"

Jophiel took the journal from Jade and looked herself. She read a few lines and turned the page before slowly gazing back up at me. The intensity of her stare froze me in place.

"You had a wraith inside your head, and Kaleus took care of it right?" she said.

I bristled, *Kaleus*? It's better than a leafy vegetable, I guess.

"Yeah. He, uh, did something and it sorta disappeared—disintegrated. I haven't seen it since," I answered.

Jade scratched the back of her neck. "Primordials don't know our languages, its presence doesn't explain the markings." Seemingly answering the silent assumption Jophiel was making.

The two of them made eye contact, silence filled the room. Were they communicating silently now?

Jade nodded slightly. "You're right."

I cleared my throat. "Hello, human here, can't hear what you're saying through the web," I muttered.

Jophiel ignored me and turned to leave through the opposite hallway, the demon's side of the warehouse.

Jade gave me an apologetic look. "Sorry, force of habit. We need to look inside your mind, your conscious mind."

My expression turned incredulous.

"I thought immortals couldn't get inside a human's consciousness, the whole loophole stuff they were telling me about."

Jade nodded.

"Only the really powerful can, with limitations. Kaleus would be able to, but he's not here. Daevas may be able to, his abilities are strong enough to work on conscious minds," she explained.

The images and sounds that I experienced while staring at him at the dinner came flashing back to mind. I had been conscious when that happened.

I backed up a step. "I don't know if I'm comfortable with this," I stated.

She came closer and clutched my hand.

"I promise Jophiel and I will keep you safe. And if it gets to be too much, we can stop. But it's very unusual that you can see and understand these symbols. There might be something else going on, and a clue might possibly be hiding inside your mind, if there is, it might help us."

I was still hesitant, dubious to the idea of a demon poking around in my head.

"Will it hurt?" I asked.

She squeezed my hand. "It shouldn't."

That just filled me with *so* much confidence…

Jophiel returned to the room with Daevas in tow. He was wearing black ripped skinny jeans and a large, oversized hoodie, dark green this time.

They crossed the room and while Jophiel stopped on the other side of the table, Daevas grabbed a couple empty chairs and positioned them to face each other.

He sat in one and motioned for me to sit in the other. I shot a panicked look to Jade.

"I'll be gentle, I promise. There's no reason to be afraid," he said.

I resisted the urge to say *that's what he said.*

I expected him to be comical and sinister, as Lillith or even Kale would be. But there was nothing but sincerity in his eyes. I hesitantly took the few steps necessary to reach the chair and slowly sat down. Our knees near touching.

"How is it you can get inside my conscious mind?" I asked, swallowing some of my dread down.

He held out his hands for me to hold.

"As a first-generation demon my powers are stronger than others. And I have a name in hell, Psychísąe. I earned it because of my very potent psychical abilities. One of my more particular skillsets is in consciousness infiltration."

I looked at both his hands before carefully placing my hands on them, afraid to make eye contact.

"What does that mean?"

His hands were calloused, but he was gentle, as promised.

"Most of what I do is alter memories and emotions. I can make a mortal feel trust instead of fear, giving more opportunities for demons to corrupt them."

Now I looked him in the eyes, terror returning to my eyes.

"*Or*…I can help someone feel less ashamed of the actions they commit. I won't be doing any of that."

I think those are the most words I'd ever heard him speak. Granted I hadn't been around him long. But compared to his counterparts, he was usually completely speechless.

He continued, "I'm just going to wander in and take a look around. I won't disturb or alter anything. It'll feel strange, but if you ever need me out, you'll only have to say so. Alright?" he asked.

I was scared, but his honesty was helping. I nodded.

He squeezed my hands slightly, the callouses on his fingers scraping mine. He turned to the other two.

"Don't disturb us unless it's important. Simply tap my shoulder. And please, don't try to communicate with me mentally, it takes a lot of focus, and I don't want to accidentally do any damage."

My eyes widened.

"Damage?!" I ripped my hands out of his. He held them up.

"Human minds can be fragile, and my abilities are strong. I can control them, but if I lose focus and pull out too quickly, I may tear a memory or two. It's an occupational hazard. I *promise*, as long as I'm not disturbed and maintain the parameters I'll set, you will be fine." He waited.

His eyes never leaving mine, he was being genuine. That didn't seem common in demons, so maybe it'd be okay.

I sighed. "Okay, just be quick, please."

He nodded, holding out his hands once more. I took them.

Jophiel and Jade took their seats a few feet away, Jophiel looked at my journal some more. Either to spare me the embarrassment of being watched, or to occupy her time while we did this.

"Ready?" Daevas asked.

I looked directly into his sea green eyes. I nodded once more.

"Close your eyes."

I did, my heart sped up in anticipation.

"Now, the first thing I'm going to do is approach the barriers of your mind. I'll wait until you let me in."

At first, all I saw was darkness. My eyes were closed, and my thoughts raced, but I didn't see anything. But then I felt something. It was like a gentle knocking on the outside of my skull.

And then I saw a wooden gate, and a figure on the other side of it. I moved closer, approaching close enough to see the grain of the wood, and Daevas. His pants were dark but not torn, and a black tank top replaced his hoodie. With more of his skin revealed I could see more of his tattoos.

The tentacles that reached up and around his neck extended into swirls and vines that went down beneath his shirt, and down his shoulders and arms. The vines wrapped around various symbols and images, ending on his wrists where they wrapped around an image of fire on the right and a snake's head on the left.

I looked back up to his face.

"What do I do now?" I asked.

I wasn't sure if I had said it out loud or not. I was fully inside my mind now.

"Now, you open the gate, and let me in."

I gazed back at the wooden gate. It looked a lot like the garden gate at my childhood home.

"Our minds usually take memories and use them to shape the inner structures of our consciousness. When a barrier to your mind was mentioned, your mind formed a gate you recognized," he said.

I must've said my thought out loud.

He shook his head. "While in your mind, your thoughts are free and clear," he explained.

"Oh," was all I said.

He motioned to the gate.

"Are you going to let me in then? Or would you like to stay here all day?" he joked.

I huffed and unlatched the gate, backing up to let him in. He walked through, now standing next to me.

He looked further into the darkness behind us.

"Shall we?"

He began walking, I had to speed up a little to keep up. It felt like we were walking through nothingness.

"Your memories will reveal themselves as they see fit. My abilities will weed out the ones we need to see."

I nodded and continued walking through the very fabric of my mind. "This is so weird. It's like walking through a dream."

"In a way it is."

We walked for what felt like fifteen minutes before the first memory appeared, or more like formed around us. The space around us shaped and moved, color and walls locked in place. Furniture rose from the empty floor, and then we were standing in my childhood home, in my playroom.

And there I was, no older than six years old. I was coloring on construction paper with crayons. I wore a blue and pink floral dress, the front of it messy and worn. My hair was pulled back into a bow.

I frowned. "Why would this memory be important? I don't even remember it."

Daevas moved closer to my younger self.

"Your subconscious remembers it." He peered over my younger self's shoulder at what I was drawing. "It seems even at a young age you had an affinity for strange symbology."

I walked over and looked too. It was rough, but there was a symbol there.

"This is an Enochian warding sigil. Not a typical childhood drawing."

Daevas looked at it a bit longer, then began walking away.

“Okay, on to the next one I think.” And like that all the furniture and walls began to disappear.

Vanishing as if wiped off a board.

I turned to catch up with him. Again, walking through darkness for a little while.

“At what age did you decide you wanted to study religion and symbology?” he asked.

“I was in high school. During an ancient world civilization class, we watched a documentary of archeologists digging up an old religious site, they talked a lot about what they learned from it and others they had explored. I found it interesting and wanted to learn more,” I explained.

Daevas unlocked another memory, the walls and furniture forming my old high school classroom. Or maybe I unlocked it, I didn’t know anymore.

The whole class was watching the documentary, and I was sitting in the second row, third seat down. The speaker in the film was highlighting some markings they found on a cave wall.

“It’s incredible. Though we may not know what these markings mean, it’s going to be a lot of fun figuring it out. Years of work lie ahead of us, but that’s what makes this so exciting,” he mused in a British accent.

At my desk, I was drawing something in my notebook, doodling really.

My teacher paused the film. "This was filmed about eight years ago, and after some work, they learned some of what these words meant."

"So, this segment right here," he pointed to the one on the screen. "they have since translated," he looked down at a piece of paper in his hands. "to be about their sun God, and the seasonal harvest that they celebrated during the solstice. Isn't that amazing?"

My younger self was shaking her bobbed head. "No, that's not right." My teacher noticed my comment and turned his attention to me.

"Heather, did you say something?"

My teenage-self lifted my head from my notebook and looked around before hesitantly saying.

"Um, I'm sorry Mr. Pirelli, those markings aren't talking about the harvest. The curved feather thing means 'to escape', and the figure with the spears coming out of its head is a monster that invaded their village and killed them. They're talking about a massive slaughter that occurred," she said.

Some of the other students laughed, even the teacher chuckled a bit.

"Well, that certainly is an interpretation I guess. But I have the reports from the scientists themselves explaining their translation. So, though I commend your imagination, Heather, let's just stick with their accounts, okay?" More kids snickered and laughed.

Ah, that was a memory I didn't like to remember. I glanced at Daevas who was watching the encounter closely.

He tapped his chin. "Interesting." He shrugged. "Shall we move on?"

Again, the fabric of that memory dissolved.

While we walked, I felt the embarrassment of that memory hit me again. Luckily, their teasing didn't deter me from going into that field of study. But it did take a hit to my social life.

I'd never had a ton of close friends in general, but after that and some other encounters, I spent more time in my own books and drawings than I did with others.

I'm sure all those thoughts were freely flowing around Daevas, so to ease some of my discomfort I asked.

"So, you're one of Lucifer and Lillith's children. That's interesting. What was growing up like?"

Daevas gave me a sidelong glance. "A lot of training."

"Training? I mean when you were a kid. What was that like?" I clarified.

Daevas shook his head. "Training for demons begins as soon as we can walk," he stated.

I looked more towards him. "What kind of training?"

He stopped mid-stride, I halted as well.

"I know that memory was unpleasant to relive and asking me about my life is a distraction for you. But a demons life story is unpleasant and gruesome. I will not be sharing those horrors with a mortal anytime soon. Besides, it'll only lessen my focus. And you don't want that right now when we still have a lot to cover. Understand?"

His gaze was edged and caustic.

Touchy subject, got it.

I clamped my lips shut and curtly nodded and we continued on our way. For the remainder of our journey, I didn't ask him questions that didn't pertain to my memories, and all the moments in-between were carried out in silence.

We walked for an average of five to ten minutes before entering into another memory. And as I got older the occurrence of strange symbols only increased.

EIGHTEEN
Kale

YOU WOULD THINK A CREATURE BORN IN FIRE and brimstone would be accustomed to the heat.

But I wasn't. The sweltering humidity was miserable, and it did nothing to ease my inner fire. Being so close to my origins made the inner flames churn inside me relentlessly.

This is why I had chosen the warehouse as my mortal getaway location. Sudbury has a more comfortable climate for my tastes, and quiet. Traveling back to hell was never voluntary, the pit was a memorandum of the suffering I went through to be who I am today, and a constant reminder of what my future held.

Usually, I would send Daevas to do my dealings with Lucifer, but today he requested Lillith and I specifically. I wouldn't subject Seere to this. Lucifer had little regard for lower-class demons, and he had a strong aversion to my making her my second.

So, to keep him from saying or doing anything that might make her feel uncomfortable, she would only be around him if I accompanied her.

I waited in the foyer of Lucifer's office. The room was carved out of the rock, which was black glossy obsidian. The walls curved upwards and rounded out at the ceiling.

A few pieces of deep, red furniture and even some charred skeletons of trees stood in the corners. The room was lit by burning embers fashioned into light fixtures. The floor was covered in black and white tiling, the white helping reflect some of the light.

His office was an iron door away, and I was to wait out here while Lillith and him got reacquainted. Despite her demotion from being his wife, and his taking of other lovers and wives, the two still felt the need to rump-and-bump regularly.

Occupational hazard of being the two most seductive beings in existence.

Another reason why I didn't like being here with the two of them. Thank the realms the room was soundproof.

Eventually the door swung open, and the two of them sauntered in. Lucifer was tall and burly, his rust-colored hair coiffed and styled, and he wore one of his regular black suits with a deep red tie. Daevas took more after him than he did from Lillith, the resemblance was sometimes uncanny.

His mouth leered towards me. I had remained standing, one hand in my pocket, leaning against the tall bar in the room.

Lillith puckered her lips to fix them, swishing her hair back and lounging on the closest burgundy couch.

"Even after all this time, you still go back to the same trash," I teased.

Lillith gave a vulgar gesture with her hand.

Lucifer laughed. "Old habits die hard. Glad to have you back home." He clapped a hand onto my shoulder.

I stiffened under the contact but leashed the inner raging fire under control.

"Is there a particular reason you called me here like a dog?" I struggled not to hiss the words.

He walked around the bar and began pouring an amber-colored liquid into two glasses.

"How is the alliance fairing?" he asked, he set one of the glasses on the counter next to me, then began mixing some ingredients together for a martini.

I glanced at the glass but didn't grab it.

"What, your whore hasn't been giving you regular updates?"

He poured the mixed liquid into a martini glass and added an olive on a stick before walking over to Lillith, handing it to her. She winked and sipped it instantly.

"Maybe if you yourself took her for a spin, you might have more respect," Lucifer suggested.

My fire swelled enough that I could taste the ash in my throat. I took a sip from my drink to tame it.

"What do you want?" I asked harshly. I was tired of the formalities and the stalling.

He stood in the middle of the room, one hand in his pocket and the other dipping his glass for a drink. It took every ounce of effort not to pull my own pocketed hand out to avoid any similarity between us, but I knew that action would only give him superiority, and I couldn't let that happen.

He swallowed his sip. "Tell me about the mortal," he instructed.

I clenched my jaw. "What about her?"

"I hear she's got a few tricks up her sleeve."

I resisted the urge to laugh at that. Instead, I gulped down the remainder of my scotch in one swig.

I tossed the glass, letting it shatter against the obsidian walls.

"If you only brought me here to play games and dilly-dally, then I'm leaving."

He pouted. “So soon?”

“I have more important things to do than to play catch up with daddy.”

Lucifer clicked his tongue. “Tsk, tsk, son. Don’t forget that you have obligations to this realm that you’ve been slacking on, don’t think I haven’t noticed.”

I rolled my eyes and walked towards the exit.

“Everything is being managed just fine.”

“By your lackies, not by you. These tasks weren’t meant to be overseen by a fifth-generation grunt, Kaleus,” he said.

A nerve, he was touching a nerve, and he knew it. It wouldn’t even get to me if it weren’t for the fact that he’s trying to get under my skin and knows exactly which buttons to push. He’s played this game with me too many times not to.

“I’ve made it very clear that you are not to speak ill of Seere.”

His voice was deadly calm, “Let me remind you, boy, that I am still in charge here. You may pretend to be in charge when you’re colluding with the angels, but here, you answer to me. Lillith answers to me. Daevas answers to me. Your *pup* answers to me.”

I flipped to face him. His face cold and unfeeling, aside from the subtle incline of his mouth.

He was goading me, and I would be a fool to fall for it.

“So, this summoning is actually just a chance for you to prod at me again. I thought we were getting over this cycle of cat and mouse.”

He shrugged. “After the last incident, it’s clear to me that you haven’t been pushed far enough. How’s that fire stoking? Is it raging to escape once more?” he teased.

I loosened a small growl from deep in my throat. "I'm in complete control." *Much to your disappointment.*

He tapped the glass in his hand with a finger, sipping it again without looking away from me. He released a loud sigh after swallowing the last of his scotch.

"If that's true, you shouldn't have any trouble sticking around a bit longer."

All I wanted was to leave. Run back to the mortal realm, hop on my motorcycle, and drive the long distance to the warehouse to clear my head. To be rid of the heat of this place and the smoldering it caused in me.

How much I longed to get away from this forever. A mortal life always seemed so much more amiable than this.

But Lucifer was right. If I were to prove that I could in-fact control the danger I possessed, leaving right now would be counterproductive.

I took a deep breath, sending a quick thread of thought to Seere, looking for that tether to sanity.

"Fine. But enough with the games and the delays. Let's get to what you wanted me here for," I demanded.

I sat in an armchair on the opposite side of the room, putting more space between us.

I felt Seere reach back, a short message. *Iaoel and I are just getting back to the warehouse. Just tolerate him until he's done frolicking.*

I hid the relief her voice gave me. Someone who knew me, jagged edges and all, and would never turn away or encourage destruction.

Lucifer returned to the bar to refill his glass.

"The wraith you captured, said it was released from Fangelsi?" he asked.

I shot a look towards Lillith, who only lazily sipped on her martini.

"That's what it told us."

He looked down for a moment, then at me. "Only archangels can open those prisons," he stated.

I furrowed my brows.

"You think an archangel is behind it?" I asked. "I assumed we had ruled them out already."

Who would unleash the very things that they imprisoned millions of years ago?

Lucifer shook his head. "It's unlikely. My siblings are loyal to our almighty father. Chamuel and Gabriel weren't even born until the very end of The Tear. They wouldn't even know how to open them."

I waited, but he stayed silent for a while, thinking. "Then how did it open?" I pressed.

He drank some of the amber liquid, before something dawned on him, a realization.

"There were a few relics from before the Paṭaippu period, before Nēram, dating all the way back to the Before."

"Before the original creation?"

He nodded. "They are certainly powerful enough to be able to negate the spells and powerful wards put on the prisons to keep them shut. If those relics were wielded by a powerful being who knew how to use them. Maybe…but a lot of those relics disappeared during Paṭukolai, right in the middle of the slaughtering."

During The Great Slaughter that led to The Tear.

This might be something—something we can work with and move forward with. We were reaching a limbo, unsure how to move ahead, only gathering information hoping something would lead us to the next step.

But this, might be the very information we *needed.*

"Is there record of these relics, what they are or what they look like?" I asked, sitting up straighter.

"Maybe, you'd have to look pretty deep into *a lot* of Scribe bases. Heaven might be the best place to start."

Seere began sending me concerned thoughts. *Hey fire-boy, you might want to get back here.*

Oh great, what now?

"How would we know what we're looking for?" Lillith asked.

She also didn't exist until after The Tear, these relics were new to the both of us.

I only reached back halfway, trying to listen to both Lucifer and Seere.

This isn't great timing, beasty.

Lucifer went to the wall of obsidian and with his finger he signed two markings, ancient markings on the wall for us to see.

"Look for Eternal sigils. They should be on anything that would be relevant from Vāļkkai to The Tear. These are the two I'm familiar with. The others are unlikely to be scribed in any written word," he said.

I studied the markings. I recall learning a little about Vāļkkai, the first corporeal beings in the universe, the almighty, his companion…forming from the various matter floating around in the void.

Daevas went inside Heather's mind, something about searching her memories. Gabriel is livid, he's become completely unhinged. If you don't get here soon, the brute might do something he regrets. Seere quickly explained.

I sighed.

"I have to go. But I'll tell the others and we'll start looking." I looked towards Lillith. "You coming?" Her eyes drifted to Lucifer lustfully.

"She'll catch up." Lucifer purred.

I resisted the urge to gag and left the room swiftly. I began walking briskly to the upper levels where winnowing would be easier.

I'll be there in a few seconds.

I shifted to the Ethereal and warped to the warehouse. As soon as my smoke and fire retreated I heard the commotion in the upper room. My own inner fire still churning and festering.

"Calm down! Everything was fine!" Jade's voice sounded.

"Fine? A demon wandering around a mortal's consciousness is dangerous! You should have waited for me," Gabriel snapped back.

Daevas' voice chimed in, low like he was struggling to breathe. "She was in no danger."

"No danger? Then why is she now unconscious? You have no idea what kind of damage you could have wrought on the fabric of her mind!"

I began running up the stairs.

"I think I do…"

"Shut up!"

"Seriously! Let him go, you stupid oaf!" Seere chirped.

"I should just smite you here and now for even trying it." Gabriel's voice was murderous.

I reached the top and rushed into the room.

Gabriel had Daevas pinned against the adjacent wall, full power and wings out in all their glory. Seere was a few steps back, daggers drawn.

Jade was behind Gabriel, not daring to get in the crossfire. Jophiel only sat at the far end of the table, watching out of boredom and annoyance.

Heather was in a chair, completely passed out, Duma was trying to assess her while also flicking his attention to the ongoing tension in the room.

Gabriel had all his might out, which meant even if they all tried to subdue him, there would be a lot of unnecessary injuries.

I stared only for a moment at Gabriel and Daevas, who glared at directly at one another. Neither willing to yield, and the longer they stood there, the more Gabriel glowed, as though ready to erupt.

Something about his grip on my friend loosened some of the stirring flame in me. And all at once the room filled with smoke and electricity.

Some of the others jumped and started at the sudden influx of power. I stepped closer to Gabriel, dragging his eyes to me.

With a mere flick of my hand, Gabriel went flying backwards towards the couches, landing hard and fast. Jade managed to dodge quickly enough to avoid injury.

Daevas sagged to floor, but he quickly regained his footing, rubbing his neck. The tentacles tattooed there now turning purple from bruises.

I squared myself between Gabriel and everyone else. He grunted, lifting himself up on his knees.

"That temper of yours is really unbecoming, feathers," I said calmly.

He growled. "I'm her Guardian. It's my job to protect her, even against you," he spat.

"He wasn't going to hurt her," I stated. He huffed.

"Then explain her current state."

When I turned to Daevas, he began to explain, "He broke my focus." Glaring at the arch-asshole, "You have no one to blame but yourself."

Gabriel went to lunge for him, but he was met by another blow from me, flinging him back on his ass once more.

"Stay put until you take a fucking chill pill," I ordered.

He glared up at me, but he didn't try to move again, his glow diminishing some.

I turned and walked over to Heather's unconscious body that Duma was still assessing. I jerked my chin and he moved out of the way.

I knelt down in front of her. First I clutched her ankles, they were steady, she was still grounded.

I clasped her hands, her pulse was steady as well, meaning no immediate trauma. I closed my eyes and focused on her. Slowly approaching the outer barriers of her consciousness.

A small wooden gate was there. I put my hand on it and sent a tendril of power further in.

"Heather?" I spoke into the void.

The wooden gate fell away, and all around me the landscape came into view.

A garden full of vegetables, fruits, and flowers, outside of a small house. A middle-aged woman with a sunhat and bright blue gardening gloves was moving a potted plant into a hole she had just dug into the ground. The woman had dark hair, and big brown eyes. She wore a floral apron that was worn and covered in dirt. She wiped the sweat off her forehead with her arm, looking off into the distance.

I followed her gaze, landing on Heather. Younger, no older than seventeen maybe. She was sitting on a porch swing reading a book. Wearing a pair of pink eyeglasses, a bright green blouse and denim overalls, barefoot.

This must be a memory.

Maybe this was the last one they were in before Gabriel interrupted and Daevas had to pull out of it.

I didn't need Heather's permission to get in here, so it must have turned into a dream after Daevas left. She was in her subconscious now.

I let out a relieved sigh and retreated out of her mind.

Opening my eyes, Heather was still unconscious in front of me. Maybe not terribly comfortable sleeping in a chair, but nothing seemed to be wrong otherwise.

My eyes lingered on her face, seeing the similarities between her and the middle-aged woman gardening, who I assume was her mother. And for a moment, just a moment, I admired the beautiful human woman before me.

But I let the moment go and turned towards the crowd, waiting for me to say something.

"She's fine."

Some of them sighed, having been holding their breaths. I locked eyes with Gabriel, who too had eased some of his tension.

"Daevas is *the best* at what he does. Despite your rude and thoughtless disruption of a very delicate process, he managed to seal her in the memory they were in. It more or less became a dream. And I'm guessing that she is still out because the memory walking was exhausting. She'll probably be out for a couple hours, maybe even a day or two," I explained.

Gabriel was standing now, wings no longer protruding from his back. He even dared to look ashamed. He looked to the floor then to me then to Daevas, clearing his throat.

"I apologize for my…recklessness."

Daevas didn't pretend to be forgiving or pleased with his empty apology, but he did see fit to give him a curt nod as a response.

Then Daevas turned to me, and I already knew what he was going to say. I held up my hand to silence him before he could speak.

"There's no need."

He hesitated, but again nodded in understanding.

I once again turned towards Heather's unconscious body. I sighed.

“I’ll take her to her room,” I slid my arm under her knees and the other around her waist, cradling her against me.

“I can take her,” Gabriel said, ready to jump in.

I tensed and backed a step. “I think you need to take a break from playing protector.”

Despite his sneering he allowed me to take her. I turned and began down the hallway.

Jade in the other room said, “I will put on some tea.”

“Make it whiskey,” Seere chimed.

The few responding chuckles eased some of the lingering tension.

I rounded the corner and carefully carried Heather to her door, spearing my power to open it.

Her duffle was open and spread on the dresser, some of her books and notebooks on the bedside table. I lowered her down onto the bed, gently resting her limp head onto the pillow. Once she was settled in, I lifted the blanket over her form.

Sitting on the edge, I just watched her for a moment. I could still feel the after-effects of my outburst. So, I took this moment in the dark quiet to try to soothe the fire once more.

I hadn’t even realized I was stroking strands of her hair as I went through my own mind and soul, fishing out every last burning ember and blowing them out one by one until I no longer felt the rage and mania.

It must be nice to be a human. Not having to worry about getting angry for fear of burning a building down. Emotions are just feelings, however unpleasant. Not a catalyst to calamity.

There’s no doubt Heather’s mortal life is anything but normal, and it is a shame she has to be a part of this. But at least when it’s over, she has the option to forget and move on.

But the frenzy will never end for me.

I must have been there a while, because Seere reached out.

Do you want us to start without you?

I assume she meant another debrief of what we found out today. I stroked Heather's hair again, letting the smoothness soothe my soul.

Give me another minute. I felt her agree and leave.

My thoughts drifted back to the words my father used to goad me earlier, and then Gabriel losing his shit. I took a deep breath and looked at Heather one last time.

"I don't know about you. But I'm starting to root for whoever started this madness."

NINETEEN
Kale

“ETERNAL RELICS?” Jophiel asked.

All of us now gathered in the large room, maintaining a safe distance from one another. Lillith had finally decided to grace us with her presence not long after the fiasco.

I nodded. “From before the original creation. Any idea what they might be since you were alive before The Great Slaughter?” I asked her.

Gabriel might know, but only from second-hand accounts.

Jophiel tapped the table, thinking. “I recall some objects that belonged to the almighty, but I don’t know if those would be what you’re referring to. As far as I remember, they went missing or were destroyed during the onslaught. That or they were cleverly stashed. I always thought Lucifer stole away with a few during The Fall,” she replied.

“He didn’t give an indication that he has them.”

Gabriel spoke, “Alright, but he said our Scribe records might tell us what to look for?”

I dipped my chin. Duma looked through the collection of scrolls and papers that Jophiel and Jade had brought back.

“None of these have the Eternal sigils on them, so they may be just informative to the primordials, but not to the relics,” he said.

"And these relics are supposed to be really powerful?" Seere asked.

Iaoel's eyes were distant, using their gift. Only after they blinked did they chime in.

"Original pieces of the Balance, belongings of the Eternals. If they got into the right hands, or maybe the wrong ones, they could do a lot of things," they said.

"Like murder a Guardian angel?" I hinted.

Jade turned to Iaoel. "Can you see these relics?" she asked.

Iaoel shook their head.

"I can see some of the effects their power left behind, but the relics themselves are beyond my abilities. They're age may be a contributor."

Iaoel locked eyes with Gabriel. "Why don't we ask the almighty? He is an Eternal after all, it'll be faster than scouting the globe for a written record of them."

Gabriel looked to Jophiel. "We'll take a visit to heaven and see if he can shed more light on them."

"Lucifer said only a powerful being could wield them properly, so who could be opening the supernatural prisons and killing immortals?" Lillith asked the right question.

All of us exchanged looks, some lingering on the archangels in the room.

"Archangels are the most powerful beings currently in existence, aside from the almighty himself," I tapped.

Gabriel glared at me. "As are you."

I met his gaze. "It's not me, feather-brain."

"Well then if we're going to start accusing archangels, maybe we should first point fingers at the only one who's rebelled in the past," he replied.

I shrugged. "Lucifer is many things, and he may be behind it yes. But when I spoke with him, I didn't see any reason why he would be. Given that the almighty spoke with him and saw no deceit, I think we can rule him out for now. What about Michael or Raphael? I haven't seen them through all of this," I replied.

Jophiel stood up, her anger rising. "Michael would never. He defines what it is to be loyal. His very duty is to maintain the Balance, he'd be the last person to disrupt it. And Raphael is too rational to do this. Archangels aren't the only beings that could wield the relics, there are other powerful beings out there capable," she defended.

"The Fallen?" Seere asked, she locked eyes with me. "We may want to put a few of them at the top of our suspect list."

For a moment, no one said anything, considering.

"A lot of well-trained angels could. The Ophanim or the Watchers are the strongest in our ranks," Duma explained.

"More than half the first-generation demons have abilities as strong as mine, any of them might be strong enough to commit the act," Daevas added quietly from the corner.

A few sighed, this was getting us nowhere.

"It seems we have a lot to do then, a lot of possible culprits that we need to narrow down. But more importantly, whoever killed Mason and is releasing the primordials, they may have a relic assisting them. What can we do about that?" I asked.

Jade said, "I think the first thing we should do is find out which relic it is. That will tell us a lot about what we can do to cease or prevent further damage."

"How do we do that, if our Guardian killer possesses it?" Lillith asked harshly.

Jade shrunk a little but didn't let it show in her voice as she clarified, "We could find the rest of them."

Nobody liked that idea, judging by the snickers, pairs of rolling eyes and groans.

"That could take years, especially when we have no actual idea what they are, or how many there are," Seere complained.

But it's more time away from the pit. I challenged internally. She only gave me a brief glance before lowering her head.

Gabriel looked at me, and while we locked eyes, I realized that he was waiting for my idea of what our next steps should be.

Perhaps my earlier show of force had gained me some footing between us. A leader willing to collaborate rather than argue. To save time, or to avoid any more conflict?

I cleared my throat, and everyone looked to me.

"So, here's what we do. Gabriel and Jophiel go to heaven and ask the almighty about the relics, find out as much about them as you can. If he knows what they all are, then we go from there."

Gabriel nodded, Jophiel only curled her lips in a small snarl.

"We're going to have to cover a lot of ground, so pair up if you can't winnow far, and go alone if you can. We'll need to check every Scribe compound, every division and even some of the other realms, like hell. We need to find what we can on these relics, and if possible, get them in our possession. Once we know which one is missing, we'll start figuring out how to stop whatever work is being done with it. It's a lot, but we have to work with it."

I locked eyes with Seere and Daevas.

"Looks like our little alliance is going to last a while longer. To save time try to report back mentally, only come back here to dump off records or to take a turn watching the mortal. Got it?"

I looked at each one of them, and each one nodded in response.

"Speaking of mortal…care to share what you learned from the earlier memory-walking exercise?" I asked Daevas.

Daevas uncrossed his legs and stood straighter. "We went back as far as her early childhood, unfortunately we didn't make it to her adult years."

Shooting a suggestive look to Gabriel, who only glared back.

"She's been seeing Enochian and other ancient languages and symbols since she herself was able to speak. It's safe to say that wraith or whatever it was that you banished from her mind before wasn't the cause of her visions."

Jade lifted a piece of paper. "She was doing her own studying while we were reading these records and she recognized what these symbols meant. When she showed us her journal, it made us wonder how much and how long she's seen these things. We *asked* Daevas to search her memories, we would've asked Kale, but he wasn't here," she explained to Gabriel.

He nodded, his only sign of understanding.

"So, she can read immortal languages, what does that tell us?" Lillith asked, she was fully laying across the couch, utterly bored.

Truly, it was a weird discovery, and if it wasn't because of another creature festering inside her mind, then what else could cause it?

Unless…

"Is there a chance she might be a *Nephilim*?" I asked quietly.

All the pairs of eyes in the room shot to me—shock written on all the angels faces.

Seere giggled, “No way.”

Nephilim were the offspring of angels and humans. For the most part, they lived normal human lives, but depending on their angel parents, some of them could do remarkable things. It’s the only real possibility.

The problem was, after The Fall, inter-relations with humans was forbidden by heaven, and though it happened every once in a while, over time the population of Nephilim dwindled to nothing but a myth.

“It can’t be, we haven’t seen a Nephilim in hundreds of years. The Cherubim’s keep close monitor of them, usually they were destined to be prophets or major history shifters,” Gabriel stated.

“Why did your flying butts stop making them?” Lillith asked. “You can’t say it wasn’t a fun tumbling.”

Iaoel answered this time, ignoring her initial seductive tone. “They disrupt the Balance, immensely. Some of the biggest disasters in human history—a Nephilim was right in the middle of it. When mortals discovered their existence, they would sacrifice them or try to tap into their angel grace for power. Restrictions had to be put in place to stop it.”

As an Angel of Sight, they would’ve seen a lot of this destruction.

“Her being a Nephilim would definitely explain why she understands the languages, not to mention it could’ve been why she saw Mason’s death. Her genealogy and grain of grace would have made the Guardian bond stronger, intensified it,” Jade said to Gabriel.

A bond she now has with *him*. Already it was intensified because he was an archangel, adding in a Nephilim grace…I shook my head, clearing away the strange sense of envy that followed that thought.

"It could also be why she was hunted by the vetala; it was attracted to her like a moth to a flame," Gabriel stated, locking eyes with me. "The angel grace of a Nephilim is rare and sticks out."

"It's a wonder none of you noticed it before," Lillith taunted.

The archangel purposefully ignored her.

"Who was her angel parent?" Duma asked.

Jade picked up her journal and flipped through it before saying, "Judging by her affinity for religion and symbology, I would venture to guess a Scribe or a Principality, they're the ones who directly deal with religion and record keeping."

Duma added, "Then again, it could've been a Nymph, they're far more solitary and fewer in numbers. Most of them off the grid entirely. They could've easily hidden a forbidden offspring from our knowledge."

Daevas and I both perked up at that.

"She did say her parents were introverted, both dedicated and ingrained in their work," Gabriel agreed.

"Her mother gardens. Nymphs are connected to the earth, right?" I said, Daevas nodding alongside me.

Gabriel pointed in no particular direction, recalling something. "She's a botanist, Heather mentioned it," he said. "A Nymph hiding right under our noses, raising children. They never cease to amaze."

"What does *that* mean?" Seere questioned.

"Nymphs are technically a part of Michael's division. They're supposed to care for plant and animal life on earth to maintain that part of the Balance. But they're secretive and often don't like working with others. A long while back nearly all of them went into hiding, refusing to report back, eventually we stopped considering them in our structure. We don't even assign angels as Nymphs anymore. You can still find a few serving as eco-spirits, protecting the wildlife around them," Gabriel explained.

"Wait, you uptight drones really let an entire sect of angels disappear from their job? I'm confused, I thought you were super uptight about that stuff." Seere scrunched her nose.

Jade leveled a wary gaze at her. "We don't exactly have the manpower to go searching for all of them. We're all stretched thin as it is."

"Whatever…"

"They also had a habit of getting in trouble, their powers are almost exclusively refined to magic and spells. They liked to share some of their magic with humans. Giving way for human witches to emerge," Duma mused—he was grinning like he found it amorous that they did such things. "It was highly frowned-upon."

Seere turned to me. "Why didn't we learn about them?" she asked me. I shrugged.

"They never interact with demons, and they're so deep in the wilderness that their existence didn't matter to our missions. Don't be upset though, I only know of them from a story or two."

Jophiel let out a loud, exasperated sigh. "It doesn't matter. We should get back to the *important* things." Her tone was cold and annoyed.

As much as I'd love to contradict her. "She's right. All that tells us is that whoever is using a relic to wreak havoc may be seeking Heather out for her rare grace. Which makes her vulnerable to attacks, so she can't be left alone. But it also means she can help us rifle through the records, saving us time as the rest of us seek them out."

I locked eyes with Seere. *Not so helpless after-all.*

"We better get started," Jade conceded.

Gabriel straightened. "I'll stay and take the first shift with Heather."

I barked a laugh. "Ha! Right, yeah, that's not happening."

"I'm her *Guardian*," he protested darkly.

I held up a hand to stop him. "Not anymore, you're not. Not until I say so. Besides, you have a trip to heaven to make, feather-boy. I'll stay with her for now. We'll all start taking turns, and then maybe when it circles back to you, I'll allow it. Got it, featherass?"

The other three angels tensed behind us. My demons, beside Lillith, did their best to hide their approval. The room felt stuffy very quickly, some of the concrete on the walls beginning to peel away in pebbles and steel arches and columns groaned under immense pressure.

"You'd be smart, hellborn, to watch what you say to us," Jophiel barked.

I tilted my head, letting my signature smirk form across my mouth. Challenging.

"This is *my* home, and you are my guests. You'd be smart about the shit coming out of your mouth before I make you choke on it," I threatened back, my tone completely calm but laced with death.

Gabriel's eyes narrowed. "We can have her moved to one of our own safe places," he countered.

I grinned wider.

“Go right ahead. And when you do, you can tell your almighty papa that it was your arrogance that cost him our alliance, and you’ll find hell’s doors closed to you and all help from demons halted. You may even find us helping your opponent.”

I let my eyes dance with fire to counter the growing gold ore that swirled in his.

I never tore my gaze from his, smirking wildly while he fought the urge to slash my throat. Oh, this game we played, it had my blood buzzing. If only the arch-asshole rode into it with the same ferocity.

“Okay…I think we can all agree that Kaleus is perfectly capable of protecting Heather for now. There’s no need for any more disputes to get in the way of our main goal. So everybody calm down, back up and let’s get going.” Iaoel broke us all out of our defensive positions.

I relaxed, stepping back first, my demons relaxing behind me. The angels behind Gabriel did the same, still looking towards him—who hesitated.

“Fine,” he said.

He backed up and turned to Jophiel.

“We should go.”

Jophiel nodded and left out the archway to winnow out.

Gabriel looked at each of us one at a time, landing on me last, lingering there with some remaining fury burning.

“Report back, don’t mess things up.”

And to me, “Be careful.”

More of a threat than a gesture of caring.

I waved at him sweetly as he ducked out. “Hope the rest of your day is as pleasant as you are.”

Seere laughed quietly behind me. I turned to her.

“You should go with—”

“I got her,” Iaoel stated, gesturing for her to follow them out to winnow.

Seere blushed slightly, earning a raised brow from me.

But Seere only shrugged. *We bonded a little.* she said mentally.

My brow raised higher, and a suggestive smile grew on my lips.

She rolled her eyes. *Not like that, stupid…not yet anyway.* and with a wink she departed from the room.

Lillith rose from the couch, “Let’s go find God’s sex toys.”

Duma began coughing, choking on air. Daevas only rolled his eyes with an exasperated sigh.

Lillith and Jade went with Daevas and Duma. All of them off to various Scribe locations, and other places in the world where records might be on the Eternal relics.

Leaving me alone, Heather still asleep in the other room, I sent a tether of power to her room to monitor her while she slept, not wanting to watch her sleep.

Instead, I snapped my fingers, changing my clothes to shorts and a t-shirt and went downstairs to the fighting ring.

While wrapping my fingers in tape, staring down the five-inch steel wall I erected next to the other equipment, I cataloged and cleared my head.

Padded punching bags were like punching through paper for me, and even the concrete walls would be littered in holes if I went at them.

Getting out some of the lingering rage would pacify my inner flame. But it would also pass time while Heather slept. Perhaps when she woke I could teach her some defensive moves, might come in handy if we're attacked again.

If she is a Nephilim, proper training could help her hold her own long enough for help to arrive if necessary.

I fisted the metal, smoke furling from my fists and floating away. I punched and saw Gabriel's face.

I hit it again, Lillith's face.

Punch—Daevas being held by the throat.

Hit—Lucifer's cold and cruel smile. The metal began to bend.

Slam—Seere bleeding on the floor.

Pop—bodies burning.

Crack—Heather's eyes.

Crash—My eyes, engulfed in flames.

My breath came out in short puffs. When I lowered my hands, the steel was bent inwards, cracked in some places. I shook my hands, some of the knuckles and fingers were broken.

But quickly the pain was replaced by intense heat, as my power wrapped around the fractures and fused them back together.

I took in a long inhale, holding it for a few seconds before releasing it slowly. Again. One more time.

Then a tap, a vibration from my extended tether. I followed it—Heather was still asleep, but she was stirring, much like the first time I watched over her. Another nightmare.

I immediately made my way towards her room, not bothering to change or take the tape off my fingers.

I entered her room and knelt beside the bed. Her face was crinkled and upset—twitching profoundly. I sure hope this isn't another internal attack. I gripped her wrist, closed my eyes, and reached into her mind. Entering her subconscious to soothe her back to a restful sleep.

TWENTY
Azrael

EVEN IN IMMORTALITY, TIME FLIES.

A million years can feel like a blink to someone who's been around for all creation. Azrael has been alive since the earth was in its infancy.

The core churning in endless heat while the damp soil crust settled and gave birth to great mountains and lakes. While the seas raged unbothered, and beasts made history through blood and breath.

Mortals lived then, early on. They were unlike the mortals of modern day. Designed differently. As they had to be. The youthful earth was then a much harsher environment, and among them the primordials roamed without restraint.

Primordials weren't gifted with the same intelligence and evolution as the mortals were. In comparison, they were savage and wild.

They were envious of the mortal's superior intelligence and insulted by them. So slaughter was their response. Cruel, brutal slaughter of an entire species. Using their archaic natures to reap mortal-kind until nothing remained. Feasting on their flesh, draining their blood, and breaking their bones down to dust.

The almighty and the seven living archangels were forced to step in.

That was billions of years ago. They marked the major event in time as Kaṇṇīr. *The Tear.* following Paṭukolai, The *Great Slaughter* in which the primordials and the battles between angels and monsters led to the extinction of the mortals in existence at the time.

The world was broken. So it was remade with beauty and opportunity.

The mortals that now dwell here were made anew as well. The almighty giving them a fresh start, and a fresh design. Made for a renewed and purified world.

Azrael was one of the eldest three archangels, and she lived through the primordial existence, through their butchering, their removal and assisted in cleansing the Earth of their stain.

Unlike her elder brothers Lucifer and Michael, Azrael was impassive, solid. She was the angel of death, her judgement determined whether souls passed to paradise or to eternal anguish.

She was order. She was justice. She was patience.

A Guardian angel was dead.

Reapers and other angel divisions began going missing. And for a little while it was a mystery. But Gabriel, who was investigating the unfolding events alongside demons, had reported back.

Primordials have returned. Released from the confinements they sealed them in long ago.

Azrael had her hands full. Her Reapers and Thrones now working double time and in pairs to gather souls, but it didn't stop some of the souls from slipping through. Now forced to wander Purgatory until they can return for them.

With the primordials showing up all over the planet, it was impossible to keep up. So much so, that Azrael had to get back in the field to help. Doing her best to impede the casualties.

She was in Djibouti now, staring out at the sinking ships in the Gulf of Aden. The ships weren't suffering from structural failures. No, they were being dragged down by a primordial called a Scylla.

A primordial creature with the upper body of a rotting woman, sharp teeth, a torso of hound heads and dragon-like serpent appendages.

Nasty, brutal and one of the worst water-bound primordials in existence.

The Scylla was extremely hard to trap the first time Azrael faced it, and it was much harder to kill.

A few Reapers had appeared with Azrael on the shoreline.

“It's already taken down five ships, and the others are too far out to escape unnoticed.” A Reaper named Polly informed.

Some of them had flown just above the wreckage to gather any information they could on what they needed to face.

“And their Guardians?” Azrael asked.

Color drained from Polly's face.

“Those that are still alive are holding it off, for now. Those who end up in the water don't come out.” She swallowed.

Azrael and the others dipped their heads in silence.

They weren't feeling them die, not the way they did when the first Guardian—Mason, died. Now, they just go missing, but one could only assume that they were dying. That's what made them hesitate. Unlike mortals—primordials were aware of angel existence, could see them, and could hurt them.

And if the Guardians were being killed, then the Reapers could be killed too. Azrael wouldn't be taking the risks of her Reapers if she could help it.

They could see from the shore as the many serpent heads ripped through the metal and wood of the ships like they were made of paper, pulling out bleeding forms impaled by their fangs.

The Reapers standing around Azrael cringed, visibly struggling with this manner of death.

All of them hadn't been around during the primordial occupation, they had no idea how to handle them. Unable to help the Guardians or to properly grab the mortals troubled souls brought them pain they had never experienced. What were they if they couldn't complete the tasks they were made for?

"What do we do?" Jared, another young Reaper asked Azrael.

Azrael didn't tear her eyes away from the carnage before them.

She wasn't sure if she could answer the question. Even during Paţukolai, they resisted killing the primordials, even while they slaughtered millions of humans, the angels couldn't bring themselves to participate in killing unless absolutely necessary.

But if they were free, and they were once again unleashing havoc upon the humans, what choice would they have? But killing it would not be easy. It would have to be Azrael.

"I'll go in and draw the Scylla's attention, do your best to get as many of the survivors out as you can. But don't get in the way, let's try to avoid more casualties," Azrael instructed.

She unfurled her wings, stretching them out—letting the air ruffle the black feathers. She hasn't flown with them in a while, she'll be out of practice.

Polly took a step towards her. "Let us help you, we can take it down together."

The other Reapers nodded, their own, smaller wings extending. Reapers weren't frequent fliers, but they had been trained to use them when necessary.

"Do as your archangel says." Uriel landed ten feet behind them, tucking in her owl-like wings slightly, but keeping them visible and ready.

They all turned towards her as she walked towards them. Her long copper hair tied back into a tight bun and her black and brown combat leathers in place of her usual attire. Her icy azure eyes locked on Azrael's black pair.

"Figured you might want help," she said, a deadly smirk forming on her face as she surveyed the Scylla thrashing in the water. "I've missed this beast."

Azrael looked her younger sister up and down. The two of them didn't usually battle together. And Azrael would be lying to herself if she didn't prefer the company of Uriel's twin Jophiel.

Both of them are equally temperamental, but Uriel had a cruelty streak that was second only to Lucifer.

"How'd you find us?"

Uriel shrugged, crouching down to view the water from a different angle, using her enhanced eyesight to survey the tangled mess ahead in a clearer view.

"I went to the Gates to meet you, they told me you were here."

"You remember how to kill a Scylla?" Azrael asked.

She hovered her hands over her arms, as they moved down scaled armor coated the flesh. Azrael's legs coated in the same armor and an ethereal blade appeared attached to her hip.

Uriel raised an eyebrow. "We're killing it this time?"

"I don't think imprisonment is an option anymore." Was Azrael's only reply as she soared into the air with one large beat of her wings.

Uriel followed closely behind.

They neared the large fishing boat that the Scylla was currently ripping to shreds. Three Guardians were fending off the serpent heads as they lunged on them, snapping their sharp jaws towards any part of their body to drag them into the water.

When dodging one of the heads a Guardian ducked out of the way only to receive a bite in the shoulder from a hound head. The Guardian cried out as blood gushed out of the wound. He flung his blade back until it sliced into the hound head.

The Scylla screamed, the decaying female form rearing upwards to attack the Guardian with her fingernails.

Another Guardian blocked her, her blade straining against the force of the Scylla as it threw more of its body weight into the blow. The Guardian behind her clutched his shoulder, blood pouring from the wound onto the wet deck.

The female Guardian was panting, her muscles straining as the Scylla leaned further. The smell of rotting human flesh on its fangs.

The third Guardian's blade looked as though it were weighing heavily in his hands as he continued slashing and cutting at the Scylla's serpent heads. When he took one side glance at his struggling fellows, it cost him.

A serpent head lunged in and bit down on his leg. As he cringed against the pain, turning to slash its head, it dragged until he lost his footing. The head kept dragging right until the edge of the boat, and then he was pulled under the water. The Guardian thrashed but was already feeling the blood loss from the bite mixed with his exhaustion.

He wouldn't make it.

Azrael lunged into the water, extending a hand towards him. He reached back and clasped her arm. Azrael sent a blast of lashing light downwards to the serpent head that still held the Guardian by the leg, the force severing its head from the body.

Azrael pulled upwards until they both jolted out of the water. Her wings not missing a beat got them back in the air. She threw the Guardian with one arm outward into the sky like a sack of grain. Polly, the reaper, not far behind her caught him mid-air, supporting his weak body with an arm around his waist and his arm around her shoulder.

Azrael didn't wait to see if he made it, she just flew straight to the boat where Uriel had landed between the Scylla and the other two Guardians. The one still bleeding badly.

She unsheathed the two long-swords from behind her back, eyeing the Scylla's rotting face with a roguish grin on her face.

"Been a long time, old friend," Uriel chirped.

All the Scylla's limbs and heads focused on Uriel, the only sign that it too recognized an old foe.

"Still just as ugly, I see."

The Scylla let out a guttural screech. The hound heads moved towards Uriel first to rip her limbs from her body. But Uriel was stronger than average angels.

She swung and dove with smooth grace, despite the slippery deck under her feet. Every attack from the Scylla missed, and occasionally resulted in a loss of a hound head or two.

While Uriel fought it off Azrael landed, approaching the two Guardians who watched, their eyes laden with shock and horror.

Azrael assessed the male Guardian's injured shoulder.

"Can you fly?" she asked. The Guardian pressed into the wound further, attempting to stand but winced and dropped again.

"I don't think so," he said.

Azrael turned to the female Guardian, her black hair clung to her head and there were a few tears in her clothing, but no obvious injuries.

"You?" Azrael nodded to her.

She nodded. "I can fly, but I don't think I'm strong enough to carry him." She made eye contact with him, and sorrow filled her eyes. "I'm too weak to winnow," she conceded.

A screech sounded behind them, when Azrael looked she saw Uriel swinging her swords at incredible speeds, lashing open the Scylla from every angle. Azrael may not need to help her. Before she could decide to carry the Guardian herself Jared dropped behind them with a soft thud.

He nodded to Azrael, reaching down to assist the male Guardian to his feet.

"I'll get them out." The Guardian groaned against the pain, but stood, the female Guardian went to his other side to help support his weight, her wings extended.

Jared looked about ready to fly when Azrael ordered, "Fly until you can winnow, then come back for the other survivors."

Jared stiffened. He sighed, lifting his remorseful eyes to hers.

"There are no more survivors." And then he and the Guardian flapped their wings, lifting the injured Guardian with them.

They flew up until they were well out of reach from the Scylla before Jared winnowed them out in a brief flash of light.

Azrael turned to the Scylla, who was bleeding sticky violet blood, but still fighting. Uriel hadn't killed it yet.

Azrael flew up to join her, "Taking your time?" she asked, frustration coating her tongue.

Uriel grinned wickedly and took another long slash cutting off the head of a hound.

"Just enjoying my last tussle with a Scylla." Uriel sang.

But this wasn't supposed to be enjoyable. Even the death of a primordial beast should be abhorrent.

Death was a regular part of Azrael's existence, but never death through enjoyment. Angels didn't enjoy killing with their own hands, at least they shouldn't enjoy it. Another reason why Uriel was one of Azrael's least favorite archangels.

Azrael extended her angel blade and began tracing the symbol for death in Enochian on it, her eternal light pulsing it to life. To plunge the blade into the Scylla's heart would permanently end its life, its death would be sealed by the sigil.

She flew higher above the Scylla, Uriel keeping its heads and forms busy. She back turned and plunged down like a bullet through the tangled limbs with the blade out, twisting around any obstacles in her path until the sharp end of the blade found its mark.

The Scylla and all its heads and limbs stilled following the blow. Azrael saw the sigil burn brighter for only a moment and then it disappeared altogether. She withdrew it from the Scylla's heart and backed away. Uriel halted her assault as well.

The open wound in its chest was the first thing to blacken and dissolve, spreading outward until the entire body of the Scylla succumbed, turning to black ash and floating away in the wind or dissolving into the sea.

Mere moments, and Azrael and Uriel were the only beings remaining in the air. The ship below rocked but stayed afloat. Uriel chuckled and slid her swords behind her back.

"Well then. I haven't had that much fun in a while."

But all Azrael could think of was the death that now leeched from this encounter, and likely from others around the world.

"Your compassion is overwhelming, Uriel." her reply dry, monotone.

Uriel shrugged, "Shall we carry on with our meeting?"

Azrael surveyed the area, seeing the debris left behind by other mangled ships and the mess that they now needed to rectify. Starting with collecting as many of the souls that fell as possible, and then moving on to alter the minds of witnesses. A mythical monster wouldn't peg well in the mortal world, so a new explanation would be needed.

"First we need to clean up," Azrael stated.

She could already spot Jared, Polly and a few other Reapers and Thrones flying to them from the shore.

"Isn't that what the insubordinates are for?" Uriel mocked.

Azrael glared at Uriel's still amused demeanor.

"Can you at least attempt to show some respect? This isn't a game, or entertainment."

Uriel rolled her eyes, waving her off. "Whatever, Azrael. Send me a message when you're ready to talk business."

Without giving Azrael a chance to stop her, Uriel soared upwards and then was gone in a wink of flashing light. Typical of her to leave when the *fun* ended, heaven forbid she actually help with the aftermath. Uriel could be a spoiled thorn in her side sometimes.

Azrael pinched the bridge of her nose, taking in a deep sigh. Not all of the archangels could be perfect, she supposed. In fact, none of them were. But Uriel was just annoying.

TWENTY-ONE
Heather

I WAS OUT FOR ALMOST TWO DAYS.

The last memory I had was of Daevas and I venturing into my family garden. And then he was gone, and I was living my memories out like dreams . It didn't feel like two days, but when I awoke it was clear that I had missed out on a lot.

I was on the lower floor of the warehouse, watching from a bench as Iaoel and Seere sparred in the center of the blue training section.

They told me about everything that had happened since my memory walk with Daevas. Gabriel's outburst, the information they learned about so-called relics that might be behind Mason's death, and the release of the primordials.

And then there was the little bit of information that I might be *half-angel.*

"A Nephilim?" I asked.

Seere chuckled as she ducked and weaved around Iaoel until she was behind them. Iaoel pivoted to block the new swing sent their way.

"No matter how many times you say it, you always sound just as shocked as the first time, chickpea."

Chickpea. Seere's new nickname for me. I'm sure it won't be the last one I receive.

“You can hardly blame her.” Iaoel stated as their blades clashed together in a loud ring.

Both of them were small in stature, but clearly that had no effect on their combat skills.

Seere wasn’t even breaking a sweat.

“Sure, but at this point if we tell her she’s actually a squirrel it wouldn’t be any different,” she teased.

I tried to not take that as an insult.

I don’t know how, but today I felt less overwhelmed by everything. I woke up feeling more comfortable in my own skin, and the butterflies in my stomach no longer bother me when I was around the angels and demons.

Maybe after so much shock, I just started to be numb.

Iaoel continued to keep Seere’s blade from moving an inch, but Seere had other plans. Before Iaoel could react Seere’s fist connected with their nose and they quickly retreated back. Not one for playing fair, I guess.

Seere didn’t miss a beat before retracting another blade, one that looked like an eastern scimitar. How many weapons did she have on her?

She kicked off her feet and immediately began running towards the shocked Iaoel. And when Iaoel saw her coming they bent to prepare, but Seere leapt over them, spinning her body mid-air.

Iaoel didn’t have enough time to react until Seere’s feet were once again on the ground behind her, and both her blades were poised against her throat.

Iaoel chuckled. “I see your reputation held no falsehoods,” they said.

Seere smirked and retreated her blades back into their sheaths.

“You should see me when I’m actually trying,” she joked.

It was a decent distraction to watch them spar. The demons and angels were faster than humans, so catching any small glimpse at their combat strategies was as exciting as watching a sporting match.

It helped ease the impending consternation that prickled my skin when thinking about what ran through my veins.

Iaoel grabbed a towel and wiped the sweat from their brow.

“So, if I’m half-angel, does that mean I have abilities, like…powers?” I asked warily.

What would it be like to have the power to summon light like Gabriel? Or even fire like Kale? To alter emotions and memories like Daevas? I didn’t even know fully what the others could do, if any potential power I had would match them.

If I did…would I even want that?

“Your angel parent was a Nymph, with an affinity for nature and basic magic. It’s unlikely that the diluted version of their power would be significant. More likely than not you may have acquired the ability to perform magic, maybe even use runes and sigils,” Iaoel explained.

Seere looked like she was ready to go again, bouncing up and down on the balls of her feet.

“But the only evidence we’ve seen that suggests that you have any angelic grace is that you understand our languages. Your grace also might have been why you saw Mason die, the Guardian bond would’ve been amplified by it,” they concluded.

Angel grace.

Iaoel had explained it to me earlier. An essential piece of the almighty's soul that fueled angel power. The only way I could comprehend it was to visualize it mentally. I imagined it like a silver fluid that mixed with regular blood.

I wondered if it were possibly to actually see it outside of the body.

I watched Seere and Iaoel reset the sparring ring back to normal. Seere's aura never appeared to me like it did with Gabriel and Kale.

The only hints I got that she wasn't human was the unnatural stillness, the predatory gaze she sometimes gave me, and the ever so subtle smell of burnt rubber that trailed from her when she walked by.

I sighed. "I guess I was hoping for something with a little more *umph*."

I rested my cheek on my fist, casually browsing through my journal for the fourteenth time.

Seere twirled a long sword around her limbs as if it couldn't touch her.

"We can't always be that lucky." She observed me, and probably saw the helplessness there.

I was half-angel and all I had to show for it was being a language translator. How pathetic. Especially with creatures like the vetala running around.

She pointed at me with her blade. "If it makes you feel any better, I'm practically as powerless as you, and I still get by just fine."

I huffed. "Yeah, you still have quite a few advantages I think. A demon is a lot better off than a weak human."

"*You* are your only weakness," she stated, even Iaoel glanced at her at that. "If you want, I can teach you a few defenses."

Iaoel stiffened and spun so fast their head might have fallen off. "That. Is not a good idea."

"Why not? She's already been attacked more than once, that happening again is inevitable, it wouldn't kill her to know a few moves that will at least give her a chance," Seere explained.

Iaoel rubbed their temples. "Even so, she still has human reflexes that will slow her down. If anything, she'll just keep her opponent entertained as they tear her to pieces. You'd be teaching a mouse how to fight off a bobcat."

"That doesn't matter. An advantage, no matter how small, can mean the difference between life and death. Even against the supernatural. Besides, she is only half-human, her odds are already better."

Seere looked at me with a wolfish grin on her face.

"What do you say?"

I gulped.

Having at least some things under my belt couldn't hurt, I supposed. But after watching the two of them tussle, maybe Iaoel was right.

"Um, I guess." I conceded.

Seere flicked the blade upwards motioning me to stand. I put my journal on the concrete floor and dusted off my pants.

I was wearing jeans and a blouse. Not exactly fighting attire. I gestured to my clothing.

"Should I change?" I asked.

Seere waved me off, putting the large blade down so that her hands were completely free. She walked onto the sparring pads.

"Your attacker isn't going to wait for you to change. You should learn how to fight in any article of clothing, even nude if you must. If you want to keep going after this, we'll spend a day in gowns so you can learn to fight like that."

"Charming," I grunted as I walked slowly onto the sparring pads.

"She's right. It's one thing to prepare for a fight, it's another to have no choice in the time or place," Iaoel chimed.

They sat cross-legged on the edge of the sparring ring, perching their face on their wrapped fists.

I looked at Seere, who looked like she was in her element. The wild grin on her face was unnerving, and the churning in my stomach began to make me regret this decision already. She tilted her head to the side, scanning my posture.

"First thing to know is you need to stay grounded, losing your footing in a fight is the quickest way to lose. Spread your feet and bend your knees. Good. Now it is important to take in as much information about your opponent as possible in split seconds. Note the sides they lean most of their body weight in, look for any potential weak spots."

She began walking towards me and I stiffened.

"Relax, I'm just going to point some out."

She put a hand on the small of my back and pushed. I adjusted my posture, and she released when I reached her approval.

"You won't likely be able to out-fight your opponent, you'll need a lot more training to do that. So for now, you should be thinking about ways to disable your opponent long enough to run away. Aim for high-nerve areas that will slow them down. These can change depending on your position. For example..."

Her foot hooked underneath my ankle and in one swoop I was on my back. She stood over me and lifted her feet to point out her ankles.

"If you're down, and you have a blade go for the Achilles heel. Supernaturals will be able to heal, but an injury like that will slow them down enough for you to get away. As soon as you do that, roll and bolt away from them as fast as you can so they can't grab you," she explained.

I noted it and nodded. I sat up and she put out her hand to stop me from rising all the way.

"If you don't have a blade, or if you're tied up, use their balance against them. Throw them off, shove between their legs or kick the back of their knees. If you have to, as they bend over to catch their balance, shove your fists or even your head upwards with all the force you can muster to break their nose."

"It'll hurt, but you'll live, and it could give you the time you need," Iaoel added. "You'd rather break a bone than end up dead."

I nodded. Seere reached down and gripped my hand—lifting me till I stood with no effort.

"Soft spots, an easy way to remember them is by using what I call *FAST KING*. Fast—F is fingers, A is ankles, S is solar plexus," she tapped the spot just at my stomach. "T for throat. King—K is knees, I for eyes, N for nose, and G for groin. Got it?" she asked.

"Fast King. Fingers, ankles, stomach, throat. Knees, eyes, nose, and groin. Got it." I repeated.

"Good. Retain that and you just might survive," she teased.

I recited it in my head over and over. This certainly wasn't knowledge I ever thought to learn, but my always-eager mind slurped it up like fine wine.

"Now if you're standing and your assailant has a hold of you, and you're facing them, gouge out their eyes. Don't be afraid to inflict as much damage as possible. If they let you go, don't be shy and jab them in the nose with this."

She lifted my hand and pointed out the area at the connecting point of my wrist and palm.

"Humans in the military learn to do this to kill their assailant, in a supernaturals case, you'll be lucky to break their nose. But a quick and hard jab to the throat will also incapacitate them. If after all that they still have a hand on you, a hard knee to the balls will do the trick."

She recited all this information and it was truly fascinating how natural it all seemed to her.

Remind me to take a self-defense class when I return to normal humanity. I thought to myself.

"If they're holding you from behind, use your heel to step on their toes, elbow to jab their stomach, and the back of your head to break the nose. Do all of them immediately after the other, don't stop hitting and jabbing until they lose their grip on you," she instructed.

Seere turned me around and wrapped her arms around me to trap me.

"Okay, now get out of my grip."

"Wait, what? Like, right now? Full force?" I asked.

"How else will you actually learn?" she asked, as if it was obvious.

I noted the way her hand gripped my wrist and her arm tightened around my torso.

"I don't want to hurt you."

She laughed and my face filled with heat.

I guess it would be silly for a human to care whether they hurt a demon or not. Even Iaoel appeared to grin with mild amusement.

"Trust me, chickpea. I've been hurt *far* worse, this will be the equivalent of a paper cut for me."

Geez…makes me wonder what sort of hell she went through growing up.

Hell, that's what, stupid. My inner monologue joked.

I sighed and readied myself to jab her.

"Remember," she said, "—fast and unexpected. Preparation is your enemy in this case."

I nodded and then stomped my heel down, but it only met concrete. I then tried to jab my elbow backward, but it met open air.

Shit.

"Nice try. *A* for effort. Don't anticipate your moves, or at least don't make it obvious, otherwise they'll see it coming a mile away. If you're taking a breath just before a blow, they'll know it. If you're choosing to do something, don't think about it long enough for them to anticipate it. Just act," she stated.

Seere released me and spun me to face her. She grounded herself and then gripped both my wrists.

"Get out of my grip," she instructed.

I only had a split second to think about my strategy. I shoved all my energy into shoving my hands downwards, but her grip held and when I shoved them back into the air her hands went up with them, still holding.

"Nice. But you gotta—"

I didn't give her a chance to continue before I hooked a foot around her ankle then kicked.

It threw her off, but I didn't think about the direction it would go. Instead of her falling back and losing her grip on my hands, instead she dragged me down with her.

She landed on her ass and I fell on top of her. She quickly spun us, never loosening her grip on my wrists, and then she was on top of me, straddling me.

Her legs hooked backwards and pinned mine down, and then she crossed my hands until they formed a cage across my chest, pinned to the concrete on either side of my head. She was laughing, and I was panting.

Well, so much for *that*.

"Excellent! You threw off my balance, I'd call that progress. But you didn't think about your own. A lesser fighter might've fallen for it enough to give you another opportunity to break free," she explained above me.

From this angle I could see all the many tattoos that covered her neck, the side of her head and trailing down her arms. They were different from Daevas'.

His were of tentacles, snake heads and fire. Seere's were barbed wire, bones and words, demonic languages written in every crevice.

I could also see the scars. Some rippled and bubbled from burns, some were sharp cuts from blades. Others were jagged and deep. Her piercings and tattoos covered them from a distant eye, but up close they were stark against her skin. I couldn't even imagine the amount of blood loss she suffered. Underneath them though, there were freckles and beauty marks.

Seere was already a beautiful being in a unique way. Without those scars—she might have rivaled the angels.

Seere noticed me staring and her brown eyes flickered an ash gray color. "I did say I've been through worse, didn't I?" she asked quietly.

"How much worse?" I countered.

Her eyes were lethal, but something else lingered there, a speck of suffering that I didn't understand.

She didn't answer, that told me enough.

Her eyes glanced sideways, distantly and then she was lifting off me. She extended a hand to help me up and I took it. Iaoel was watching us closely, but no worry was written on their face, only keen observation.

They hadn't missed a thing, but they weren't going to push it.

"We'll pick this back up again later. I need to be somewhere," Seere said as she walked towards the pentacle on the other side of the room. "In the meantime, do some strengthening exercises. Gaining some muscle will help you more in the long run," she instructed.

She blew a kiss towards the Angel of Sight. "Iaoel, my sweet, keep the bed warm for me," she cooed.

Iaoel snorted and shook their smiling head. "See you later, Seere."

A small pillar of ash smoke surrounded Seere for a moment and then disappeared along with her. A simpler winnow style than Kale's or Gabriel's. Iaoel was still shaking their head when I returned my gaze to them.

"Where'd she go?" I asked.

Iaoel shrugged, stretching their legs out in front of them.

"Probably off to join the Prince wherever he's off to. She can't get far on her own without him."

The *who*?

"Prince?" I called curiously.

Iaoel's gaze locked on mine and then widened with realization.

"Oh! Right. I guess no one told you. Kaleus—he's the Prince of Darkness," they said plainly.

I raised an eyebrow, still confused.

"The Heir Inferno?" They stated. I shook my head.

"He's the son of Lucifer. The *antichrist* if you want to reference a derogatory religious depiction."

Oh. My eyes bulged. I've been spending time with the devil's son?

"But I thought he wasn't a demon?"

Iaoel nodded. "Maybe that half-angel part of you is keener than we thought, it was trying to tell you something. He is Lucifer's son in the loosest definition, Daevas is one of Lucifer's *actual* sons. Technically Kaleus is no one's son. He wasn't born, he was created," Iaoel explained.

"Created from what?" I asked.

My heart was racing, the *antichrist*...no wonder his power is so much stronger than the others. And like most of the seeds of knowledge these immortal freaks were giving me, this bit was only increasing my long list of questions.

Iaoel bit their lip and narrowed their eyes.

"I think I'll leave the rest of the story for Kaleus to tell. I might have told you more than he might be comfortable with. Who knows, he might've had specific plans on how he was going to share this information with you and when. He does have a pension for the theatrics."

"Wait, why can't you just tell me now?"

Iaoel stood quickly and briskly made their way over to the pentacle.

"Seems my shift is over. Jade is upstairs getting lunch ready. I would recommend you spend your time doing what Seere instructed. Exercising will pass the time anyway." They waved as a pillar of light encircled them.

"Hey! Wait!" but they were gone.

And I was alone on the sparring pad. Within moments I could hear Jade upstairs humming.

I huffed. "This is why I prefer to be alone."

I sighed and walked over to the stairs. If I was going to work out, I was definitely going to change. As I slipped past a distracted Jade in the kitchen and walked down the hallway towards my bedroom door, I thought about what Iaoel had said.

Kale was the *prince* of hell? And not born like the other demons—but *created.*

In the religions I had studied, I recalled mentions of the antichrist being the spawn of the devil, meant to inherit the Inferno and bring about the apocalypse on earth.

When I entered my small concrete room, my instincts overpowered me and instead of changing I flipped open my laptop.

In my Christianity religion folder, I searched key words antichrist and *son of Lucifer*. The first results that popped up were relating to the bible prophecies that encircled his name. He was mentioned with many names.

The Little Horn and *The Prince Who is to Come* in Daniel, *Master of Intrigue*—that seemed about right.

In Thessalonians they call him *The One Who Brings Destruction*. I read further as it spoke of the antichrist's personality and nature.

"Daniel: seven-eight, 'This little horn had eyes like human eyes and a mouth that was boasting arrogantly.', okay, he is a bit arrogant can't argue with that," I recited out loud.

Most of what I found stated that he would spout falsities and blasphemy to claim power rather than through sheer force. Most of it sounded like religious babble, even describing him as a beast with horns, but perhaps these depictions were where the humans began going off the rails.

“—'and the dragon gave him his own power and throne and great authority.’ Revelation: thirteen-two.”

Dragon? Lucifer maybe?

So Kale wasn’t a demon. He wasn’t an angel. He wasn’t human. But he was something entirely different.

But what exactly?

And whatever he was, I wasn’t sure I should trust him?

TWENTY-TWO
Kale

WE WERE WORKING WITH WHAT information we had, which wasn't a lot.

We didn't know what these relics were, where they were, how many we had to find, or the potential power they possessed. We'd be lucky if digging through millions of years' worth of archives were actually going to give us more to work with.

My head was pounding. I couldn't shake the feeling that this was only the beginning. Like we were still at square one, while our adversary was a hundred squares ahead of us.

I would give my left arm just to know who was behind all of this—if it were one person. At least I could work with that.

How did I get involved in this anyway?

It was only a week ago I was going about my long and miserable existence as usual. Moving from one legion to the next inspecting their progress and reports. Boring as usual.

I was in the middle of teaching a mouthy lower-class demon a lesson when it happened. When even in the lowest pits of hell the echoing sounds of a scream and a rumbling deep in the dirt halted everything.

I didn't have to be summoned then. I willingly went to my father's office, Seere and Daevas in tow. Even the devil was stirred crazy, unsure how to comprehend the event that had occurred. Lillith was there, along with four of Lucifer's most trusted Fallen.

Lucifer was listening to the Opsalis. An orb stolen from heaven during the Fall that can tap directly into the supernatural web without permission. Satan was the only one allowed to use it, and it gave him the ability to listen and gain key information inconspicuously.

The Opsalis was usually locked up in Lucifer's vault, alongside rows of angel wings he took from the Fallen as proof of their loyalty after the Fall—and also as leverage when they didn't comply.

Only the holder could decipher the messages inside, to the rest of us outside the only evidence we saw of it working was the swirling of gray fog and golden streams inside it. Lucifer was listening intently, not paying attention to the others in the room.

The four Fallen that were there—Abaddon, Ipos, Sytry and Cain. Lucifer's high commanders. Many of the other Fallen contributed to demon breeding and soul acquiring. Not these four, they were what gave hell its reputation.

Abaddon dipped a small bow when I entered, the only one of the four that I had established a working relationship with. When or if I ever take over this realm, he'll likely be the only one that continues to work in my order.

I would happily demote Sytry and Cain, I was already shaping Seere and Daevas to take over for them when the time came. Ipos would be a pain, but I would take her over Lillith any day.

Seere and Daevas blended into the background, seating themselves on the couches against the dark walls next to Lillith. The swirling of the orb slowed to a stop, and it was only then that Lucifer deigned to acknowledge our arrival.

"It seems the Balance has been tipped in a rather intriguing manner." Lucifer grinned coldly as he eyed us all one by one.

It was rare that all of us would convene in the same room for long. An annual meeting usually was all we could manage, and it was done in a much more spacious venue where we could argue without melting the walls.

I crossed my arms across my chest, tapping my foot impatiently.

"Spare us the dramatic pandering, Lucifer." My voice was tight and low.

On my way here I had formed the cold exterior mask that I wore around him, constantly soothing the churning magma under my skin so he wouldn't see it.

That was always what it needed to be. Any sign that my inner fire was out of control was an opportunity for him to exploit. So, a cool calm was the only thing I would give him. That I would give any of them.

Lucifer chuckled. "A Guardian angel is dead. Murdered it seems."

I furrowed my brows and even felt the click of confusion come from my connection with Seere.

"Really?" I asked.

I turned to the four Fallen, who didn't give any indication of guilt or shock. Abaddon however, had enough curiosity in his expression to tell me that this was unusual.

Another reason I didn't like this particular group, their range of expressions were limited to utter boredom and icy calculation.

Lucifer glanced between them as well. "I'll leave it to Sytry and Ipos to investigate internally. Though I am already confident that none of our kind are to blame. In the meantime, I've been requested to meet with the almighty to discuss the matter."

"He's allowing you into heaven?" I asked pointedly.

Lucifer gave me a knowing smirk.

"The almighty isn't that stupid. Neutral territory," he replied.

Neutral meant that they likely were to meet in the mortal realm. I felt electricity spark up my veins, but I reigned it in. Lucifer didn't spend time among the mortals, but I did.

And in a way I considered it my territory, with no real claim to it. But I used it as a getaway from the hellhole.

Cain spoke next, "Will you be needing company, my liege?" he asked.

Ever the faithful dog. Or a crafty one. Lucifer seemed to have a similar thought process when our eyes locked.

"I know it's been a while since you've been on the surface, Cain, and you're just itching for another opportunity to shed blood. But I have no need for company, and I'd rather not have to deal with ending you when you attempt to escape," he purred.

Cain didn't show that he was disappointed or shocked. He only nodded numbly.

The last Fallen that escaped Lucifer's control had much better resources available to succeed. Cain was a brute, and not worthy of his position in my opinion. But I didn't decide those things—not yet anyway.

Lucifer went to the wall behind his desk and pressed his palm to it. A hiss sounded and then numerous sigils and wards glowed red across the wall. And then a door-sized section disappeared inward. Lucifer stepped a few feet inside the stone hallway and set the Opsalis on a shelf on the inner side.

When he stepped out of it the wall resealed behind him, the wards glowing once more before fading and the wall once again solid.

His vault was locked with his very essence, more than his blood. Not even Daevas or any of his other blood relatives could open it. But I could...as I was created with a piece of his essence.

I could. But I wouldn't. Not when the risk outweighed the rewards. Maybe one day when the circumstances were reversed.

"In the meantime, I'll leave Kaleus in charge." I held my breath. Crafty asshole. "You can handle the pit while I'm gone, can't you son?" he teased.

I wish I could melt those cunning eyes right out of their sockets. I responded by nodding, maintaining my cool composure even as the tips of my fingers sparked.

Ruling hell. That was my destiny.

Lucifer had never intended on being in-charge of that realm forever. It was a means to an end. He never revealed any of his true motives and intentions for the future with anyone, not even when I was the most loyal among his followers.

No, Lucifer invented what it was to be conniving and scheming.

He would tell half-truths in order to get others to do his bidding. It was how he convinced other angels to follow him to hell. One would assume that he wanted more power, as most of those with power wanted.

But I always thought it was more than that.

There was a time when all I wanted was my father's approval. I wanted to help him cripple the world and stand beside him in the ruin and rule alongside him.

I was a boy, and all I knew was fire and chaos. I had to learn the hard way that things aren't black and white. Evil can't be defined in only one way.

Lucifer learned something too from those early years. That I had acquired more traits from him than he intended, and that those traits and values were weapons that could be used against him.

The rebellious archangel learned the hard way that his creation wasn't someone that would be bent to his will.

I was so lost in my thoughts that I didn't hear Seere arrive, not until I heard her panting behind me. She coughed.

"Took you long enough," I chuckled.

She was bent over, taking in long deep gasps of air.

She glared up at me. "Oh I'm sorry, your *high-fuck-ness*. You know I can't get far on my own, it's not my fault you asked me to travel five thousand miles without warning. Someone had to stay with the mortal, so I had to leave without my angelic partner."

Seere finally caught her breath and walked up to stand next to me. She peered down off the glacier we stood on into the crack in the earth. The crack was so deep we couldn't see the bottom.

"So, this is Tyurma huh?"

"Yup," I answered.

The icy wind whipped past, hitting our faces like a thousand tiny needles. She shivered.

"Couldn't you choose a warmer prison to check out? Jeez, this makes me miss the pit."

I shook my head, grinning. "Nothing would make me miss the pit."

I waved my hand towards her, sending a small flicker of fire to bubble around her. I would have to continually use a bit of my power to maintain the bubble around her while we were here.

At least it would let me siphon some of the pressure off.

Seere, being a lower-class demon, couldn't summon enough power to keep herself warm in harsh climates such as this. She could pass as human if she wished to, but she would be bored.

I could see her joining a traveling circus or even entering a fight club to let off steam and burn energy. But even then she would have to hold back.

And that, would be a torture of its own for hell's most honed wrath demon.

I looked back down into the crack and held out my hand for her. "Shall we?"

She looked down and didn't look thrilled. "Are we winnowing in?"

I shook my head.

"We get to slide in." I waggled my eyebrows. Her pupils widened.

"Slide? What do you mean, sli—"

"Let's go!" I didn't give her another second to change her mind before I clutched her hand and jumped, dragging her down with me.

To her credit, she didn't scream, instead she gasped for air as we free fell into the icy fissure. As our bodies neared the jagged ice edge, I put a wall of hot air between it and us to slow our fall and to melt the ice enough to slide.

Down the frozen glide we went, far past where the light leaked in until there was only darkness. I let some embers escape my skin to help light the way, and after a few minutes of slick dropping our feet touched the bottom.

We stood and brushed off our clothes, the leather keeping us from being soaked, and the bubble of hot air I had around us easily dried any remaining moisture off. Seere tossed her blonde braids behind her shoulder and looked around.

"Still a child at heart, fire-boy," she joked.

I laughed.

"Always, beasty."

We stilled when we both felt it. The stirring. It was ahead of us, in the shadows. It was like the sound of shifting sand. Even the air felt shifty and dry. It was warmer down here, as if the ice above did nothing to freeze the beings down here.

“What exactly is imprisoned in this one?” Seere asked in a whisper.

The hairs on my arms rose, and even my fire dulled like it was shrinking away from what lay ahead. This place was more ancient that I was, older than even some of the archangels, feathers included. And whatever was in here predated the world he knew.

I swallowed down the heaviness gathering in my gut.

“From what I remember, there’s at least one Nuckelavee in here, some Chenoo, a few Strixes I think. I don’t remember the others,” I explained.

Seere eyed the space ahead of us, feeling that ancient energy I felt as well.

“I definitely didn’t pay enough attention in this part of our history lessons,” I chuckled.

“I reviewed some of the information before coming here, just to refamiliarize myself. Don’t worry, they aren’t hard to kill if we need to.”

She was by my side as we walked towards that energy, until we came face to face with a massive wall made of black chain links. It rippled and flowed like it was affected by the smallest change of air.

Beyond it, we could see nothing. But that didn’t mean nothing was there.

Seere reached out and touched the chain and quickly retreated her hand while sucking in a quick breath.

“Mmm, yeah don’t like that,” she said. “Felt like a white-hot needle shot through my spine,” Seere described as she shook out her hand.

“The prison is sealed by archangels, so I’m guessing a demon trying to mess with it would do that,” I teased.

She stuck her tongue out at me and crossed her arms.

“Well, it looks like it’s still sealed to me. These beasts haven’t gone anywhere since they were put here,” she said.

I nodded. “Not yet anyway.”

I stared past the chains and could have sworn I saw a feathered tail slither just beyond sight. The images of the primordials that we had were limited and not incredibly detailed, but perhaps the tail belonged to the Nuckelavee.

This place was eerie enough to make my stomach churn. I could only imagine what the other prisons were like if this one unnerved me so easily. It would certainly be interesting to have been around when these creatures walked the earth freely.

Would they make hell look like a kids bouncy house?

Who am I kidding, that’s terrifying too.

I eyed the chain wall. The metal resembled some of the black rock that fell from other worlds. Perhaps the archangels needed something not of this world to hold them. No doubt every inch of the prison was spelled and warded to keep them from trying to escape.

But some of them were opening, the seals of other prisons were being burst open. Who could accomplish it?

Curiosity soaked my skin, and I lead with it as I knelt and pressed my hand on the ground just an inch from the chain barrier. I summoned inside myself to the deeper core of molten ore that churned without end.

I speared into it just enough to pull out a thread of it and led it through my veins . It traveled up through my chest and down my shoulder and arm. I halted it at my wrist, the heat of it already started to sear the skin above it.

“What are you doing?” Seere asked.

I eyed the chain wall again, looking at the flawless black metal and every curve it made around each of its links.

“I’m trying something, just to see.”

I inched my fingers closer to the bottom links, and barely touched it. That one touch vibrated across the entire barrier and then rippled back to me. Through the connection, I saw every link, every bond that made it whole.

I didn’t feel pain though, not the way Seere described it. It was almost like it was testing me, and somehow I had passed its test, and therefore was not to be harmed by it.

Interesting.

Seere’s voice said in my head, *I hate it when you say that.*

Or she may have said it out loud, I wasn’t sure. I didn’t feel completely in my own body, part of me was now in the chain.

The piece of molten core I threaded to my wrist was melting its way through my skin, so I loosened it once more—letting it split evenly across all my fingers until it rested against the tips in smaller orbs. The orbs then touched the chain links where my fingers connected to it.

I heard a hiss come from the contact, but then the entire chain wall began to ripple continuously, getting faster the longer I held my hand there.

Seere backed up a step from the wall.

“Um, Kale, what are you *doing*?” she asked again.

I didn't answer her. I was too focused on the feeling of the chains as they responded to the fire by clicking open, one by one, downward. Slowly as the chains unlocked from top to bottom, the wall began to disappear into nothing.

I was too busy watching and feeling the experience that I didn't notice the swishing sound of something beyond moving. But I did hear the metal ring of Seere's blade as she freed it from its sheath into her hand.

Something pale blue flashed in my peripheral vision, I turned in time to see Seere swing her blade in time to stop the frozen bodied Chenoo that lunged for the opening. It fell back with a gurgle but didn't lunge again.

That's when I saw it, the owner of the feathered tail I saw earlier moved forward to where we could see it.

A Nuckelavee.

With the body of an enormous bear, only instead of fur it was covered in a rainbow variety of feathers, and its muscles underneath bulged. Its head jutted out like a wolf's and it had four large canines that were as large as an elephant's tusks. Its feathered tail whipped back and forth as it eyed Seere at the largest point of the still-opening chain wall.

As its tail swished closer past me, I saw that amongst the feathers there was also a sharpened barb at the end, with a bead of venom seeping from the tip.

Shit.

"Kale! Close the damn gate!" Seere yelled as she freed another blade to prepare for a potential attack.

I turned my gaze back to the links I still held and focused on them.

Close. I thought.

Nothing happened.

The Nuckelavee got closer, drool seeping from its mouth and its tail swishing faster. If it hit her, what would that venom to do her? Could we even heal it? I closed my eyes and shoved my consciousness into the braided chains.

Seal. Lock. Fucking close, damn it!

The chains only hummed in response, and then I realized, I used my molten core to open it, and the chain sucked it right up.

I would need another thread to close it.

I heard the ringing of Seere's blade swishing in the air as the creature neared but I kept my eyes closed as I reached back into myself for another thread of my inner core.

It took immense focus to draw from my core without accidentally unleashing too much of it. I wasn't about to lose control now.

As the thread worked its way to my arm, I heard Seere let out a small squeak as she lunged out of the way of the poison-tipped tail that whipped towards her.

I felt the heat of the thread as it slid through my veins into my hand and up into my fingers. Seere shuffled again, grunting with the effort.

"Fucking hell," she muttered.

I opened my eyes to press the core back into the chains when I saw more of the Chenoo and even a Strixe heading for the opening while Seere was busy with the Nuckelavee.

I broke my focus just barely and used my hand to shove a wall of fire between them and Seere. They recoiled away from it. Enough that I could let it down and concentrate back on the chains. I felt the ripple and hum of the chains as the thread of core worked on them.

Lock. I thought again, and this time the chains listened.

I felt and heard every click as its motion reversed and the disappearing links reappeared upwards, sealing the opening as it went. The Nuckelavee was whipping its tail through the opening again, Seere ducking each blow.

As the links formed, they touched its tail. It let out a rattling roar in pain and then backed away. Its tail now tucked closely underneath as it shrunk back into the darkness.

Within a few seconds the chain wall completed its formation once more, sending one last shimmering ripple as it secured in place.

I took my hand off of it and took in a deep breath. Seere was gawking at it, panting for air as well.

She sheathed her blades and turned to glare at me.

"You just *had* to open it, didn't you?"

I shrugged. "I didn't actually think it would work."

She rolled her eyes. "I could have died!"

"But you didn't," I chuckled.

I rose onto my feet and brushed the icy ground from my pants. She trotted over to me at punched me in the shoulder.

"Ugh, you're such a—" she sighed and didn't finish the sentence.

I looked back at the chain barrier as it once again flowed in an invisible breeze.

Seere bit her lip. "So, you can open the prisons, that's new."

I snorted. "Yeah. Interesting, but not exactly helpful in our current investigation. I'm sure it'll just put me higher on Gabriel's private suspect list."

"I'm pretty sure you were already at the top of it, right below Lucifer," she joked.

I nodded in agreement. I had each of the archangels on my own suspect list as well, along with half of the Fallen. Better to prepare for the worst than to just assume they were all innocent.

The primordials behind this prison have since returned back to the darkness beyond it, retreating into their eternal cell. Let's hope whoever is opening them doesn't get them all open.

This was one of the milder prisons, and these particular monsters weren't nearly as high on the lethal food chain. If these got out, what would the others be capable of?

I knelt down again and began drawing lines, circles, and dots on the ground.

Seere jolted. "Don't you dare open it again," she snarled.

I laughed. "Relax, I'm just installing an alarm. If someone comes to unseal this one, the alarm will alert me, and hopefully if that happens, I can get back in time to reseal it and catch our guardian slayer," I explained.

Once the symbol was finished it glowed for a second and then faded. I stood and extended my hand to my best friend.

"We should get back," I said.

She looked up towards where we slid in and her face crinkled in wonder and disgust.

"And how do we do that exactly?" she asked.

"Winnow, of course."

She glared. "I thought we couldn't winnow in and out of here?"

I grinned like a wildcat.

"Don't be absurd, of course we can. I just wanted to slide in."

I giggled when she began smacking me like the little spitfire she was.

“You stupid, arrogant fire-hole!”

She joined my laughter for a minute before we calmed down and clasped hands.

“Ah, but you love me.”

Seere snorted, tossing her braids behind her shoulder.

“I hope you choke on your balls while I shove them down your throat.”

I threw back my head and laughed whole heartedly as I shifted us into the Ethereal and bent air and space until we reached the warehouse floor.

TWENTY-THREE

HEAVEN WAS LIKE ALL THINGS—LAYERED.

There was the part of heaven specifically designed for the mortal souls—paradise. Then there was the layer where the angels grew and trained, from there they would descend into the other realms for assignment. Other layers included the Eternal Depository, the Creation Suite, and the Empyrean Manor.

The layers were like rooms, separated only by doors that the almighty had fashioned out of pure energy. The rooms, along with all the realms of the universe, were held together by the careful threading of the almighty Eternal and the Balance. Constantly working in sync to allow for life to thrive.

Before, the universe was unchecked and chaotic. Energy buzzed about with no real direction or purpose. But God found a purpose in his creations, and now his creations were in danger.

He spent most of his time in the Empyrean Manor these days, monitoring the situation as best he could while still keeping everything intact. Luckily, it wasn't as bad as it could be. A few attacks here and there, but nothing that his angels couldn't handle.

The flap of wings signaled Michael's arrival on the terrace. The almighty remained inside, swiping past the screen he was watching. Michael walked in through the open doors and found him. His wings already tucked in tight.

"I see you've made some improvements. Upgrading?" he asked.

God swiped again, smiling. "Even heaven needs to keep up with the times. How is the rest of the universe fairing, Michael?"

"No immediate conflicts to be found. Seems to be centered on earth," Michael explained.

The almighty nodded and swiped his screen again. Human populations weren't slowing down, and his angels were keeping the attacks from becoming public, masquerading them as other disasters to keep the panic at bay.

Fangelsi and Nessus prison were open, that much they knew. The creatures that came from those prisons were smaller, but dangerous, nonetheless.

"Are you sure I can't be of more assistance here?" Michael asked, he still stood close to the terrace doors. His arms folded and back straight.

God shook his head. "Gabriel and Jophiel have it covered."

"Even with the attacks?"

He lifted his gaze from the screen to lock with Michael's.

"We have some angels at our disposal to keep the primordials at bay. Only a couple prisons have been opened. We'll manage. Though, it would be helpful if you could go to Fangelsi and Nessus and get those seals back up, I can instruct the others to try to capture the primordials and get them back."

"I suppose I could do that," Michael replied.

"Michael," Gabriel said as he and Jophiel walked into the room from the hallway. "What are you doing here?" he asked.

Jophiel was already pulling out a chair and adjusting her pantsuit to sit in it. Michael straightened further upon facing his youngest brother. Gabriel couldn't help but feel that all-too-familiar sense of smallness.

In the alliance, even alongside a being like Kaleus, Gabriel felt equal and important. But in the presence of his more revered and far more experienced brother, Gabriel was next to nothing.

"Checking in, reporting the status of the universe. Offering help where I can," Michael said simply.

The almighty flicked his eyes between the two and then to his screen again.

"I was just suggesting to Michael that he try to reinstate the seals on the open prisons. Maybe we can contain the primordials before it gets too hectic," the almighty explained.

"Containment didn't seem to work the last time. Those prisons were meant to be permanent," Jophiel said.

Michael nodded. "I'll look into some stronger wards and barriers, maybe we can increase their efficiency this time."

Michael shifted on his feet a bit before turning back towards the terrace doors, his wings beginning to unfold once more.

"I'll take my leave. Notify me if you should need my assistance," he said to Gabriel.

Gabriel felt a subtle jab from that comment. Although he knew Michael didn't intend it, in his eyes Gabriel was nothing more than a boy. Compared to his battle experience, Gabriel had yet to leave the training ring.

Gabriel nodded instead of replying. And then with one flap of his wings, Michael was gone. When Gabriel gazed back at the almighty, he was staring at him. "You have news of the Guardian's killer?" he asked.

"Only an idea. Perhaps a tool they are using to aid their violence." Gabriel answered.

The almighty's brow rose. "Oh?"

"We have a few questions for you. Lucifer mentioned that there are relics, Eternal relics that had great power. And that anyone with these relics could enhance their own abilities. Could you tell us what you know of them?" Jophiel asked.

God's eyes reflected instant recognition. "The Eternal relics? I haven't thought of those objects in some time."

"You think our adversary could have found one? Used it to kill Mason?" Gabriel pegged.

God nodded. He scratched his chin, lost in thought.

"The relics were remnants of the universe's energy, what was used before any of the Eternals, angels or archangels existed to keep the Balance.

During the earliest Creation, we split them into fragments and scattered them across the realms to as a foundation for the Balance," he explained.

Gabriel sat down in an open chaise, processing this new information.

"A safety precaution, in-case our abilities and forces fell through and there was nothing else to hold it together. Really, after the Tear, there wasn't any need for them. I've completely forgotten about them until now."

The almighty paused, looking at something on his screen and then swiping it away.

"I suppose, if a supernatural being had hold of one, then they could potentially yield their raw energy to an advantage."

"You said you split them?"

"Originally, it was one object, we called it the *Vil Kal*. While the Eternals were still forming, the *Vil Kal* is how the Krλnn mended the universe. But once we, the Eternals, completed our physical forms, we took to maintaining the Balance. Splitting it into pieces and scattering them seemed a safe way to disperse the energy for optimal coverage, in the event of a failure."

Gabriel narrowed his brows. "I'm afraid I don't fully understand."

The almighty waved him off. "It is difficult to explain the happenings of the Before. The Krλnn and *Vil Kal* preceded the Eternals, and most of what it is comprehensible," he explained.

"And the split pieces…"

"Are what *you* call the Eternal relics. Before you ask me, Gabriel, what they are, I cannot help you. Once they were split, the relics took different forms, what they were when they were split is not what they are now."

Disappointment and dread flooded through Gabriel's heart with the weight of a thousand worlds. How can the alliance have any hope of finding them?

How did the Guardian killer find one?

"If you're asking about them, am I to assume you are trying to locate them?" he asked.

Jophiel and Gabriel nodded in sync.

"At least to narrow down which one our unknown Guardian killer has and hopefully be capable of countering the power they've gained from the one they have in possession," Jophiel added.

"I haven't handled them in a long time. Their whereabouts are unknown to me," the almighty stated.

Gabriel sighed. So much for that.

"Although—" God started. "A long while ago, not long after the Fall, I did give Chamuel the only one that remained in heaven. Lucifer was running off with objects of great power from our Depository on his way out, objects like the Opsalis. I gave Chamuel the relic to avoid Lucifer getting his hands on it and corrupting it in hell."

Gabriel and Jophiel exchanged glances.

"We have to pay Chamuel a visit, then," Jophiel mutter

The almighty nodded.

A sweeping shrill came from the screen. God rushed around his desk and swiped. The images appeared on a bigger screen for all three of them to see.

Images of Azrael and Uriel fighting off a *Scylla*, debris of sinking ships and injured, bleeding angels.

"The Scylla was imprisoned in Sheol. That makes three prisons open now. The situation is growing worse," the almighty stated.

Gabriel observed the images. It looked like it had caused a lot of damage, and a lot of souls would've been lost.

"Do they need assistance?" Gabriel asked.

He pulled on his thread to Azrael. He asked and she answered.

"No, they took it down. But only three angels made it out alive," the almighty replied.

"What else was in Sheol?" Jophiel asked, observing every detail of the images before them.

"Most of the large, water-bound primordials. Leviathans, nyaids, hags. We had the cyclops' in there, as well," God answered.

Three leviathans if Gabriel's memory served him right. Sharp-toothed sea-serpents, slippery and very hard to catch. During The Tear, they only managed to entrap three. The others had to be killed.

Hags were the size of human heads. They were a grotesque form of water-goblins. Their skin was mud brown and leathery, with ten tentacles each. If they got their grip on you, those tentacles would inject microscopic barbs that would hook inside and release a venom that would start digesting you from the inside out. It was through those putrid tentacles they would consume their prey. But they traveled in schools, and they were highly territorial.

Nyaids were a lot more elusive, more singular. But would inflict an equally terrifying death. They had no real solid form—more they were a patch of milky goo. In the time they lived on earth freely, they would float atop the surface of water, almost like a patch of seafoam. As soon as a living organism touched it, the Nyaid would wrap around its body like a second skin—cutting off the air and nutrients.

Nyaids were slow eaters, they would keep their prey encased until it eventually rotted. That's how the archangels were able to catch them, once a nyaid had hold of prey, it was incapacitated until it finished its feeding process.

The cyclops was as the Greeks described. One eyed giants. They used to live in caves on the shores of rock islands where mortal sailors would seek shelter from the oceans fury. Cyclops' were a lot less versatile and frightening. Brute force and an appetite were all they needed in their world. Their small brains actually made them some of the easiest primordials to imprison.

Primordials were cruel creatures without bounds. Basest of monsters with one unifying instinct, to kill. Some for simpler reasons such feeding. But others with larger brain capacity indulged in the pain they inflicted.

Humans in comparison were more civilized. They felt empathy and were family oriented. The combinations of these creatures didn't work out well.

In today's times, humans would be completely unprepared for the horrors they would be facing.

Jophiel stood from her chair. "Well, we shouldn't waste any more time."

Gabriel nodded and looked back at his almighty father.

"How many pieces did you split the *Vil Kal* into?" he asked. "That would help a great deal."

"Six."

He nodded once more before following Jophiel to the door.

"Gabriel, Jophiel," he said, halting their departure. "Keep your search for the relics discreet. We do not need any other supernatural beings looking for them. It would also be best to try to keep Lucifer from attaining any further knowledge on their whereabouts," he instructed.

"If he is the one who brought them to your attention, he likely hopes to gain possession of them through your alliance. Be selective with whom in your alliance you pursue them," the almighty finished.

Jophiel scowled. "I couldn't agree more." Then she locked eyes with her younger, more amiable brother. "To Paris, then."

Paris. The city of love. And logically Chamuel's current location.

PART THREE
PRESENCE OF MIND

TWENTY-FOUR
Heather

I SPENT SO LONG RESEARCHING the antichrist, that I hadn't realized that no one had come to check on me for *hours*. When I finally glanced away from my computer screen and at the clock, I realized how long I was in my room completely undisturbed.

Either that meant everyone was too busy to notice my absence, or maybe they assumed that I needed some alone time. Either way, I was grateful for it.

I had actually changed my clothes, intending on working out like I had planned before I got lost in my computer. Some comfortable, leggings, a sports bra, and a track jacket. After tying the laces on my running shoes, I swooped half of my cropped hair into a bun.

It had been a while since I went running. Over a year, really. My academic life always seemed to consume my time, I spent more time indoors than I used to.

My mom would scorn me silly if she knew that. The woman *hated* being inside, if she wasn't writing her books, she was in the garden, knee-deep in the dirt.

Which I suppose made more sense now that I knew she was actually a Nymph. The garden had been her connection to the angel life she led in secret.

That thought made me sad. I wished she'd have told me who she was. Perhaps I could've been closer to her, maybe if I had tried harder with that relationship, she would've felt comfortable sharing such a huge secret with me.

But even as a kid, I didn't like getting involved in the garden. The most I could manage was lounging in the porch swing reading while she busied herself amongst the flowers and vegetables.

I regretted our distance. After learning so much.

I reached for my phone on the desk and clicked it open. Scrolling through my contacts until it landed on my mom's. After taking a deep breath I pressed the green dial button and held it to my ear—listening to it ring…and ring.

"*You've reached the home of Joseph & Eileen Coleman. We're not available at the moment, but if you'd like to leave a name and number, we'll try to call you back at our earliest convenience.*" And then that familiar shrill beep.

I sighed. "Hi mom, it's Heather. I was just calling to check-in; see how you're doing. Hope your new book is turning out okay. Don't worry about calling back, I'm doing fine. Say hi to dad for me and I'll talk to you later. Love you. Bye."

That wasn't an irregular thing for us.

My parents were engrossed in their careers and activities, phone conversations were usually sparce and short in content. They trusted me to make smart decisions, and I know they would be there for me if I needed it. But beyond an emergency situation, I was on my own.

After putting my phone away, I made a mental note to try again later. Maybe one day I'll find a chance to speak with my mom about her origins. But for now, I shouldn't worry about bothering them.

I made the trek out to the main warehouse floor. To find no one around.

Surely there was someone here, but maybe they were resting or doing research of their own. I could only hope that whoever was on watch was an angel rather than a demon.

I eyed the workout equipment on the one side of the large steel space. There were plenty of things I could do, but I didn't feel any particular pull to any of them. Then my eyes drifted to the back door at the far end of the warehouse. The door that led outside.

Nobody exactly said that I couldn't *leave*. They more like implied that I should remain here for my own safety. But what harm could come from running a couple miles around the area?

I glanced around the warehouse, at the open archway to see if anyone was nearby. But it was quiet, no sign of anyone around.

What if I ran and didn't come back?

The question rang in my mind. Surely it wouldn't take them long to find me. But maybe I could get far enough to at least return some sense of normalcy. Maybe I could duck inside a restaurant or bar and steal away a few hours of regular mortal existence.

Even something as simple as that could greatly improve my whole outlook on all of this chaos.

I quietly walked to the door and touched the handle. Trying not to breathe too loud so I could hear any sounds behind me. Nothing. Good.

I pressed the latch, and it easily clicked free.

Unlocked.

I guess if you're assuming that any intruders would be supernatural, they wouldn't be using the door. I watched the archway as I slowly eased the steel door open, wincing when it made a *squeak* for a moment.

But no one came. So, I continued through it and kept my eyes on the archway until I finally clicked the door closed behind me.

Once I turned to face the outside world, I saw that this warehouse wasn't the only one around. Instead, it was in the middle of an entire warehouse district of whatever city we were in. Away from the main streets of town.

It was well-past sunset, the moon rising higher in the sky, with barely any residual light coming off of the horizon.

Boy, does time get away from you when you're living in a steel box with painted windows.

The florescent streetlamps were flickering on. I walked at first, getting an idea of which direction would lead me out of the warehouse district and into a city street. Making a few wrong turns into dead ends, I finally found a city road.

Looking back one final time, I tightened the small bun on my head and took off into a jog down the road towards the mass of city lights ahead.

A few miles. I could do that.

I didn't bring headphones, jogging without music. Instead, I just listened to the wind in my ears and for any potential dangers around me. After about half a mile, I stopped feeling nervous and just relaxed into the run.

My lungs burned from the exertion, but I was thankful for it. I shouldn't have stopped doing this, I missed the way it made my blood flow. There was a freedom in running, in being able to go anywhere on your own two feet, with only yourself as your limit.

If I returned to the immortal insanity behind me, I would need to convince one of them to do this with me regularly. As I'll likely receive a verbal lashing for going out alone this time around, I'm sure Gabriel will be worried if he finds out. Hopefully, the archangel stays busy long enough not to notice.

Archangels.

God, this world I was thrusted into made me dizzy. I wasn't even sure what my life would be like after all of this madness was over. Would I be able to return to my normal life? Studying religions would be a joke at that point. To know *so* much, and not be able to say anything about it.

How could someone even maintain relationships after something like this? With every person I meet, all I'd be thinking about is how there's a Guardian angel attached to them somewhere.

Even worse, demons spend time among humans.

Knowing *that*—could I ever really trust another person? Could I even live amongst others knowing that I wasn't even fully human?

I wouldn't be a part of either world. I'm something in-between. So really, I don't belong anywhere.

I shook my head to empty those thoughts out. No point in stressing about that now. One thing at a time. For now, I needed to help in any way I could. After that…I'd figure it out. Somehow.

I was close enough to the city limits to see the details of the local shops. A gas station was lit the brightest, and a single car sat there with an old man filling up his tank. People seemed friendly enough here so far. I passed a few streets, saw people leaving a restaurant hand-in-hand.

The further in I ran, the closer into downtown I became. Where things seemed to buzz with life more. Multiple bars and pubs lined the main street I turned onto, with some piano-bars and restaurants busy with customers.

I even passed by a small quartet playing in a small park area at the center of the city, a small crowd gathered listening while sipping on something hot.

It was brisk here. My track jacket barely giving me enough coverage, but the cold only motivated me to keep moving, keep the blood pumping.

No one bothered me, any who looked at me only offered polite smiles and went about their own business. I think this would be a pleasant place to live, especially if I weren't all too aware of the warehouse full of angels and demons only a few miles east of downtown.

I stopped at the edge of an intersection, waiting for the light to change. I took the break to catch my breath and stretch out my already sore calves. Glancing around I saw a couple through a window enjoying a slice of chocolate dessert. My heart tugged at the sight.

Why hadn't I spent more time dating when my life was normal? Now that I knew my life will never be the same, I felt a little rage at myself for not giving those few suitors a better chance. I may have been a solitary individual, but it wouldn't have hurt to let more people in. To have friends.

I sighed and checked the light once more; it was about to change.

I glanced back at the window briefly and nearly shrieked.

In the window I saw Kale's reflection, watching me. I whipped around to where he should have been next to me, but I didn't see him. My heart thundered in my chest, and as soon as the light changed, I bolted.

Stupid. I was stupid for assuming that I could do this alone. I was being followed the *entire* time?! I rushed around another city block and looked around frantically but didn't see him.

But the hair on my arms stood up, I *felt* him.

I needed to go somewhere, anywhere. My eyes locked on a small diner at the edge of the street still alive with customers. I went for it. As soon as I slipped in, I felt the warmth inside, and I immediately moved into a booth in the back corner. Trying to control my breathing.

A tall, older blonde waitress came up to me. "Hello honey, anything I can get you?"

"Um, can I get a coffee please?" I asked.

She smiled and nodded. "Sure thing. Anything to eat? Our cherry pie is our specialty."

I turned my head to the door. "Sure, I'll take a slice."

She nodded and walked away. I scanned the entire diner, looking for that devilish smirk, but saw only humans. I looked out the window, down the dark street but saw no sign that he had followed me.

But when I turned back in my seat I nearly jumped out of my bones. "Fuck me!" I squeaked.

Kale was sitting across the booth, an arm draped over the back of the seat and the other tapping on the table. He was smirking at me, and it infuriated me.

"Well, if you insist. But I'd suggest a change in venue unless you *like* having an audience," he purred. "If so, me likey."

I growled. "Do you have to just pop up like that? There are people here."

He shrugged. "No one noticed. Why are you so jumpy?" he asked.

I sighed deeply, my shoulders tense.

"You followed me," I stated.

"Were you trying to run?" he giggled. "Are we that bad?"

My eyes widened only for a second before I caught myself and avoided his gaze.

"I just wanted to go for a jog. I didn't think I needed a babysitter for that."

"I agree. But with another prison open, I still have to keep you safe. But I didn't want to make you uncomfortable. Which is why I stayed in the Ethereal realm instead of revealing myself, it was only when you took off in a panicked run that I figured I'd drop the act," Kale explained.

He picked up the small dessert menu from its placement behind the condiments and perused through it.

"I am curious, you shouldn't have been able to see me while I was Ethereal, unless somehow you crossed into it accidentally. If I had to guess, I'd say maybe Nephilim grace made it possible for you to have barely crossed the veil. It's impressive. And not impossible."

The waitress returned and plopped down a plate of cherry pie with a dollop of whip cream on top and poured coffee into a mug.

"Can I get you anything, sonny?" she asked Kale sweetly.

The son of Lucifer offered the old woman such an authentically human smile, it almost made me forget just how dangerous he was.

"I would *love* to try this lemon tart, if you still have some?"

She blushed. An elderly woman—*blushed.*

"Coming right up!" And then she was skirting off to the kitchen.

I gaped.

"What?" he asked me as if that didn't just go against everything I now knew about him.

"Nothing. I just wonder how nice she would be if she knew the devil's son was who was talking to her," I blurted.

His eyes darkened, the smile that remained on his lips crept away from their deep color.

"I see. Someone told you." His head tilted, regarding me like I was a mouse for him to devour. "So that is why you're skittish. Are you afraid of me now, then?" he asked with only a hint of humor in his voice.

I scowled at him. "What I wanna know is why you felt the need to hide it? I assume everyone else knew all along."

He hummed and poured a little salt on the table.

"It didn't seem important."

"That's debatable."

Kale chuckled as he drew shapes in the salt with his finger.

"Does it really make a difference whether I'm a demon or something else? I think it just makes me that much more interesting."

I shifted in my seat, angling more away from him. "It makes a difference to me."

"Oh yeah? In what way?"

I opened my mouth to speak, but words didn't come out, so I closed it again. He wasn't looking at me, his gaze was solely fixed on the salt he was pushing around. The old waitress returned and set down a small plate with a round yellow tart on it.

"Enjoy."

Kale smiled that human smile again before she turned and walked away. He picked up a fork and dug right in, shoveling the tangy dessert into his mouth. His eyes spotted my pie and he jerked his chin towards it.

"Their cherry pie is marvelous. Positively sinful. I wouldn't let it go to waste," he stated.

I made no move to pick up my fork, instead I looked out the window at the street where the busyness was already dying down to barely anything.

“At what point did you start following me?” I asked.

He chewed as he spoke, “As soon as you left the warehouse.”

“How did you know I left?”

“I had a tether of power on you, it jerked me awake when you exited the compound,” he answered.

“A tether of power?”

“I can send small ribbons of my power outwards, sort of like a net. That way, I can keep track of those around me. Comes in handy when your home is chock full of angels.”

“Oh. Okay.”

I wasn’t quite ready to dig deeper into that. But it made my spine lock knowing that he had his own little alarm system in place for me without my knowledge.

My brows furrowed. “You were asleep?”

Kale rolled his eyes and chuckled, licking his fork clean.

“Yes, unlike the angels I actually do need to sleep. Only for a few hours at a time, but I think we can both agree the beauty rest is working for me,” he smiled teasingly.

He picked the crumbs off the plate and popped each one into his mouth until it was completely clean, then he pushed it aside and slid my pie towards him.

“If you’re not going to eat it…”

“Why isn’t Gabriel back yet?” I asked.

He gave me a knowing smile. “I don’t know, he hasn’t checked in since he went to heaven.”

“Isn’t that something we should be worried about?”

His grin widened. “Not yet. Travel in the Heavenly realm is more complicated, I’ll let you know when we should be worried. Are you missing your white knight that badly?” he teased as he took another bite of pie.

I glared and crossed my arms. “He’s better company.”

He pouted and put a hand to his heart. “That hurts, honey-eyes. How will I ever recover from these wounds?” he chuckled. “Surely I’m not that bad to have around? You didn’t seem to mind when we were flirting in the library.”

I bristled at the memory. “I didn’t know what you were then.”

“You didn’t much trust me then either, yet you still talked to me. I think you liked the danger of it.”

“Which comes with your kind, no doubt. The hellborn are the masters of temptation, right? Maybe I should start asking if you had me under some kind of thrall then?” I countered.

His eyebrows raised. “Oh, and if you were, would you assume that you are free of it now?”

I straightened my spine and lifted my chin. “Believe me, I won’t be falling for your mind tricks anymore.”

He snorted. “We’ll see about that.”

We stared at each other for a moment, but I broke eye contact first, looking back out the window into the dark street. I heard him finish the pie, and he even got a hold of my coffee and downed it in one gulp.

And then he just sat there. I could feel his eyes on me, but I refused to look at him.

I spotted a group of women coming out of a bar across the street. They were wearing skin-tight dresses or low-cut tops with skinny jeans. Some of them clearly inebriated. They giggled and laughed together as they began walking down the street.

They were enjoying a normal night out on the town. Completely unaware of the invisible world of monsters and supernatural beings that lay just beyond their eyes.

I missed that ignorance, that freedom.

"You'll get used to it," Kale stated quietly.

I didn't deign to look at him, I just continued watching the humans.

"Used to what?" I asked, equally as quiet.

"Feeling different. Feeling separated from all of them. Eventually, it'll just become your way of life," he explained.

"You would know?" I asked pointedly, lacing my tone with disdain.

He wasn't fazed. "I'm the only one of my kind. I pretend to be on equal ground with demons, even with the archangels. But I will always be something else. There isn't even a name for what I am. Not a real one. They can call me the antichrist, the Little Horn, Prince of Darkness, Heir Inferno. The list goes on and on. But they're all just using placeholders for something no one understands."

I gave him a side glance, not meeting his gaze. "What about Lucifer? He *created* you, right? Wouldn't he know what you are?"

In my peripheral vision I saw him shake his head and turn it away from me.

"Lucifer experimented with something he himself didn't fully understand, and the result was me. In his mind, I'm a weapon for him to wield against his foes, nothing more."

Although I heard the hint of sorrow in his voice, I told myself it was nothing but a ruse to gain my rapport.

"But there have been others like me, in the past. Iaoel said that there used to be Nephilim all over the world. But after the...Fall, they eventually disappeared, right? I am only alone because of that, but it's possible for others to come into being," I said.

I meant the words to pick apart his logic, that we weren't the same and he couldn't use that as a way to build trust with me.

His smile didn't reach his eyes.

"Think of it anyway you like, my point still stands. Eventually, over time you will stop letting it bother you. Maybe if you're lucky, you'll feel normal again before the end of your life cycle."

I turned to look at him finally, and though he still held a firm smirk on his lips, it was dulled. A phantom mask he held over something else I couldn't pinpoint.

"Is this some backhanded attempt to make me trust you? Or pity you and let my guard down? You think if you tell me a little bit about your daddy issues and try to claim that we're not all that different from each other, that suddenly I'll negate the fact that you're supposed to be evil incarnate and we'll go skipping through fields of flowers singing My Little Sunshine?" I bit out.

All humor erased from his face, replaced with cold, brittle irritation.

"You find out one thing about me that you don't like and suddenly you know who I am, based on a fable?" he accused.

"This one fact isn't something small like that you put pineapple on pizza."

"No," he snapped. "But I'm sure if it were something small and stupid like that, you'd still manage to find some way to spin it so you could use it as a justified prejudice."

I huffed. “I only just barely started getting used to the idea of angels and demons. Now I have to wrap my head around…whatever it is you actually are.”

“Oh, thank you, I guess we *hellborn filth* should be grateful for your tolerance.”

“That’s not what I said.”

“No, you said I’m evil incarnate. For someone so religiously educated, I’m honestly mystified that you’re being so quick to believe an old book of fairytales.”

“I never said I believed it. You’re twisting my words!”

“And now what?” he continued on with a level of lethal calm that made my skin crawl. “Now that you realize how far down in the pit I really come from, how deep my origins truly go, now you’re already swaying-lenience is beyond redemption? How fucking righteous do you have to be?”

My breath caught in my throat, and I felt a twisting uneasiness coiling in my gut. I didn’t know how to convey what exactly it was about this knowledge that was bothering me. But it definitely wasn’t *that*.

“I’m not saying that that is *who* you are—”

He snarled, “You don’t know me at all.”

“Yeah, that’s what I’m saying!”

He ignored me, and just kept blowing through another rant.

“You don’t know any of us. Your religious studies are biased and mostly made-up bullshit. Yet you still refer to them as fact, as if you haven’t already been plunged into the immortal world that goes against every teaching ever written.”

He chuckled darkly. How did this go wrong so quickly? How can I get him to *understand*…

"Next you'll start believing that the almighty god actually knows all and can wipe the humans off the map with a flick of his hand. Well, guess what, princess, nearly everything you've ever learned is wrong."

His finger pointed out towards the skies.

"Your precious angels are *just* as flawed as the hellborn, even the gilded archangel knight you've got on a pedestal, has glorious flaws that render him as imperfect as me."

I was still as a board, my chest closing in on itself. I don't think I've ever been in a situation like this. I felt terrible and confused all at once, wishing I could just shrink into a dark corner and never move.

But Kale continued his monologue, "Religion is an *illusion*, Heather. It gets its strength from depriving you of your instinctual desires and making you small. Its teachings and all of the purity posse put you in a box and tell you that your confinement is a blessing from the heavens."

His nostrils flared as he spoke, and small sparks of lightning flicked across his fingers.

I pressed further back into the cushioned seat, fear rushing through my veins. I really don't know Kale at all. What he is like when he is angry. I'd seen him defend me against a monster—*two monsters*.

But he was also the *Heir Inferno*. A hellborn Prince. What if his earlier camaraderie was an act?

Kale read my body language, his pupils dilating as he registered the fear in my eyes. And then something shifted in him, his shoulders slumped slightly, and he sat back, almost defeated.

"I would never hurt you, Heather. I need you to know that."

Kale's tone was firm, but also broken in a way I didn't understand. Remorseful even.

I swallowed the lump in my throat and nodded—choosing to believe him…for now.

He was quiet for another moment, waiting for me to relax some before his gaze turned distant again, and then he resumed his speech.

"Religion tells mortals that I'm the epitome of darkness and evil. That my very *existence* is to bring chaos to the world. Maybe they're right. But I'll tell you something about evil, Heather," he paused, tapping his finger on the table—slowly.

"Evil, it only exists when people abuse their free will. It comes when we *choose* to give in to it. We all make choices every day that define us."

I said nothing. His tone growing heavier as he went on.

"I don't let what I am, what *they* say I am, define me. So, you can choose to hate me or to trust me as you see fit, I don't care. But maybe take those religious biases with a grain of salt. *Choose* to have an open perspective. And maybe not get yourself killed while you're at it, okay?"

I was staring at him, and he at me. We sat like that for a few moments, not saying anything. Eventually I looked away from him when the waitress placed the bill on the table and walked away. She may have said something, but neither of us seemed to notice.

The atmosphere between us was thick. I wasn't entirely sure where I should go from here.

His words hit a few chords, that was for certain. But I hadn't yet made up my mind. I needed time to process.

While I did, I might be better off with the angels, ideally Gabriel or Jade.

Eventually I swallowed and said, "Maybe the angels should take over protection duty for now."

He kept his facial features neutral, but orange flame flickered in his pupils.

He straightened his back. “Sorry, but you’re not staying at the Marriot hotel. We all have responsibilities beyond just protecting you, and unfortunately the angels have more to get done than the hellborn do. So I can’t guarantee that we can *accommodate* for you.”

He looked me up and down, and then a mask slid over his features, taking all of the previous emotion with it.

“But we will do our best to stay out of your way.”

With nothing else to say, I dipped my chin once in thanks.

Kale’s jaw was tense, but other than that he had become a cold and unfeeling statue.

“I’d suggest you start your jog back to the warehouse before the storm comes in.”

Before I could respond he disappeared in thin air. Probably simply crossed into the Ethereal realm, but still remained on watch. I sighed and looked down at the bill, he had conveniently left a few bills on it to pay the tab.

When? —I had no idea.

I slid out of the booth and walked out of the diner, which had since emptied out, leaving me as the last to leave. As I stepped onto the dark street, I looked up to the sky to see dark clouds beginning to cover the light of the moon. I could smell the rain in the air, only a few minutes and I’d be drenched.

It’d be much faster if Kale winnowed us back to the warehouse. But after our *talk* in the diner, I knew that wasn’t an option.

So I tightened my bun and stretched my legs before taking off into a jog back towards the warehouse district.

A town sign told me where we were. *Sudbury*, Ontario. Canada.

No wonder it was so cold here. Just as I was passing through downtown again the rain started. First as a sprinkle and then as I reached the edge of the town towards the city road I had originally came from, it turned into a full downpour.

I could see my breath as I continued running down the side of the road. Thinking about what Kale had said in there.

Religion is an illusion. He wasn't wrong about that, I used to believe that. I knew it to be just a way for people to make sense of the world and the universe in ways they could comprehend.

It puts you in a box and tells you that your confinement is a blessing. That's what I did, wasn't it? I put him in a box and decided that that was who he was. Maybe he was right, I was being biased without a real reason. I wasn't trying to, but inevitably I had judged him. And I didn't give him a chance before doing so.

I made a mental note as my skin felt heavier from soaking in the rain. I would give him a chance; I would give them all a chance. I'd observe and remain as open-minded as I could.

After that, after I was fully convinced that he genuinely could be trusted, after that—I would apologize to the Prince of Darkness.

TWENTY-FIVE
Kale

YOU'RE SURE LETTING IT bother you a lot.

Seere said internally while I was punching the concrete wall. She was sharpening her favorite double-sided blade. She had been waiting for me at the warehouse when I returned from my thrilling late-night experience with Heather.

Naturally Seere realized right away that I wasn't happy, no longer in the good mood that I'd left her in. She questioned me about the experience, and I just let her see the whole memory. I immediately wrapped my hands and began working my fists on the wall.

I didn't even bother looking at her when I responded. *It's fine, Seere.*

I could hear the ring of the metal as she ran it with the stone, sharpening its edge.

That's a big 'ole pile of horseshit fire-boy, and you know it. What I wanna know is why. This isn't the first time you've been judged for your name. Hell, we've heard a lot worse in the past. So why are you letting a dumb human get under your skin? Seere asked.

Forgive me if every once in a while I get upset when someone hates me for no logical reason. I sneered.

I punched again, hard enough to crack the wall.

I felt her vibrant chuckle ripple through my blood. *Gabriel hates you. And you don't seem bothered by that, actually you seem to devour it like it's candy.*

Feathers actually has a good reason for his prejudice. He was there during my last blowout remember?

I smiled at the memory. That was a dark time in my life, and I had paid the consequences. I've managed to keep myself under control since then.

Gabriel was there, yes. And he gave me enough of a fight to spark my interest. I'll have to provoke him hard enough one of these days to settle the score. But it wasn't the time for that.

My tether remained on Heather during her run back to the warehouse, I was completely aware of where she was. I didn't feel the overwhelming need to watch her in person, in-fact, just thinking about her made me grind my teeth.

It was with that tether that I sensed when she finally reached the warehouse. And when she unlatched the door to walk in Seere whipped her head to her. Heather was soaking wet and shivering from the downpour outside. But I didn't care.

She walked in and closed the door behind her and glanced over at us. Sure I could've winnowed us both back here after we'd left the diner, but I would be lying if I didn't say that I wanted her to suffer a little bit for her unfounded prejudice.

To give Heather credit, she didn't shy away from me and Seere's sharp gazes as she strutted past us.

Seere was itching to say something snarky, instead, she just stared at Heather pointedly for good measure. The sight of it threatened to break through my resolve, I could have laughed at it.

It was juvenile, and hilarious. But when I looked back at Heather our eyes met, and that hot fury tasted like coal as it burned my throat.

Heather held eye contact, and dare I say her eyes betrayed her by showing signs of regret for the things she said before. She eventually turned away and slunk upstairs to dry off.

Seere snorted, making me look at her. “After all this alliance shit is over, you want me to kill her?” she asked, half-serious.

I chuckled, “Tempting. Ask me again when the alliance shit is over.”

A column of light flashed and then Duma and Daevas appeared in the pentacle. They spotted us and immediately made their way over to our side of the room.

“Where did you just come from?” I asked, mostly towards Daevas.

Duma was the one who answered though, “We visited some Scribes in Beijing.” He lifted a few pieces of parchment. “This is all we could find on the Eternals. Not mention of the relics, but they had those symbols on them. So maybe they mean something.”

I took the parchment from him and looked down at it. It was a timeline, outlining the first creation and some of the first things created during that time. Including the formation of earth and its surrounding planets.

I sighed, “I don’t know how much this will help, but it can’t hurt to factor it in.” I handed it to Seere, who read it over some. She wasn’t as fluent in the angel languages as the demon and human ones.

Duma crossed his arms and remained a generous distance from the rest of us. Daevas took some glances around the room, observing his surroundings as though he hadn’t been here hundreds of times.

“How’s Heather?” Duma asked simply. Seere did her best to suppress her chuckle but both of them noted it. The twitch of my brow probably didn’t help either. “What happened?” he asked, genuinely concerned.

I sighed, bored. “She decided to make a run for it earlier, don’t worry I reeled that fish back in. I would suggest being aware that she’s a flight-risk,” I said.

Daevas smirked slightly as he watched me speak. That demon never missed a thing.

“She’s got a rebellious streak.”

I shrugged. “A stupid one more like.”

Duma looked up at the open archway towards where Heather had left, and then back at me.

“Not enjoying your own protective detail, Prince?” he asked, a knowing smile on his face.

Even though the angel might’ve just been trying to include himself in their humor. His implication didn’t miss its mark.

“I can handle it,” I stated.

I kept my expression neutral, but Dumdum read between the lines.

“Would you prefer Gabriel resumed as her Guardian, if it is bothering you so easily?” he asked.

Oh, this bastard is asking for it.

Seere chimed in, “As much as the human would probably love that, let’s not forget that you angels have a tendency to overreact.”

Duma snorted. “The Heir Inferno seems to be on a hairline trigger himself.”

“Would you like to go head-to-head with that trigger, Dumdum?” I challenged.

Gabriel could hold his own in a combat with me. But this lesser angel would be easy to reduce to rubble. And I would enjoy doing it.

Duma laughed. “You are just itching for a fight, aren’t you? I’ll pass. Some of us have to remain impartial and collected.”

"I think he's afraid to lose," Seere giggled.

If he gave in to our goading, I might've just let her have her fun with the angel.

Duma tilted his head and smirked at her. The action of it was very demonic and interesting to see on an angel's face. Then a knowing glint flashed across his eyes.

"Not in the slightest, *Jazar Danti*."

The air in the room tensed, but not because of me. Seere's eyes widened and then turned murderous. Her old nickname, the name she earned in the pit as a teenager when she fought her way from the bottom, taking down powerful demons and even putting some of the Fallen to shame.

Dante's Butcher.

Not a name Seere picked for herself, but one she was forced to uphold. Lucifer had attached a spell to the name, had it inked into her bones to make it permanent. Whenever someone dared to invoke the name, she was compelled to accept the challenge regardless of her physical state.

To challenge the Jazar Danti, was to ask for death, or brutal pain. Lucifer laid out the rules in the spell explicitly. Seere would have to fight with only her hands, but her opponents could use whatever weapon they desired.

A fighter could only win when one of them yielded or if death claimed Seere's challenger. But if Seere yielded, every wound she had every received, every scar—would reopen. And she would have to suffer all that pain again for a full twenty-four hours, before her healing would seal them up again.

The only loophole given was that she would never die from her challenges or her wounds.

My father was a cruel man, and he forced this on her because she and I bonded in the pit. With her help, I was finally able to defy his will. For thirty years following his punishment he placed Seere into the fighting pits, and every day as soon as she had healed from the previous challenge, he made one of his higher demons or one of the Fallen challenge her.

He made me watch every fight as they tore her apart. It was punishment for us both. Eventually he let her out—bored of it. But the spell still remained, and even though demons in hell rarely challenged her after that, it still happened from time to time.

But with an angel, Seere couldn't kill them and they healed much faster than her. On her weakest days she would be forced to yield.

But this was not one of those days. And Duma was invoking the challenge.

"I see you angels know more about what goes on in the pit than you let on," I stated.

Even Daevas had tensed his entire body. He didn't know Seere then, but after her release from the pits he made a point to know her. Especially when he knew what she meant to me. That was one of the main events that resulted in Daevas switching his loyalties from Lucifer to me. Though, there was still progress to be made there.

Seere stood to her full height from where she was, crouched and stepped onto the sparring pads. She began clicking her knives and daggers off, tossing them to the side. Never breaking eye contact from the Spectral.

She eventually freed all of the weapons and remained without them to aid her. She opened her arms towards Duma. "Shall we see how good your training is, shiny boy?" she asked with the lethal calm she only spoke with when she was gearing up for a bloody fight.

Duma hesitated, shooting me a wary glance before he finally stepped onto the sparring pad. He was my height, standing a foot and a half taller than Seere. She scanned him up and down, assessing his weak spots.

"No weapons? You know you're allowed to use them," Seere said.

Duma widened his stance and raised his fists. "I'm best at hand-to-hand. Seems only fair to be on equal ground anyway."

Seere chuckled darkly. "Among monsters like us, there is no such thing."

She closed the distance between them and sent the first punch, he dodged it with his forearm and countered it with his own upper cut. But she spotted it and caught his wrist before it connected with her chin. She spun and flipped him over her tiny body, using his weight against him.

He hit the ground with a grunt but didn't miss a beat as he swung a low kick, knocking her down as well. She went with the backwards motion and got her hands underneath her in time to catch herself and instead swung her legs over through a back handspring, kicking his chin in the process.

Duma reared back for a moment, but lunged back in. Punching her in the gut before her arms lowered. She grunted, blocked the second jab, and turned to elbow him in the nose.

It connected with a sharp crack, but Duma got ahold of her elbow and twisted the arm behind her back.

Before she could get out of it, he slammed his feet to the back of her knees with a sharp crack and she dropped to the floor. Seere threw her head back, connecting once again with his nose, and he let up just enough that she was able to twist. She led with her back and hooked a turning leg around his neck and dragged him down.

But he was fast. His knee bent forward and slammed into her skull hard. She reared back and didn't react fast enough when his other knee repeated the action. Her lip split open on her teeth, and blood began to pour.

His legs flipped her around, and then Duma was on top of her, punching without holding back. She blocked a few, but not all. She let down her guard so she could grab around his neck and his shirt, and tightened. Using his own shirt to choke him. While trying to get her off he rolled to the side, and she didn't hesitate.

She shoved her head into his nose again, and then released him, putting some distance between them. She panted but sucked in air quickly, venting as trained. Duma coughed and slowly stood. Blood dripping from his nose down to his mouth, but it had already begun to heal.

They smiled at each other, then both rushed back in. They both punched, blocked, and lunged. At one point Duma sent a solid fist into her open side, and she kicked him right in the balls. But the angel didn't falter, sending another jab towards her face. She caught it and twisted his wrist, and we all heard the small crack that resulted.

He winced and shoved into her stomach hard enough to send her flying onto her ass. She landed and raised her legs over her head and back to propel herself back onto her feet. Then she took off into a sprint towards him and leapt to wrap her legs around his neck. She twisted and released, flinging him across the mat into the ground.

A flash of light on the other side of the room signaled someone's arrival.

"Ooh, what I miss?" Lillith chirped.

Iaoel and her quickly joined us, watching Duma and Seere spar.

"What's going on? Why are they fighting?" Iaoel demanded, worry laced in her tone.

I looked at them. "Duma invoked the challenge," I replied.

Lillith chuckled, a hand on her hip. "I always loved to watch the butcher brawls."

I glared at her, she responded with a wink. I turned back to the fight, neither still backing down, but I knew Seere was getting tired.

She would never admit it, but fighting an angel required more energy than with the demons.

But she had fought worse.

She had him on the ground again, pounding his head against concrete. Snarling with her teeth. He kicked her in the stomach, and it took the breath from her. Duma didn't stop while he was ahead, he jumped and kicked again, throwing her back. Then he spun and kicked her head twice with each foot as he soared in the air. She stumbled back.

He lifted his leg and kicked her stomach again and again. Each time she stumbled further and further back. She was choking and gasping for air with each blow, unable to recover fast enough to block them.

Come on, you've done better than this. I urged internally.

I felt her hiss back. *Bite me, fire-boy.*

Duma spun and kicked again, and the force threw her to the ground. And then his knee was on her neck, the other holding her legs down and his arms locked hers tight. When she struggled against him, he jerked.

Seere cried out as one of her arms broke with a loud *crack.*

She was seething. As she puffed for air she spit out blood on the concrete. She couldn't get out of this, he had won. And now she could only yield.

"Duma," Iaoel warned sternly.

Duma's sharp face turned towards the Angel of Sight, and then recognition flashed through his eyes. He wasn't thinking about what her yielding would do to her, he was solely focused on winning. Which is why he didn't hold back, and why he had gotten the upper hand.

But what I didn't understand was why Seere let him? I'd seen her fight much stronger opponents with less strength and succeed.

Duma turned to gaze down at the wrath demon, his brows still tight in focus, but his expression was softening.

"I'm going to yield," he said to Seere.

She growled, and it was the voice of her demon form that spoke, "Don't do me any fucking favors."

He released his grip and stood.

"I yield," Duma stated, ending the challenge, and saving Seere from the pain that she was meant to endure from the loss.

Seere growled, more like screeched as she got to her feet.

"Coward!" she spat, splattering blood on his face.

He didn't flinch, he just stared back at her with calm indifference. After a second of staring at her bleeding fury, Duma turned away and walked towards the stairs.

"We're done here."

Iaoel glanced between all the demons in the room, and then they joined Duma up the staircase, through the archway.

Lillith clicked her nails and took a long audible sigh.

“It’s so much more entertaining when they actually claim their victory. Perhaps I should mention to Lucifer that you need another decade in the pit, Seere. You seem to need a reminder to keep up your training,” she prodded.

I lunged for Lillith, ready to melt the skin off her bones. But Daevas intercepted and wrapped his arm around my torso, halting my momentum. To keep from burning him, I reigned in the licks of flame and electricity that dared to escape the barriers that held them at bay.

But my eyes remained on the mother of demons—bloody, painful murder on my mind.

“She’s not worth it, Kale,” Daevas insisted, his voice low and soothing despite the heat that radiated from my body.

Lillith was smiling at me seductively and it took every ounce of my will not to shove Daevas aside and strike her with a bolt of lightning. Slowly, I slid my gaze to my friend, he was steady as a mountain in a storm.

He only lowered his gaze when mine calmed and a deep breath released from my chest.

“Lillith, make yourself useful and go read the materials brought in today,” Daevas instructed.

She winked at me but did as she was told. It wasn’t until she was already beyond the arch that Daevas backed away from me. Both of us turned to Seere. She was already loading her body weapons back into their hidden sheaths.

She grabbed a towel and wiped the blood from her face, the wounds slowly healing over.

“I’m fine,” she said aloud, reading my mind.

“I know you are,” I replied.

Daevas had started the process of cleaning the blood from the floor and sparring pads. I walked over to approach Seere.

"You threw that fight," I demanded. *Why*? I emphasized down our connection.

Seere rolled her eyes. "I did no such thing."

"I've seen you destroy a Fallen twice as equipped as Duma in the pit. I've seen you fight with a severed artery," I pointed to the mat, "—*that* was child's play. Did you want to yield?"

She sniffed, wiping the last of the blood from her nose.

"You think I would *want* all my scars to open again? You think I want to be writhing and bleeding for an entire day over some stupid, arrogant angel?"

"I can't think of another reason why you let him win," I settled.

Seere didn't earn her name by losing so easily in a tussle. Hell, she had fought better while both her hands were bound by white hot chains. Maybe she wanted to feel pain, maybe she did need a reminder of who she was and of what she had endured.

Could she really be feeling so powerless among all of us that she was looking for the only vice she had to give herself?

"There was no chance that one of these self-righteous fuckers would've actually let me yield. Even *they* wouldn't go so far to inflict pain on a demon like me. They're merciful cowards. I knew what I was doing," Seere explained simply.

She started to walk towards the stairs. I caught her hand, holding it tight as she turned and faced me.

"We don't need to go back there, Seere." Seere locked eyes with me, and we both felt the lingering ache there from our shared experiences during that dark part of our history. She knew what I meant.

I held her hand up to my chest with both of mine.

"Don't ever throw a fight again."

She rolled her eyes, but I tightened my grip for further emphasis, pulling her closer.

"Don't *choose* that agony. Ever."

Seere looked down, ashamed. "Kale—"

"Promise me," I interrupted.

Our eyes met again, and she saw the need in my eyes. I needed her and she needed me. I would not watch her destroy herself, just as she would beat my ass whenever I let my own demons consume every piece of me.

She sighed. "Through hell,"

I nodded. "And everything in-between."

I kissed her hand, and she squeezed mine.

"Together," she finished.

TWENTY-SIX
Heather

HE WAS SWEET WITH SEERE. Tender.

Something you wouldn't expect from a demon, or rather the *devil's son*. It contradicted everything I had thought and even claimed before, everything that religion wrote, and even the way the angels treated all of them. Already, he was proving himself to be an anomaly—unlike anything I expected.

The others hadn't noticed when I slipped onto the staircase during their conversation. At first all I heard was Duma telling Kale and Seere about the information he found. But then it progressed rather quickly into a sparring match. Or something.

I wasn't entirely sure what had actually caused Duma and Seere to start their fight, but I was surprised by how violent it got.

When Seere and Iaoel sparred, it was light and more or less just a mild exercise. But this was combat. Some of it too fast for me to even track.

It wasn't much of a surprise that the angel ultimately won, but then Kale said that Seere threw the fight. I heard him describe some of the states she had been in during previous fights, and her capability to win even under extreme physical duress. She must have truly been holding back if Duma was so easily able to take control.

But why did he yield? And why was she so mad about it?

When I heard the others coming up the stairs I slipped around the corner and pinned myself against the wall. Duma and Iaoel noticed me, but paid me no mind, going to their rooms without a word. Lillith didn't notice me when she went to the opposite hallway, didn't even turn her back.

From my position I could hear Daevas and Kale speak with Seere, hear the genuine concern in their voices. They cared about her deeply and were not happy to see her fail.

Whatever their history, my curiosity was peaked. But after what I had said to Kale at the diner, I didn't think they'd be willing to share their life stories with me anytime soon.

I didn't blame them one bit.

I stiffened when Kale came around the corner and stopped right in front of me. I hadn't heard him come up the steps. He stared at me with so much indifference, it chilled my bones to the point of breaking.

Yeah, I deserved that.

"Enjoy the show?" he asked coldly.

I closed my eyes shamefully. "I—"

He didn't give me a chance to continue before he turned and left down his hallway without a word. I let out a long breath and ran a hand through my hair.

I guess that was going to be our normal for a while. I would have to think of something to make it up to him, so he would be able to look at me without wishing I were dead.

"It won't last forever," I jumped when Seere spoke, she was next to me.

I put a hand on my chest, my heart pounding from the jump scare.

"I really wish you all would stop appearing out of nowhere."

She chuckled and went to the fridge. She pulled out a beer and popped off the cap with the flick of her finger. Obviously, these beings didn't need bottle openers. She dipped it back and chugged half of it in one long gulp.

"What won't last forever?" I asked.

Seere hopped up to sit on the kitchen counter. She put down her beer and braced her hands around her nose and in two short cracks fixed the bones back into place without so much of a wince. I cringed.

"You could just apologize, you know? Kale's not as hard-shelled as he comes off as," Seere said before she took another shorter gulp of beer.

For second I flicked my gaze to the hallway he went before returning it to the small blonde in front of me. Her dark skin already bruising where she had originally been cut during the fight. She was healing, but slowly.

Seere noticed my stare and smiled. She pulled out another bottle of beer from the fridge and held it out for me.

"I like you," she said.

I raised an eyebrow and took the beer from her hand. "You don't know me."

My stomach tightened when I recalled Kale saying the same thing when I said that I didn't trust him.

Seere chuckled and flicked the lid off my beer. "I can tell a lot about a person without knowing them."

"Even after what I said…?"

She waved me off. "You said something mean, were a little bit of a judgmental bitch, yes. But in all fairness, nobody likes us at first. It comes with the territory of being hellborn."

She pointed in the direction Kale disappeared to. "He likes you too, otherwise what you said wouldn't have bothered him one bit," Seere explained. "Let's just say it gets tiring being hated, we're used to it, but I think Kale saw an ally in you—if not a friend."

He wanted to be my friend…and I messed it all up.

"I don't hate you," I told her.

"You're well on your way," she countered.

I stared down at my beer and finally took a sip of the barley water. I sat in one of the stools, fidgeting with the bottle.

"Was he right?" I asked. She looked at me confused. "Did you throw that fight?"

She groaned. "I had chances, perfect opportunities to take him down without much effort that I chose not to take."

"Why?"

Her eyes locked onto mine with the preciseness of a missile.

"I was bred to be a monster. With no choice but to kill or be killed. Sometimes I have to remind myself that I can choose to be something different. I can choose to inflict pain or endure it. I was prepared to endure it today."

"Endure it how?"

She winked. "That's a story you'll have to earn. Did you really mean what you said about only wanting angels on watch?" she asked.

I shrugged. "I was...upset. It was a petty request," I admitted, tapping on the glass.

She nodded and jumped off the counter.

"Good. Because I'm volunteering for the morning shift, and you and I are going to work."

"Work?"

I had a feeling I wasn't going to like the work she had in mind. Her widened smirk told me enough.

"Five a.m. I want you ready to go on a short run. After that we'll spend time doing core exercises and weightlifting. Then we'll get back to our self-defense lessons."

My eyes bulged. "Oh great," I moaned.

She giggled—dumping her empty beer bottle and trotted to the left hallway.

She waved as she ducked out. "See you bright and early, chickpea!"

After finishing my own beer, I took one look at the clock and winced, heading to my own room to try to get at least some sleep before five in the morning.

I thought about what she said. Would simply apologizing undo all the harsh things I had said to him earlier? Even if he did forgive me, I wasn't sure I deserved to be forgiven just yet.

Maybe Kale needed to be angry at someone to let off stress, and I could be that for now.

Seere said that we could choose to inflict pain or endure it. As tough as the son of Lucifer may have been, it didn't erase the fact that at the diner I chose to inflict pain on someone who hadn't done anything to deserve it.

Really, when I considered the fact that I'd seen the demons more often than the angels, and that they had been pretty helpful in this whole ordeal, I shouldn't have been so quick to judge them.

Yup. In no way did I deserve to be forgiven just yet. Kale could be mad at me for a while, I could endure it. And maybe I would learn something from it along the way.

Maybe…just maybe, in time we could be friends—it wouldn't hurt to try.

If I no longer fit in the normal, mortal world, I would have to find some way to live in the dichotomy of my existence. I could start here, alongside these immortal beings.

TWENTY-SEVEN
Gabriel

THERE WAS NO ONE ELSE LIKE CHAMUEL.

His personality contradicted all the other archangels in so many ways, it was difficult to see him as one. He was the gentlest of us all and didn't have a harsh word to say about anyone. In addition, Chamuel had the least amount of power. As the second youngest, it would make sense for the diluted power to leave him with barely anything. But I proved that to be wrong.

So maybe it had something to do with the fact that Chamuel was so kind and passive. That maybe a key component of the archangel might was in their assertiveness. Or maybe it was conviction. The three eldest by far had some of the surest conviction in their actions. Michael with his loyalty, Lucifer with his volition, and Azrael with order.

All nine of us held a specific value above all else. All nine values working together to support a just system. Chamuel fulfilled the compassion element. Jophiel encompassed the value of honesty—and she wore it well. She was never afraid of saying exactly what was on her mind. But she was fair, and unless her opinion was needed, she would usually restrain herself.

Chamuel was a free spirit. He didn't have an official office or location. He spent most of his time in the field alongside his Amors and Cherubims. It made finding him a little more difficult. Jophiel had managed to get a hold of him through the supernatural web, he was in Paris.

Jophiel and I winnowed instead of flying, landing in the Champs de Mars garden just outside the Eiffel Tower. There is where we found Chamuel—in front of a canvas, paintbrush in hand, painting a portrait of a young couple in front of the Tower.

He wore a pale blue dress shirt tucked into jeans with the bottoms rolled up to reveal blue checkered socks against brown dress shoes. Brown suspenders and a pink bowtie finished off his ensemble. His tight-curly brown hair styled neatly.

His back was to us, but he heard us approach. "It's important that even while chaos threatens to overcome all that is good, we remember to take a moment and appreciate the beauty that is always enduring. Don't you agree, Gabriel?" he asked.

I observed the portrait. A marriage proposal in the city of love.

"I agree. We should always make time to remind ourselves of what it is we fight for," I replied.

"This couple—they haven't met yet. But two years from today they are destined for this exact moment. They each individually have to overcome an obstacle that will ready them for the life they deserve. That's what I love most about my job. Not the matching, or when one's destiny is fulfilled, no. The things they endure to get there. Humans are so adaptable and unyielding. Even when they can't see their ending, they pursue without hesitation. They love without reason and they dream without limit. I envy them at great lengths sometimes," Chamuel admitted.

Jophiel cleared her throat. "Chamuel, we have serious business to discuss with you."

Chamuel half-turned to us. "Jophiel, a moment is all I ask. Take one small moment to breathe and clear your mind before plunging into the doom and gloom of this unfortunate situation," he begged.

Jophiel frowned. "Not all of us have the luxury of time."

"Then *make* time."

She looked at me then, a silent request to stop this nonsense. But Chamuel wasn't lazy or inconsiderate, in-fact he was very thoughtful and sympathetic.

I gave her a nod and sent a message internally. *Just bear with him for a little bit.*

Jophiel rolled her eyes but agreed. Chamuel didn't specify what we were to do, instead he only finished the last of his painting and then began slowly putting away the supplies—by hand.

While we waited for him to complete his task at an excruciatingly human speed—causing Jophiel to look like she was in agony, I took a moment to observe our surroundings.

Paris was a beautiful city, but not nearly as it was long ago. There was a long list of places in the world that I would rank above it in elegance and majesty. The sun was beginning to set on this side of the world, causing the sky to turn to a blend of purples, pinks, and oranges.

It's been a while since I'd spent time on earth among the mortals. I was too busy in heaven, training other angels for their positions. Even heaven couldn't rival some of my favorite places in the mortal realm. When I was young, while the earth was still fresh from its restoration following The Tear, I used to love going to Thailand, particularly a small cove in Krabi.

Before humans returned with their new designs to populate every corner of the world, angels could practically live there out in the open unnoticed.

A smile grew on my face when I thought about the times I would join other trainees and jump off those cliffs into the turquoise water. A rare time when I could forget my duty, my position and just live.

I'd have to go back one day, when things calmed down.

Sudden surprise shot through me when vivid images flickered in my mind at the thought of it. In them I saw Kaleus, there at the cove, doing some stupid backflip into the water. Seere pushing Iaoel off and jumping not far behind her.

Lillith sunbathing in an overly revealing scrap of fabric, Daevas and Duma just treading water, watching. Jade and even Heather laughing from the shallows.

They were all there, and they were getting along. I was on top of the cliff, the next to jump. Kaleus shaking out of the water only to look up and challenge me to attempt a better stunt.

Friends. Spending a day together cooling off after a long day. It was a normal activity—even human. Something that didn't exist for any of us. All getting along like we weren't polar opposites ready to rip each other's throats out.

What is this? I blinked and my eyes adjusted back to where we were. Back to the setting sun in Paris.

Chamuel was staring at me, and Jophiel was nowhere in sight. "Where's—"

"I sent her to stash my art supplies," Chamuel explained.

When our eyes met again, I saw the knowing smile in them. Those images—they weren't products my own imagination. "Why did you show me that?" I asked.

Chamuel watched me closely. "We all have our destinies to fulfill, Gabriel."

"Are you saying *that* is my destiny?"

He shook his head. "It was a glimpse into what you could have—if you take the right turns, make the right choices. A possible future if you want it to be."

I crossed my arms. “I’m not even sure what that was supposed to tell me. That I could have a normal life, a leisure day with my enemies?”

Chamuel chuckled and watched the sunset with a small amount of awe.

“It was a scenario, that shaped from your thought process. Pulling from some of your deepest desires and mixing it with something you already knew.”

“My deepest desires?”

He shrugged. “It is in the nature of us all to seek companionship, Gabriel—friendship. An archangel’s life can often be a lonely one,” he sighed. “You may not see it now, brother. But some of the members of your alliance were always destined to cross paths with you. For one—their destiny will be intertwined with yours for all eternity. Again, *if* you choose to go down that path.”

I didn’t fail to notice that he neglected to tell me *who* that was supposed to be.

“I thought you only received visions of destiny for mortals.”

Chamuel smirked then. “Everyone always underestimates my abilities,” he chuckled to himself. “We’ll have to find time to discuss this another day.”

Before he fully finished his sentence Jophiel winnowed back in to where we were.

Chamuel nodded to her. “Now, what can I do for you?”

Jophiel glanced at me before answering. “The almighty told us that he gave you a relic during The Fall.”

He blinked, his first sign of recognition. “Yes, he did. That was a long time ago. What of it?” he asked.

“We need it,” I clarified.

Surprise widened his pupils. “For what exactly?”

Jophiel and I proceeded to explain to Chamuel the information we had on the relics, what Lucifer told us, what God told us, and our reasons for seeking them out. We explained that our angel killer might have a relic and may be looking for others as well to gain power. We told him everything, even our discovery of Heather’s genealogy.

Chamuel listened, not interrupting for even a moment. A picture of patience and humility that surpassed all of the eight other archangels.

After we finished, he took a moment to think, scratching his chin and adjusting his bowtie.

“Forgive me, but I don’t entirely see why you need the Love relic from me.”

Both of our brows narrowed in confusion.

“The *Love* relic?” I asked.

Chamuel smiled knowingly, “Yes. That’s the relic I was given. Now answer my question, why do you *need* the relic in your possession?”

Love relic. We’ll have to learn more about it later.

“What do you mean?” Jophiel asked.

“Well, isn’t it enough knowing that I have it? It’s one less relic that your perpetrator might have. Why do you need it in your possession?” he asked.

Jophiel and I exchanged glances. “Are you opposed to giving it to us?” I asked.

Chamuel looked away again, thinking, his head tilting to the side as he did so.

"The relic was given to me to keep it hidden, for safekeeping. I may be a little more frivolous than the rest of you, but I do follow orders. I wouldn't be a good protector if I gave it to the first person who asked for it," he explained.

"Do you not trust us?" I demanded, some wariness growing in my gut.

He shook his head quickly. "Of course I trust you. But you can't blame me for trying to be logical about it. Do you intend on using the relic for a specific purpose?"

Jophiel looked like her own resolve was faltering. "We may in time. If our opponent wields a relic, or even two, we may need this one to counter against them."

Chamuel looked at her intently. "You don't even know what it does or how to use it. If you did, you might think differently."

"We have the best intentions, Chamuel."

"Your intentions are to use it as a potential weapon against another weapon. Horrible events have happened with the best intentions," he countered.

We were all quiet for a moment. Just staring at each other. Chamuel was being rational and protecting an object of great power from those who might seek to exploit that power. He was justified. But it didn't stop me from being offended by his mistrust.

"What is the Love relic capable of?" I asked gently.

Chamuel's eyes softened. "It's not a weapon. Its only capability is to restore and sustain. It has healing abilities far greater than our own. And I'm afraid, even if you tried to wield it, you might fail. It is like a living thing, it requires you to be pure in your intentions while using it, otherwise it won't give you the power it possesses."

Something about the way he said that touched a nerve, and he noticed that it did. He put a graceful hand on my shoulder and looked deep into my eyes—his full of sympathy.

"There are obstacles you too must face before you're ready for your destiny, Gabriel. You have not yet experienced true suffering and humility."

He broke our gaze to also look at Jophiel.

"This ordeal is going to become much bigger than any one of us imagined. Your alliance is going to be tested." He turned back to me. "You will need to trust those you see as enemies in order to overcome it."

"You say that as if you know what we're facing. If you do, I would advise you to disclose that information to us," I instructed.

He shook his head. "Not everything comes that easily. I can't see the specifics, only the broad implications and possible outcomes. Even the Angels of Sight can't see anything beyond that. As I'm sure you already know, Jophiel. All I see for certain is…this is only the beginning."

The Angels of Sight were Jophiel's division, *creation*. But destiny and creation went hand-in-hand, and so did their divisions. Really, with Chamuel's premonition abilities, it would have made sense for the Angels of Sight to be a part of his division. But they also saw death and pain. Chamuel could see those too, but in choosing compassion and love over his innate gift, he defaulted to charge over destiny. Whatever he saw that was dark and painful he ignored it, letting the AOS deal with it.

Jophiel sighed, watching the last of the sun dip past the horizon. "You're beginning to rival our father with foreboding crypticism, Chamuel."

Indeed. But they all knew too well that even those with the Sight didn't see everything. And what they did see wasn't always conveniently helpful.

Chamuel chuckled. "I apologize for not possessing the same level of candor as you, Jophiel. But in my line of work, being completely forthcoming can alter the future, and not always in a good way."

It seemed we were not going to be acquiring the Love relic today. Chamuel was solid in his reasoning, and we truly couldn't blame him for it. I didn't feel an overwhelming need to push him on it, maybe because the mysterious predictions he gave me were putting me out of my right mind, or maybe I was just tired of arguing.

I took one last look at the city of love and then clasped my arm in Chamuel's.

He nodded to me, "When you truly need it, I will give the relic to you. Until then, I wish you luck on the rest of your search."

"You wouldn't happen to know where the others are, would you?" Jophiel tried.

Chamuel shot her a sympathetic glance. "If I hear anything I'll let you know."

I smiled genuinely at my older brother. "It was good to see you otherwise."

Jophiel scoffed and rolled her eyes. She winnowed out without another word. She was never one for heartfelt exchanges. Chamuel shook his head at the empty place where she left. "She's always a joy to have around."

I chuckled. "Better than Uriel."

Chamuel nodded in exasperated agreement. "Yes, I completely agree."

I went to leave but Chamuel called my name to stop me.

I half-turned back. "Yes?"

"The human. Is she truly a Nephilim?" he asked.

I nodded. "I'm surprised you didn't know, isn't that part of your division?" I teased.

He laughed. "More Jophiel's than mine. But even the almighty misses things from time to time, brother." His expression dulled slightly. "I can't see her destiny."

I figured that, the AOS couldn't see it either.

"Whatever her future holds, it's shadowed by something. Keep an eye on her."

I snorted at that. "The hell prince isn't making that easy. For the moment, I've thoroughly been *grounded* from Guardian duty," I chuckled.

Chamuel smiled widely. "Kaleus is an anomaly in this universe that has always intrigued me. Leave it to the Heir Inferno to finally humble you a little."

"I would hardly consider his arrogance a humbling tide to weather."

"If you say so," he said with an eyebrow raised.

I narrowed my eyes at the compassionate archangel. "Whatever you're plotting, Chamuel. Leave me out of it."

His hands flew up in the air. "I don't plot, little brother. I simply others towards the destination they're meant for. Speaking of, I need to return to my responsibilities, I've had to donate nearly half my angels to help against the primordial attacks, so I've had a lot of backlog to catch up on. Farewell, Gabriel."

In an orb of dusty pink light, Chamuel winnowed to who knows where, leaving me behind in the Champs de Mars. Even after all of that cryptic destiny-talk and his refusal to hand over the relic to us, I still felt a sense of warmth after visiting Chamuel.

He had a way with people that was unparalleled. The angels that were assigned to him always seemed the happiest amongst the rest.

I suppose being in charge of matching together soulmates and helping mortals find their destinies tends to foster a more optimistic workplace environment than say the Gates of Judgement.

Still though, it was nice to feel even a fraction of his kind presence, if only for a moment.

And as Chamuel said when we arrived, it is important to make time for those moments even while the world is crumbling around us.

TWENTY-EIGHT
Heather

SHE WAS TRYING TO KILL ME.

That was the only logical explanation. Why else would she make me run six miles, spend not one but *two* hours doing core exercises, and then another hour of weights.

I got a measly thirty minutes to catch my breath before she forced me onto the sparring pad with raised fists.

I tried; I really did. But I felt like jello.

I was flat on my back, after thoroughly just having my ass kicked. And I mean literally, she kicked my ass with her foot and I was on the ground. Seere giggled as she stood over me, the demon hadn't even broken a sweat. *How was that possible?*

"Come on, chickpea! We're just getting started," she teased.

I was panting like a dog, every inch of me slick with sweat. My head felt hot, my arms and legs trembling. "I…can't…feel…my…legs," I gasped out.

She laughed and tapped my calves with the toes of her boots. "Oh you poor baby. You wouldn't last a day in the pit. They'd eat you for lunch."

She didn't force me to get up, instead she just simply sat down next to me, pretzeling her legs together. Seere fiddled with one of her blonde braids, humming a small tune. It was cheery, sounded kind of like a pirate song.

I swallowed. "How old are you anyway?" I asked, my voice was hoarse, desperately thirsty for a gallon of water.

"In human years or immortal years?" She only paused her humming to ask.

"Human, please. I'm nowhere near ready to comprehend immortal years," I clarified.

She hmphed. "Fair enough. I'd say I'm about one-thousand, five hundred…and nineteen—years old? That sounds about right. You lose count after a while."

I tried not to choke a bit on that. Taking another steadying breath. "What is that like? Living for *centuries*? I mean, wouldn't you get bored?"

"All the time. But in hell time moves slower. What may seem like mere days down there can be years up here. There were a few decades here and there when I didn't see anything but the brimstone walls of the Inferno, and when I came out again, it was an entirely new century. You wouldn't believe how difficult it was to adapt to the new fashions and slang," she joked.

Something pinged in my chest at what she said. *Decades*. There were decades where she only knew hell, I hadn't even reached my third decade of life. To spend that amount of time in notoriously the worst place imaginable, even without knowing exactly what she went through, I couldn't imagine.

"Kale mentioned when we first met that he was like three-thousand years old. Is that true?"

"Three thousand, two hundred and ninety-seven, I think."

"But didn't you say you grew up together?"

She nodded. “We did, sort of. I met Kale when Lucifer threw him into the legion fighting pits to train his body. He saw how the other demons treated me and how I dealt with it. Even as a young demon, I didn’t let those bastards tear me down. Kale was the only hellborn who didn’t treat me like dirt.” She snorted at the memory. “I think he became my best friend when he willingly let me carve him up like a stuffed pig after I had a hard day.”

Seere seemed unfazed by the mention of it, as if talking about her demonic upbringing wasn’t anything to cry about.

But Daevas had told me something during our dream walk nearly a week ago that made me wonder if that attitude and humor was just an act.

A demons life story is unpleasant and gruesome.

Even Kale had implied the other night of their shared past, while he tried to talk to her about her thrown fight. *We don’t need to go back there, Seere...Don’t choose that agony.*

What horrible things did they endure in hell?

“Who else is here?” I asked, mostly to distract myself from the horrible images my mind had begun to conjure with those thoughts.

Seere and I had been alone all day, mostly. The only time we saw others was when they winnowed in and dropped off information and then disappear again. But even then, Seere kept my focus on our fitness routines.

She shrugged, leaning back on her wrists. “Kale’s in his room, being a brood. Duma is around here somewhere, probably avoiding me. Everyone else is out collecting research,” she answered.

“Why would Duma be avoiding you? Because of the fight?” I asked.

She smirked. “I can’t think of another reason.”

I swiped a piece of stray hair on my forehead and cringed at the thick layer of perspiration there, wiping it off with the bottom of my damp V-neck.

"Why did you two start sparring anyway? I didn't see that part."

Her eyes darkened. "He spoke my demon name. By saying it aloud he invoked a challenge of combat that's spelled to it," she explained.

"Your demon name? Is that what happens when someone speaks a demons name? They have to spar with them?"

"No. Just mine."

"Why is that?"

Seere winked at me. "I told you yesterday that was a story you'd have to earn."

I gestured to my trembling body. "And I haven't done that?"

She laughed. "This was just a warmup, chickpea."

I groaned loudly and laid my head back down, which got her to laugh some more. I stared up at the ceiling of the warehouse. Some of the steel was rusting, and there were cracks in some of the concrete beams. I had a feeling those cracks weren't caused by anything of the natural world.

Seere got up on her feet only to flip over into a handstand. Then she started doing pushups in that position.

"Please tell me I don't have to join you in doing that," I begged.

She huffed amusingly, "I'm a wrath demon."

"So…?"

"So we can't sit still for very long, otherwise every muscle in our body starts to shake, and then we spin off into a killing frenzy. It's not pretty. I have to keep myself active to ease the pressure," she explained.

A *wrath* demon, huh? "There's a name for everything, isn't there?"

"Yup. The angels have names for what they all do. Demons—they have names that in a way refer to their heritage but also to their claiming abilities."

"Claiming as in…?"

"Souls."

"Right." I massaged my temples. "I'm going to have to start writing all this shit down, I can hardly keep up with the angel encyclopedia," I said.

She had to have done over fifty pushups in her handstand when she lifted one and continued one-handed. Crazy person.

"Eventually, stuff will just make sense. But it'll be years before you understand everything. Don't sweat it, chickpea, you're doing great," she assured.

"Why are you being so nice to me?" I asked suddenly, I didn't look at her, but even from my peripheral vision I saw her drop back to her feet and tilt her head at me.

"Am I supposed to be mean to you?"

"I mean—you're a demon. Aren't you supposed to be constantly trying to tempt me towards evil or convince me to hail Satan or whatever?"

She laughed. "The faster you get over those religious stereotypes, the sooner you'll understand the hellborn."

I sat up and looked at her. "But what about my soul? Isn't it a part of your job to try to 'claim' it as you said?"

Seere winked at me. "Who said I wasn't?" she teased sarcastically.

I rolled my eyes and released my hair from its messy bun.

"Technically, part of my current job in this alliance is to protect you, and also solve a murder. So, claiming your soul is not on my to-do list, but also Kale doesn't make his inner ring collect souls like Lucifer does. It's an outdated job requirement. One of the changes he will try to change when he takes over the pit."

"He's going to take over hell?"

She shrugged. "In theory, he is the Heir Inferno. But it's not likely Lucifer will hand over the reins anytime soon, not until he achieves his own agenda."

"His agenda?"

"Never mind. Don't worry about that, it's our problem to deal with at a later time."

I nodded, dropping it—even though my mind pocketed the nugget of information for later.

"I guess I just didn't expect the demons in this alliance to attempt to befriend a human. In the grand scheme of things, it seems like it would be a waste of time."

"Well, I wouldn't count on Lillith planning a sleepover anytime soon. Although on second thought, she totally would, it just wouldn't be the type of sleepover you'd want to participate in, if you know what I mean."

We both chuckled.

"I have exactly *two* friends in this entire universe," she stated a lot more seriously, causing me to look into her eyes.

"I don't like hell. Hardly anyone does, but I have specific, *personal* reasons to avoid the Inferno. This alliance is giving me time away from it. That fact alone puts me in a more pleasant mood that can't be shaken by something as dumb as a human who was a tad-judgmental or a few quick-tempered angels. I see this short time as a temporary freedom. And maybe while I'm enjoying it, I can maybe make some additional friends that haven't seen me at my worst, you know?"

She looked at me and smiled, my throat was tight.

"I can be cold and hateful when I want to be, trust me." Seere shook her head. "Right now, I'd rather be nice for a change. Sue me."

I smiled back at her, whole heartedly. I truly misjudged all of them. I was beginning to see why Kale liked Seere so much. She was easy to be around, easy to talk to.

Seere's gaze turned mischievous when she finished with, "Except with getting you in shape. That is not something I'll be nice about. Now get up, it's time to work on chokeholds."

I whimpered and slowly dragged myself off the floor into my wobbly legs.

We both turned when a large golden flash of light appeared in the pentacle, and then Gabriel emerged. Every muscle in my body awakened, and my heart skipped at the sight of his face.

He looked around and locked eyes with me, and then a warm smile grew on his face.

"Hello," he greeted.

Just the sound of his voice warmed me all over. I was barely breathing.

"Hi back. Haven't seen you for a few days," I responded.

He exited the pentacle and began walking over to me. “Sorry about that. Trips to heaven take longer than other forms of travel. Jophiel and I had to make a couple other visits along the way. How have things been here?” he asked.

“Fine.”

He looked me up and down, and my cheeks burned realizing that I was soaking in my own sweat and probably looked like a hot mess.

“Have you been exercising?”

Seere hummed. “I’ve been teaching her some self-defense maneuvers,” she replied, she was watching the two of us like we were a comedy special, twirling a small throwing knife between her fingers.

“Was that something you *wanted* to do?” Gabriel asked me as he stepped closer. “Or were you—"

Seere scoffed. “We didn’t force her, mother hen. It never hurts to be prepared.”

Gabriel was right in front of me now. He reached across the distance between us to gently touch my elbow. The touch sent sparks up my arm and down my spine. I tried not to blush from the reaction.

“Are you doing alright?” he asked gently, now looking down at me from his height.

“I’m sure she’s giddy as a school girl now that you’re here, Lancelot.” Kale’s voice filled the warehouse as he jumped from the top of the archway. Landing the twenty-foot drop like it was nothing.

Gabriel glared at him, but Kale’s eyes were on me. His mouth was twisted in an evil smirk, but his eyes were cold. Still angry with me.

He beelined straight for the pentacle and whistled while gesturing with his hand.

“Let’s go, Seere,” he instructed.

“And where are you going?” Gabriel asked.

Seere joined Kale in the pentacle, clasping her hand in his. He sneered at us.

“I’m tired of watch-duty. I need to kill something,” he said rudely, pointedly glaring at me.

I breathed as a column of orange and red fire surrounded Seere and Kale, taking them away from the warehouse. Gabriel’s gaze lingered briefly on the now empty five-pointed star painted on the concrete floor before finally sliding back to me, a curious curve on his face.

“What’s that about?”

I bit my lip and shrugged. “Don’t worry about it.”

I read in his expression that he wanted to ask about it further, my response only increasing his concern. But I didn’t want to talk about that right now.

“So, a lot has happened since I last saw you.”

“Yes. I’m sorry I wasn’t there when you woke from the memory walk. I needed some time to calm down,” he started.

I nodded. “They told me. It’s okay.”

He smiled and jerked his head towards the archway. “Hungry?” he asked.

My stomach growled loudly in response. “Starving.”

He chuckled and took my hand as we walked up to the kitchen. It was a real effort not to read too much into the handholding. I knew he meant it to be a comforting sentiment, but it made my heart do jumping jacks.

“Any more nightmares?” he asked as he reached into the fridge and pulled out a water bottle. He handed it to me then returned to pull other ingredients from the fridge.

I’d never been happier to see a bottle of water. I chugged half of it in one sitting, wiping the stray droplets off the corners of my mouth before answering his question.

“A small one a couple days ago, but other than that, nothing major. I’ve stayed distracted enough.”

He was putting together a ham and cheese sandwich. For someone who didn’t eat, he didn’t seem shy when handling food.

“And how are you taking the news of being a Nephilim?”

I took another chug of cold water. “Surprisingly well, though that could just be that after everything else I’m becoming thoroughly desensitized.”

“At least it explains a lot of things. Like why your brain hasn’t fried from the knowledge of our existence,” he countered.

“True. I did have a question about that though.”

“Ask away.”

He folded the sandwich together and cut a diagonal slice before sliding the plate onto the counter in front of me.

“Thanks. If I’m half-angel, does that mean I am immortal too?” I asked.

He brushed his hands clean of the wheat seeds from the bread.

"It depends. Some Nephilim in the past could live angel lifespans, but some of them didn't. We don't know why, but it tends to be random. You'd probably have to speak to the almighty to get a more accurate answer on that."

I raised an eyebrow. "Like, in-person? Or would I have to pray?"

"In person," he chuckled. "Being half-angel gives you some privileges that mortals aren't granted. Although, Azrael might be able to tell you as well. She would have to look at how much angel grace is in your blood, and then compare it to her books."

He paused and scanned me up and down again. The look was contemplative, not wanting—but it made me blush, nonetheless.

"Do you want to be immortal?"

"I don't know, I've heard it can be boring."

He threw his head back and laughed. I don't think I've ever seen him laugh so openly, it was beautiful and warm like a fresh sunny day.

"I suppose that's an accurate factor to consider."

I smiled and ate my sandwich. He tidied up the kitchen while I did, both of us not speaking while doing so. I wasn't sure how much the others had shared with him about the events of the last couple days, there was a lot to discuss about the things this alliance had learned a few days before that.

God, it had been a week.

Only a week since my life was turned upside down. It felt like two months. It just made me understand what Seere said about time moving slower. We were still on earth, but it felt like time was moving slower with these ethereal beings.

They weren't much closer to finding Mason's killer, and I wasn't able to offer much help. I could feel the weight of the stacks of books and papers that now piled on the dining table left of me. I hadn't looked at them since the day Daevas went into my head.

Such help I'd been. *I ought to make that my next priority, after taking a long hot shower of course.*

"They told me that you went to visit heaven to ask about the relics, how'd that go?" I asked.

Gabriel turned to me. He sighed and shook his head. "Not as well as we'd hoped. He only knew where one of them was, and when we went to get it, we were refused."

"By whom? Who had it?"

"Chamuel."

Chamuel. He was the…Jade said he was essentially the cupid of the archangels. Right.

"Why did he refuse to give it to you?" I asked.

Gabriel walked over to the dining table and looked down at the collection of records that had accumulated.

"He says that until we actually need to use it, there isn't a logical reason why we should have it in our possession. Which he's not wrong about. At least we know where one is. It's progress at least."

He picked up one of the scrolls and sat down to start reading. A few lines in he paused again, staring at nothing in particular, his brows pinched tight.

"I'd like to apologize," he stated.

"For what?"

He looked up at me, those ocean blue eyes gentle and remorseful.

"For reacting so irrationally when I found out Daevas was rummaging through your consciousness. It was my fault that he broke his focus, and if he hadn't managed to lock you in a memory my poor reaction could've been harmful to you. I'm sorry."

"I'm not upset about it."

"I know, but it doesn't excuse my behavior. Surprisingly enough this is my first time being an official Guardian. As an archangel, everything is stronger. The Guardian bond is more intense for me than it would be for say Duma or Jade. I've had bad experiences with some of the demons in this alliance, and I let that hatred fuel the already powerful protective bond. My reaction was rash and unprofessional. You may not fully understand it, but that was a failure on my part. It went against my training and I feel displeased with it," he explained.

"I don't really get this whole Guardian bond thing. Is it supposed to just be about protection or is it a psychic connection? I'd like to understand it," I stated.

"The best way I can describe it is to compare it to the bond between a mother and child. A mother's amygdala actually creates new neuropathways to hardwire her brain to better protect her child. It's like that. It is a psychic connection, but it's also chemical, in a way."

I didn't think I liked the idea of our *bond* being analogous to a mother-child relationship…

He went on, "For a regular angel, it keeps them aware of their mortal assignments and protects them from harm. For me, it clouds my judgement and hard-wires me to go against my rationality in order to keep you from potential harm," he tried to describe.

"So, I'm like your child?" I asked with a grimace.

He laughed lightly. "Not that literally no. It's just a similar comparison to make sense of it. I'm just saying that there will be times when I have to fight against it in order to make any rational decisions. I didn't expect or prepare for a reaction like that a few days ago, so it took me over in the moment. Now I know better, and I will be more careful and aware of it. I promise to restrain myself in the future," he promised.

What if I don't want you to restrain yourself? Butterflies swarmed my stomach at the unexpected thought. *Get yourself together, Heather.*

"Iaoel said that being a Nephilim also intensifies the Guardian bond, and that's why I experienced Mason's death," I said. Thinking about Mason and his pain was as effective as an ice-bath.

Gabriel nodded. "I'm not entirely sure what it is you feel between the bond with me, but I'm guessing it's stronger than it would be for a full-blooded mortal."

"I trust you. Before I even knew you, I trusted you full-heartedly. I felt that way with Mason too, like I have known you my whole life." I explained.

"That doesn't surprise me at all. The essence of angel grace evokes rapport in mortals, your angel grace combined with a full-angel's in a bond would make that much stronger."

Not to mention everywhere he touched me my skin warmed up like a blanket and made my senses sing with excitement. But that wasn't something I was about to say out loud.

Gabriel had returned to reading the scroll in his hands. I finished the last of my sandwich, sneaking side glances at the golden archangel.

After a few minutes I cleaned my plate in the sink. Gabriel scrunched his eyebrows and distantly looked at the wall. Another facial expression that I was beginning to learn that meant someone was talking to him telepathically through the angel web.

"Oh," he mumbled out loud.

"What?"

"Duma was just explaining to me what happened last night, with Seere," he replied.

Oh right. "Yeah, Seere and him had a little fighting match. She said that he invoked her demon name and then they had to do it."

Gabriel nodded. "Duma regrets his part in it."

"Seere's demon name…do you know it?" I asked.

Gabriel's eyes locked on mine, and warning was in them.

"I do. But I won't say it out loud, and it's probably best that you don't know it."

"Can you write it down?" I asked. He shook his head.

"I know you're curious, but I don't think we should risk you saying it out loud unintentionally. Even if she yielded to save you from the fight, I don't think you'd enjoy watching what that would do. You'd feel guilt for a great deal of your life after that experience," he explained.

"What do you mean? What happens when she yields to the challenge?" I asked. If Seere wasn't going to tell me, maybe he would.

Gabriel looked away, listening to someone for a moment and then dragged his darkened gaze to me once more.

"You've seen her scars?"

I nodded. Some clean cuts, but others jagged and bubbled as if from burns.

"If Seere ever loses and is forced to yield to the challenge of combat invoked by that name, every scar and injury she's ever endured in her past reopens and her healing doesn't resume until a full day has passed. Seere can't die from it, but she would feel all that agony. It's a spell Lucifer tattooed into her flesh that she can never escape from," he explained.

Oh god…

Gabriel grimly nodded when he saw the horror in my eyes.

"If you ever doubted Lucifer's cruelty, that punishment is a decent reminder of his proclivity for it. I would leave it be though, especially to Kaleus. He's very protective of Seere. Pissing him off would make Lucifer look like a saint."

"Noted," I breathed.

I understood now why Duma yielded even when he was winning the fight. He knew what his victory would mean for the demon and chose to save her from it.

Even when Seere was willing to *choose that agony.*

There was so much about these immortals that continued to surprise me. I had certainly taken my mortal existence for granted, and now I wasn't sure I would even be able to go back to it—knowing what I knew.

To return to the mundane human life where I was one final away from my master's degree, readying for a trip to China.

To begin my career in religious studies and anthropology as though these awe-inspiring and equally terrifying supernatural beings hadn't come in and swept the world I knew away.

Gabriel returned his attention to the scroll and, standing in the living area, I remembered how filthy my skin was—just sitting in my own sweat, probably reeking of it. But Gabriel didn't seem to notice or acknowledge it. Either way, I desperately needed a bath.

“I’m going to shower. You still going to be here when I’m done?” I asked.

Gabriel nodded. “I’m back on Guardian duty for the rest of the day, so yes I’ll still be here.”

He smiled at me and I smiled back. And then I left down the hallway towards my room for a change of clothes.

I would wash away the dirt, grime, and sweat from my skin. But I would never be able to wash away the last week.

TWENTY-NINE
Kale

IT WASN'T ENOUGH TO JUST BURN THEM to mere cinders.

That was easy, effortless. I wanted to feel the life leave their bodies. But even that wouldn't be enough to satisfy me, but it'd have to do. Seere and I winnowed straight to Tasmania near where the Nessus prison had burst open.

This prison had a lot of smaller primordials inside that were now wreaking havoc on the locals.

Among them, my personal favorites were the Eriking and Leapers. Leapers were little, no bigger than the palm of your hand. Their skin was green and scaled, reptilian and lizard-like. With only three fingers on each limb pointed into a claw. They had long tails that they used to climb, and small-sharpened teeth.

Humans would likely describe them as miniature dragons. But they swarmed like bees, climbing up their victim's limps and then clawing through the skin enough to tear open veins, capillaries, and arteries. With so many of them on you at once, you would bleed out before you could get them off.

The Eriking was worse. With no real physical form, it was a mist creature that would whip around its victims without being noticed. Their favorite method of killing their prey involved plunging into their airways and stealing the oxygen from them. It fed on your air, on the nutrients that you needed from it. Which it could easily get without killing you. But that was the thing about primordials, they didn't *need* to kill you—they enjoyed it.

Something they and the hellborn had in common.

Seere made herself busy with the Fafnir. A lion-jaguar combination beast with pitch black fur, yellow eyes, and razor-sharp talons.

She played with it, letting it chase her and pounce only to disappear before it could rip her to shreds. It was vicious, but its size made it slow.

And Seere was very, very fast.

She moved with such stealth, giggling each time it pounced and failed as though she hadn't been beaten in a childish squabble with an angel only the day before.

Whereas I was taking my time tracking the Eriking. Letting it think that it was luring me to my death. It would be sorely mistaken. Small strings of my shadows worked into an invisible web around the trees and brush, and every time the misty primordial touched one it sent a vibration to me. I knew where it was at all times.

I'd forgotten how much fun hunting could be. The action in hell has long since fizzled into barely anything. The universe had settled into a calm that was boring for creatures like me. And after I had put restrictions on myself for violent acquisitions, I'd become restless.

This alliance was something new, something to occupy my time. But with information filtering in slower than a snail, I was growing bored again. Until we had more information and a direction to go in, we would be waiting.

There were three prisons opened now. And the primordials that escaped were giving us all something to do. While the angels were in a rush to take care of the problem quickly, I was in more of a mood to relish in the challenges these nasty creatures offered.

Each one was unique in such ghastly ways even my own imagination couldn't have come up with. And the method needed to kill them was usually just as unique. I would be lying if I said it wasn't intriguing to find out what made these things tick. Afterall, these creatures had never encountered a thing such as I.

The Leapers had been following me for quite some time and, now that I was standing still, listening, and watching the Eriking float around me, they took their chance. I felt them as they began climbing up my legs like ants, circling my limbs until all twenty of them had found the best access points to vital veins.

I smiled to myself, letting them do as they wish, even taking the opportunity to look at the little lizards up close. Their drawing depictions didn't do them justice—missing details such as the yellow skin between their spines and ridges on their necks.

I was still connected to Seere while she fought. *If these little dragons weren't about to try to slice me open, I would keep one as a pet.* I joked internally.

I felt her chuckle. *I don't see why you can't. Can I keep fluffy over here?* She asked.

I laughed internally. *I'm afraid he would be much harder to sneak into the pit.*

A vibration to my left notified me that the Eriking was closing in. Maybe it was sensing my distraction. *Good.* Let it come closer.

I heard what sounded like a tiny chirping noise come from a Leaper that had made its way to my neck, no doubt ready to open my carotid. A bunch of identical chirps came from the other Leapers, and then I felt them start to slice. Or at least try to slice.

I had already hardened my skin before they got there, slicing through would take more effort than that of miniature lizards. I let them try for a minute, and then I released the fire from my skin. I smelled the burning flesh before I heard their little cries.

Over the course of a few seconds the tiny beasts were nothing more than ash floating off my skin. All of them save for the one on my neck, who I left unharmed. It clung to my skin but couldn't break through. I reached up and grabbed it in my hand. It chirped and thrashed.

I looked at the small creature, waiting for it to calm down. Eventually it looked up at me and snarled.

I chuckled out loud. "I think I'll call you Absonath, Abson for short."

I saw it then, the purple mist of the Eriking curling around my feet. It was so similar to my own smoke, curling and moving against my skin. Quick as an asp the mist plunged for my airway but was stopped short when I projected my own smoke against it, blocking its path.

It tried to move around it, but I willed my smoke to cut it off again and again. Honestly, I wasn't sure it would work. It was a gamble to see what one could do against it.

The Eriking retreated back and fumed together into a form, the mist opening up where a face would be. I heard the sound of a whispered wind come from it as it faced me.

"What are you?" a whisper of wind asked. If I weren't fully focused on it, I wouldn't have heard its wispy voice.

"Not mortal," I answered plainly.

I willed my smoke to encircle me and loosened the shell I had over my form. Ochre fire leaked through the cracks of my corporal form. I felt the smoldering core churning because of it, I had to keep my focus to not release it fully.

With my form lowered, I let the Eriking see a glimpse of what I was underneath. Let it see the liquid fire simmering in my eyes. The purple mist solidified further, showing a more distinct form.

If there was anything in this world similar to me, this came closest. A dark-purple mist primordial to counter my fire and smoke.

“So this is your form?” I asked.

With no face I couldn’t read any expression it might have had. It only remained in front of me, seemingly assessing me for weakness. But I was doing the same. It couldn’t get past my smoke, which made me wonder if its weakness was what it took from its victims. Air, oxygen. Could it be that simple?

“How do you die?” it whispered.

I snorted. Clearly it wasn’t as smart as I had originally guessed if it was stupid enough to ask.

“I don’t know,” I answered honestly. “Perhaps I don’t.”

Its form was breaking, suggesting that it couldn’t hold it for long. I had been hunting it for a while now, it would be now or never to finish it off.

“But you do,” I stated.

Its mist began to break away from its form in response—but I was faster. I surrounded it with a vortex of smoke, spinning and closing in on it with a trap. Everywhere it tried to escape it was cut off from the air.

The only sounds of its distress were the increasing whooshing of wind. I wrapped my smoke around tighter and tighter until nothing else remained. Until even my smoke dissipated into nothing.

I lifted the hand that still held the Leaper and looked at it. It had wrapped its tail around my index finger and had watched me kill the Eriking.

“I hope this means you’ll be a good pet, Abson?”

The creature responded with a chirp and then twisted until it perched on the back of my hand and finger, like a large ring.

"Good," I said.

"Just wait until Heather sees that thing," Seere quipped.

Right. *Heather*. The main reason I had left to kill monsters.

I could already see her laughing and smiling like a love-sick teenager next to Gabriel. Much happier among the bright and shiny angels than with someone who was born in darkness and torment.

"Scowl any harder and your face will be stuck like that," Seere stated.

I rolled my eyes and walked through the trees and brush to search for any remaining things for me to kill.

Seere followed me, humming her favorite song. We passed the body of the Fafnir, now gutted and soaking the ground in its oily blood.

I summoned a small flame in the opposite hand Abson was in and flicked it to the furry body, setting it ablaze. We couldn't leave evidence of the primordials for mortals to discover.

When we had arrived here, there were enough creatures to keep us busy for hours. Making plenty of noise—it was now quiet. Our work done.

It was unlikely that these were the only Leapers, Eriking, and Fafnir to escape from Nessus, and honestly, I was considering going and finding the rest. If only to delay our return to the warehouse just a little while longer.

I couldn't blame Heather for wanting to get out of it for a while. Even I had begun to feel stifled and stir-crazy inside. I wasn't even going to give her a hard time about her evening jog.

In-fact I would have offered to run alongside her, use the opportunity to feel a little more human myself. But she made it pretty clear that she couldn't stand to be around a creature like me.

Though she didn't seem to have any problem spending time with Seere afterwards.

"She is sorry about it." Seere read my thoughts, which were no doubt flowing freely down our constantly open connection.

I sighed. "I don't care."

"Keep telling yourself that."

I halted. "Seere, let it go."

She folded her arms across her chest. "I will when you do," she countered.

I pinched the bridge of my nose, my shoulders tense.

"I don't have to do anything. I don't have to listen to you, or be nice to her, or forgive her. Because there is no reason to. Whether she meant what she said or not, it is what it is. I tried being nice, I tried being friendly, and in the end, she learned what I was and decided that that was all she needed to know. I don't blame her. We are monsters, Seere. She'd be stupid *not* to steer clear of us."

Seere glared at me. "You can be a real hypocrite, fire-boy."

I gave her a smirk that didn't reach my eyes. "Aren't we all sometimes."

"You are always up my ass about being insecure and down on myself. Yet here you go doing the exact same thing. What happened to not letting your demons eat you, Kale?" she demanded.

I glared at her but didn't say anything.

She continued, "We have a chance here, to make friends, to gain allies in heaven. With all that your father is plotting, don't you think that would be a good idea?"

“He’s been planning that shit since the beginning of time, Seere. It’s not going to actually happen, I’m in better control.”

“Barely. All he needs is one chance to break through that calm exterior and he’s in. As soon as your guard is down, he’ll use it to your advantage. These angels can help you, stand with us against him when that happens. Daevas and I can’t fight Lucifer, let alone the army he has behind his back.” Fear laced the edges of her tone.

We’d always been planning for that eventuality. Lucifer wanted power—he created me specifically for that purpose. I did everything I could to maintain my distance and control over my own abilities.

But Lucifer didn’t get his reputation from allowing his *property* to defy him. He knew how to pull the right strings, press the right buttons to get what he wanted out of anyone.

Yet another reason I tried to keep Seere with me at all times, especially around him. She was one way he could control me, and the moment he truly knew that would be the day I’d have to take a stand against him.

But I couldn’t do it alone, and Seere was right. Seere, Daevas, and I—however strong we all were—were nothing compared to Lucifer’s arsenal.

Having angels on our side could mean the difference between victory and an eternity of bending to the devil’s rule.

“We’re still a long way from that, Seere,” I replied simply, offering her a sympathizing smile.

She didn’t look convinced. “We need to make friends, Kale. Heather is a Nephilim, which means her rare kind of grace is a powerhouse of energy. Having her as an ally could be exactly what we need. Plus, being nice to her would make us more favorable with the angels, especially Gabriel. An archangel in our corner would be *huge*.”

"So actually, you want me to be nice to Heather so that we can someday use her for our own gain?" I asked.

She shrugged. "There are other reasons. But that is the big one, yes. But more importantly, you need to stop believing the things she said or implied."

"Why? Nothing she said was wrong."

My best friend sighed, and then grabbed my hand and held it to her chest the same way I did with her the other night.

"You are nothing like that. I would know."

Her words only reminding me of all we had been through together. Every hurdle and obstacle we faced in our many centuries in the pit. Who I was before I met Seere, and how much she brought me out of the raging fire from which I was created.

"Promise you'll at least try to let them in."

After a moment of staring into her black eyes, I nodded.

"I'll consider it."

She looked down at the now pile of ashes of the fallen Fafnir.

"Besides, you need more friends. You're getting needy," she teased, elbowing my ribs.

I chuckled. "Hey, you knew what you were getting yourself into with me."

She shook her head, clearly amused. "Unfortunately."

We both chuckled. She reached for my hand to return back to the warehouse when someone else's winnow signature appeared in front of us. A silvery light with popping sparks, which could only mean one person.

Fan-fucking-tastic. Seere groaned down the connection.

"I see you two had fun," Sytry said, smirking widely as he looked around at the leftovers from our destruction.

I tensed, Seere did as well next to me. But I quickly schooled the cold, unfeeling mask onto my face before Sytry locked his gaze back onto the two of us.

The light-skinned Fallen angel had black hair, black eyes, and wore a turtleneck underneath a suit jacket. Sytry was part of Lucifer's inner circle. His demon offspring were the slave demons. Masters of the mind that could entrap a mortal soul with their own unique way, and in doing so would enslave the mortal for eternal servitude.

The mortal's minds would be twisted and warped until they became husks of who they once were, zombies willing to serve their masochistic masters.

Their very purpose went against everything I believed in. Giving no choice to the mortals before committing them to their fate. Finding pleasure in torturing their bodies and souls for all eternity.

I took a steady breath, blocking out the haunting images that threatened to penetrate the carefully constructed wall in my psyche. I could feel Seere sending me what comfort she could down the connection.

Sytry was a menace, one I would happily get rid of when I have the authority.

"What brings you to the surface, Sytry?" I asked calmly, coldly.

He tapped his foot against the ground. "Lucifer sent me. We haven't received any updates since you last visited."

I raised an eyebrow. "I'm afraid you've got the wrong person, that's Lillith's job. Take it up with her."

Sytry gave me a knowing smile. "It seems that she is not collecting enough information to be of interest. Her reports are thin. Care to share what news you have of the relics?" he asked.

Of course, Lucifer would share that information with his circle. Especially the ones who were most loyal. No doubt he had them searching for the relics as well.

It was quickly becoming a race to find them, and whether it be Lucifer's goons, the alliance, or our Guardian killer to find them first—we could only hope fate was in our favor.

"When there is news worth sharing, Lucifer will be the first to know." The lie flowed effortlessly from my lips. Then again, I didn't care if he believed me.

Seere had freed a throwing knife into her palm, but kept it hidden from his view. Always ready just in-case we needed to battle our way out. Not that Sytry would last against my fire if he tried, but Seere may not be that lucky.

"How are you Seere?" Sytry asked her all too charmingly.

She squared her shoulders. "Just cheeky, Sytry."

"Not going to ask me how I am?"

His hand rested arrogantly in his pocket, perfectly at ease. But he was unknowingly lessening his presence trying to mimic Lucifer.

"I don't care how you are," Seere said, completely uninterested.

She'd come a long way since her first few decades as my second—when she was more timid and had a hard time hiding her insecurities around the Fallen.

"We heard about your recent challenge. Losing to a lower-class angel is rather beneath you and being mercifully saved from the consequence no less. Lucifer isn't happy with his butcher."

His butcher. The only thing keeping me from incinerating Sytry where he stood was Seere's voice in my head.

He couldn't handle me even if I were his. She was attempting to make light of the comment. Despite its implication of ownership.

But Sytry said other things too. Proving that Lillith had been feeding Lucifer and his brutes *everything*. I'll have to remind that bitch of her place.

Seere smiled wickedly at the Fallen angel. "Shall we spar, Sytry? Do you think you'd do better this time around?" she asked pointedly.

His eyes flared with anger, but only for a moment before that aggravating composure returned.

"I'm surprised to see you're actually still around and kicking. Isn't the end of your life cycle fast approaching?" he asked.

Seere didn't let him see her falter, and neither did I. But I felt it in the connection. It was true that as a fifth-generation demon, Seere wasn't supposed to live as long as she has.

She'd be lucky to last until her second millennia, if even that.

But we agreed not to discuss it. We both would rather not dwell on her shorter lifespan.

The fact that she had lived this long made me hope that her unique skills would negate her fate. Or maybe I could find a way to keep her around longer. Another reason why angelic allies would be helpful in the future.

"Is there anything else we can do for you, Sytry?" I asked.

Sytry cocked his head to the side and darted his eyes between us. Cruel amusement rose the corner of his mouth.

"Lucifer expects a report soon. I wouldn't make him wait much longer," he suggested.

I clasped Seere's hand in mine.

"Noted. Have a safe trip back to the pit. Would you do me a favor and send Lillith our way, she has actual work to do," I requested.

Sytry bowed his head slightly in response. It was all the confirmation I needed before I bent space into the Ethereal realm and aimed for the warehouse.

He's a fucking asshole. Seere said down the connection.

He won't be smiling forever. I replied.

Seere squeezed my hand. *Allies, Kale. We need allies.* She emphasized.

The smoke and fire cleared from around us, now calmer since I'd left off steam, revealing an empty warehouse floor. I could hear voices from beyond the archway. Belonging to an archangel and a mortal who both were not who I wanted to see just yet. But I had no other choice.

I turned to look down at Seere, still holding her hand. Sytry's visit was a reminder of a darker time, filled with blood and vacant eyes that never failed to rip me open. I was working to close that door before it could fully open again.

Seere tightened her grip on my hand and even squeezed my arm with her other hand.

"Don't let your demons eat you," she whispered.

I nodded. And then heard a small chirp that reminded me of the lizard Leaper still attached to my finger. I lifted my hand and chuckled. I'm surprised Sytry didn't notice him.

I asked him, "Ready to meet some people?"

THIRTY
Gabriel

"WHAT THE HELL IS THAT?"

Heather shrieked as Kaleus showed us the tiny primordial he had wrapped around his index finger.

Kaleus chuckled darkly, rotating his hand to show it off more. "It's a Leaper."

"Is there a reason you have it attached to you like an accessory?" I asked.

Kaleus reached down with his finger and stroked the green and yellow spines on its back.

"Well after I burnt all of his buddies to a crisp, I had a thought that maybe it could be interesting to have a primordial as a pet," he explained plainly.

"It's a *he*?" I implied.

He grinned from ear to ear and lifted his finger higher to 'present' it. "I named him Abson."

"Wha—" she stopped short. Kaleus glanced at Heather and saw the fear on her face and his smirk grew larger, deadlier.

"Don't be afraid, he's completely harmless. Well, unless you let him near a major artery. I wouldn't suggest doing that," he winked.

Seere huffed a laugh as she popped off the cap of a beer from the fridge and began drinking.

I looked at the Leaper and then at Kaleus. "It's dangerous to have here, Kaleus," I stated.

He waved me off. "Relax, Abson and I have an understanding. I'll keep him contained while I'm not around, okay?"

Heather was staring at it, slightly horrified, but also curious. Among all the primordials, Leapers weren't nearly the worst, especially when they were alone. In a pack, they are lethal, but one less so.

"Keep it on you or in a different location," I ordered. "No matter how small, we shouldn't risk Heather's safety."

Kaleus rolled his eyes. "I suppose I can agree to that. What are you two up to?" he asked, bored.

He snapped his fingers and the Leaper disappeared, no doubt into some enclosure elsewhere. He went and sat on one of the kitchen island stools, Seere sat on the counter next to him.

I gestured to the pile of parchment we had acquired over the last few days.

"Trying to weed out anything important," I answered.

"How did your visit with daddy go?" Kaleus asked.

I told him about the information the almighty had given us, and then about Chamuel and what information we had gotten from him.

Seere was the one who responded when I finished.

"So we have nothing. All that time and we're still barely moving?"

"Knowing where one relic is located is something. The others may find something too, and we have all of this to read through. We just have to keep looking," I replied.

Seere turned to look at Kaleus, he locked eyes with her. They were communicating silently.

Kaleus sighed and held his hand out towards the table. “Fine. Give me something to read.”

And so that’s what the four of us did for an hour. Well, three of us. Seere regularly got bored and did something else, eventually completely disappearing altogether. Duma and Daevas eventually came in from their perspective hallways and joined us in our reading.

Iaoel and Jade returned to the warehouse, bringing additional reading material along with them. Jophiel hadn’t come back, but she had sent me a message that she was attending to her division for a little while, taking a break from the alliance at the same time. I couldn’t blame her; we were all a little tense.

It was close to five-thirty when Jade rose from her chair and walked into the kitchen—pulling out various pans and ingredients.

“Anyone hungry?” she asked.

Angels didn’t need to eat, but that didn’t mean we couldn’t enjoy a good meal when we wanted to. Heather and the demons on the other hand needed the nutrients.

“Depends on what you’re cooking,” Kaleus stated.

His attentions remained on the parchment he held in his hand, but I noticed that every time he spoke Heather’s gaze would shift to him, watching his every move.

No doubt that he noticed as well, but he pretended not to. Something had clearly happened between the two, but Heather didn’t feel inclined to tell me exactly what.

I’ll admit, my imagination wasn’t helping either. It took extreme effort to suppress the growing anger and worry in my chest when I observed the two. They kept looking at each other, but remaining their distance.

I was gone for a few days, and already I felt left out of the loop.

I knew I should probably respect Heather's privacy. But to have the son of Lucifer looking at her like an enemy stirred the Guardian bond to the point of shaking.

Jade was speaking, but I wasn't hearing the words. My senses were honed-in on every breath the Prince made, and every watchful gaze Heather shot him.

Kaleus' eyes shifted, catching my stare. I felt the tap in the front of my skull, his request to connect.

I let him in. *I know I'm gorgeous, feathers. But the staring is getting a little creepy*. He stated.

My jaw tightened. *Did something happen between you and Heather?*

Kaleus' bored expression upturned into his signature smirk. *Jealous*?

I rolled my eyes. *I'm serious. Your mood has changed with her.*

It was his turn to roll his eyes. *We got into an argument.*

Anything I should know about? I asked.

If she didn't tell you then I would venture to guess the answer to that is no. He replied simply.

I scowled. *Well, whatever it is. I expect you'll be professional from now on.*

Internally I heard him snort. *You and I both know that professional is not in my vocabulary, featherbrain. Besides, other people expect me to be entirely unprofessional, so...I can't let them down.*

You're insufferable.

I looked back at Heather to see her watching me. It seemed she had begun to realize the times when I communicated telepathically. It would certainly be nice to be able to do so with her, a much faster method of communication, and a lot more personal.

Jade was cooking, and Duma had gotten up to help her. By the smell of cumin and turmeric, she seemed to have opted for a type of curry.

Heather sighed as she tossed aside a piece of paper and picked up another.

"This is all we've collected from nine of the Scribe outposts," Duma said. "We still have a lot more to visit."

"How many Scribe locations are there on earth?" Heather asked out loud.

I was the one to answer, "There are hundreds of small ones, but the largest ones—there's about sixteen."

"What about the prisons? How many of those are there?"

Daevas answered this time, "Twelve. Scattered around the world."

Heather bit her bottom lip, thinking. "How many of them are open?"

"Three so far," Kaleus replied quietly.

"Nessus in Tasmania, Fangelsi in Angola and most recently Sheol in Cyprus," I explained. I looked at Kaleus. "You went to Tyurma to check it, right?" I asked.

He nodded. "It's solid. I put an alert sigil on it to notify me if it's opened," he answered.

"So, if the Scribes record everything in both immortal and mortal history, then why aren't we finding a lot on the relics?" Heather asked.

"These outposts, old information gets buried underneath the new. And a great deal of the Scribes are too young to know about the relics, let alone know exactly where we can find records of them," Duma explained from the kitchen.

Heather scrunched her nose. "Can't you just like look up key words and let the system find the information, like a computer?"

Some of them chuckled at that, the loudest among them being Kaleus and Jade. "The larger archives are older than the computer age, they haven't upgraded yet," Jade said.

"So, we're just looking for a needle in a haystack, and using a magnet isn't an option," she commended.

I nodded. Heather clicked her tongue.

"So much for organization," she muttered.

We locked eyes and I smiled warmly at her humor. "It's a work in progress," I chuckled.

She huffed and looked aimlessly at the scattered paper on the table.

Her expression shifted to something saddened. "This is sounding like it's going to be a longer trip than originally planned," she stated quietly.

I offered her a sympathetic look. "I'm sorry. We'll get you back as soon as we can."

Kaleus snorted, causing us to both look at him.

"If being human will even be enough once you're done with us," he joked. Though his tone was humorous, his expression was cold—disconnected even.

Heather looked down sheepishly, a distant memory flashing in her eyes.

"We'll see, I guess," she muttered.

I reached across the table and touched the back of her hand with my fingers.

"You may turn out to have an immortal lifespan, and if that is the case, we can find a way to make it just as enjoyable as your mortal life would have been," I offered.

Heather looked up at me, the skin of her cheeks reddening slightly. I resisted the irrational urge to touch them, instead just broadened my gentle smile for her. She nodded and smiled back.

I heard Kale's barely audible scoff followed by his muttering, "*Bâlbâi-mă.*" Romanian. *Gag me*. His favorite language since I first met him.

Heather must have heard it too, cause her eyes shifted to his for a second and back to mine. Then they scanned me up and down, pausing at my shoulders.

"Do all of you have wings?" she asked suddenly.

The room stilled for a moment as they all registered her question.

Jade scooped some rice into a bowl and handed it to Duma before replying first.

"Angels do. Though they're much smaller and less vibrant than the archangels'. And we don't use them often. Most of us find winnowing to be much faster. We really only use them in combat situations," she explained.

"Can I see them?" Heather asked bluntly.

The angels all exchanged glances, "I suppose. After we eat, we can go up to the roof." Jade agreed. Duma and Iaoel nodded in agreement.

Heather hesitantly smiled and stood to clear the records from the table so that we could eat on it.

Before I stood to join her, I turned to Kaleus, feeling a strange emotion vibrate along the connection that was still open between us.

His expression was unreadable as he observed the Nephilim, and it was no easier to understand what he was feeling internally. But whatever it was, it triggered to the surface bits of those images Chamuel had shown me.

An image of Kaleus laughing in the reflective blue water, splashing it towards Heather's gleeful face and then at me with just as much excitement.

Maybe Chamuel's vision wasn't just a possibility for me, but also for the Heir Inferno. Perhaps the Prince also had a buried longing for friendship—for peace and normalcy.

Maybe the two of us weren't as different as we thought.

Thinking of me, feathers? I'm touched.

I rolled my eyes mentally. *And you're snooping.*

You had the connection wide open, my friend.

The rest of the group was grabbing a plate of food while the Heir and I conversed mentally. Heather was watching the whole exchange from the corner of her eye.

What kind of naughty positions do you think she's got of the two of us going through her head right now? I can think of a few fun ones.

I grunted in exasperation before abruptly cutting off the connection and putting up a sizeable wall for good measure. But I could still hear Kaleus chuckling from the corner of the room as I went to join Heather at the table.

THIRTY-ONE
Kale

RELUCTANTLY DAEVAS AND I followed Heather and the rest of the angels up to the roof after dinner.

Keeping our distance, we stayed on the opposite side of the building while they all lined up along the edge of the other side a few feet apart. Gabriel remained next to Heather, facing them.

First Duma loosened his wings, simple and white with hints of pale blue in the feathers. Then Jade unfurled hers, which were slightly smaller, her feathers were ombre, turning from white to a light orange color. Iaoel's were different, theirs were dark gray with speckles of white and brown and equal in size to Duma's, stretching out past their arm spans.

Once all three had spread their wings out, Heather went to each one and looked them over with admiration and awe.

Angels were beautiful creatures. How could they not be? Even the creepier Cakti and Ophanim had beauty. Sure, demons did as well, but only in their humanoid forms. If humans saw demons in their raw form, they wouldn't be able to collect souls.

Our attractiveness was a mask, a glamour to lure in prey. Angels were beautiful naturally, even when their personalities were dull and often irritating.

Once Heather had seen her fill of their feathered ailerons she backed away.

"What is it like to fly?" she asked.

Jade rustled her wings, feeling them out as if she hadn't had them out in a long while.

"When we're first learning, it's terrifying. But eventually it becomes very freeing," she explained. Jade extended her hand towards Heather. "Do you want to see?" she offered.

Heather's eyes bulged and she retreated back a step. "What? Like, fly with you? Oh no, I don't want to fall."

I snorted, but Daevas and I were too far back for her to hear. As if they'd let her fall. Although she could definitely use a good long drop to scare her a bit.

Daevas had his arms folded, leaning against the edge of the roof, he was observing the exchange with indifference, but I knew better. He was aware of everything, always ready to step in if needed.

Gabriel touched the small of Heather's back when she backed away from Jade. A comforting touch, but irritatingly gentle to watch from here. "You'd be completely safe. If you'd prefer, I can take you for a flight around the block. I think you'd like it," he offered.

Ugh. Gabriel's golden kindness was disgusting sometimes.

When Heather turned to look at the archangel, he unfurled his gold/white feathered wings. They were nearly twice as wide and large in comparison to the lower-angels'.

Her eyes lit up like fireworks at the sight. And for a moment the steady flame beneath my skin burned hotter, threatening to break past the skin barrier.

"You're sure it's safe?" Heather asked, taking in every detail of Gabriel's glorious wings.

Gabriel held out his hands for her, ready to embrace her. The angels behind them already turning towards the edge to take off.

"More than sure," Gabriel replied.

Heather was hugging herself, scanning Gabriel up and down, his open embrace. Almost identical to the one he offered that first day we brought her to the warehouse.

Even then she was in awe of him, behind all that fear and uncertainty—she trusted him without doubt. But the human couldn't bestow that same faith in the hellborn. In me.

She nodded, pressing her lips together in anticipation as she stepped into his embrace. Gabriel gently spun her so she would be able to see, then wrapped his large arms around her waist, lifting her feet on top of his.

The archangel looked almost as excited as her. Like this was his first time flying for enjoyment with another person. The two looked positively giddy.

Gross.

He leaned down to whisper something in her ear, and when she nodded, he lightly beat his wings—lifting off of the ground. Heather clutched close to him as they slowly rose.

The angel was taking it slow to ease her nerves. And then his grip tightened around her before he flew horizontal, following the other angels who had already taken to the skies.

Daevas and I stayed grounded, watching the ethereal beings fly around in circles a hundred feet above the city. I could hear Heather's surprised shrieks and excited giggles from where I was standing.

Lightning sparked from my hands to my feet, barely staying contained. I had to focus on my breathing to keep the churning magma from escaping my shell as I watched them.

"You alright?" Daevas asked coolly.

He was watching them too, but as someone who never missed a thing, of course he noticed the small bursts of energy coming from me.

I swallowed down the ash that had started to build in my throat.

"I'm fine."

He nodded and tapped his foot on the ground. "I know better than to push you—"

"Then why does it sound like you're about to?" I snapped.

Daevas continued, unflustered. "Seere told me about Sytry's visit."

"What about it?"

"Is it something we need to be worried about?" he asked.

I shrugged. "No more than usual. I've been ignoring Lucifer's nagging; he's feeling left out."

Daevas nodded once. "And Lillith?"

I suppressed my growl. "We keep her in the dark. Don't give her important information unless it's something Lucifer would guess on his own," I instructed.

"I'm assuming that includes the locations of relics?" he clarified. I nodded. "We have a long way to go from where we are now. This isn't going to be an easy task. Not to mention the Guardian's killer may be well-ahead of us."

"We'll make do."

Daevas glanced at me then, his eyes contemplative. I met his gaze.

"What have you observed from our heavenly compadres?" I asked.

Daevas' straightened; a trained warrior ready to give his reports.

"Jophiel is distant, she will never fully trust any of us. We should tread lightly around her."

I nodded. Information I had already gathered myself, her general disdain for us was clear enough the first day of our alliance, but it hadn't improved over the last week.

"Iaoel has dealt with demons before, they have an open mind. I can see them being a potential ally. Jade is almost as open minded. Her position makes her an influencer, and her priorities are in the safety and protection of those she cares for. Duma is one we would need more time with. Right now I would say he's loyal to Gabriel, he would follow his every order," Daevas explained.

I had Daevas on assignment to assess whether these angels could be trusted and if they could potentially help us if we needed it. We may never need them, but I wouldn't be the son of Lucifer if I didn't plan for the potential future.

"Gabriel is a tough one to measure. But his Guardian bond with the human is making him vulnerable and possibly pliable."

"If we managed to get him on our side, would he be able to influence Jophiel and some of the other archangels?" I asked.

Daevas shook his head. "Possibly. From what I've heard, his older siblings see him as the unexperienced child among them. Only a few actually take him seriously and value his input. But maybe after this alliance, if we succeed, that will change."

I took all the seeds of intel Daevas had given me and pocketed them for later. Locking them in the vault of my mind where no one, including Seere, could access.

I watched the four pairs of wings soar and bank in the air around each other. Leisure flying. I'd seen them use those wings in combat, the flying was much sharper and more precise.

Some of them could weaponize their wings, adding armor that could cut through stone sharper than a laser.

Maybe it wasn't necessary to learn all I could about these halo-wearing immortals. But from the moment I saw Lucifer convening with his entire inner circle following the death of the Guardian, I knew that he was plotting something. Using the chaos and confusion to find a weakness in the heavenly realm that would aid his schemes.

Which could only mean that he would find his use for me soon. And I wasn't about to fall into his control again anytime soon. So, we needed allies. People we could call for aid when the time was right.

Possibly, if we played our cards right, we could be helpful enough to earn ourselves some favors. However we chose to play it, every moment counted. So that when the time came, we wouldn't be alone when we freed ourselves from the devil's grasp.

"Spend more time with Duma. Get to know him, discreetly. Do what you have to, to gain his trust," I instructed.

Daevas remained calm, but I knew his micro-expressions well enough to know that he wasn't thrilled with the order.

"Go with him tomorrow to Dalekaya Skala. Search the archives yourself, don't expect a Scribe to know what we're looking for," I ordered.

He bowed his head. "Of course."

We were quiet for a moment, watching as Iaoel and Duma landed back on the roof. They retracted their wings once more before heading back inside, paying us no mind. Gabriel, Heather, and Jade had stopped flying around, instead just hovering and talking with each other in the air.

I was able to narrow my vision to see them with better accuracy. Well enough to see Heather's flushed skin and the now more obvious golden glow coming off Gabriel's skin. Clearly, he had enjoyed himself to let loose some of his hold on his power.

"What about the Nephilim?" Daevas asked.

"What about her?"

He nodded in her direction. "Are we to befriend her as well? A Nephilim is a decent weapon to have in our armory should we need it," he stated.

A weapon.

That's what they had begun to see her as the moment we realized she was Nephilim. That she was a weapon to be wielded against our enemies.

To be wielded for power. White-hot anger began to surge in my core, I could feel its churning liquid bubble and hiss against its restraints.

"No," I growled. "We leave her alone."

"What do you mean?"

"I *mean*, regardless of her potential power or the advantages that it would give us. She is half-mortal, and she wants to return to that life. Who are we to deny her that? Leave her be," I explained.

My eyes remained on her from my distance. It didn't matter if she could make the difference between us succeeding in our separation from Lucifer or failing—only to be bound in chains until Lucifer found use for us.

The idea of using her as a weapon, the same way Lucifer would use me, wasn't going to happen. I would not do that to another person.

If I had the chance to live a normal mortal life, I would take it.

Gabriel, Heather, and Jade turned towards us and began to fly closer.

Daevas cleared his throat. "You know I'm here if you ever need to talk," he said quietly.

I gave him a side-glance and nodded in response. He dipped his chin back before heading back into the warehouse.

Jade landed first, smiling from ear to ear as she approached me. Gabriel and Heather landed seconds later, Heather stumbling to regain her footing.

“You should join us next time, Kaleus,” Jade suggested with a wink, gently elbowing me in the side.

I offered her a small smile in return that didn’t fully reach my eyes. “I don’t think you’d be able to keep up with me.”

Jade laughed lightly. “That sounds like a challenge.”

“If you want it to be.” I winked. She chuckled and started for the roof door.

Heather was catching her breath from the whole excitement when she looked at me confused, having just caught me and Jade’s short conversation.

“You have wings too?” she asked.

I shrugged. “I can fashion them if the situation calls for it. They’re nothing like the angels’, not as aesthetically pleasing,” I replied.

When her eyes locked on mine the molten core churned hotter. But I kept my expression neutral. A vast improvement from the death stares I’d given her recently.

I still felt the sting of her earlier words, the implications of them. Still saw how easy it was for her to fully trust an archangel but be so dissentient towards me after learning what I truly was.

It was truly disappointing—we were similar in so many ways. We were both the only ones of our kind, for the moment at least. Neither one of us really fit in anywhere, and we both could be used as weapons.

Maybe that was what actually bothered me.

I finally found someone who could relate to my situation. And she so quickly hated me like everyone else.

I was so lost in thought that I hadn't realized we'd been just staring at each other in silence for a while. It was Gabriel putting a comforting hand on her shoulder that broke our eye contact.

"Jade and I are being requested to return to our division to help with some crowd control," he said.

"You gotta leave again so soon?" Heather asked.

I almost rolled my eyes from the disappointment in her voice.

He tucked a loose strand of her hair behind her ear, "I'll try to be back sooner next time," he chuckled lightly.

I'm gonna vomit if these two don't stop their gushy touching. I practically screamed down the bond to Seere.

I heard her giggle. *You need to get laid, fire-boy.*

The archangel turned to me and opened his mouth to say something—but I cut him off.

"Yeah, yeah. Protect the mortal, no funny business, let you know if anything happens. Get outta here already, featherbrain."

Gabriel glowered at me but shook it off and extended his wings once more, beating them once and shooting back into the skies. Heather watched him fly until he disappeared beyond sight before lowering her head to look at me once more.

I could see the words forming in her eyes, but before she could open her mouth to speak, I turned and walked towards the roof door.

"Kale—" she called.

"Save it."

I had the roof door half-open when she said, “Please.”

I don’t know why I paused, but I did.

“I’m sorry. What I said the other night was stupid. I shouldn’t have let fiction influence my opinion of you. I know there’s a lot I have yet to learn, and I’m going to try to be open minded. I just wanted you to know that I’m sorry.”

I gripped the roof door tighter, almost to the point of bending it. I knew she was genuine; I knew since she returned soaking wet that night that what she said was purely human, and that she actually didn’t say a lot—rather I too jumped to conclusions. I knew I wasn’t even all that mad at her for it—not really.

It was a misunderstanding. So why did I feel angry?

It all just reminded me that I was hardly worthy of the friends I already had. And I shouldn’t expect anyone who hadn’t experienced our level of hell to see through the flames.

I wouldn’t share any of those facts with her though.

No, I would spare this mortal the pain which often came with being friends with a hellborn. Save her from the real demons within.

I will stick to the cinders of beasts where I belong.

In the end, the only response I could give her was, “I know you are.”

THIRTY-TWO
Heather

THE NEXT DAY WE DIDN'T WASTE ANY TIME pouring ourselves back into the pile of papers.

Us being me, Seere and Iaoel at least. Duma and Daevas had apparently gone to visit the Mosco Scribe archive, Gabriel and Jade were still off taking care of Guardian angel business.

I hadn't seen Lillith for a couple days, but Seere implied that she was spending a lot of time in hell as of late.

Kale was here as far as I knew. But still avoiding spending any unnecessary time around me.

After my apology, I could tell that he needed more time to forgive me. But when he looked me in the eyes, his expression was beginning to soften. At least I knew we were beginning to move forward.

The most I could do with the records was to jot down anything I could understand. My journal was filling up quick with random symbols that didn't make any sense.

Some of them were the demonic language—Aļik, among other demonic and angelic languages that I definitely wasn't fluent in.

It was frustrating that some of the ethereal languages struck some recognition, my half-angel blood managing to form words and phrases from them. And then others would be complete gibberish to me. If translating was a part of my Nephilim abilities—it sure wasn't as helpful as we needed it to be.

After we poured over what was collected, we were managing to make a dent. But with seven other outposts to visit, our pile was only going to get bigger. And unfortunately, what information we were finding was leaving us with next to zilch.

“Are there any other places that records of the relics could be other than in a Scribe post?” I asked.

Iaoel flipped a pager over, scanning relentlessly through the information. “Heaven. But we’ve already checked there.”

“And Hell’s records are copies upon copies. And small in quantity,” Seere added.

She rolled the piece of parchment she had in her hand into a tight ball and threw it over her shoulder. It landed perfectly in the waste bin next to the kitchen counter. Seere did a small fist-pump victory dance.

Iaoel rolled their eyes. “Could you please not do that? We do have to return these.”

Seere fiddled with her braids. “That one was about some dumb shrine of muses in Egypt. Trust me, no one will miss it.”

“Someone might seek out that information in the future,” Iaoel countered.

Seere snorted, “Not likely.”

Indeed. A lot of what we were reading was of mundane events and places, hardly helpful to our situation. If they really kept all of this information, I was beginning to think the angels had a hoarding problem. Along with their obvious organization issues. I mean, would it kill them to digitize?

Shrine of the Muses.

I straightened in my chair. Where have I heard that before? It sounded so familiar, but my brain felt so foggy from overreading, I wasn’t sure I’d manage to conjure up that information.

And maybe I shouldn't, if Seere had determined it to be useless. Still though, the nickname referred to something right at the tip of my tongue…

Wait a minute…

"Shrine of the Muses?" I clarified as I stood and went to fish the ball of parchment out of the trash.

Seere watched me with a raised eyebrow. "Yeah. What of it?"

"Wasn't that what they called the Library of Alexandria?" I asked.

Iaoel lowered their paper to look at me. "It's one of the Library's nicknames. But a large portion of it burned down in one-forty-five B.C."

I unraveled the ball, smoothing out the wrinkles on the paper so I could see its writing more clearly. Most of it was written in Greek, which I was relatively familiar with.

But that wasn't what caught my eye—right alongside it on the edge of the paper were five small fading sigils, one of them was what they told me was the sigil for the Eternal—Irul, which explained why they grabbed this piece in the first place.

I traced the lines and circles that made up the other four.

I didn't know what they meant, but as my fingers grazed over them I felt a strange pull that I didn't fully understand. It was like a small thread in the back of my mind was being tugged on.

Darkness dwells where one can't see.

"I think we need to go to Egypt." I stated, not able to take my eyes off of the curved lines.

"Jophiel and Jade already went to Egypt, they didn't find anything," Iaoel replied.

I shook my head. "They went to Cairo, right?" I asked. They nodded. "We need to go to Alexandria. It could be nothing, but my gut is telling me that we'll find something there," I explained.

Seere furrowed her brows. "Something like what? The ruins are a tourist attraction now."

"Heather could be right. It *was* once one of the largest collections of knowledge in the mortal world. We've been focusing our search on immortal archives, but what if we should be also looking in mortal locations too. I know some of the Nymphs hoarded information and hid it when they dispersed. What better places to put them than in normal human libraries, where someone wouldn't even bother taking a second glance at them," Iaoel said.

Seere shrugged and got to her feet, adjusting her buckles and belts that held small, sharpened weapons in them.

"I guess it couldn't hurt to look. But you're navigating." She pointed at Iaoel. "I can't focus with all those crowds taking selfies and wearing bright colored Hawaiian shirts," she giggled.

Iaoel nodded and stood as well. Both of them started walking towards the archway.

"Can I go?" I asked.

They both paused mid-step and looked back at me. "You should probably stay here, in-case there are primordials nearby," Iaoel replied.

"Oh come on, she'll be fine. Let her come along," Seere argued.

Iaoel looked at Seere disapprovingly. "It could be dangerous for her."

Seere scoffed and waved them off, "Last I checked, the Egyptian prison is still sealed shut. So it'll be fine. Besides, the poor girl is starving for some sunlight."

She looked at me and winked.

"Gabriel wouldn't allow it."

"Well, Kale says it's fine. And he's the one I take orders from. So she's coming."

Seere didn't give Iaoel another moment to object before she clasped my wrist and dragged me out the archway and down the stairs with her.

Iaoel hesitated, but eventually sighed in resignation, following us down to the pentacle. Thank God I wore my sneakers today.

Seere stopped us in the center, keeping her grip on my wrist. Which was surprisingly not that hard for someone of her strength.

I leaned over and whispered in her ear before Iaoel reached us.

"Did Kale actually say yes to this?"

Seere snorted quietly. "Like I'd actually need his permission to do *anything*."

Well then. I was a stowaway.

When Iaoel entered the pentacle next to us they gripped Seere's free hand and looked us both up and down.

"We'll keep this portion of the report out," they stated.

Seere elbowed them. "You got it. I owe you one anyway."

Just as I realized that this was the first time I'd winnowed with someone besides Gabriel, a thin field of light surrounded us, and the wind whipped my hair more fiercely than it did before. It felt like I was on a rollercoaster, doing bends and loops at sharp speeds.

The feeling was making my stomach jolt. This was a lot more jarring than it was with Gabriel.

It lasted longer too. Instead of a few seconds, we winnowed together for about two minutes before it finally subsided. The fading light revealing the rising sun on the Mediterranean's horizon.

We were on the coast just outside of the modern building of the Library. I turned to stare at it, and the ruins close by.

"How big was the original Library?" Seere asked. I looked at her and she shrugged. "It was before my time."

"Huge. We'll have to find an entrance into the old structure, see if there are any hidden chambers or tunnels," I answered.

For once I was in my element. I had learned about this place and could actually contribute more than I had been just sitting at that dumb warehouse table. The feeling was exciting.

Iaoel looked the structure up and down. "The best place to start would be inside the Bibliotheca. Let's go."

Once inside we were faced with hundreds of shelves, and an endless stream of study tables. It was a very modernized looking library, large and expansive to accommodate hundreds of knowledge seekers and tourists. But there were no immediate signs of anything old.

The three of us walked further into the library, passing a couple additional spaces where there were exhibits of some of remaining artifacts from the original Library.

But still no sign of even a basement door.

"Maybe I was wrong," I mumbled.

Seere touched my arm to stop me. I paused and looked in the direction she was looking—at Iaoel. Who had gone completely still and wasn't blinking.

"What's happening?"

"I'm assuming since they're an Angel of Sight, that they are having a vision," Seere explained.

"Well I hope it's a vision about where to go."

"You and me both, chickpea."

We waited while Iaoel stared off into nothing. I was expecting their eyes to go white or something when they had a vision, at least that's what I envisioned when Gabriel told me what they were.

A full minute passed when Seere spoke again, sighing audibly.

"Holy hellfire, it must be a long one."

"Are they usually not?" I asked.

Seere grinned to herself. "The first day this whole alliance started I went with them to Reaper's Creek, remember?" I nodded. "Iaoel had a vision of me, of what exactly I have no idea—anyway, that vision only lasted like twenty seconds," she explained.

"How do they work exactly?"

She threw her hands in the air, exasperated. "Hell if I know, chickpea. You should ask them," she said as she pointed to Iaoel still as a rock.

I sighed and approached their motionless body.

"Iaoel?" I called. I waved my hand in front of their face, nothing. I placed a hand gently on their shoulder. "Iaoel?"

Suddenly they blinked and the air they had been holding in came whooshing out of their mouth. Their eyelids fluttered and then their pupils focused on me, finally seeing me in front of them.

"I know where we can get in, come on," they said, immediately walking again.

They led us to the back of the building where the crowds had disappeared, until we reached a door that read, Μόνο το προσωπικό.

Staff only.

I read it over and raised an eyebrow at Iaoel. "You're sure?"

They rolled their eyes. "So little faith, even now you know of our existence." I shrugged and nodded.

We all took one last look around us making sure no one saw us before Iaoel broke the lock with the push of her thumb.

"Breaking and entering isn't very angelic," Seere teased.

Iaoel smirked back at her. "Perhaps your methods are rubbing off on me, hellborn."

Seere's eyes twinkled. "Speaking of rubbing, remind me to break out the oils later," she purred seductively.

I didn't say anything, even though I felt extremely awkward suddenly taking on the role of the third wheel between the two.

Iaoel chuckled and turned to walk through the door.

I let Seere go in front of me and mumbled behind her, "Are all you demons such shameless flirts?"

Seere laughed louder than I expected. Made me worry someone might hear us.

"Just you wait, chickee-dee. When Kale is done being mad at you, you'll find yourself at the receiving end of flirting that'll make you blush so hard, it'll make your feathered prince charming look like Charlie fucking Brown."

"Oh joy," was my only response.

She continued to giggle quietly as we found ourselves descending a metal spiral staircase.

Down a story we stepped into the basement, which looked more like the electrical room. Translucent cabinets revealing row upon row of blinking lights of every color. Iaoel kept walking though, so Seere and I kept following as they led us through another much older door that took a little pushing to get open.

And by little, I'm sure to a human like me it would have been impossible.

Through it we were going down a tunnel, large pipes running along all sides. After turning a couple corners the equipment gradually got older, and unused. Even the smell of the place aged. Wet mud that reeked of mold and sewage. I cringed against it.

The ground softened and electric light became extremely limited. Before long, the walls of the tunnel hardened into what looked like aged stone.

"It's not much farther," Iaoel informed.

"What's not much farther?"

They didn't answer, but when the space opened up, they didn't need to. The tunnel opened into a semi-large antechamber, where the walls were lined with stone shelves and other dark doorways that led to alternate locations. There were rotting wooden boxes and broken pottery scattered around the space.

There were four dark pathways, one of which had collapsed—given the fallen stone covering its entrance.

Iaoel pointed down one of them.

“Each of these should lead to another room like this, it goes on for a while. But there should be some scrolls here and there. Most of this was canvased when they were doing the renovations, but they missed some things,” they explained.

“How do you know?” Seere asked.

“My vision showed me. But unfortunately, it didn’t specify which chambers to go down. We’ll have to split up.”

My eyes widened. “What? Why? Is that a good idea?”

Iaoel gave me a sympathetic look. “There’s nobody down here but us. You’ll be fine.”

I suppressed a scared whine and looked between the angel and the demon.

“I don’t know how much you immortals keep up with pop-culture. But usually when the gang splits up, that’s when the axe murderer picks them off one by one,” I explained. “And I’d rather not be cut to bits in some underground ruins never to be found again, thank you very much.”

Seere chuckled. “Guess it’s a good thing you have an axe murderer for a friend.”

She had an axe in her hand now.

I put a hand up and shook my head, “I’m not even going to ask where you were keeping that. Look, I would really rather stay with one of you.”

A flashlight appeared out of thin air into Iaoel’s hand, they approached and handed it to me.

“I know you’re scared, Heather. But that’s just your human-side talking. Now would be a great time for you to embrace your angel-half. Your first lesson in overcoming your panic.”

I gripped the flashlight, which I assumed came from the Ethereal realm—if Kale could put my car in there, no doubt a flashlight was no problem.

Seere agreed. "You said you wanted to come. Coming on these excursions means you have to help. It's just an ancient library, if you can't handle it just yell for one of us and we can be there lickety-split."

I gulped, my throat dry. I closed my eyes and tried to take a deep breath. I'd never done something like this before. Sure I'd gone on anthropological digs, but there was usually an entire team of experts, with extremely bright light fixtures, and everything was already scavenged.

I didn't fully know why I was suddenly so afraid, feeling like the ground beneath me was about to disappear. But the idea of entering that darkness alone…

"Heather," Iaoel said. I opened my eyes, they were still facing me, Seere not far behind them.

I exhaled. "I'm sorry. I just have a bad feeling about this."

Seere's eyebrows narrowed. "You are the one who said that your gut was telling us to come here," she stated.

"I know. I don't know how to explain it. It shouldn't be so hard for me to walk down a simple passageway. But I'm terrified. I'm more afraid now than I was when that vetala thing almost ate me, or when I met all of you. Shouldn't that mean something?" I asked.

The fear that was clenching its claws around my heart was irrational and I couldn't break away from it.

Iaoel glanced back at Seere with a worried expression. Seere met their gaze then shook her head and stormed between the two of us.

She gripped my shoulders and looked me dead in the eyes when she said, “Listen to me for a second, Heather. Fear is a very powerful enemy. It will do anything and everything to chain you down. But *you* are stronger. You can overcome it. The only way to do so is to face it head on. Okay?” she asked.

Reluctantly I nodded.

“Okay, now I’m going to give you something that always helps me overcome fears grasp. I want you to repeat after me: I am afraid and I don’t care.”

“I am afraid, and I don’t care.” I repeated hesitantly.

“Because I am a badass and *nothing* can conquer me.”

THIRTY-THREE
Heather

I'M FINE.

There is nothing to be afraid of. You're just being a baby. There is nothing down here but rock and dirt. You can do this.

We had split up, each of us taking one of the available passages. The goal was simple, go through and grab anything that looked important. Which wasn't much. Iaoel was right about them previously combing through these and taking whatever survived. Because all I was seeing as I walked down the dark hallway was stone and broken pieces of equipment and pottery.

The fear I felt remained, it actually began to get stronger the further into the dark I went. It was only Seere's words chanting over and over in my head that kept my feet moving forward.

The wrath demon should consider switching careers to motivational speaker. I'd read hundreds of books and heard tons of speakers in areas like philosophy and history, and none of them had managed to inspire me as much as Seere did.

I mean, who says stuff like that?

I am a badass and nothing can conquer me.

I had hoped that after all this was over Seere could tell me about her life. If she could overcome as much agony and fear that I could only imagine came from being born and raised in hell, then surely I could conquer this dark library.

The only light in my vision was now sourced from the flashlight in my hand. The passageway narrowed the further into it I went, until it eventually opened up into another antechamber like Iaoel said it would. I scanned the entire room with the light, similar to the other one, only this one had less excavating equipment.

I took a steadying breath to fight the waves of fear that continued to clench around me. My imagination was running wild as I looked over every inch of the space with the flashlight. I wasn't a huge horror movie fan myself, but that didn't mean I wasn't sometimes forced to endure them.

Every moment I feared that the light would land on a figure crouched in the dark or light up a gruesome bloodied face that would eat me alive and leave my bones for the others to find later.

I shivered against the images. *I am afraid and I don't care.*

After scanning the entirety of the chamber and finding nothing I locked light on the two additional passages that led into more harrowing darkness.

I am a badass and nothing can conquer me.

I was going to start worshipping the sun after this.

Two paths…which one to take? Neither one of them seemed appealing, to be honest. Why did I want to come? Serves me right for trying to be helpful. But I was getting tired of that steel and concrete warehouse. A change of scenery, even one as dark and nerve-racking as this one was in a way refreshing.

Left or right. *Come on, Heather—just pick one*. I looked at the doorways carved out of stone for both of them and pointed my flashlight down them. But neither revealed any signs that would tell me which one would be the best pick. What if I entered the wrong one and just ended up in an endless maze of stone whereas the other could be where pertinent information is stored.

I sighed audibly. "Well this is a fucking pickle," I said out loud, my voice echoed in the darkness.

I pointed my light into the left hallway and noticed that my fear dulled slightly. Hm. I turned towards the right hallway and again felt the talons of terror squeeze my senses. Back at the left, they released. So maybe the left hallway would be my best bet.

Just as I began to cross the threshold into the left one, I felt that thread in the back of my mind again, and it tugged me backwards.

The hell?

I paused and turned to look at the right hallway again. The dark emptiness felt like it was growing from it. Every instinct in my body was telling me to go into the left, follow the one that felt safest. All of them except that strange tug.

I swallowed and approached the threshold of the right. My chest felt so tight and even my vision wavered slightly upon staring into the void. Why would I be more afraid of this one than the other? They both were equally ominous—it didn't make any real sense.

The tug pulled harder, this time forward.

Maybe this fear was a sign. Maybe it meant that there was something important down here, and the part of me that was angel could sense it. So maybe this fear wasn't a human reaction at all, but more of an alarm sounding in my body.

So, with another deep-steadying breath, into the right passage I went.

At first it was as simple as putting one step in front of the other to overcome the growing ache in my stomach. But as I was engulfed completely in the darkness of the passage the air became thick, making it harder to breathe it in.

I tried to make as little sound as possible to keep my ears open to any potential threat that I couldn't see. But the only sound I heard was the thumping of my pulse as it quickened the further inside I went.

Heather. A whisper said. I whipped around and shown the light towards the airy sound—nothing.

My heart pounded. *My mind is playing tricks on me. The fear is overcoming my common sense.* I panted for air when I heard the airy whisper again.

Sați.

What the actual hell?

I circled around, pouring the light of the flashlight over every surface around me. There was nothing. I swallowed the lump in my throat and took another couple steps forward. *It's all in your head.*

Don't let it conquer you.

When I only heard silence the hairs on my arms rose. I spun around again and again. Checking my surroundings every second. And soon, I had forgotten which way I had come from. Everything looked the exact same, solid stone wall.

Shit. Where am I? I needed to get back; I knew this was a bad idea.

Every muscle in my body felt tight, and soon I was struggling to breathe. Panic beginning to rise. I touched my hand against the stone wall to stay standing. My vision was blurry, and my skin felt prickly.

I need to get out. I need to get out.

Then my flashlight started to flicker and dim.

My panic rose. "No. No, no, no, no."

I tried shaking it and banging the side of it, but the light sputtered and then went out completely. Leaving me in pitch darkness.

I felt for the wall again, cold stone meeting my hand. I couldn't hear anything by my frenzied breathing. I was trapped, and I had no idea which way would take me out and which one would bury me further underground.

My breath hitched with every harrowing thought that swam through my mind, turning each time I thought I heard something.

Help. Somebody help me.

"Seere? Iaoel?" I spoke out loud, my voice was quiet, breathless at first. I gulped down, clearing my throat some.

"Seere!" I yelled. I heard the name echo into the darkness, but I didn't hear a response.

I pinned my back against the wall and slid down until I was sitting. Both of my hands touching the surface for stability. My knees clenched against my chest.

Stay where you are so others can find you. First lesson of being lost.

"SEERE! IAOEL!" I screamed louder.

Please find me. I begged internally. God, what I would give to be able to use that stupid supernatural web right now.

My hands touched something cold, and I felt for it again—the flashlight. I had to get it working. It must have rolled away because my hands scanned for it and didn't find it.

"Shit," I muttered. "Seere! My flashlight is dead! I need you!" I called out again.

If they were looking, maybe the sound of my voice would help lead them down the right passages.

Unless they were too far into their own passages to even hear me. I certainly couldn't hear them. Damn these old Greeks who created such a soundproof library.

I tried to gulp down air, even as my throat felt like it was closing up.

"You're fine. You're not hurt, they'll come find you. You're afraid and you don't care," I recited to myself. "You are a badass and nothing can conquer you."

I felt like a child, terrified of the dark. My fingers felt around the cold ground for the flashlight. I winced as something sharp cut me. A piece of broken pottery maybe. Or maybe the flashlight broke and a sharp piece was poking out.

I gave up on searching for the flashlight and clutched my legs, hugging my body as close as I could. I closed my eyes, a more comforting darkness than the one in front of me.

Nothing can conquer me. Nothing can conquer me. Nothing can conquer me.

I chanted it in my head, even whispered it out loud over and over. But the fear never subsided, and there were no sounds of Seere or Iaoel coming to find me.

I was stuck here alone. *All alone*.

Something touched me, something wet and solid. I opened my eyes and though I still couldn't see anything, I felt it. Slick, slimy vines touching my legs, my arms, my face.

And a whisper that sucked all of the life out of my soul.

"*Finally*." The voice wasn't human, and I wasn't safe.

And then I was screaming.

THIRTY-FOUR

"HEATHER?!" Seere called as she rushed back to the main chamber.

She'd heard Heather yelling and it was based on the sheer terror in her voice that motivated Seere to go back for her. Maybe asking her to go alone on the human's first trip wasn't a good idea.

But Heather needed to start conquering her fears at some point, otherwise this alliance would be the death of her.

Once Seere reached the original antechamber they had split from, she went to go down Heather's passage when a figure appeared. Seere backed away when she saw Iaoel coming through it holding Heather in their arms. Heather was cradled in close—her eyes were closed but eyelids fluttering frantically.

"What happened?" Seere asked.

Iaoel was smaller than Heather, but their angel strength didn't struggle to hold the human's weight.

"I'm not sure. I heard her screaming. When I went in to find her, I found her like this. She's not responding," Iaoel explained.

Iaoel put Heather down so that they both could assess her. Heather's muscles were twitching frantically, but she never opened her eyes.

"Heather?" Seere asked. "You alright?" but the human didn't reply. "She seems catatonic."

“Something mental then. Maybe she’s in a dream,” Iaoel theorized.

Seere shook her head. “Why would she suddenly start dreaming? What did you see down there?” she asked.

“Just her huddled on the floor. Her flashlight was five feet away, working just fine. I don’t know if she saw something or what. But I still don’t sense someone else down here, I can’t make sense of it.”

Seere touched Heather’s forehead. It was hot to the touch, a fever. Seere didn’t have any mental abilities besides some feeble shielding that Kale helped her develop when she was younger. And Iaoel’s didn’t extend beyond their visions and the super-web.

“We should get her to Kale. He’ll be able to see what’s going on.” Seere said.

Iaoel nodded. “My thoughts exactly.” They cradled Heather under her arms and legs and lifted again. “Let’s go.”

Seere gripped Iaoel’s shoulder and then light surrounded them. Her eyes remained on Heather’s unconscious body while they winnowed through space. Heather’s eyelids were fluttering and twitching nonstop.

Whatever she had seen or heard in that passageway, they’d have to return to it later to inspect it. But for now, they needed to help their Nephilim.

A few minutes passed and then the light cleared, they were inside the pentacle.

Before Iaoel could take a step they too collapsed to their knees. Seere caught Iaoel quickly enough to steady them so they didn’t drop Heather.

“You okay?” she asked.

Iaoel panted. “Yeah. I think there were wards down there, winnowing through them nearly knocked the wind out of me.”

“Wards? Why didn’t we sense them?” Seere demanded.

Iaoel shook their head. “They must’ve been old enough to be barely noticeable. I wouldn’t have even realized they were there if I hadn’t been carrying you two with me.”

“People only ward places when there’s something to hide.” Seere stated. Iaoel nodded in agreement.

“Or if they’re trying to keep something in.”

Kale’s voice echoed through the large room, already having sensed Seere’s distress through their connection.

“What happened?” he demanded.

He jumped directly off the top of the stairwell and crossed the distance to the pentacle within seconds.

Iaoel still held Heather to their body. “We don’t really know,” they answered.

Kale looked over Heather’s body and then locked eyes with Seere. “Show me.”

She let him into her memories. Replaying every moment since they decided to go to Alexandria up until the moment the winnowed back. Hours of memories that compiled and played out to Kale in a matter of seconds.

Kale nodded when he received all the information.

“Hand her to me,” he instructed.

Iaoel didn’t hesitate to exchange Heather’s body into Kale’s waiting arms. He walked out of the pentacle towards one of the tables covered in weapons and workout equipment on the other side of the room.

“Clear off the stuff.”

Seere did so, Iaoel helping until there was nothing left. Kale lowered Heather's unconscious form onto the metal table, his eyes puzzled as he watched her eyes.

His brows narrowed. "I can't see what's going on."

"What does that mean?" Iaoel asked.

"It means I'm going to have to shove my way in. Whatever she's seeing is blocking control of her own consciousness," Kale explained.

He pulled up a chair and sat next to the table, gripping Heather's hand. Iaoel gripped his shoulder, he looked up at the Angel of Sight.

"Wait a minute. Remember the last time, we should wait until Gabriel comes back. He doesn't want anyone going into her head again," Iaoel said.

"That isn't his choice to make."

"*He* is her Guardian. When she is unable to make a choice, he's the one to make it."

Kale grunted. "Even if I agreed—which I don't—he could take hours, days even. I need to go in and figure out what's going on now. We can't risk whatever is in there ripping the fabric of her mind apart," he argued.

Iaoel hesitated, looking around the quiet warehouse. Gabriel gave specific orders to the angels following the last incident. No one was to go walking through Heather's consciousness without his permission or without him being present.

If the other angels arrived before the demons did, they would be hostile. Iaoel had seen it in a vision. This wasn't going to be pretty, but Kale was right. Waiting could be the worst thing for Heather.

Iaoel's hand was still on his shoulder. "Remove your hand, angel. I won't tell you twice," he warned.

They nodded and retreated back.

Kale turned again to the human, with his hand in hers he closed his eyes and focused on the entryway into her mind. Where the wooden gate should have been there was a huge stone wall. With not a single crack in sight.

Kale pressed a hand against it. He felt rumbles. She was behind it along with whatever else was causing this.

Kale opened his eyes and looked at both Seere and Iaoel, who were watching them intently.

"I'm going to have to throw all my energy into this to break past it. Do not, I repeat, *do not* interrupt." He locked his gaze on Seere in warning. "My physical power is going to be on auto-pilot. Including the barriers that keep it under control," he instructed.

His expression was grave.

"If you see the signs, you know what to do."

Seere nodded in understanding. Iaoel was curious but didn't question it.

Seere flicked her gaze to Iaoel. "If the others get here before Gabriel…"

"Do whatever you have to. I'll try to be quick," Kale ordered. Seere and even Iaoel agreed.

He closed his eyes again and began the slow process of breaking through the wall that now bordered Heather's mind.

Seere sighed and went to the weapons now scattered on the floor and started clicking some in place on any free sheaths and buckles she had on her leathers. Iaoel turned and watched her.

"You really think you'll need those?" they asked.

Seere shrugged. “If it’s me against angels who are ten times more powerful than I am, I’ll need all the help I can get.”

“You say that like you’re alone.”

Seere gave them a pointed look. “Are you willing to go against your own friends, your brothers and sisters? Even if the fight gets bloody?” she asked.

“I’m hoping it doesn’t come to that.”

“That doesn’t mean we shouldn’t prepare for it to. And I will do what I have to. I don’t expect you fight,” Seere said. Her focus completely on tightening and locking in all her weapons and straps to ensure stealth.

“Maybe Kale will finish before anyone shows.”

“Have you not seen this then? Have you seen where this goes? Cause that advantage will help a lot,” Seere suddenly asked.

Iaoel shook their head, peering back at Kale and Heather, now both deep in her consciousness, unaware of the world around them. Iaoel had seen a lot of things, some of them couldn’t be shared with anyone. Or it risk their futures changing to something worse.

“I will do my best to persuade them against violence,” Iaoel stated simply.

Seere chuckled darkly. “That’s comforting, love.”

THIRTY-FIVE
Kale

THE WALL WAS THICK, whatever erected it—it wasn't Heather's doing.

She was still too new, untested in mental capabilities to achieve something this strong unintentionally. What the hell was Seere thinking taking Heather along? Especially without telling me. The moment I had known they were gone I began communicating with Seere.

But she assured me that everything was fine and that there was no danger. So why was Heather now locked inside her own mind?

I pressed both my palms against the stone and pushed, but it didn't budge. I could feel the rumbling behind it vibrate my skin.

I sighed, pressing my forehead against it.

"Heather? If you're in there, I need you to help me get in." I said into the stone.

Even with a wall, it was her mind—she should be able to hear me.

"Wherever you are, whatever you're seeing, focus on the sound of my voice and come to it," I instructed.

I felt a stirring that was different than the rumbling, something smaller. It must be her.

"Come on Heather. Follow my voice."

“Kale?” a soft voice asked, muffled behind the wall.

“Yes, it’s me. I’m here.”

The rumbling was smaller, like it was farther away. “How are you here?” she asked.

“We’re in your mind, Heather. Your body is safe in the warehouse. I need you to bring down this wall for me,” I instructed.

Even with a wall between us I could sense her when she touched it.

“This isn’t real?” she whispered.

“It’s real, it’s just happening in your mind. The wall,” I pushed.

“I don’t know how to bring it down.”

I sighed and looked over the stone once more.

“We’ll have to do it together. Heather, I’m going to throw some of my power into it. What I need you to do is focus your mind on creating a crack in it. Whatever built it still lives under the rules of your own mind, if you focus hard enough you should be able to break it. Okay? Can you do that?” I asked.

“I—I’ll try.” she replied in a small voice.

I nodded. “Okay, when I say so, start visualizing cracking the wall.”

I closed my eyes and retreated deep into myself. Going deeper and deeper until I was staring at the liquid, molten core that churned and boiled.

In here, this power was also mostly just my mind. My inner core a visualization that manifested my abilities through my consciousness instead of my real fingers. But whatever I did in here would affect my physical body, which was why I needed Seere to keep an eye on me. In-case my outer shell was compromised.

I reached into the core and pulled out not one but two threads of it. Leading them out through my veins, up my shoulders and down my arms until the two strings pooled into my palm. Only the thin barrier of my skin keeping its heat at bay, but I was going to have to let it come through.

I took three deep breaths as I allowed the magma to melt through the flesh and touch the stone. The rumbling returned stronger underneath my fingers, sensing the threat. I pressed my palms hard into the wall and the threads of core started doing their job. I could feel the stone underneath beginning to shudder and break under the intense heat and pressure.

"Now, Heather," I gritted out. Stealing away just a moment of focus to instruct her.

Bits of sand and stone started to crumble and fall at my feet. The balls of core spread out further, the stone beneath it began to crack and tremble.

"It's working." I heard Heather say, her voice a lot closer and less muffled than before.

I just needed it to open enough for me to slip through. The distant rumbling was getting deeper, nearing us. Bigger pieces of stone broke off and dropped to the ground, and then the crack was opening. I grunted against it and began retreating the threads before they could break all the way through. If they accidentally hit Heather…I couldn't let it happen—even in her mind.

Once the threads of core were once again deep inside, I pushed my hands against the growing crack, using blunt force to break through. As soon as I saw a glimmer of Heather's golden-brown hair, I flung myself through the opening.

I collided with Heather, throwing us both to the ground. She yelped and then sat up quickly. Behind me the crack shuddered and then closed again. We'd have to find another way out. Taking care of whatever was in here might do the trick.

I panted and locked eyes with the scared mortal. She looked terrified, and the space of her subconscious was darkened, the ground beneath us brown dirt.

“You okay?” I asked.

She nodded. I looked around, the rumbling now beneath us.

“Do you have any idea what’s in here?”

She shook her head. “It’s been changing forms. The first time it looked like liquid tentacles, the second time it looked like that vetala but not. I haven’t seen it since, but I’ve felt it coming,” she explained. “All this time I thought I was still in the Library. That that wall was—"

I nodded, surveying our surroundings. “Iaoel and Seere found you in the passages after hearing you scream for help, you were practically comatose. They brought you back to the warehouse so I could help you.”

“I don’t even know when I passed out. But I guess that explains why that feeling went away.”

“What feeling?”

“I was so scared in the Library. The fear was eating away at me. But not long after I saw the first form of whatever this is I stopped feeling that terror. I mean, I’m still scared. But it’s not as overpowering as it was before,” Heather explained.

“The Library apparently has old wards on it. Your fear might’ve been the way your limited angel grace reacted to them. But wards usually mean something important, maybe whatever is terrorizing your mind right now was being contained in the Library somehow,” I stated.

I stood from the ground and held my hand out to help her up.

“Like a primordial?”

I shrugged. “Maybe.”

Then I started walking in the direction of the rumbling.

“Where are you going?”

“We have to find this thing and take care of it if we want any chance of getting out of here,” I replied.

“We can’t get out the way you came in?” she asked.

“That wall is strong, and my physical body could hurt others around it, including you if I spend too much of my power in here,” I explained. “So, this is the next best solution.”

She sighed, “Okay.”

Heather rushed to catch up to me and grabbed my arm—clinging to me. I looked down at her. She scowled.

“I know you’re still mad at me, but deal with it.”

I chuckled. “I’m not mad at you.”

The space around us wasn’t empty, just dark. When my eyes began to adjust, I could see that it was a field—a dead field. A structure was in the distance but was still too far away to see. That seemed like the best direction at this point.

“You’re not?” she asked.

“You said you were sorry,” I said plainly.

She huffed. “I know. I just thought—you seemed like you needed more time to forgive me.”

“Oh, I haven’t forgiven you yet. I’m just tired of being mad about it,” I clarified.

A large rumble sounded, causing us to pause. I scanned all around us but after a moment of silence and no sign of anything I got our feet moving again.

"You know, what I said wasn't even that bad. One second I was expressing how I felt, then next you were yelling at me. I've apologized and I'm trying to be more open minded, but in all fairness, you weren't the only one to jump to conclusions. So why you're taking your time forgiving me is beyond me," Heather argued.

I resisted the urge to laugh in her face, instead I only smiled—keeping my eyes on lookout for any threats.

"That's the thing about forgiveness, honey-eyes, it's not up to you when I decide to bestow it. I could hold-out for eternity if I wanted to. You've done your part, now let me do mine in peace."

"Are you going to make me wait for eternity?" she asked.

I looked at her then. "If you don't leave it alone, then yes."

She huffed. "You can be a real hardhead. I make one mistake—a misunderstanding really—and you hold it over my head?"

"Who said I was holding it over your head?"

"You! You still avoid looking directly at me, acting like I've insulted your ancestors and shit on your bed!" she gasped and frantically looked around when she realized how loud her voice was raised.

I chuckled when she eventually looked back at me for a response.

"You humans are so petty."

"Petty?"

"Just because you feel bad about your actions, you think the only way you can feel better about yourselves is by having your feelings validated. When you have yet to realize that really, princess, this isn't about you," I explained, crossing my arms.

Her honey-brown eyes glinted when they stared at mine.

"I just want—" she stopped herself and looked away distantly. "Never mind. You're right. It's not fair of me to expect you to just smile and move on like what I said didn't hurt you in any way."

"See, now that's your problem, right there," I snapped, backing away from her a step.

Her brows narrowed and her nose scrunched in confusion.

"You think that you've deeply wounded me, but it's in that thought process that you're assuming you know who I am and what I feel. I don't care that you think; I might be an evil son-of-a-bitch. I've lived with people assuming the worst of me for a lot longer than you've been alive. If I were 'hurt' every time that happened, I would be one fragile-as-fuck immortal, don't you think?"

We had stopped walking, even when I could now see the outline of a rotted gazebo a hundred yards away.

"You're acting pretty fragile right now."

"I'm not mad that you reacted the way you did, finding out what I was. That comes with the territory. I was mad because you automatically dismissed all of my actions that contradicted that view of me. You caught onto the idea that I was a monster before actually considering everything else."

She backed away another step, no longer clinging close to me.

I groaned, the inner part of me still unable to convey what it was that was bothering me.

"Now, however, I'm mad that after all of that, you're now acting like you've deeply wounded me and need to tip-toe around my feelings. Pick a stance, Heather. Stop swinging back and forth," I finished with a gruff. So many more things still left unsaid.

Heather glared at me and tucked a piece of hair behind her ear.

"What do you want from me, Kale? Do you want me to see you as a creature of evil or as someone who feels pain?"

"Fucking hell, Heather. Do you hear yourself? I'm not some tortured soul that only *you* can piece back together, okay? This isn't like your books, okay? No one is just one thing. We're all complex. That's the real world, full of real monsters right in front of you."

Why am I like this?

"So even you think you're a monster? Yet you hated me for thinking it?" she asked pointedly.

I suppressed a low growl. "We're all monsters in our own way, princess. The only difference is those who pretend they're not and those who savor it."

She scoffed, "Do all you have such a dark and twisty way of looking at things? You say you're not a tortured soul, and yet with everything you just said I would beg to differ. You wanna know what everyone is seeing, what even the angels see? They see people with great power and strength who grew up in *literal hell* and decided that the only way to survive was to be broody and perverse about everything. It's juvenile, is what it is. Even humans go through a loner phase, Kale, but at least most of us get over it."

I wanted to agree with her. I did. But I didn't know how to let that wall down.

Heather continued, "You're just stuck in it. You've settled yourself with the idea that this is as good as it gets. That the only way to endure your eternity is to pretend like you love being a spawn of Satan. You tease and you play. And then you get mad when others don't immediately dismiss it as fiction."

Her nose crinkled in frustration…and it was adorable.

"You say I'm swinging back and forth, but you are too. Who are you really, Kale? The Heir Inferno, or something more? Make up *your* mind and then *be that*."

I was frozen. Heather finished her rant, and we just stared at each other.

If only she knew how badly I needed to hear someone say what was going through my thoughts each and every day.

And how she did exactly that.

I remained calm, my instincts telling me to slide on that cold-indifferent mask that I wore in hell. But I fought against it.

I was deep in the consciousness of a Nephilim who had just unknowingly laid me bare. A Nephilim whose mind was being attacked by an unknown threat who still hadn't shown themselves. Now wasn't the time for me to completely shut her down.

This conversation could continue later.

"As fun as this conversation is, Heather. We'll have to take a raincheck on it." I broke contact to look at the gazebo ahead of it. I nodded towards it. "Ever seen that before? In your dreams?" I asked.

She looked at it and tilted her head to the side. "No. I haven't."

"What about in real-life?" I asked.

She smirked. "I thought this was real life," she teased, poking at my earlier statement.

I held back my chuckle. “Focus, human.”

“I’m half-human,” she corrected with a teasing smile.

I snorted, “Right, so what should I call you then?”

She shrugged. “My name would suffice.”

I shook my head. “Nope, I use nicknames.”

“I know, you call Gabriel ‘feathers’ and ‘featherbrain’ all the time.”

We began walking towards the gazebo once more.

“Don’t forget ‘Lancelot’, ‘Buzzard’ and…let’s just say I have infinite names for that arch-asshole.”

Heather surveyed the dead field, some fear returning to her eyes.

“Why do you tease him so much?” she asked, using the casual conversation to distract her from our situation.

“One of these days I’ll tell you all about my first encounters with Gabriel. Then you’ll understand why he’s my favorite plaything,” I replied.

With no more than twenty feet between us and the gazebo, the ground shook. More than just the rumbling that we had been feeling pretty consistently—this time the ground quaked, throwing off our balance slightly.

Heather and I both jutted out our arms to steady ourselves. When the shaking stopped, we both felt it. Our sixth sense telling us that we weren’t alone anymore, and that if we turned around, we would see whatever was causing her catatonic state.

I didn’t turn at first, I kept my eyes on the gazebo.

"Heather, here's what's going to happen," I said low. Quiet enough that only she could hear. "Without looking back, you're going to run for the gazebo and get as low as you can. Wait there until I tell you otherwise, okay?"

In my peripheral vision I saw Heather nod slightly—taking in a slow deep breath.

Inside her consciousness I didn't have weapons, and my power wasn't at full strength. So, I would have to rely on my training and only use my limited power when absolutely necessary. I bent my knees to ground myself and took in a long deep breath.

"Go."

She bolted and I spun around.

A black shadow, built into a figure stood almost three feet taller than me. The shadows seeped and spread out from the bottom of the figure, whipping around like tentacles. The motion reminded me of the Nuckelavee's tail.

It was like the shadow read my mind each one of those tentacles' edges hardened into a sharp barb, rearing up to strike with the speed of a deadly viper.

Ah. Charming. I thought to myself and then quickly lunged to the side when one lashed towards me.

THIRTY-SIX
Heather

"CAN'T YOU JUST ZAP IT or fry it with your powers?" I called out.

Crouching low in the gazebo, I watched Kale dodge each whip of the shadow's barbed tentacles. What the hell was this thing anyway? And what was it doing in my fucking head?

Kale made a sound that resembled a struggled huff as he lunged away again.

"I'll remind you that we are in your head! Not the real world," he responded back.

"You did it the first time!"

He grunted when he had to roll to evade a sharp blow. He crouched no more than ten feet away from the gazebo. The thing was gradually pushing him closer to it and to me.

"Would you like to try?" he teased.

I should just shut up so he could focus. But talking to him was keeping me from trying to help. If I did, I would be a distraction and a burden. Not actually helpful. Staying back was my only option at this point.

When a black tentacle jutted out and hit the gazebo there was a loud smack and then the wood broke, splinters falling to the ground next to me. I yelped reactively and moved away from where it hit.

Kale flung out his hand and a small ball of lightning shot towards it. The tentacle twitched and then retreated.

Kale was panting.

“If I knew what the hell it was, I could fight it better. But it’s too fast for me to anticipate its moves.” He ducked when another shot aimed for his head.

“Can it actually hurt you?” I asked.

He retreated back a step when it came closer. “In theory, no. But even the mind can be damaged. I have no idea what it’s capable of.” He gasped as he barely evaded another shot.

It shot out four of its tentacles this time, two straight for him and the other two slammed into the gazebo again. Breaking one of the columns holding up the frame. I ducked away from the falling wood. Kale grunted as he blocked one and caught the other against his forearm.

Despite its shadowy appearance, its tails were apparently solid. And strong, given that Kale’s muscles were bulging and pushing against the strain it took to hold the sharpened barb away from his face.

A sizzling sound hit my ears before the smell did. Then I saw it, a red and orange glow covered Kale’s arms. They burned through the flesh of the tentacle until the barb fell off it onto the ground with a thud. Kale breathed and backed away, the glow disappearing from his arms.

The fallen tentacle shriveled back and then as it raised again nearer to its wielder, the shadows and liquid formed a sharpened edge once again.

“So much for that,” Kale muttered more to himself.

So his Inferno abilities didn’t do much against a creature that could morph and change at will.

Instead of lunging for Kale again, the shadow creature pulled all of its sharpened tentacles back—standing more than ten feet tall—staring at us.

For a moment it was quiet, unmoving. I didn't take my eyes off it, and neither did Kale.

"What's it doing now?" I asked.

Kale was a few steps away from the gazebo, amongst the broken shards of wood that had fallen around its entrance. "I don't know."

The son of Lucifer was watching every move and detail of the thing while it was still. His stance balanced, low to the ground, ready to lunge if he needed to.

I sat up further from where I was crouched on my knees. Gripping the railing for support as I got fully onto my feet. As I stared at it, trying to find details in the shadows, a face maybe. I could feel its attention directly on me, and even without a face I still felt like I was looking directly into its eyes.

A minute passed or ten—I couldn't tell anymore. Eventually the shadow began to move again. Not quickly like before, instead its liquid limbs slowly widened, the airy form spreading outwards until it was wider than the gazebo, and then it began curving inwards.

To completely surround the gazebo.

Kale kept his eyes on it as he closed the distance between us and joined me in the center of the white gazebo.

He gripped my wrist and placed me behind him as the shadows surrounded the front entrance and slowly was oozing around the edges.

"The only way we're getting out of your consciousness is if we can put this thing to sleep or kill it. But I honestly have no idea how," he whispered to me.

"I feel like I've seen this before."

"In your dreams?" he asked.

I nodded. "That may not be helpful. But if I've seen it before…"

"Then it may have been in here all along," Kale finished my sentence. "And if it changes form like you said, then maybe everything Gabriel and I have seen in your nightmares were all the same thing."

"I thought you got rid of the first one you encountered," I said.

I still remembered that day. An all-white room and then a shape that was only barely dark enough to see. The feeling of it when it touched me, the cold mist. And then the reddened, eclipsed landscape that took over when a dark figure with red eyes sent bolts of shocking lightning at it until it disintegrated into nothing.

That dream felt like a lifetime ago. And what I thought had been destroyed that day may very well be what was currently cocooning us in a dome of smoke and shadow.

I swallowed as what little light was already here began to sputter as the shadows and mist closed around us. It wasn't touching us, more like circling, consuming the gazebo in a globe of shadow.

"Maybe all I did then was put it to sleep. Maybe the wards in the Library woke it up again," Kale hypothesized.

"I'd really like this thing to be out of my head," I sighed.

Kale didn't say anything to that. What could he say? They weren't sure what it was, so there was no way of knowing if it could be expelled from my consciousness.

"But if that's not possible, do you think you could put it back to sleep?"

"I could try," Kale stated.

He tilted his head around to get a full view of what now covered the gazebo in a churning dome.

"The other day I killed an Eriking, that primordial is a purple mist that sucks the air from your body as a means to kill you," Kale started to explain.

"What a pleasant story, so comforting right now," I replied.

Kale tightened his grip on my wrist as a way to tell me to listen.

"The only way to kill it was to surround it in my own smoke and cut off its air as well. What gave it life was also its weakness," he continued. "What this thing is doing right now is looking a lot like what I did to the Eriking."

I gave a half-hearted laugh. "So what you're saying is, this thing is about to suffocate us?"

My already jittering nerves and fear were growing in my chest. Suffocation was an awful way to die.

"We're still in your head, remember? Our bodies *shouldn't* be in danger. But that doesn't mean it can't convince us that we're suffocating. We can't let it make us believe that what is happening in here is also happening in the real world," Kale amended.

"How do you suggest we do that? This feels very real to me." I asked, eyeing the swirling shadows that I now noticed also had ribbons of silver, red, and gold in it.

It had gotten so dark that if those shadows weren't moving, I wouldn't see anything.

As if reading my thoughts, Kale's skin began to glow with the same dim orange color of hot coals underneath a campfire.

"I thought your powers were limited here?"

"Are you complaining?" he demanded.

"No," I said quickly. "I was just wondering if you're wasting it by giving us light instead of using it against the shadow monster."

Kale chuckled lightly. "All I'm doing is lessening some of the power I use to reign it in. So actually, I'm conserving energy this way."

"Reign it in? You make it sound like you could lose control of it at any time."

"There's a lot to my power that is difficult to understand."

I nodded slightly. "Someday you'll have to explain it to me."

"Someday if you're lucky. Just not now."

Kale still held my wrist, and the temperature of it was distinctly hotter. Nearing on the edge of painful, but I didn't resist against it. The heat was an anchor for me to stay sane in the moment, even if it made my hand clammy. Even my back was sweating with our backs against each other.

He didn't seem to notice, still watchfully observing every motion of the shadows—looking anywhere for a potential weakness or threat.

"It's really taking its time with killing us," he said.

"Do you *have* to say it like that?" I begged.

His shoulders shrugged upwards. "Sorry. I'm not a fan of sugar-coating things."

It was quiet between us for a moment. And, as I watched the shadows relentlessly circle us in our dome-like tomb, I tried to think about other things to keep the terror and helplessness at bay.

"Talk about something, distract me, or I'm going to start freaking out," I stated.

"I thought my presence was distraction enough," he replied, I could hear the flirty smirk in his voice.

"You and Seere…what's the history there?" I asked suddenly.

I felt his back stiffen and then he laughed. The sound was strange in contrast to our current predicament.

"By your tone I'm guessing you mean are Seere and I a couple?"

I didn't reply, just waited patiently for his answer.

He chuckled once more. "When we first met, I had an interest, but I'm not Seere's type."

"I thought demons were all very *open*."

Kale huffed, "We are. Doesn't mean we can't have preferences. I would think by now you would have seen Seere's preference," he said suggestively.

I have. She flirted with Iaoel unabashedly, and Iaoel usually indulged her with equal treatment.

"What is it like to grow up in hell?"

"Exactly as you would imagine, well—actually much worse, but I'm sure your imagination can come up with an answer to that one."

"Seere's scars—"

"Now *really* isn't the time to talk about that, honey-eyes," Kale interrupted. The heat of his skin increased slightly.

I took a deep breath, beads of sweat rolled down my face from my forehead. With the shadow closing us off from the outside air, Kale's heat was making it unbearable.

The shadows around us slowed their circling—drawing my attention. Was this a sign that our end was getting closer?

We both stilled when the shadows started hardening into a solid wall. Soon everywhere around us no longer churned and swirled, instead we were entombed in dark stone.

For a moment all we heard was the sound of our breathing. Then a small tapping started. It was as quiet as a raindrop, then it slowly increased in pace and quantity.

And it was above us.

Both mine and Kale's head slowly raised to look up towards the ceiling. Something was hitting the top of the gazebo.

Light taps at first, slowly getting stronger. Soon chips of paint and wood crumbled and dropped with each tap, and then the wood splintered and bent inwards against the force.

I gulped. "Kale…"

Kale gripped my arms and shoved me backwards just as a large black glass shard punched through the wood straight down towards our heads. It was so fast it jutted two feet into the floor of the gazebo, barely missing us.

My hands caught the railing behind me, steadying me as I gasped for air from the force of Kale's shove. The shard was between us now, its material looked like crystal more than glass the more I looked at it.

Kale wasn't looking at it though, he was looking up at the ceiling where the taps continued.

"Move!" he yelled as more shards crashed through the weakened wood down onto us.

I raised my hands over my head to protect myself and dodged side to side to avoid a direct hit.

It was a miracle that none of the shards hit me, but I knew that luck wasn't going to last forever. The taps and pounding changed direction, no longer above us but around us. Kale noticed the change as well, looking around to try to pinpoint the loudest taps to anticipate the first shards.

"To your right," he said.

I rotated left, avoiding a shard, as it shot past me on the right. Kale jumped away from his right as a shard shot past just below his left knee. I focused my ears as best as I could to listen for the loudest taps, avoiding shards as they zipped through the wood. The frame of the gazebo was being shredded open. I would be surprised if it stayed standing much longer.

I jumped when my back slammed into Kale's chest, I whipped and gripped his forearms.

"We need to get out of here, we can't dodge them forever."

A much stronger tap sounded right next to our heads, loud enough that our eyes bulged in sync and we both dropped to our knees a mere second before an entire line of sharp darts shot through, both of us panting.

"I'm open to ideas." Kale said.

I looked around and saw that in some parts where the shards burst through light was flooding in. Cracks in the shadows, openings. I pointed to them.

"Maybe we can get through one of these openings."

Kale huffed. "They're hardly big enough for a person to get through."

"Help them along then," I suggested. I looked down at his glowing arms. "Let the fire out, let it burn a way through."

Kale shook his head. “Even if I can manage to do it, it will spend most of my mental reserves. It’ll leave us vulnerable,” he explained.

A sharp tap beneath our feet and we were moving to avoid the shards that now were starting to shoot upwards.

“We’re vulnerable now!” I yelled.

Kale grunted in agreement and gently pushed me off of him.

“Fine. Leave yourself some space,” he instructed.

He approached the nearest wall, avoiding shooting darts and shards as best as he could. He placed his palms against the edges of the cracks and dipped his head—eyes closed.

I watched as his skin cracked and split and what looked like molten lava started to pool through the openings towards his hands.

The shooting shards halted, and with them so did the taps. The creature doing this knew what we were trying and began shifting its focus on it. The molten fire went into Kale’s fingertips and then from there began burning and melting away at the edges of the wall.

A hissing noise signaled that it was working, but I didn’t have a chance to celebrate it when the taps resumed. This time they were all a solid constant covering every surface around us. The structure of the gazebo moaned against the pressure.

If I had to guess, we only had seconds before shards of crystal and glass impaled us from every direction.

“Kale, hurry!” I yelled.

He opened his eyes and looked around, realizing the trouble we were in.

He pulled his hands away from the wall, the liquid fire in his hands coming with it. I was about to tell him not to stop when he swore.

"Shit. We don't have time. Get down!" he yelled.

I did as he said, crouching into a ball. He knelt down, hovering over my body as he planted his hands on the floor on either side of us. I kept my eyes down, watching what his hands where doing.

I heard the shattering of wood as the sharp black darts whizzed towards us.

Fire erupted from Kale's hands, whooshing upwards and around us, shielding our bodies from the incoming danger.

I felt its heat around me, could smell the sulfur and coal as it burned. The fire was consuming all the air, making it hard for me to breathe. I glanced up at Kale's face—his eyes were tightly closed, the muscles of his face tense in concentration. His skin was darkening, and the veins on his neck were beginning to glow.

His power was threatening to burst from him, to erupt from every inch of him, and he was fighting against it, keeping its energy in his hands. His breath was ragged, coming in short bursts.

I watched in awe as his skin continued to shift and crack like the hardened surface of a volcano, lava threatening to burn through.

How close was he to showing his true form? And if he couldn't keep it under control, would I even survive long enough to see it?

His face started to relax, and that's when I realized that the shield of fire had receded. I looked around to see that there was black dust and sand spreading away from us as if from a large blast. And that we were no longer in the gazebo.

No, the gazebo had burned along with all of the shards and shadows. Leaving only the two of us in a barren field.

When I looked back at Kale, he was taking in short panting breaths, his skin no longer cracking open, and all evidence of the fire gone. His eyes were closed, and his forehead was close to the ground.

I stood and surveyed our surroundings, no sign of the shadow creature. Maybe he managed to kill it—or put it back to sleep at least.

"Well that worked," I muttered.

He chuckled lightly, the sound was struggled. "Yeah, but now we have another problem," he replied.

I looked back at his crouched form. "What?"

He sat up and winced, his hands clutching his right side where a shard of black crystal had stabbed him deep. He tried to rise again but groaned against the pain.

I gasped and knelt in front of him. "Shit. Can you heal?" I asked.

He shook his head. "I just spent everything I could spare in here. At this point, I can't even get us out."

He cried out when I pressed against the wound to help stop the bleeding.

He winced with each breath, clenching his fist against his forehead. I took another glance around our location—my mind. Whatever he did may have eliminated the one danger, but in reality, we didn't even know if that thing was actually gone.

And we might be stuck in here.

THIRTY-SEVEN
Seere

SO FAR THEY WERE LUCKY.

No one had yet returned to the warehouse in the fifteen minutes that Kale had been inside Heather's mind. They would soon find out how much that luck would last. Seere had already pulled out a piece of charcoal and started drawing binding wards on Kale's arms. Small and simple ones that would keep his fire under control if he couldn't do it himself.

Iaoel sat on a stool a few feet away from them, waiting for a vision or for someone to show. Their eyes never leaving the two now unconscious figures.

Once Seere finished her work, she touched the charcoal to the floor and drew a circle around the two, and then marked five protective runes on its edge.

"I have a bad feeling," Iaoel stated. They hadn't spoken for a while, so the sound of their voice made Seere stiffen.

She gave the AOS a side glance. "I can't say I have the warm fuzzies either."

"They should be done by now."

"It must be more complicated than anticipated."

Iaoel looked towards the pentacle. "Jade says they're almost done in heaven."

Seere sighed. "Great. Well let's hope they're delayed a little longer," she replied.

Seere was already prepared for a fight if it were necessary, but it would be much preferred if they could avoid it. Plus, if a fight ensued, it would throw off their progress in making allies with the angels.

Looking Iaoel up and down, Seere knew that they were likely to be their easiest prospect, as they were already warming up to her with ease.

But the others were wild cards, they needed more time with them to develop rapport. Time that Seere wasn't sure she had much of anymore.

Kale needed others on his side, people he could call friends. Especially when Seere left his life, he would destroy himself if he dealt with that loss alone.

"Can you see when people are going to die?" Seere asked Iaoel out of the blue.

Iaoel's eyes widened in surprise. "Not always. It depends on its relevance. Usually we only see mortals ends. Why?"

Seere shrugged. "Just curious."

Iaoel narrowed their eyes in suspicion and then they softened when they observed Seere fidgeting with her braids, a nervous movement that meant she was anxious. "You've exceeded your life expectancy, and your end days are worrying you?" Iaoel asked, though their tone was less in question and more in statement.

Seere shifted her gaze to Kale, her best friend. "I'm not worried about dying, Iaoel."

"You're worried about your friends."

Seere nodded quickly. "You couldn't see my death, even if you tried?" she asked.

Iaoel shook their head again. "I can't control what I see. I'm sorry."

She waved them off. "No worries. I guess not knowing just makes things more interesting."

Seere whipped to fully face Kale when she heard the sound of sizzling. She walked closer to see some of the binding wards on his skin burning under intense heat. Seere barely touched his forehead and quickly retreated the hand to avoid a burn herself. Iaoel was tense on their stool, watching.

"He's expelling more power than he should be in there, leaving little to protect his physical form from the fire underneath. His outer shell is beginning to breakdown," Seere explained.

"Those wards aren't helping?" Iaoel asked.

Seere clicked free a small knife. "They're holding for now, but I should place some deeper ones to help."

For good measure Seere put on a pair of leather gloves before she began carving the wards into his hot flesh. He'd heal from them easily enough.

Seere could withstand the burns if she needed to, but she scarred when healing, and she didn't feel the need to add to her extensive collection when she didn't have to.

She carved out three of them. One on his arm, one on the back of his neck, and the other on his knee. They should hold him long past when the charcoal wards burned off.

Iaoel began to approach the table. "He's not burning Heather is he?" they asked.

Seere took off her gloves to check their held hands. Both of them were mercifully cold in contrast to the rest of him.

"No, whatever he's doing, whatever power he still retains is keeping her unharmed."

“Gabriel will be happy about that.”

Seere glared at the AOS. “Kale is a lot more capable than you all make him out to be.”

Iaoel threw their hands in the air in surrender. “I meant no offense, Seere. I’ve seen how much the Prince has grown over the years.”

A sharp inhale drew their attentions back to Kale, who was now tense, his body trembling. Lightning and fire licked across his shoulders and feet. Not long afterwards the charcoal marks burned completely off, smoke following in their wake.

Seere and Iaoel tensed as his veins began to light up, fire surging just under his skin, threatening to break through. Seere’s heart thundered in her chest when she saw blood begin to pool from a wound in his side.

Even the carved marks began to sizzle. Seere and Iaoel backed away as the protective circle around Heather and Kaleus began to glow a deep orange color, the five protective wards pulsing, being hit again and again with flame.

“That’s not a good sign,” Seere said out loud.

Iaoel eyes were wide, no longer sitting on the stool.

“Where’s Daevas?” they asked.

“He’s with Duma.”

“Call him back, he may need to go in and help,” Iaoel instructed.

Seere didn’t look convinced that that was a good idea. “Duma will try to stop him.”

“Well it’s a good thing you’re armed this time.”

Seere rolled her eyes and then reached into her own mind for that taut connection she occasionally used with Daevas.

Daevas, wherever you are right now, we need you back at the warehouse. She said into it.

Immediately she felt him accept the connection, What's wrong?

Seere sent the memory to him as a better means of explaining and then followed it with, Try to get here before Duma, or he'll get in your way.

Daevas didn't hesitate before saying, I'm on my way.

Seere locked eyes with Iaoel who asked, "Is he coming?"

Instead of replying, Seere pointed to the pentacle at the very moment a column of dark smoke and flickering embers signaled Daevas' arrival.

He didn't waste any time before rushing towards them, his face collected and calm, but urgent. Daevas took in the entire situation, observing the circle and protection marks that still pulsed.

He then looked over Heather and Kale, his gaze pausing longer on Kale's wound that was now leaving a pool of blood on the floor.

"He shouldn't be hurt out here," he stated.

He crossed the protective circle and paused as a wave of heat hit him. He took a deep breath and moved closer to Heather's unconscious body, standing on the opposite side of her from Kale.

A pillar of light flashed across the room and then Duma was charging for their group. His eyes already assessing what was about to happen.

"What on earth do you think you're doing?!" the angel demanded.

Seere intercepted his path and put a hand up to his chest to stop him. "That's far enough."

"Gabriel forbade you from doing this again, why weren't we informed?" he asked Iaoel directly.

Iaoel maintained their distance, choosing not to be involved in the physical portion this argument would most likely end up in.

“Duma, you have to understand—” Iaoel started.

“Understand what, Iaoel? That you went against direct orders and let the hellborn son go inside the mortal’s head? And what is Daevas about to do? Is he going in too?”

Daevas half-turned to the angel. “Yes, to get them both out. If you were wise you wouldn’t try to interrupt,” he said.

“I can’t allow you to do that,” Duma stated firmly.

Seere tilted her head with a feline smile across her face.

“Get a move on Daevas,” she said without looking away from Duma’s angered expression.

Daevas nodded and gripped Heather’s free hand and closed his eyes. Duma watched and pressed further against Seere’s restraint. But it was too late, the demon was in.

Duma looked at Iaoel with fury and then turned that sharp glare towards the small demon before him.

“Let me through,” he ordered.

Her smile grew, an eyebrow raised. “Not gonna happen,” she purred.

Another flash of light and Jade appeared in the pentacle. Her eyes scanned the room and then did a double take when she saw all of their bodies, tense and unmoving.

“What’s going on?” she asked, rushing over to us.

"Heather, Seere, and I went to the Library of Alexandria to find some clues. But Heather was affected by something there, some old wards that reacted badly against her angel blood. She is locked in her own consciousness. We brought her back her so that Kaleus could figure out what was going on and bring her out of it," Iaoel started to explain.

Jade's eyes flicked to the three inside the circle. "Kaleus is bleeding," the angel stated plainly.

"Something is going wrong inside. We needed Daevas to go in and help," Iaoel finished.

Jade observed Seere and Duma, facing each other like territorial apes.

"Why didn't you call for Gabriel and me?" Jade asked.

Seere was the one who answered. "The urgency of the situation determined a different order of priorities," she said with a smile.

Her feline eyes daring Duma to make a move. Duma's attention shifted when a double-edged sword slipped into Seere's free hand—ready to strike.

"Well he knows now. And I'd like to see you stop all three of us when he arrives," Duma challenged.

Excitement flicked across her dark eyes. "Or I can put you down before he arrives," she countered.

Duma and Jade physically tensed.

"Seere, there doesn't need to be violence right now," Jade stated, her gaze flicking over to Iaoel for support.

"I agree. So back up and let them work."

"Put down the sword," Duma retaliated.

Seere raised the sword, pressing one of the sharp ends against his chest and then used it to push him back. He willingly backed up but only as far as she pushed.

“Not. Gonna. Happen.” She enunciated every consonant.

“You’re saying that if I try to get past you, you’ll utilize your weapon against me?” Duma asked carefully.

Iaoel locked eyes with Jade, both of them knowing what that action would mean. Seere never lost eye contact with the Spectral angel who had only a couple days ago invoked her demon name, bloodied her on the mats and then yielded like a coward to save her pain.

Today was not going to be a day that Seere would go easy on him.

“I’m saying, that if you so much as even try—I will carve you up into little angel pieces and lick your blood off the blade while you slowly heal on the floor.”

Seere leaned in closer to say in a quieter voice. “And that will be just a glimpse into the real Jazar Danti.”

Seere was taking a risk in saying her own name, though it wouldn’t invoke the challenge, it would ultimately result in a punishment she would have to inflict on herself later. But it was worth it to solidify her threat. If only to stall them just a little longer.

In reality, it would be better for her to incapacitate the two of them now before the archangel arrived. Against him she would be shark bait.

Duma’s stance was wide and there were weapons scattered around the floor around them. Seere could see his strategy before he even had thought of it himself. And, at the moment that he quickly ducked to grab one, Seere didn’t hesitate to swing her blade.

But the metal didn’t hit flesh, instead it was intercepted by a staff—held by Jade.

Jade pushed against her blade to throw Seere back a bit, and Seere willingly stepped back. She freed another sword from her side to fill her other hand as Duma armed himself and joined Jade's side to go against the wrath demon.

Seere smirked as she bent her knees lower, her stature tiny compared to the two.

"Challenge accepted." And then she lunged.

THIRTY-EIGHT
Heather

I WAS PRESSING THE WOUND as hard as I could, but it was still bleeding, the shard still inside it should have been staunching some of the blood loss—but it was not.

For what was supposed to be an imaginary wound, it sure seemed real. Especially when Kale was beginning to look sickly and pale.

"You're worrying me, Kale," I muttered. His eyelids fluttered and he coughed.

"Save it for when we actually have reason to worry," he responded.

I looked down at my fingers, now soaked in the crimson liquid. Images of Mason's death continued to flow right alongside this experience. What if Kale was dying? Could he die in here?

"Remember that in here your thoughts are wide open, you might as well be saying them out loud," Kale stated weakly.

"Sorry."

Kale grunted and looked down at the wound then winced when it hurt to do so. "I'm not going to die. I might just pass out."

I sighed. "Mason died like this. What makes you any different?" I asked.

He put a hand over mine, staring up into the nothingness of my mind above.

“I’m a very different creature than Mason was. Much stronger too.”

I snorted half-heartedly. “We have no idea what the hell that thing was. You can’t be sure that it wasn’t capable of killing even you,” I argued.

“Even if I did die, I’m not so sure that would be a bad thing,” he coughed.

I chuckled darkly. “I should have known you were one of those suicidal types, goes hand-in-hand with your grim state of being.”

He chuckled this time. “I was created for the sole purpose of bringing chaos to the world. I’m sure even the angels wouldn’t shed a tear if I no longer were a problem for them.”

“Do you want to cause chaos?” I asked.

His eyes met mine. “Is this your subtle way of trying to find out if I’m truly trustworthy or not?” he asked.

I shrugged. “As you’ve pointed out multiple times, I don’t know you. But there’s no time like the present to remedy that.”

He laughed lightly. “That’s a long and tiring journey to take, halfsie-darling. I don’t think you’d have the strength.”

I rolled my eyes. “Well at the moment, I have more strength than you. So try me.”

Kale shook his head. “Not today, honey-eyes.” He took a short breath that I believe was meant to be a long one. He wasn’t far from unconsciousness.

Unconsciousness. Was that even possible when you’re in someone’s consciousness?

“Are you always this dense?” I asked.

"You ask a lot of questions," he stated. "It gets annoying after a while."

"It's keeping you awake, isn't it?"

He groaned, wincing from the motion. "Can you take the shard out, please? It might be what's halting my healing."

"Or it could cause you to bleed out," I countered.

He waved his hand lazily in the air. "I'm bleeding out anyway, just do it."

I sighed and eyed the black crystal shard still embedded in his abdomen. I lifted a hand to it and gripped it right above where it protruded, it was icy cold to the touch. He winced and groaned.

"Quickly, please," he begged in a voice that was definitely not human.

"Okay, on the count of three. One—" I shoved it out before continuing to save him the anticipation. He cried out and pounded his fist against the ground next to him.

Once he regained his composure after a few breaths he said, "Thank you."

I tossed the shard away from us and pressed against the bleeding wound once more.

"Is the Prince of Darkness actually thanking me?" I mocked.

A low growl sounded from deep in his throat. "Don't push your luck."

"Are you healing now? Do you feel any better?" I asked.

He looked down and then closed his eyes. I assumed he was focusing on his power.

“No,” he grounded out. “My power in here is still weak, it should be enough to heal—but it’s not.”

“Great,” I grumbled.

Kale turned his head, looking off at nothing. “Good news is I can sense Seere again. But that’s about all the good news I have,” he explained. “Looks like our alliance is being tested.”

“What does that mean?”

He didn’t get a chance to answer before the sound of crashing thunder vibrated around us. I winced, resisting the urge to cover my ears. The initial crash of it settled, but the rumbling didn’t, the ground shaking under our feet.

I made a pained sound. “You have got to be kidding me,” I whined.

Kale was looking around. “Guess I didn’t get rid of it for very long.”

“We can’t fight it in this condition.”

He shook his head. “No, we can’t. I can barely stand, let alone set off another blast. Even if I could, my physical form would be toast.”

Heather? A deep voice called, echoing around me as if in a large dome.

“Wait! Do you hear that?” I asked.

Kale winced when he tried to turn around. “Besides the rumbling of our fate?”

“No, shh.”

He stilled, not making a sound. *Heather? Kale? Where are you?*

“It’s Daevas! Why can’t you hear him?” I asked.

Kale breathed. "You have to let him in, until then I can't hear or see him."

"But I'm not in control in here."

Kale shook his head. "You always have control of your mind. Focus on his voice to pinpoint where he is and let him inside," he instructed.

"But the wall—"

"Just do it!" Kale snapped.

I sighed and closed my eyes. *Daevas*? I blinded sent out into my thoughts.

Heather! Where are you?

I don't know, some dead field. How do I let you in? I asked.

You already did by reaching out. I'm only seeing rock structures, a dead field? he asked.

I sighed audibly. *We were in a gazebo, but it's pretty much blown to smithereens at this point.*

"He says he's near some rock structures. I have no idea what he's talking about," I told Kale out loud.

"DAEVAS!!!" Kale screamed out loud.

I blocked my ears from the sheer volume of it. My head was beginning to hurt from all of this.

We waited for a couple seconds in silence.

"What the hell is going on in here?" Daevas asked from the opposite direction we were looking.

We both whipped our heads around and in sync sighed with relief. "Thank god," I said.

"As helpful as his presence would be, God's unfortunately not here." Kale rolled his eyes. "Did you see anything strange on your way?" he asked Daevas.

Daevas shook his head, crouching to assess Kale's state. "I can feel the ground shaking, but nothing appeared. You look like shit," he stated.

Kale snorted. "Thanks. Things as bad as they feel on the outside?"

"Your injury is real, and not healing. Plus, Seere is currently holding off Jade and Duma from ripping into the wards she put in place on you. We should get out of here before Gabriel arrives, he's on his way—and he may not be happy."

"What about the wall?" I asked.

Daevas placed a supporting arm underneath Kale's, putting one of his arms over his shoulder and heaved him upwards. The Prince moaned loudly against the pain.

"What wall?" Daevas asked once they were steady.

"So it's down. Good, that'll make it easier to get out of here," Kale groaned.

Daevas looked between us confused. "You'll have to tell us the story later. Let's go." He began walking away from the field towards where he originally came from.

"Can't you just blink us out of here or something?" I asked.

Daevas huffed, not turning to me. "Not without shoving you into a dream. If you want to come out with us, we need to go to the edge of your consciousness," he explained.

I sighed and began following. "So many rules," I muttered quietly.

I heard Kale chuckle and the two of them exchange a small look.

"She's not gonna like all the other forty-million rules of our world," Kale mumbled.

"Not one bit," Daevas agreed.

The field must have just been a chamber of some kind inside my mind, because as we approached a darkened fog ahead of us, I could see the edge where the dirt of the field stopped abruptly and then turn to gray concrete or stone.

I followed Daevas as he carried Kale further into the darker fog, slowing down when we started passing what looked like ancient stone ruins that used to be buildings. Crumbling columns that resembled those of the Acropolis and Temple of Zeus in Athens.

"Am I the one who creates these locations?" I asked quietly.

"Your mind naturally fills space with things it's familiar with. If you're not in a memory, your subconscious will fill in the blanks. Sometimes the spaces take an emotion or stress and morph it into a landscape. If I had to guess, I'd say that dead field might have been concocted from your fear or the anxiety you were feeling," Daevas explained.

"And this one? These ruins?"

"You tell us," Kale coughed.

I was about to tell them about the ruins' resemblance but I stopped short when another thundering roar rolled past us, closer this time. All three of us turned to look behind us to see a growing mass of shadow in the distance, moving towards us.

"We really need to go!" I yelled.

Daevas turned again and tried walking faster, but Kale was weak and dragging his feet.

I tried not to look back as I kept behind the two. My instincts screaming at me to run, but only Daevas knew where we were going. Rushing ahead would help no one.

We passed by a broken stone wall that used to be part of a building. At least that was what my mind fabricated it to be. Daevas stopped, causing me to glance ahead. It was an edge, complete darkness with no end in sight.

I walked up to stand next to him and looked down. It was like the world just ended, and a sheer drop into darkness was all that remained.

The ground shook again, and I turned back towards the mass of shadow and smoke that was quickly advancing.

"Now what?" I asked, having to raise my voice over the sound of the ground breaking.

Kale's eyes were barely staying open, his body going lax. Daevas had to use both hands to support him.

"Grab hold of me," Daevas instructed.

My eyes were still on the growing shadow creature, fear tightening its grip on my chest. I couldn't look away from it, sensing its faceless form staring me down once more.

"Heather! Grab onto me!" Daevas called.

I blinked and turned away from it. I reached out my hand and barely gripped the fabric of his shirt.

"Go now!" I yelled.

Daevas nodded. The ground beneath my feet shuddered and then it was breaking apart. Daevas and Kale's physical forms began to fade, but the ground between us split.

I stumbled back, losing grip on Daevas. He turned just in time to see that I was no longer connected; it was too late, he was already fading away.

"No!" he yelled.

I swayed as my feet lost balance and then fell onto the ground. Flying dirt and dust flooded my vision, choking the air from my lungs. I blindly flung out my hand to reach for him again but the distance between us grew too large.

The thundering of the earth was so overwhelming I couldn't hear anything else, not even the sound of my own breath.

Eventually the dust cleared enough for me to open my eyes. For me to see that Daevas and Kale were gone.

I gasped and rolled to face the creature right at the moment I saw it rear up above me and descend upon my fallen form. And, as its fluid-like shadow cocooned around me, the sound of my scream was cut short.

THIRTY-NINE

"DUMA, JADE—STOP THIS! There's no reason to fight." Iaoel tried to reason with them, but their efforts were overshadowed by the clashing of steel and iron.

Seere wasn't holding back, moving quickly to combat two different and skilled opponents. She had to hand it to the angels, their training was effective.

She spun and twirled, kicking Duma hard enough to send him flying a few feet away only to have to do a back handspring to avoid getting hit by Jade's staff.

The Guardian Master huffed as she spun the staff to throw off Seere's footing. Seere tossed her blades and punched Jade's gut, and when that caused Jade to bend over Seere reached up and gripped both ends of the staff.

Both of them pushed and pulled, equally trying to use an end to break from the other's grasp. But they both held firm. Jade shoved her knee up to break Seere's balance, but Seere anticipated the move, using her own leg to catch Jade's in mid-air.

Hooking it and pushing the staff towards her at the same time. Jade lost her balance and fell onto her back.

Seere didn't miss a beat before mounting Jade's fallen form, pinning down her legs with hers, and pressing the staff against Jade's throat. Jade struggled but didn't make an immediate move to shove her off.

Seere kept her focus on the Guardian Master, even as in her peripheral she saw Duma recovering and approaching to pull her off—or to use the opportunity to get to Heather's body. When he strode right past the two of them she had her answer.

Duma saw his chance and he took it. Iaoel made a step to stop him, but hesitated.

"Duma, stop. You cannot interrupt."

"Stay out of this, Iaoel. Since you're so good at it already," Duma snapped.

Duma easily broke the protection wards on the floor, releasing the barriers that would have kept him out by burning him.

He reached his arm out to grab Daevas' shoulder when he halted; frozen as a set of long, sharp nails wrapped around and pinned against his throat.

Iaoel gasped when they saw Lillith poised behind Duma. In all of the ruckus none of them had noticed that the mother of demons had quietly snuck into the room. Her stealth allowed her to get the better of them.

The red-headed temptress had one clawed hand gripping Duma's bicep, her lips right at his ear.

"Make one move, pet. I dare you," she purred in his ear.

"Unhand me," Duma grounded out through his teeth.

She chuckled darkly. "Careful, angel. I may not be able to kill you, but Aspis won't hesitate to put you to sleep for a little while."

Duma tensed as the small snake necklace she wore came to life, slithering onto his collarbone and neck. Hissing softly as it readied for the order to strike.

Lillith leaned in closer till Duma could feel the heat of her breath.

"And her bite hurts a lot more than mine." She nipped at his ear for good measure, but Duma remained still.

The serpent continued a path up and down Duma's collar bone.

"I'm not entirely sure what started this little tussle. But from what I can see, the Heir is hurt, both him and Daevas are busy inside the Nephilim's mind, and our last remaining demon is showing you chastity-fuckers what it's like to bleed. So why don't we all calm ourselves and take a deep breath," Lillith suggested.

No one spoke, but the tension in the room remained.

Lillith smirked and opened her mouth to speak again when a bright golden light filled the room, and then Gabriel was walking towards them all.

"Enough. Angels, stand down," Gabriel ordered his angels.

But the demons also slowly began to relax. Lillith's serpent retreated back to her neck and solidified under an unspoken order, Seere straightened, releasing the staff from Jade's neck.

Slowly Lillith and Seere backed away from their opponents, Jade and Duma regained their footing putting distance between them by moving closer to the archangel.

Gabriel took a look at each and every one of them, ensuring that they all weren't about to attack once more—before he landed his gaze on the three inside the now ruined protection circle.

"How long have they been in?" Gabriel asked no one in particular, his attention flicking between the bleeding Heir and the Nephilim laying on the table. Worry etching lines into his skin.

Iaoel was the one who answered, sounding quieter than before. "About thirty minutes."

"Why didn't you wait for Gabriel to get here before going in?" Duma demanded.

Gabriel held up a hand to silence his angelic comrade. "It's fine. Iaoel made a judgement call and I trust that it was necessary. If both Kaleus and Daevas had to go in it must be serious."

"But—"

"There is a time and place for this argument, Duma. It's not now." Gabriel interrupted.

The Spectral stiffened and when he met the steady gaze of the archangel he nodded in understanding and relaxed. Duma backed away to stand outside of the group, folding his arms and taking steadying breaths.

"Tell me what happened," Gabriel instructed Iaoel.

So they did. Both Seere and Iaoel contributed to telling Gabriel every detail of what had happened since before the Library.

While listening, the archangel took his time assessing each of the three, spending more time on Kaleus to inspect the mysterious wound that had no obvious source.

It looked like a stab wound, but according to Seere and Iaoel's reports the wound showed up randomly while Kaleus was apparently using excessive energy.

Gabriel stood at the head of the table and pressed his fingers lightly to Heather's temple.

When he focused on her mind he was met with only blockades. He was only able to get inside one's subconscious while they slept, their consciousness was beyond his abilities.

Everyone jumped in surprise when Kaleus and Daevas simultaneously gasped for air—jolting out of their mental state with wide eyes. Gabriel knelt next to Kaleus and gripped his arm.

"What happened?" he demanded.

Kaleus coughed and winced, clutching at his side. He bared his teeth and glared at Daevas.

"That's what I'd like to know," he said pointedly to his third.

Daevas' eyes were on Heather's still unconscious face, looking distressed. "She lost her grip at the last second."

"Then go back and get her!" Kaleus yelled.

Daevas still had a grip on her hand, already trying. His brows bunched together in further anguish.

"I can't. The edge of her consciousness crumbled away as we left."

"What does that mean?" Gabriel demanded.

Daevas looked up at the archangel. "I don't know. I haven't seen that happen before. Whatever is in there is defying all the rules of body and mind. There's no way we could prepare for it," he explained.

"What did you see?"

Daevas shook his head and looked at Kaleus, who answered.

"My guess is that it's a primordial of some kind. But it didn't resemble anything I've heard of. And it changed form. What I saw was a shadow silhouette that could solidify into shards of black crystal and glass." He gestured to his bleeding side. "Which is what did this."

"Did any of it hit Heather?"

Kaleus rolled his eyes and waved a hand over her unbloodied body. "Does it look like it hit her?"

Gabriel glared at the Heir. "And now she's stuck in there?"

"I'd go back in myself, but my mental powers are spent," Kaleus stated.

Gabriel looked back at the still face of the human, her eyelids no longer fluttering and twitching like they were before. "What you described doesn't sound like any primordial." He spun to face Seere. "Why was she so afraid to go alone in the Library?" he asked her.

Seere bristled, rolling her shoulders back. "I assumed it was just nerves. But then after we realized that the place had wards on it, we thought maybe her fear was just her body's reaction to them. Like her angel-half was signaling her in some way," she explained.

"And you're sure that you didn't see anything when you found her?"

Iaoel was the one who replied. "Just her flashlight on the ground."

Kaleus groaned. "I know where your thoughts are going, featherbrain. But I don't think whatever is in her mind came from there. If it changes form, wouldn't it make more sense for it to be what we both have seen in her dreams before?" he asked.

Gabriel had wondered that himself. "Why was the Library warded?" Daevas asked.

Iaoel shrugged. "We didn't find anything worthy in it. Maybe something used to be there that needed to be protected, but those old chambers have been excavated a long time ago."

"A relic maybe?" Gabriel guessed.

Kaleus coughed. "Maybe. We'll have to go back there at some point." His hand pressed hard against the wound, blood still dripping into the large pool of it that now lay beneath his chair.

"You're not healing," Gabriel stated. Kaleus shook his head. The archangel knelt again, motioning for him to move his hand. When he did, Gabriel hovered his hand over the stab wound. A golden light protruded from his palm towards it.

Gabriel's brows narrowed in concentration as he attempted to heal Kaleus' injury with his own power, but nothing happened. He sighed and lowered his hand. "I can't heal it either."

"Should I try?" Jade asked.

Gabriel shook his head, "If it's beyond mine and Kaleus' powers, it's unlikely to respond to yours. You may need to heal the old-fashioned way," he sighed. "We need to get it cleaned up and dressed."

Seere reached his side and began to help support him up, Daevas rushed to the other side and helped. Kaleus winced before jerking his head towards the Nephilim.

"What about Heather?"

"Maybe I can take her to Azrael, see if she can—"

Gabriel was cut off suddenly when Heather shot up, gasping loudly for air.

She coughed, clutching her throat. Gabriel was at her side in an instant, putting a hand on her back to support her. She sucked in air with so much force like she had been drowning.

"Heather? Are you alright?" he asked.

Everyone in the room had moved closer, worry written on all of their faces. Kaleus resisted getting closer, leaning on his two friends for support.

Once Heather's breathing regulated, she looked around frantically, seeing each and every one of their faces.

Horror and fear were written all over her, but with each face she locked onto it eased. Lingering on Kaleus and his still bleeding body, and then it stopped lastly on Gabriel.

She touched her face and neck, running hands through her hair as if reminding herself that she was alive.

"How—" it came out in a rasp at first, she swallowed to clear it a bit more. "How am I, how did I get out?" she asked.

This time she looked at Daevas for an answer. He extended a free hand and lightly touched her ankle. "What happened after Kale and I disappeared?" he asked.

Heather's eyes bulged with confusion and dread. "That was—" she paused and looked around again, "How long after you did I come out of it?" she asked quietly.

"Only a couple of minutes," Kaleus answered, watching her closely—even as his skin looked paler than death.

Heather looked down, her gaze flicking around without direction—counting internally.

"Heather."

She looked up at Kaleus.

She read the weariness on his face, and the question behind all of the others as well.

"You disappeared, and then…" She closed her eyes and shuddered.

A tear streamed down from each of her eyes before she opened them again and answered.

"It felt like I was in there for *weeks*."

FORTY
Heather

I COULDN'T ANSWER THEIR QUESTIONS at the moment.

Every muscle in my body was still trembling feverishly. I had to beg them to leave me be for a little while, let me collect my thoughts, remind myself that I was in the real world again and not in my head. Kale and Gabriel both read my discomfort and sent everyone away.

Minutes. I was in there for only a few minutes?

Seere and Daevas took Kale up to his room to clean up the damage on his side that wasn't healing anytime soon. Gabriel helped me up the steps, and when I asked if I could take a bath he told me there was only one bathroom in the warehouse with a bathtub. He led me into a dark room and then into the bathroom attached to it.

I waited, leaning against the sink counter while he filled it with hot water. I stared off into space, my skin cold whenever I let the memories consume me over again.

I jolted when Gabriel touched my arm, drawing me from my thoughts.

"It's okay," he said. "You're safe. The water is ready. Do you need anything? Food? Something to drink."

Just the thought of food made me queasy, so I shook my head in response. He nodded and swept a stray piece of hair away from my face.

"I'll leave you be then. Just call if you need anything." He leaned forward and gently kissed the top of my head and then was gone, closing the door behind him as he left.

I stared at the full tub of water, the steam that rose from it and shivered. I took a deep breath and undressed. The bathroom wasn't huge, or extravagant. The tile was white and black, the walls a pale blue color. In the far corner there was a standing shower with glass doors. Across from it a simple porcelain toilet and the sink was made of simple wood topped with a white stone counter.

There wasn't a mirror. Strange.

I jerked back at the first dip of my feet in the hot water, but then finally relaxed into its warmth. The tub was deep, completely covering my body in water without having to sink down low.

I sighed as it chased away the chills that still coated my skin. I took some time to clean off, and then I just sat there, holding my knees close to my chest.

It was so quiet. Only the sound of water dripping off my hair broke through the silence.

Minutes. Goddamn. I massaged my temples with my fingers, easing the headache that had been there since I awoke.

I closed my eyes only for a moment but behind them all I saw was that shadow creature staring back at me. I shot my eyes open and shook my head.

I'm out. I'm safe. I said to myself. It's over. At least this part of it is over. If this is what happens when I join the angels and demons on their searches, then maybe staying here was for the best.

I would need some time before I'd be ready to experience something like that again. I imagined that wraith that they brought back prisoner last week.

Gabriel said that other primordials were so much worse than that one and the vetala. I brushed my wet hair back behind my ears. Was that thing in my head a primordial too?

Darkness dwells where one can't see.

The wraith said that just before they killed it, when they asked what I had to do with all of this. Was the wraith talking about this shadow creature than lingered in my subconscious?

I missed my home—my apartment, my bed. Being able to take a soothing bubble bath and then eating a slice of strawberry cheesecake while binge watching Criminal Minds on Netflix. I missed the smell of coffee and the sounds of chatty college students in the Bistro café just outside the science building.

I missed soaking in the sun at the lake, reading a dystopian thriller, then cooling off in the green mucky water. Hell, I even missed only feeling nervous when I sat down in an old wooden desk to take a test, the feeling of a pencil in my hand and the flipping of paper as other students turned over the page.

Small mundane things that seem so outside my reach now.

A life without shadows and blood.

Blood. So much blood.

Blood staining my fingers as I desperately tried to staunch its flow, to stall the end of a life. Feeling the warmth leave their body, the light empty from his eyes…

My vision cleared, refocusing on the water in front of me. A drop fell from my face into the bathwater below my raised knees. I reach up and touched my cheek. I was crying.

I let loose a sigh and wiped my eyes clean. The water in the tub had gone cold—I hadn't realized I had been in here that long. I braced my hands on the edges of the tub and lifted myself up—wrapping a clean towel that was folded on a small shelf by the door.

I looked around and realized that I hadn't brought any clean clothes with me.

I didn't even know whose room I was in.

A black cotton robe hung on the door hook. I touched the fabric; its soft surface was warm and comforting. I wrapped my hair in the towel and put the robe on, securing the tie tightly. It wasn't terribly large or thick.

The hem reached down mid-calf, but the arms were a bit longer than expected. I rolled up the cuffs to my wrists and turned to check myself in the mirror only to stop short, remembering that there wasn't one in this bathroom.

I gathered my dirty clothes in a pile in my arms and turned the handle on the door. It opened into a larger bedroom. The walls were made of the same concrete as the rest of the place, only in this room there were more rusting steel columns and pillars, adding a touch of red and orange to the dreary gray color of the cement. A large wooden canopy bed stood in the center against the wall.

And laying in it was Kale.

"Oh! This is your room," I gasped.

He was sitting up, his chest bare and his side bandaged up. "I see you found my robe," he stated.

I touched it just above my heart. "Sorry, I didn't bring any clean clothes. I'll wash it, I promise."

He chuckled and only winced a little from the motion.

"It doesn't bother me when beautiful women wear my clothes, although I wouldn't have minded if you came out naked," he teased.

I huffed a laugh and walked towards the bed. "How are you feeling?"

"Shouldn't I be asking you that?" he countered.

I put my pile of clothes on the floor at the foot of the bed and continued up the side, sitting on the bed beside him.

"I'm not the one who got stabbed."

"No, but you are the one who got left behind." I tried not to feel the sharpness of that statement.

"It wasn't Daevas' fault. He had his hands full with you, how was he supposed to know the ground would disappear beneath us," I chuckled.

I looked at his bandages and reached my hand up to lightly touch the outside of it. He flinched only a fraction, but it was enough for me to pull back.

"You're still not healing?" I asked.

He moaned, cracking his neck. "No. My powers are nearly back to full strength, but no healing. Of all the things I envy about mortals, this is not one of them."

"Since when do you envy mortals?"

He smiled distantly, fidgeting with the dark green silk sheets. "It's a long story."

I nodded and left it at that. I was beginning to tell when Kale wasn't up for telling me a tale of his life. I could wait, I was just grateful to be on better terms with him.

"Gabriel's probably waiting to hear what happened in there," he stated.

I turned to glance at the closed door, then dipped my head and sighed. "I'd like to pretend it didn't happen a little while longer."

Kale nodded, an expression of grim understanding on his face.

"I want to tell you that shit like that doesn't happen often, but I think this is only the beginning of these adventures. We still have a long way to go."

Kale had changed so much since I first met him, in that already I was seeing his mask fade away. He still teased and flirted, but something was changing in the way that he was starting to speak to me like I was a friend, more tenderly.

The way he spoke to Seere sometimes. And how Gabriel has spoken to me since the beginning.

"I'm looking forward to it," I replied simply.

"Liar." He tapped my elbow with his.

I offered him a small smile, and then my eyes scanned lower down to his chest. Seeing those tattoos more up close, and the patterns they drew. The first thing I noticed was the upside-down cross on his neck.

I pointed to it with raised eyebrows. "A little on the nose with that one?"

He smirked. "Just in-case people forget." He winked.

Seere, Daevas, and Kale all had some form of flames embedded in their tattoos. But altered in other images—Daevas with his talons and tentacles and Seere with barbed wire. Kale's started as chains, that intertwined and formed various symbols and images.

Skulls, claws, teeth. All with veins of red and orange inside. The tattoo trailed down his neck, shoulder, and chest. Some thorny vines broke off from one end and encircled what looked like a small Hawaiian flower just over his heart.

"What's the flower for? It's so much softer than the rest," I asked.

Kale touched a finger against it, his eyes darkening in thought. "A reference to something that meant a lot to me," he answered plainly.

Something about the light I occasionally saw around him dimmed and swirled like smoke. I was starting to think that what I was seeing wasn't his power leaking from him, but maybe something only I could see.

Whatever it was, it told me that he didn't want to explain further. And I also got the sense that it was a reference to someone not something. But I didn't push, not when he looked sad just thinking about it.

I returned my eyes to the tattoos, following the symbols and lines and then smiled at what I saw peeking out of the bandages against his ribs.

"Is that a phoenix?"

Kale attempted to look down at it but grunted when the effort caused pain. "Yeah."

At least it was more of the shape of a phoenix. Outlined in black, its center red and orange. A tribute to his inner power perhaps. I tapped his arm playfully.

"Maybe we should start calling you feathers," I teased.

He laughed. "I'm sure your favorite archangel would just love that."

Our chuckles eventually died out, fading into solemn silence. After a minute I put my hand gently on his wrist.

"Thank you for all you did in there. I'm sorry you got hurt because of it."

Kale rotated his wrist so he could lightly grip my own. "It is kind of part of my job now to keep you safe at all costs."

I rolled my eyes. "I mean it. I haven't been kind to you lately, I've been stupid and naïve. And now you're hurt because of me."

"You could always give me a blow job to make up for it," he teased sarcastically.

I smacked his arm which caused Kale to laugh out loud. "You're an ass."

After he was finished laughing, he gripped my hand again, turning more serious.

"I'm sorry I couldn't get you out of there. I was trying to get Daevas to go back in as soon as I realized that you didn't come out with us."

I shrugged. "I was mere moments away from coming out anyway, I don't think going back in would have made a difference."

"Well, if it makes you feel better. We're thinking that that shadow monster was the same thing Gabriel and I dealt with on two separate occasions in your dreams. And that those wards in the Library might have triggered it or broke it out of your subconscious. So, if we go somewhere and you feel that petrified fear again, we'll know to get you clear of it before it can happen again," he explained.

I huffed, fidgeting my fingers against the skin of his forearm. "I don't think I'll be going anywhere with any of you anytime soon."

"Why not?" he asked.

I gave him my best *are you kidding?* look.

"I think I'll keep my powerless half-blood ass where it's safe from now on."

"And what is safe? This warehouse? Even here there's a risk of danger. You can't just hide out in fear of the dangers of the world because life is fucking short—especially for you. Featherbrain might agree with you staying cooped up in here for your own safety. And if that's truly what you want to do, then okay. You do you. But don't avoid it, do it *because you're afraid*," Kale argued.

Our eyes were locked on each other's, and I think this was the softest I've ever seen him look at me.

"Keep training with Seere—hell, I'll even train with you if you want, get stronger, test yourself and soon enough you won't be as powerless as you are now. And when you feel up to it, you can come with us on one of our searches. Within reason of course—I'm not taking you to hell. You don't need to see that."

Kale squeezed my hand twice.

"And if twinkle-toes gives you a hard time—I'll back you up. Seeing how I'm the only one who can put him on his ass when he needs a time-out," he chuckled.

I smiled, feeling warmth coming back into my core, erasing the cold memories of what I experienced in my own mind.

"You still have to tell me that story." The one about how he and Gabriel met. The one he promised to tell me while we were fighting against shadows and crystal inside a white gazebo.

Kale tilted his head and smirked at me. "You're stalling, *draga-mea*," he sighed, looking towards the door. "Your white knight is trying desperately to be patient, but any longer and he might burst," he informed.

I shook my head. "Do you think I'll ever be able to use that super-web thing?" I asked.

"*Super-web*?" he laughed lightly. "Maybe in time if we work on what little powers your half-angel grace has given you. But trust me, it's annoying as fuck. I wouldn't recommend it." He groaned as he started shoving me off the bed. "Now get out of here and let me sleep, human!"

I giggled and stood, snatching up my pile of soiled laundry and opened the bedroom door to leave. I took one look back at the son of Lucifer—at his scrunched-up face as he painfully attempted to adjust into a laying position, and I couldn't resist the warmed smile that spread across my face.

I closed the door behind me and started walking down the dimly lit hallway, realizing that I hadn't been down this side before. I took in the details of the rusting steel beams and cracked concrete walls.

Passing other rooms, stopping to take in the subtle carvings, objects and pictures that hung on them identifying their owners.

A spiked ball mace hung on one of the doors. I guessed that must have been Seere's room—since she seemed so adept with weapons.

The door that I assumed to be Daevas' only had a demon-sigil carved into it, and then a few plain doors down from his there was a poster of a naked woman holding leather whip on one hand. Lillith, I presume.

I continued on until I eventually entered into the main living area, seeing Gabriel, Jade, and Duma standing around the kitchen island talking. They turned to me when they heard me approach, Gabriel immediately walking over to me.

I put up a hand to stop his approach.

"I just need a few more human moments, and then I'll be at your disposal," I begged.

His eyes dipped then, scanning me up and down. No doubt seeing the robe I wore that didn't belong to me.

Gabriel nodded. "Of course. Take your time."

I closed the distance between us and stood on my toes to reach his full height. Planting a quick peck on his cheek, ignoring the butterflies in my stomach.

"Thank you."

EPILOGUE
Lucifer

LUCIFER OBSERVED FROM HIS REGULAR viewing area, watching with cold amusement as Beelzebub snipped off another appendage from the poor soul's hand with a rusty pair of scissors.

The following struggling scream filling Lucifer's darkened soul with a small trickle of pleasure. The Fallen stalked around the bound body only to position another finger for removal. His red eyes glowing with delight as he leaned down to speak in the damned mortal's ear.

"Beg for mercy," Beelzebub instructed with a lethal calmness.

The mortal's face was stained with tears and splattered blood. He sobbed through his bit, shaking his head frantically.

"P-p-please. I'll do anything," his muffled voice begged through the fabric tied around his lips.

Beelzebub glanced up at the window, seeing Lucifer's approved gaze before pinching the shears in one fluid motion, taking another severed finger with it. The human screamed and sobbed in agony.

Lillith came into the viewing room, looping a sensual arm through the devil's, putting a red-nailed hand on his chest, and running her tongue up the side of his neck.

Lucifer grinned. "Back so soon, my love?" he asked.

She giggled against his ear, sucking on the lobe before responding.

"I have news."

"I sure hope this news is far more interesting than the ones you've been bringing me as of late," Lucifer said.

"Oh it is. It includes a situation in which your dear young Heir was nearly-fatally wounded," she purred.

Lucifer fully turned to his seductress then, wrapping his arm around her waist and gripping her chin.

"Oh really? Do tell."

She bit her lip and pouted. "Mmm, what will you give me for this little tale?" she asked, nipping at his bottom lip.

The devil growled and then shoved Lillith hard against the charred volcanic wall. His pupils churning a deep crimson, seriousness laying in them.

"How about a swift lashing?"

She giggled. "It's been a while since you've whipped me, lover."

His grip on her chin tightened. "And I'll be happy to indulge you, but first—the information," he instructed.

Lillith rolled her eyes and sighed audibly. "The Nephilim went with a couple of our *alliance* members on a record-search. She came back in a catatonic state. Kaleus went into her consciousness and whatever he found there managed to injury him—badly," she sighed again before continuing. "Daevas went in and had to pull the poor sucker out. Not long after the fragile little half-blood emerged as well."

"So far, the only intriguing portion of this story is the bit about Kaleus getting harmed," Lucifer said coldly.

Lillith poked his chest. “I’m getting to it. Supposedly, they went to an old human library that they suspected held some information about the relics. According to Kaleus’ puppy-dog, the girl experienced nearly excruciating fear beyond any reasonable level, and when she went off alone this happened. The angel that was with them says that the old archive was warded.”

“Warded?”

“Yes.”

Lillith sensually traced a fingernail along the collar of Lucifer’s shirt. Already desperate for their layers to come off.

Lucifer’s took in all the small details of the story, some bits of his memory clicking into place as he did.

“Did they find anything while they were there?” he asked.

Lillith shook her head, starting to kiss his neck. “They’re intention is to go back another time.”

Lucifer gripped Lillith’s cherry-colored hair and pulled her back to look at him. “Well done, my tart. This is tasty news indeed. I’ll have to give you an extra reward for it.”

She licked her lips and sighed, “I knew you’d like it.”

“There’s just a few things. First—where is it they went exactly?” he asked.

“The old Library of Alexandria.”

“Ah.” He traced her lips with his finger. “Second—I want you to delay their return to it for as long as possible, at least until I tell you it’s clear, can you do that for me?”

She moaned in pleasure when his pelvis pressed closer to hers. “Of course.”

"Good, and third—keep this meeting a secret from Kaleus. In-fact, from now on, make him think you're not reporting back to me, and only report back when he's not watching. Be discreet. The less attention you draw to yourself the better," he ordered.

"As you wish."

Lucifer chuckled darkly, dipping down to bite that sweet spot connecting her neck to her shoulder. She moaned in reply, causing him to move further up, kissing as he went.

"Wards don't cause an angel to feel overwhelming fear, not even a Nephilim. No, that terror the half-blood felt was leading them right to it," he mumbled against her skin.

She pulled him closer. "Leading them to what?" she asked in a whisper.

Lucifer pulled back to stare at his beloved, holding her jaw in his fingers.

"This information is confidential Lillith, to the highest degree. You understand what would happen to you if you shared this information with anyone else, correct?" he asked.

She nodded, some of the pleasured fog between them lessening as she focused. The punishment for sharing information that was spoken in confidence with the Lord of Hell was always specific to the offender. In Lillith's case—her skin flayed, and her raw flesh boiled for five days.

"Our faithful, rag-tag alliance, my heart, has unknowingly located a relic. A particularly powerful one at that. And I plan to take full advantage of the opportunity that Nephilim has presented me," he informed.

Her eyes widened. "How do you plan to do that?" Lillith asked.

Lucifer pinned a finger against her lips, shushing her into silence. She responded by sucking on it.

"All in good time, my goddess. Now, I remember mention of a whip," he purred. "Shall we break out the nipple clamps and strap-on as well?"

Lillith smirked with wicked delight and giggled as the devil lifted her into his arms and led them out of the viewing room and down a hallway of screams.

Understanding the Realms

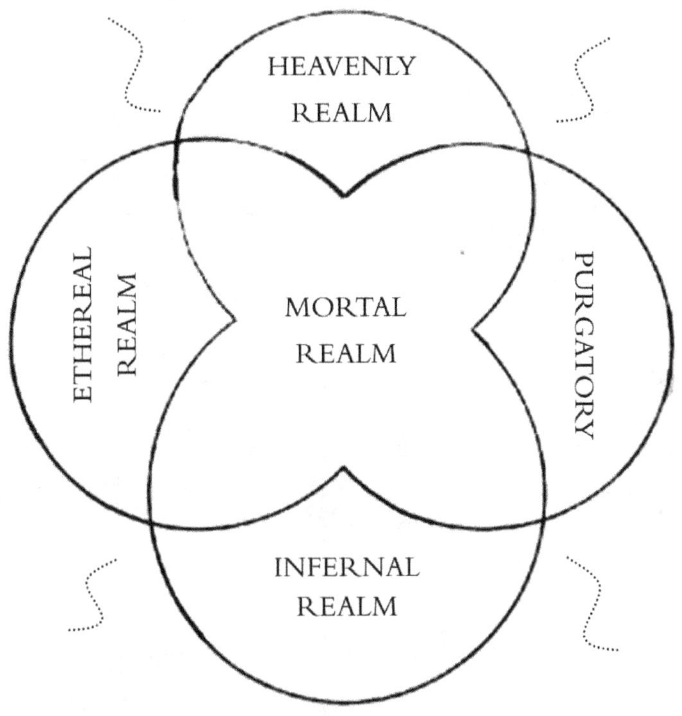

The **Ethereal** & **Purgatory** realms run parallel to the **Mortal** realm. Supernatural creatures can view the Mortal realm within them, but are unable to interact with it. The Ethereal realm is more or less a void in which time & space are irrelevant, and beings may pass in and out of it easily. Purgatory is more restricted, entrance and exit is limited to certain gate checkpoints.

The **Heavenly** & **Infernal** realms are veiled above and below the Mortal realm, only powerful supernaturals can interact and affect the Mortal realm from these realms. Formidable warding lies between them, reducing access to only those given approval.

The **Beyond** is the empty void of space, it is outside the confines of time and reality. Any and all beings may venture into it—at their own risk. The **Between** serve as the border lines between the physical realms. Those who serve on the borders constantly dwell on these lines, helping or preventing other souls from entering a realm.

The Paranormal Pyramid

Archangel Divisions

Archangel	Division	Realm	Primary Workforce	Secondary Workforce
Lucifer	Perdition	Infernal	The Fallen	The Hellborn
Michael	Worlds	Beyond	Ophanim	Nymphs
Azrael	Judgement	Between	Reapers	Thrones
Raphael	Archives	Ethereal	Scribes	Principalities
Uriel	Limbo	Purgatory	Watchers	Cakti
Zadkiel	Miracles	Heavenly	Seraphim	Dominions
Jophiel	Creation	Heavenly	Angels of Sight	Virtues
Chamuel	Destiny	Mortal	Amors	Cherubims
Gabriel	Training	Heavenly	Spectrals	Guardians

AUTHOR'S THOUGHTS

I can't even describe how much joy it gave me to finally finish this book. About nine months before I started working on this series, I went through a difficult family conflict that brought upon severe depression. For months I was living like a ghost, thinking only of what had happened, and what I could have done differently to change it. I had spoken to multiple therapists that tried to help me work through it, I'd talked about it with my husband and mother-in-law so much it eventually became the same conversation on an endless loop. I found myself questioning my entire existence and couldn't look to the future without grieving all of the moments I was meant to have that would no longer happen.

I used to be an avid reader and loved to write my own stories as a teenager, but all of that came to a halt when I went to college and got busy. But also, I lost confidence in myself, thinking I wasn't a good enough writer to make a living from it. But it was during this difficult spiral when I decided to pick up one of my story journals and start jotting down ideas. Out of nowhere the characters in Alliance came to life in my head. I wrote an outline draft in a matter of days, and with it I could breathe again. But I was nowhere near done. The outline draft, plot and character descriptions only got more in depth.

When COVID-19 came into our lives, bringing all of our social interactions to a stop, I lost my job. I still was going to school but doing so online. I found myself with way too much time on my hands. So I continued my work on Alliance, and even sparked ideas for other stories as well.

I finished the first draft of Immortal Alliance right in time for my birthday in August 2020. Although there was still so much editing and reviewing work to do, accomplishing such a huge feet brought life back into my soul, and my spiral was done. Now when I look to the future, I don't feel overwhelming grief and pain, instead I see possibilities and hope.

I found perspective in Heather. I found strength in Seere and trust in Gabriel. I found a sense of resilience in Kale, and order in Azrael. There is so much growth that all of these characters go through, some of which will always remain behind the gates of my mind. And I hope that others will find a place in this story in which they can fight their inner demons and be a badass.

Thank you, Immortal Alliance, for teaching me that **nothing can conquer me**.

ACKNOWLEDGEMENTS

First and foremost I need to thank my husband, Ian. He has been with me every step of the way, going over every tiny detail of this series, working out the kinks and brainstorming with me to create the story structure. Even when he may not have desired to hear more about it, he listened to me go on and on about the characters, their relationships, the world building—everything with a fine-tooth comb and provided feedback. This man is my gravity, holding me to the ground and keeping me focused. Even if he knows this story inside and out, backwards, and forwards, he still didn't hesitate to be my first initial editor, and he will always be the opinion I care most about. Thank you, my love, I couldn't possibly to this without your love and support.

S. Wunderink, for her editing work on this book. I got lucky and found her through booktok (tiktok), and we connected right away. It was amazing how she jumped right in and gave me constructive, honest, and reassuring feedback about a book that started out so impactful for me. Thank you for all your hard work, this success is also yours.

I'd like to thank one of my best friends, AnnElise for her words of encouragement. She has done nothing but encourage me to keep going, hype up my progress and make me smile. She is an inspiration to me, always a positive beam of light in my dark and dreary world. I couldn't ask for a better friend or support system.

Of course, I have to thank my mother-in-law, Cyndie. She too has listened while I hash out my infinite number of ideas. All while she provided endless support and encouragement. She has and always will continue to remind me that I am loved and how big a part I am in their family. Cyndie, thank you so much, I truly love you with all my heart, and I promise, grandkids are on the agenda.

Gregory, thank you for being my first official *beta reader* on this book. As an avid reader yourself, I knew that your opinion would be reflective of what I am hoping my readers capture while reading this series. Thank you for your open-mindedness, your support and encouragement.

My college professors—Ramon, Emily & Kathryn have been inspirations for me since day one. Ramon reminding me that all of our stories are important and his feedback to my work only further inspired me to keep improving. Emily for her endless light of encouragement. A woman who puts equality and mental health above all else. I was working as her assistant director on a theatre production when the idea for this series captured and hooked me in. Emily only added to my excitement and helped me believe in myself. Kathryn, my mentor, my friend. A sparkling dazzle of energy who will always be one of the greatest people in my life. Thank you all for your support and encouragement.

My student teaching mentor teacher, Mr. Higgins. During my three months of student teaching and finishing my degree I was also in the final editing process of this book. Higgins gave me encouragement and spread word like wildfire. I'm not one to brag about myself, so to have someone in my corner boasting about this major accomplishment was a huge deal for me. Thank you Higgins!

ABOUT THE AUTHOR

A.CATHERINE is an indie author residing in the Pacific Northwest. Recent cum laude graduate from Central WA University with a Bachelor of Fine Arts in Theatre Education and a minor in Family Science. She intends on pursuing a Master of Fine Arts in Creative Writing in 2022.

Storytelling has, and always will be the core of who she is. Whether it be on the live stage, in the classroom, typed up in a computer or between the fragile pages of a journal—storytelling is her passion. She is happily married, a mother of four fur-babies; two cats and two dogs, a teacher, an avid reader, and a lover of the Performing Arts.

CPSIA information can be obtained
at www.ICGtesting.com
Printed in the USA
BVHW080927270721
613003BV00007B/275